A
Mack Murphy
Thriller

The Wolf Hunter

BOOK 1
DESOLATION

A
Mack Murphy
Thriller

The Wolf Hunter

BOOK 1

DESOLATION

Terrence O'Malia

DEFIANCE PRESS
& PUBLISHING

The Wolf Hunter: Book 1 Desolation

Copyright © 2024 Terrence O'Malia
(Defiance Press & Publishing, LLC)

First Edition: 2024

Printed in the United States of America

10 9 8 7 6 5 4 3 2 1

All rights reserved. No part of this publication may be reproduced, distributed, or transmitted in any form or by any means, including photocopying, recording, or other electronic or mechanical methods, without the prior written permission of the publisher, except in the case of brief quotations embodied in critical reviews and certain other noncommercial uses permitted by copyright law.

This book is a work of fiction. Names, characters, places, and incidents are either products of the author's imagination or are used fictitiously. Any resemblance to actual persons, living or dead, or locales is entirely coincidental.

DEFIANCE PRESS
& PUBLISHING

ISBN-13: 978-1-963102-13-0 (Paperback)
ISBN-13: 978-1-963102-12-3 (eBook)
ISBN-13: 978-1-963102-14-7 (Hardcover)

Published by Defiance Press & Publishing, LLC

Bulk orders of this book may be obtained by contacting Defiance Press & Publishing, LLC. www.defiancepress.com.

Public Relations Dept. – Defiance Press & Publishing, LLC
281-581-9300
pr@defiancepress.com

Defiance Press & Publishing, LLC
281-581-9300
info@defiancepress.com

CHAPTER 1

The Boeing CH-46 helicopter banked hard to the right and started dropping altitude. The pilot strained through his night vision goggles to identify the landing zone about fifty kilometers from the Pakistan border. Staff Sergeant Mack Murphy was jarred awake by the sudden loss in altitude, and he immediately began preparing for the landing. The diesel exhaust invaded his nostrils as he scanned the faces of the men surrounding him. Seeing the six other warriors put his mind at ease. He closed his eyes briefly and scrubbed his mind of everything that didn't belong on a patrol through Taliban country.

"All right, amigos, time to earn your paychecks," Captain Richards said into the mic on his headgear. Captain Richards didn't usually go on patrol, but the most recent intelligence briefings had suggested the beginning of a counterinsurgency, and he had to see it for himself. At least, that is what he told the battalion commander. The truth was Captain Richards, call sign 'Apollo,' wanted some action.

The six Marines all gave him a thumbs up as they stood. The chopper landed abruptly, and the men were jostled inside the belly of the helicopter. Apollo pumped his fist as a signal to move out, and the men obeyed. The moon was nowhere in sight as the seven Marines ran down the helicopter ramp and into the darkness. They found their position and dropped to the valley floor until the sound of the rotors was soft in the distance. Slowly, they each stood and checked their microphones. Once communications were confirmed, they fell into a single file line and slowly began picking their way along the valley floor.

The sound of the helicopter was replaced by the constant chirping of crickets as the men waded through the scrub grass. Staff Sergeant Murphy was at the back of the line, and he listened to the wildlife for any sign that the seven Marines weren't alone.

Sergeant Wayne Sass, a scrappy kid from the Bronx who loved to fight, was on point. His senses were on high alert. He concentrated on the smells, the sounds, and the wind as he crept through the rocky terrain. Captain Richards was second in line, just ahead of Staff Sergeant Spencer Williams, the team's RO, or radio operator. The fourth man in line was Gunnery Sergeant Scott Martin, call sign Spartan. He would have been in charge if Apollo hadn't decided to come along for the ride. To the men in Force Recon, he was simply G-Mar, and he was not happy to be riding shotgun, but he kept his thoughts to himself. He knew Apollo was the best there was, but no Marine likes the back seat. Behind G-Mar was Corporal Liam O'Malley, the team slack man. Just behind O'Malley was Jeremiah Echols, the team's Chief Hospital Corpsman, or HMC as the Navy called them. He was the only Navy personnel on the patrol. It didn't matter what his rank was, the team Corpsman was always called 'Doc.'

The crickets stopped chirping just as the seven-man team fell into a rhythm, and the valley floor grew eerily silent. Mack's inner voice started screaming at him, and he knew something was wrong.

"Hold up. I don't like this," Mack whispered into his mic. Everyone in front of Mack took a knee.

"What is it, Mack?" G-Mar's voice crackled in Mack's earpiece.

"It's too quiet. I don't like it," Mack replied.

G-Mar was just about to speak when automatic rifle fire rang out on the valley floor. As the men dove for cover, two things became abundantly clear; the Taliban had been close enough to hear them land, and the seven-man recon patrol was horribly outnumbered.

Game time, Mack thought as he hit the deck and looked through the night scope. The AK-47 muzzle flashes looked like a thousand fireflies in the distance. All seven men were battle-hardened, and they knew not to return fire when they were outnumbered. The enemy would lock onto their position, and the same seven muzzle flashes would give away their small numbers. Mack estimated that the fireflies were coming from about one hundred meters. Too close for fire support, but what other options did they have? Something niggled at Mack's brain as he listened to the AK-47s, but he couldn't quite put the pieces together. He ordered his brain to think as he watched the men picking their way toward him. Several seconds later, the last tumbler clicked into place.

How do they know where we are? He finally thought.

How did they find us? Williams thought at the exact same moment.

"Apollo, do you want some fire support?" G-Mar asked calmly over the sound of bullets exploding into the rocks all around them.

"It's too close; we need to try to pull back a little before we engage," Apollo replied.

"Roger that."

"Mack, do you have any targets?" Apollo spoke into his microphone loud enough to be heard as another volley of bullets slammed into their position. Mack was the team sniper, and he was carrying the Remington Arms Mk13 Mod 5, chambered for the .300 WinMag. It wasn't technically the Marine Corps' sniper rifle, but Apollo didn't care what the bureaucrats thought; if Mack preferred the .300 WinMag, then Mack got a .300 WinMag.

Mack peered through his night vision scope and saw a few dozen robed men shuffling their way down the shallow ravine that separated them.

"I have targets, Captain. Permission to send these haji's back to the Stone Age," Mack replied as he slowly adjusted his scope to battle zero range.

"Listen up," Apollo said. When Mack goes hot, everyone falls back 400 meters directly south," Apollo rattled off a new grid coordinate and grabbed his rifle. "OK, Mack, get some."

Mack squeezed the trigger, and a split second later, he felt the familiar kick as the rifle butt slammed into his shoulder. He watched through his night vision scope as the Taliban fighter's head exploded into a cloud of green mist. He was firing as fast as he could find new targets and aim. Mack dropped five Taliban with five shots. *One shot, one kill*, Mack said to himself quoting Carlos Hathcock, the most famous Marine Sniper of the Vietnam War. He was exchanging the five-round magazine when Sass slapped his shoulder and yelled, "We need to book it bro, there's rag-heads everywhere."

Mack nodded in agreement after squeezing off one more round. One more green-faced Taliban toppled to the ground as Mack pushed himself up onto his knees.

"Go. I got you," Sass barked.

Just as Sass unloaded with his M4A1 in short, well-controlled bursts of fire, a rocket-propelled grenade came whistling through the air directly toward the two men. They instinctively dropped to the ground and covered their heads. The RPG screamed through the air less than a meter over their heads before detonating into the rock behind them, close enough to feel the heat, but neither man was injured.

That was close, Mack thought just as Sass let loose with another short burst of semi-automatic fire. Mack jumped to his feet and started up the ravine as Sass covered his retreat.

"We are going to have to call in some danger-close support," G-Mar said to Apollo as he grabbed the handset from Williams. "Zeus, this is Spartan. I need fire support at four-two-Sierra-Whiskey-Bravo-four-niner-zero-seven-fife-niner-six-fife-two-six. Say again, that is four-two-Sierra-Whiskey-Bravo-four-niner-zero-seven-fife-niner-six-fife-two-six. How do you copy? Over."

"Negative, Spartan. That is too close to your location. Over," Zeus replied.

"This is Spartan; we're being overrun. I repeat, we need fire support. Two hundred foot mobiles, maybe more closing fast. Danger close. How copy?"

"You're too close for the big stuff; I'll see if I can get a Cobra diverted to your position," Zeus responded.

"We need it *now*, Zeus," G-Mar shouted into his mic. After what seemed like an eternity, Zeus replied. "Put your heads down; Cobras will be on seen in five mikes. Light up your positions and stay low, Spartan."

G-Mar cupped his hand over his ear to hear the incoming traffic. "Spartan copies, Spartan out."

G-Mar looked through his night vision goggles (NVGs) down the ravine, and his heart skipped a beat. "I guess all the intel about the insurgency was right after all," he said to nobody in particular. The Taliban were quickly scrambling their way onto the ravine floor, and he wondered if they shouldn't pull back even farther.

"Pop some I.R.. We have two Cobras coming in heavy; we have to hold them off for five mikes," G-Mar screamed to be heard over the sound of rifle fire. Everyone knew what he meant. Each man carried a few plastic sticks that could be cracked to release an infrared glow that was only visible wearing night vision goggles. He whispered a silent prayer that the flyboys would be ahead of schedule and squeezed his carbine at a group of advancing Taliban.

The team returned fire in short bursts to avoid letting the enemy see too many muzzle flashes. It was pitch black, and a muzzle flash was visible for miles. The enemy was on the ravine floor and starting the 100-yard climb up the near side as the Marines kept returning fire.

Mack took two sticks and cracked them to activate the infrared glow. He launched one as far forward as he could and then threw the second one as far to his right as possible. They were only visible wearing NVGs, so the helicopter pilots would know where the friendlies were. Mack was about to squeeze off another shot when a red tracer round whizzed past his head from his right flank.

"We're getting cut off," Mack shouted into his mic.

"They are trying to flank us, Sass. Don't let that happen," G-Mar yelled.

"I hear ya boss," Sass hollered back as he altered his sector of fire about 45 degrees to the North and began sending lead presents downrange.

That's an M-60, Captain Richards said to himself. *What an unfortunate twist of fate,* he thought as he watched the United States military-manufactured tracer rounds all flying about ten feet too high. Soviet-made tracers were usually a greenish hue, but the ones coming downrange were definitely red. The US had supplied the Mujahideen with military supplies for almost twenty years in the 80s and early 90s. Now those same weapons were being turned against them by the Taliban—Whiskey Tango Foxtrot.

Mack saw movement out of the corner of his eye as he slammed another magazine into his sniper rifle. A line of machine-gun fire pocked the ground two feet from his head, so he rolled to the right and started pulling the Beretta out of his drop leg holster. He had the gun out and was bringing it onto the target as the man's face ripped off his head in a dazzling spray of green mist. Instantly, the body dropped to the rocky ground, only taking time to die on the way down. Mack turned and saw Echols firing from a crouched position just twenty feet away.

Gotta love Doc, Mack thought shoving the pistol back into his holster and quickly started scanning for more targets. Mack pulled the trigger again; this time, no recoil. *JAM,* Mack said to himself as he tried pulling the bolt back to clear the rifle. As he cleared the .300 Win Mag round out of the ejection port, he saw another black-robed man running up the rocky slope about fifteen meters from his position. He dropped the MK 13 and pulled his Beretta back out of the holster. Mack drilled a 9mm jacketed parabellum through the man's thigh. The man let out a scream as he fell to the ground. On his way down, he pulled the trigger on his AK-47, sending out a stream of bullets in Mack's direction. Suddenly, Mack felt a burning pain in his right shoulder. Before Mack could fire again, the man's head snapped back sending a dazzling spray of green mist into the air, and he fell limply to the ground. Mack could hear the M-249 SAW firing over his shoulder and he made a mental note to thank O'Malley when they got back to the rear.

Mack grabbed at his right shoulder with his left hand and felt the unmistakable hot and sticky liquid. After a quick inspection, he was satisfied that it was only a laceration from the bullet. *Good to go*, he thought and yanked another magazine from his vest, slamming it into the magazine well. *Never try the same magazine twice in a firefight. If it jammed the first time, it only stands to reason it will jam the second time*, Mack heard the voice of his sniper instructor from years ago speaking to him. As Mack stared through his scope, a flash of light burned his eyes, and he had to look away. He had been so preoccupied trying to avoid being killed that he hadn't heard Apollo announce the arrival of the Cobra gunships.

He was about to ask what had happened, but he had the answer a split second later. The Cobra Attack Helicopters were there ahead of schedule and were raining down hellfire and brimstone from its AIM-9 Sidewinders, Hydra 70s, Zuni Rockets, and the M197 three-barrel Gatling guns. The two Cobras came up from their South and lit up the battlefield like a Friday night football game. Mack saw the carnage in the valley below them, and the sight struck him. Dead bodies were sprawled out on the valley floor like they had been thrown from the helicopter. The sight burned an indelible picture into his brain that he instinctively knew would never be erased. The smell of propellant was thick, and the view of all the dead bodies in the green hue from his rifle scope was macabre.

Mack forced himself back into the fight. He began searching for targets when his eyes went blind again from a flash of light, and he felt the air get sucked out of his lungs. The rocket hit about thirty yards from his position. Luckily, the missile was heading away from him when it hit the ground at an acute angle, propelling the blast farther away from him. The next thing he felt were pins and needles in his lungs as he fought for air. Then his world went quiet. The sound was the last thing to hit him, and when it did, it blew a hole straight through his right eardrum. The microphone in his left ear had protected it from the concussion. Disoriented and gasping for air, he tried to regain his equilibrium. His NVGs further disoriented him so he flipped them up. He heard voices coming his way, so he reached for his Beretta, but it wasn't in the drop-leg holster. He quickly flipped his NVGs back down and scanned the earth around him.

"Mack," G-Mar screamed.

Mack heard his name but couldn't figure out where it was coming from and why he couldn't hear anything else. He spun to his right and saw G-Mar yelling at him, but he couldn't hear what he was saying. He swiveled his head the other way and put his hand behind his left ear.

"We gotta move. The Cobras dumped everything they have and are heading back to Bagram. The Tallies are regrouping, so we gotta go."

Mack bent to retrieve his Beretta which was lying on the ground.

"You good to go?" G-Mar said.

Mack just nodded. *I can't hear, but at least I'm alive,* he thought.

G-Mar nodded back and said, "Let's move."

The seven Marines humped another two clicks in the direction they were initially headed with no further attacks. G-Mar and Captain Richards were sure that the insurgents had retreated to the safety of the surrounding mountains and would not be regrouping for the rest of the night. Echols quickly dressed Mack's wound and reassured him he wouldn't die. HMC Jeremiah J. Echols was from Arkansas and had enlisted in the Navy when the judge gave him the option. He was pulled over while driving home from a friend's house in a car that had been reported stolen. The car belonged to a New York attorney who had been in the Ozarks on vacation when young Jeremiah hot-wired it. His father had pulled some strings and got Jeremiah's record expunged, but by the time the ink was dry on the paperwork, he was at the Great Lakes Training Facility in Michigan.

"Lucky cracker," Echols said. "You know, if you had been a brother, you would have died right there on that hillside. Brothers are always getting killed in wars, while you Crackers just get bruised and win medals."

"The Captain's still alive. So much for that theory," Mack said with a grin.

"That's because even these rag-heads are smart enough not to mess with Apollo," Echols said, chuckling to himself. Captain Richards didn't pick his call sign for any Greek God; Apollo came from the Rocky movies. He bore a striking similarity to the actor who played Apollo Creed.

"Hey, Captain, we got some goat-humpers on our nine o'clock," Sass announced softly into his mic. A split second later, all seven men were in position with weapons scanning the terrain. The team spread out in a line to cover the sectors of fire from the approaching Taliban.

"Looks like they are going to walk right past us about 200 meters away," Apollo said quietly into his microphone. All six men instantly heard him through their earpieces.

"Can I send these culchies a few bangers?" O'Malley said with his characteristic Irish brogue. Corporal Liam O'Malley was the slack man on the team, but that didn't mean he wasn't well respected. The slack man was the junior man on the team who was responsible for carrying everything that needed to be carried, including the M-249 SAW machine gun. They gave him all the heavy gear to hump, but O'Malley was more than capable. At just over six feet tall and weighing in at a smart 210 pounds, Liam was more like a pack mule than a Marine. He had grown up on the streets of Dublin before his family emigrated to the US when he was a senior in high school.

"O'Malley, we're not in Dublin. Speak English?" Apollo said.

"No disrespect intended Captain, but I believe I was."

"I think he is asking if he can shoot these mother …"G-Mar started to say, but Apollo cut him off.

"Negative. Let's be Recon Marines for a change. Let's try to get a headcount and do some snoopin and poopin." Everyone knew what the Captain meant. Stay quiet, gather intelligence, and only engage if necessary. "Let's see where they're going," Apollo said again as he peered through his night vision goggles.

Fifteen minutes later, Sass watched the line of Taliban soldiers walking past him through his NVGs. Halfway down the column of Taliban fighters, he saw something that made him momentarily stop breathing. He reached down to key his mic but thought better of it. The Captain had ordered strict radio silence. He studied the man in the middle of the column for a closer look. The man looked to be about thirty he guessed, but he couldn't tell. It was hard to tell a man's age in Afghanistan, and it was even more difficult through NVGs. He was carrying an AK-47, and he was wearing night vision goggles.

Not good, Sass said to himself. "If he could see the Taliban, the Taliban could see him." He was lying prone behind a cluster of weeds that were a scarce commodity up this high in the mountains, but the facts were the facts. Sass was holding his breath, hoping that the Taliban fighter he had just seen was the only one that had NVGs. He was just about to let out his breath when he saw it. Further up in the column of Taliban, the man carrying the M-60 had an infrared dot on his head. Before he could think, Sass had keyed his mic.

"Turn off all I.R. Say again, turn off all I.R. now."

The whole team heard it and slowly reached up to push the buttons on their AN/ PEQ-2 infrared sights mounted to their rifles.

G-Mar had just lit up his night vision scope and found the man carrying the M-60. He placed the infrared dot on the side of his head and was tracking him when he heard Sass over the comms. He slowly reached up to turn off his infrared, but as he did, his rifle dipped, and the I.R. beam drew a line in the sand two feet from the man with the NVGs.

Sass saw the man jerk his head up the slope to the right and step off the trail. He barked out some orders, and men began scrambling.

"Do not engage," G-Mar said over his comms. "I say again. *Do not engage.*"

A second later, the hillside lit up with muzzle flashes as AK-47 and M-60 rounds slammed the dusty earth surrounding the seven-man team on the crest of the hill. Sass continued to watch the man with the NVGs. He hadn't fired even though he had given the order. He flipped up his NVGs and looked at the man through the night vision scope mounted to his rifle. He saw the NVGs and realized why he wasn't firing. They were a first generation, Russian-made model. They were great if you wanted to see in the dark, but too much ambient light would render the wearer temporarily blinded, and AK-47s had a very bright muzzle flash.

The shooting began to trickle off, and Sass saw a man stomping past others to get to the man wearing the NVGs. He saw them waving and heard them shouting in what sounded like Arabic, but they were too far away to understand what they were saying. *Arabic?* he thought. He had taken part in the initial push to Baghdad in 2003 and was familiar with the language.

The last AK-47 was silent now, and the group resumed their pace along the valley floor. Captain Richards counted over 125 insurgents as he saw the last man shuffle past his position. A quick estimate told him that the force they had encountered earlier was probably over 200 strong. That was disturbing, but what really disturbed him was the weapons they were carrying. He counted at least fourteen RPGs and three mortar tubes. The Taliban never traveled in numbers like that. The entire point of guerrilla warfare was speed and mobility. Travel in small groups, strike hard, and then get out.

Apollo realized that the counterinsurgency had indeed begun. The weapons were flowing across the Pakistan border and the men they were fighting that night were not Afghani. They were most likely Arabs from Iran, Syria, and Saudi Arabia. Apollo had visual evidence that the intel was accurate. He continued to watch the line of soldiers filing past him. Some of the men were not men at all; they were boys. Some of them looked like they were no older than ten. He saw the M-60 with the ammo belts wrapped around an insurgent's neck, which explained the tracer rounds. If they started shooting, he wanted to take out that gun first. Just as the last man trudged along the trail, Captain Richards keyed his mic.

"SitRep, over."

One by one, the men on the team checked in. Mack told Apollo that he had taken a round to the right shoulder and blew out an eardrum earlier, but it was OK. The bleeding had stopped, and Echols had already bandaged it. Everyone else was all right until they got to Williams. Spencer Williams was wiry with an athletic build and came in just a shade under six feet. He had been to every training school Mack had been to over the past two years, and the two were like brothers. Spencer was the starting quarterback for Columbia University the day his girlfriend fell sixty-seven floors inside the South Tower of the World Trade Center. He had been in the Marine Corps reserves, but after the love of his life died he just couldn't seem to focus on school, so he left his studies behind and went looking for revenge. He never talked about it with anyone but Mack.

"I took a round to my left side, but it will be fine. It's not bleeding," Williams said.

"On my way, Spence," Echols said and slowly retreated up the side of the hill. He didn't stand until he was well over the rise, so his silhouette wouldn't be visible to the man with the NVGs.

Twenty minutes later, Williams was patched up. Sass had filled in everybody regarding the NVGs, and how the guy wearing them had spotted the I.R. laser. They didn't dwell on whose it was. It could have been any of the lasers mounted to their carbines. The point was that they had gathered actionable intelligence. The enemy was getting wiser too and much better supplied than two years ago.

"I guess the NVGs explain how they knew where we were earlier," G-Mar said to nobody in particular over his throat mic.

"Copy that. All right, we need to know where they are heading," Apollo said into his mic.

G-Mar was about to respond when Mack's voice cut him off.

"It looks like they are coming back," Mack whispered into his throat mic. He had just picked his way over a boulder and was peering through his scope when he spotted movement on the ridge to the east. He cursed to himself as he instantly realized what was happening. The insurgent wearing the NVGs was not new to this game. He knew that the Americans were on the ridge, but when there was no return fire, he played it cool. He ordered his men to continue down the trail until they were far enough away. Then he backtracked and came up the ravine and headed West in a classic flanking maneuver. *Chalk one up for the douche bags*, Mack said to himself. It was standard operating procedure for an infantry unit, but Jihadists were known for their brutality, not their infantry squad tactics. The seven-man Recon team would have to play this game like chess instead of checkers. "We're getting flanked again," Mack said through his mic as he climbed back off the rock.

"Pull back, everyone!" Captain Richards said, and he pulled the map from his chest pocket. He jabbed his finger at the map as G-Mar bent his head close to look at it through his NVGs.

"We need to make it here by 0300, and then we will call in fire support if they are stupid enough to follow us," G-Mar said, agreeing with Apollo's idea. "We need them to follow us, so don't get too far ahead. We need to keep them in our sights but far enough away to avoid those rockets."

Everyone peeled off and headed down the embankment on a path that would intersect the trail where battle-hardened insurgent fighters had just shuffled past. Mack watched the enemy pick their way up the path for another few seconds before heading back down the boulders to rejoin the team. They crossed the path without incident and slowly began picking their way up the rocky slope. Fifty minutes later, at their new rally point, they set up a hasty perimeter. Mack called in their position over the secure satellite phone and then started working on his sniper hide. He had to conceal his muzzle flash as well as he possibly could. They had mortars, and Mack had already learned not to underestimate this group. Walking in mortar fire to an effective kill zone took just a few minor adjustments.

Twenty minutes later, Mack saw the first soldier scurry across the road. He estimated the range at 1200 meters. Well within the 1300-meter distance his sniper rifle was capable of, but *Who needed an MK 13 when you had a satellite phone and the entire United States Marine Corps in your back pocket* Mack thought.

"We have company, gentleman," Mack said into his mic. The insurgents just crossed the road and were heading up into the rocks.

"Apollo, we have some back-door visitors as well," O'Malley added.

Captain Richards was moving now. He crouched down next to O'Malley and peered through his scope. He clicked his throat mic and said, "We gotta quit underestimating these towel heads. They flanked us again. Listen up. We may have a Little Bighorn going on right now. I need up-to-date information on all troop movements. This one is going to be up to the flyboys tonight, gentleman." The rally point he had chosen was the highest peak for miles. It was good high ground, but what he hadn't known earlier was that it was also very exposed.

Mack kept the satellite connection open as the men called out any troop movements. The whole mountain was about to be lit up like a Christmas tree. Mack had heard about the special forces unit blown up by friendly fire during his first deployment to Afghanistan. A group of

Green Berets with ODA-574 dropped a JDAM right on their own position and killed three berets and five Afghani. The rumors were flying that the incident happened because the officers wanted in on the fight. Mack was glad when Captain Richards allowed him to call in all fire missions over the secure satellite phone.

Mack reported the last of the enemy positions, disconnected the satellite connection with Bagram, and smiled to himself. It was going to be quite a show. They were keeping the night's work in the family, so to speak, as two AV-8B Marine Corps Harriers with the VMA-223 were en route accompanied by his two favorite Cobra pilots that night. Mack conveyed the news to the rest of the team and advised everyone to find some good cover. He told them he ordered takeout and to watch for a parachute from one of the Cobras. Everyone knew what Mack meant, and they all replied in the affirmative. The takeout was a resupply of ammo, water, and whatever else they could get into the small box that would be dropped over their position. Mack saw the insurgents advancing up the road and figured they numbered close to fifty. The other seventy-five insurgents were coming in the back door. Mack grabbed the satellite phone he had been carrying and made a split-second decision. He would get his butt chewed off when they returned to base, but he had to make one more phone call. Mack powered on the device again and pushed the digits from memory. After fifteen seconds of pings and pauses, he heard her voice.

CHAPTER 2

Renée Murphy gave the cashier one of her enormous smiles as she unloaded her purchases onto the conveyor belt. The teenage girl working the register gave her a fake smile in return and then rolled her eyes as she began scanning the items. Renée saw the girl roll her eyes, but she let it go. It was her third trip to the grocery store this week, so she had seen the same cashier twice before. She was dressed all in black with black lipstick and black fingernail polish. Everything about the young girl screamed *leave me alone*. Renée figured there wasn't much to make the young girl happy, so she just pulled the items from her cart. Going to the store used to be easy for Renée, but carrying four bags of groceries became infinitely more difficult now that she had twin three-month-old babies to look after. She flashed one more smile, revealing a perfectly aligned and magnificent set of white teeth at the young man putting her groceries into the bags, and then she pushed the shopping cart toward the exit. Renée knew that smile would get a much bigger response from the young man.

She had just turned twenty-eight, but her black skin didn't look much older than the smooth skin of the babies staring back at her. Renée transferred the babies to the stroller that she had left at the front of the store and headed toward the Ford Excursion for the short trip to her mother's home. The Excursion belonged to Mack, and it was his pride and joy. It had been brand new only five months earlier and still had the faint smell of a new car. Renée's little, two-door BMW didn't seem very practical anymore after the twins came along, and she planned to trade it in.

She was in a quiet suburb outside of Cleveland, Ohio, and her life as a new mother was good. Breastfeeding was a bit of a challenge at first, with two bellies to satisfy, but being the mommy of twin girls was a blessing beyond her wildest dreams. The girls were fraternal twins, and each child bore an uncanny resemblance to one of their parents. Renée was still employed with the Central Intelligence Agency, but she was on maternity leave. She had been with the CIA for almost six years when she saw that little pink line at the end of a plastic stick that would change her life forever. As she clicked the first car seat into the base in the back seat of the Excursion, her phone rang. Renée gave Brianna, the oldest twin by twenty-two minutes, a huge smile and kissed her on the forehead. As Renée fished the phone from her pocket and glanced at the caller ID, her smile was rewarded with a saliva-filled grin complete with a few bubbles. She was strapped into her seat so well she looked like an F-16 pilot. She laughed out loud as she pushed the button to answer the call.

"Hey, baby," she said as she closed the back door and made smiley faces at Brianna through the window.

"How are my girls?" Mack whispered.

"We are just fine," she said feeling a little apprehension beginning to take root. "And why are you whispering?"

"I'm at the theater," Mack whispered. Theater was the code word Mack had devised to let Renée know he was in an ongoing operation. For the last two months, Mack had been calling almost every day on the secure, Iridium satellite field phone. Renée had procured the phone from the CIA to give to Mack before deploying. It worked better than the Marine Corps' issued device, so he used it for work as well.

"Is it a good movie?" Renée said, falling into the prearranged dialogue that they had worked out. If Mack replied that the movie was boring or a new chick flick, Renée could breathe a sigh of relief. It meant that things were going smoothly, and he was indeed bored. If he said the movie was a real thriller, she knew to put the phone to each little girl's ear so that Mack could tell his daughters that Daddy loved them ... possibly for the last time. Renée held her breath and said a silent prayer waiting for the three-second delay that came with communicating via a satellite phone from halfway around the world.

"It's a real thriller," she heard Mack say softly.

Renée felt the wind rush out of her lungs as she held the phone to Aubrey's right ear and said, "Here's Daddy."

Mack spoke in a soft fatherly voice, "I love you very much, and I can't wait to see you when I get home. Be good to your mother, and never forget your daddy loves you more than life itself." Renée repeated the process with Brianna, who was still blowing bubbles and cooing softly; then Renée put the phone back to her own ear.

"How good is the movie?" Renée said, willing herself not to cry.

"The best one I've ever seen, babe," Mack said. Before Renée could reply, Mack said, "I love you, Pep, but I gotta get back to the movie."

"I love you too," Renée said, her voice finally cracking, and the tears that were forcing their way out couldn't be held back any longer. "Be safe; you come home to me, Mack. You have three girls that love you very much."

"I will, Pep. I promise," he said, using the nickname he had given her on their first official date, and then he disconnected the call.

"Bye," Renée said softly as the sobs came. She had no idea what was wrong with her lately. Despite being as happy as she could ever remember, she cried almost every day. She blamed it on her hormones, but deep down, she knew that she missed Mack more than she cared to admit. Mack had only spent a month with his new daughters before he deployed. Standing on the tarmac, she watched him as he hugged and kissed the girls one at a time before putting them back into the stroller and boarding the C-17 back to Afghanistan. She cried even harder when she remembered that day and how difficult it must have been for him. As Renée finished buckling Aubrey into her seat, she thought back to their first date aboard the USS Peleliu three years earlier.

*****

Renée was aboard the USS Peleliu eight weeks after the September 11th attacks. The President and Secretary of Defense were pushing the CIA to start gaining a foothold in the region, as it had been far too long since the US had an embassy or even a CIA presence in Afghanistan. She was to link up with the Marines going into Afghanistan to secure a base of operations against the wishes of the CIA Director, Maxwell Kaine. She would also start recruiting assets the minute she hit the ground. The North had several CIA operators working with the Northern Alliance, but the South was virtually untouched.

The plan called for an overland assault of about 400 miles via CH-53 helicopters to a small airstrip known as Forward Operating Base (FOB) Rhino. She was to be part of the initial insertion team, tasked with surveilling the area ahead of the Fleet Marine Force's arrival. Two years of training had begun to pay off. She was looking forward to the mission, but she was unsure how the Marines would take the news that a female spook was going to be with them on the initial insertion. Just three days before the invasion, Renée was tasked with briefing the Marines about the satellite phones and other communications equipment that the CIA had provided for the op and explaining to them her interpretive assets. The briefing was with the First Marine Divisions Reconnaissance team and 7 snipers from STA (Surveillance and Target Acquisition) Platoon.

Renée felt every eye in the room on her as Major Keels laid out the plan in intricate detail. It was not a new feeling for her. She had always been beautiful, but up until now, the eyes boring into her had never been a room full of battle-hardened Marines. After a brief introduction, the Major gave Renée the floor.

As Renée stood and walked to the front of the room, one of the Marines let out a long whistle. The other Marines were about to do the same when the Major ordered the men to "lock it up."

Renée saw the Marine who had whistled at her, so she turned to face him and said, "Thank you."

"Good afternoon, gentleman, my name is Renée Shaw, and I am with the Central Intelligence Agency," she said in a commanding voice that didn't allow for any question regarding her authority.

"There ain't any gentlemen in this room. I can tell you that for sure, ma'am," a voice said from the back of the room. The Marines all chuckled out loud until the Major called for silence again.

"I am quite certain that you have been given some bad intelligence, whoever said that," Renée replied sarcastically. She plowed on with her briefing as she pulled out the encrypted satellite phones and handed them to the Major. The Major then passed them out to the senior men who would depend on them once they arrived in Afghanistan. Renée spent the next fifteen minutes walking them through the phones' functions. She rattled off codes to dial to get the right locations. She passed out a dozen code sheets that went with the twelve phones she distributed and encouraged everyone in the room to memorize them. The pieces of paper were to be collected before they could leave the briefing.

"These codes will change every two days once we land in Afghanistan, so you will need to memorize long strings of numbers." Nobody picked up on her use of the word *we*, so she plowed on. "I realize this may be hard for some of you," she said as her eyes met the Marine sergeant who had whistled earlier, and the rest of the Marines roared with laughter. She was about to end her briefing, so she silently steeled herself for what she was about to say.

"Does anybody in this room speak Pashto or Dari?" she asked.

"I can say al-Qaeda," said the same voice from earlier. Only a few daring souls chuckled at that comment, and the room fell silent once again.

"Well, then I guess I'll just have to go with you all," Renée said with more confidence than she felt. There was silence for an uncomfortably long time. The Major, who had a dumbfounded look, was about to say something when Renée cut him off. "Those orders are from the White House; I would choose your words carefully, Major Keels," Renée said. She knew she had stepped in it when everyone stared at the Major, but she didn't let it get to her as she retook her seat.

"Well, I guess it won't be so bad; you're a lot easier on the eyes than this group of jarheads; that's for sure," Major Keels responded somewhat sarcastically.

Renée decided to give the Major a little victory and didn't respond. She had learned how to deal with overly confident men, and she knew she had to let them win now and then or they turned into sore losers. She knew the mission had to take precedence over everything else, so she quietly stared at the Major before giving him a wink to let him know that she appreciated the comment.

The meeting broke up, so she collected all twelve pieces of paper, inserted them into her briefcase, and turned to leave. As she approached the hatch, a very handsome Marine returned to the room. She had noticed him earlier in the briefing, but didn't give him much thought. He was a man of above-average height, probably around six feet tall, with curly black hair tapered to bare flesh around his ears and nape of his neck. He just stood there in the doorway and stared at her.

"Can I help you?" Renée said, trying to find a name tag. Marines in Reconnaissance and STA Platoon did not wear their names on their uniforms like other Marines did. She remembered somebody saying that earlier in the day.

"Murphy. Sergeant Mack Murphy, ma'am, with Sniper Platoon

First Marines. I'm pleased to make your acquaintance again," Mack said as he extended his hand.

"Sergeant Murphy, it's nice to meet you too," she said, accepting Mack's hand. "What can I help you with?" Renée had heard the word 'again,' but she chalked it up to being introduced earlier during the briefing. Renée was nowhere close to being ready for what Mack Murphy was about to ask her, and when he got down on one knee and asked her if he could have the honor of escorting her to the enlisted man's club that evening for drinks, she started to laugh. The stress and pressure of the briefing had caused her to let her guard down momentarily, but she quickly got her emotions back in check.

"Not the response I was hoping for, but I am encouraged by your lack of rejection thus far. I have been shot down before, believe it or not. But before you answer," Mack said with her hand still in his, "I need to tell you something."

"What do you have to tell me?" Renée said, still smiling and growing a little uncomfortable at how long he had been holding her hand.

> *How do I love thee? Let me count the ways.*
> *I love thee to the depth and breadth and height*
> *My soul can reach, when feeling out of sight*
> *For the ends of being and ideal grace.*
> *I love thee to the level of every day's*
> *Most quiet need, by sun and candle-light.*
> *I love thee freely, as men strive for right.*
> *I love thee purely, as they turn from praise.*
> *I love thee with the passion put to use*
> *In my old griefs, and with my childhood's faith.*
> *I love thee with a love I seemed to lose*
> *With my lost saints. I love thee with the breath,*
> *Smiles, tears, of all my life; and, if God choose,*
> *I shall but love thee better after death.*

Renée stood for a long time staring down at the handsome man on one knee. How did he know that was her favorite poem? Here was a man she took to be just another one of the Neanderthal Marines who had been making crude gestures at her since the day she landed on the Iron Nickel, as the sailors referred to the *USS Peleliu*. The giant number 5 painted on the quarterdeck had earned it the nickname. He finished speaking, and she knew he was waiting for a response.

"How did you know I was a Shakespeare fan?" she finally said, trying to see if he honestly did know what he was talking about, or if he had been put up to the stunt by one of his Neanderthal colleagues.

"Why you aren't a Shakespeare fan at all, my lady. You have much better taste than that. You are an Elizabeth Barrett Browning fan, and so am I. Her 43rd Sonnet happens to be my favorite."

Renée was impressed that he knew who her favorite poet was, but she chalked it up to a good guess. "How do I know you aren't just a typical Marine looking to get into my pants a few times before you tell me, 'It's not you; it's me?'"

"You are going to have to take my word for it, but the odds are slightly in your favor," Mack said, grinning.

"Why is that?"

"Typical Marines don't know who Elizabeth Barrett Browning is, much less quote an entire poem. Most Marines don't know any poems without the F word in it, which makes me not your typical Marine. Plus, that's not my style."

"Yes," Renée said.

An awkward silence soon filled the room as Mack got off his knee. "Yes, what?" he finally managed to say.

"Yes, I will go to the enlisted club with you tonight," she finally said.

Mack jumped up and down as he pumped his fists in the air like Rocky on the steps of the Philadelphia Art Museum.

Renée understood the meaning and giggled softly.

"Okay, you do realize that there is no enlisted man's club on the ship, so would you settle for cold sodas in the mess hall tonight around 1900?"

"I hadn't realized that," Renée said, "but don't get too excited, Jarhead. Most men never make it to a second date, and nobody's gonna make it all the way without C4," Renée said with a hint of playfulness in her voice.

"C4, as in the plastic explosive?" Mack said, sounding confused.

"C4 as in color, cut, clarity, and carat," Renée replied and held up her left hand. She wiggled her ring finger to make sure he knew where she stood.

Mack smiled and raised his pinky. "Pinky swear, I will not even try to kiss you tonight."

Renée offered him her pinky finger, and they shook on it. "I'll see you tonight, Sergeant," Renée said and flashed the smile that had captured Mack's heart the first time he saw it three and a half years earlier.

Ten minutes before 1900 hours, Mack strolled into the mess hall. He poured himself a glass of soda from the fountain machine and took a seat at the very back. At 2000 hours, he was reasonably sure he had been stood up when Renée came walking into the mess hall.

"I thought you had stood me up," she said, laughing as she passed a dozen Marines staring at her and sat down across the table from Mack.

"I thought the same thing," he replied.

"I've been sitting in the officers' mess for the past hour until it dawned on me that you did say the enlisted man's club. The skipper here has been encouraging me to eat in the officers' mess since I arrived," Renée said.

"I am sorry to disappoint you, but I am not part of the gentry, milady," Mack said in a sad attempt to mimic a British accent. "I am but a poor yeoman."

"Well, you are certainly full of surprises. I had no idea you spoke the King's English."

Before Mack could respond, she interjected, "Where is that glass of soda you promised me?" Mack just smiled at her and stood to get it.

"Are you a diet soda girl, or do you like the hard stuff?" Mack said as he stared at her face. She was so breathtakingly beautiful it was hard not to.

"Do you think I need the diet soda?" Renée replied playfully.

Mack just went to the fountain and filled a large plastic cup full of regular soda and brought it back to the table. He handed her the plastic cup but stayed glued to her face.

"Thank you," Renée said, "and a wise choice, by the way."

Soon, Mack realized he had been staring for too long, so he dipped his head and went for it. "Do you not remember me?" Mack said with a conspiratorial tone.

"Uhh, I …" Renée stammered.

"We have met before, you know. I believe it was at the Green Leafe Café while you were at William & Mary. Computer Science and Global Studies, if memory serves me correctly."

"That would have been … what, at least four years ago?" Renée said.

"Three and a half, to be exact. April 9th, 1998, I believe it was. I asked if I could take you out for a drink, and you said *no*."

"I said *no* a lot of times when I was at William & Mary; how do you remember the exact date?"

"It is not every day that a man gets to sit next to the most beautiful woman on the planet, especially after being around a bunch of Marines for almost six weeks. I was up in Newport News with some friends right after we graduated Sniper School at Quantico."

"But how do you remember the date?" Renée said more forcefully.

"I uh … I have a pretty good memory," Mack said, somewhat embarrassed. He wasn't trying to brag, but it was true.

"Really," Renée said. "A photographic memory, I would say to remember the exact date."

"Something like that," Mack mumbled under his breath.

"I have met a few people who claim to have a photographic memory, but when pushed to prove it, they realize that it is not truly photographic but just exceptionally good. A true photographic memory is pretty rare."

It is, Mack thought, but he didn't dare say it out loud. "I guess I just have a good memory," he finally replied.

Renée stared hard at Mack. She was about to press him on it when the memory flooded back to her. "I do remember that. You quoted me some poetry back then too."

"You were made perfectly to be loved, and surely I have loved you, in the idea of you, my whole life," Mack said, quoting Elizabeth Barrett Browning again.

"I do remember you. I asked if you were a Barrett Browning fan, and you said, 'Of course; they are my two favorite rifles.'" Renée was laughing now, and Mack had begun chuckling as well.

"That's how you knew who my favorite poet was." Renee said excited that she had the answer to the question she had been asking herself all day. "But seriously, when did you remember that?"

"What I do, and what I dream include thee ..."

"As the wine must taste of its own grapes," Renée finished the Browning quote before he could.

"I remembered you the second I saw you today." Mack shifted in his seat, leaned forward, looked her in the eyes, and said, "For a man of low estate, when in the company of beauty so great, will ne'er forget the lady's face, that stopped his heart in its place."

"Not sure I know who said that ..." Renée searched her memory. "Was it Yeats?"

"Sergeant Mack Murphy," he said sarcastically.

"A warrior and a poet, I see." Renée liked him so far.

"We Irishmen are known for that."

Renée smiled and flashed her brilliantly white teeth. "Is that so?"

"But I am only half Irish," Mack said.

"And what is the other half?"

"My mother was half Blackfoot and half Cherokee."

"Mack Murphy really doesn't strike me as a Native American name," Renée said, wondering if he was joking.

"Well, my real name is Makoyii Kanati Murphy, but you can call me Mack for short. But again, enough about me. I want to know what nationalities collided to create this stunning beauty," he said as he gestured toward Renée.

"Does your name carry any special significance?" Renée pressed ignoring the gesture. "I have studied Native American culture a little bit, and they don't just pick names based on societal trends. They usually carry ancestral significance. Am I correct?"

Mack wasn't sure why, but he liked her more every second. He hesitated a moment before answering her. He wasn't sure she was ready for the answer, but he had been rolling the dice all day. *Why stop now?* he thought. "It literally means the one who hunts the wolf. Makoyii is the Blackfoot name for wolf, and Kanati is sometimes translated as Great Hunter."

"The Great Wolf Hunter," Renée said without the slightest trace of levity.

"I guess you could say that," Mack said, trying not to blush.

"And what does the name Murphy mean?" she added sarcastically.

"Sea Warrior," he replied trying not to smile.

"The Great Wolf Hunting Sea Warrior," Renée said with obvious fascination.

"Something like that, but enough about me. I want to hear about Renée Shaw."

Renée paused for a moment as well. Not because she didn't understand what Mack wanted but because the irony was not lost on her. In her line of work, there were three types of people. The masses were referred to as sheep. Well-intentioned but completely ignorant people who went about their lives as though the world were full of rainbows and unicorns. The second group was referred to as wolves. The murderers, thieves, dictators, sociopaths, and psychopaths were all lumped in with the wolves. Osama bin Laden was the most notorious wolf at that time and the reason the Iron Nickel was preparing for an invasion of Afghanistan. Then there were people like Mack Murphy. The sheep dogs, or those who protected the sheep and hunted the wolves. She had no doubt that Mack was well aware of the significance, but she was silently impressed by his lack of false bravado.

"Well, my grandfather on my dad's side was as Black as you can get from the Mississippi Delta. He married my grandmother when he was stationed in Korea, so my father was half Black, half Korean. Pure-blooded Afghani on my mother's side."

"So this is a homecoming for you," Mack said, clearly fascinated.

"In some ways, I guess. I grew up speaking the language with my grandparents, but I guess I never really considered it my homeland." Renée was silent for a moment, studying Mack's face and tracing the scar above his right eye. She wondered where he got it or, more importantly, who had given it to him. She didn't ask. Mack was about to say something, but Renée beat him to it. "Do you think this could ever work?" she said and then tried to force a frown onto her face even though she wasn't feeling sad.

Mack was confused by the statement. At first, he asked if she was talking about the upcoming mission. Renée shook her head silently. It became clear to Mack that she was talking about the two of them. He lifted his eyes and indicated by his facial expression that he now understood the question.

"Well, you'd have to find me a job with the CIA, and we'd have to get stationed in the same country preferably, but I think it would work out."

Renée just smiled again and said, "No, silly, this." She put her hand on top of his, and when Mack saw the stark contrast between the two hands, he smiled.

"Well, I have been wondering about that question for the past three and a half years, and the only thing I can come up with is that it has worked for the saltshaker for hundreds of years," Mack said, smiling.

"The saltshaker?" Renée said, puzzled.

"The saltshaker doesn't go anywhere without pepper. I guess you could say they are pretty much inseparable, and the world has accepted that," Mack said, trying to look serious.

"You were doing so well, and then you had to go all corny cliche on me," Renée said with her best attempt at being offended. "Does that make me pepper? Are you comparing me to an insignificant plastic container filled with little flecks of black spice?"

"Yes," Mack said, doubling down. "But when I think of you, I would probably say Jalapeño pepper 'cause you are definitely spicy." Before Renée could respond, Mack cut her off and said, "I shall now refer to you as Pepper, or Pep for short. How would that be?"

"I like it, but I don't think I will call you Salt. A guy named Mack doesn't need a nickname anyways."

"Milady, you can call me anything you want, as long as it is for the rest of my life."

"You are so corny. No wonder I told you *no* back at the Green Leafe."

"I thought it was because you had another boyfriend. At least, that's what you told me. Are you saying you said *no* because I was corny?" Mack tried to fake a horrified look, but it wasn't working.

That first date was all it took. Renée hadn't thought in a million years that she would fall in love with a White man, but after two hours of conversation and several glasses of soda, she had indeed fallen in love. He was ruggedly handsome yet still maintained a boyish smile. He was intelligent and brave, no doubt, but his soft-spoken nature and easy-going smile were what she liked the most. She wasn't sure what she thought about snipers, but he was definitely a man of action. Killing people didn't seem to suit him, but she had no doubt he would be good at it. He wasn't pretentious; he wasn't trying to be somebody he wasn't. He was just Mack. Her last boyfriend had been a lawyer who worked for a big law firm in DC, and as Renée mentally stacked Mack against him, she wondered what she had seen in him at all.

"Well, it's getting late, and I have some things left to do before we go," Renée said as she started to stand.

"Yeah, me too." Mack stood and thanked her for the beautiful evening.

"It was fun," Renée said and turned to go.

"One more thing," Mack said. "It's about the mission."

Renée looked at Mack and saw what she thought was that good old-fashioned bravado coming out, so she cut him off. "Is this where you tell me that you'd feel better if I stayed on the ship and didn't risk getting my nails broken out there with the men?" Renée said a little more sarcastically than she wanted. Men were all the same, she thought and then cocked her head to the side as she waited for Mack's response. He had been caught off guard, and Renée saw it.

"I was just going to say that you will have to teach me how to use that phone again because I don't think I heard a word of your briefing this morning. I was too busy looking at how beautiful you are." Before Renée could respond, Mack said, "That way, I can teach the other thirty guys how to use them too."

Renée smiled and stuck out her hand. "I'm sorry. That wasn't how I wanted to end the evening."

"That's not how I wanted the evening to end either, but a pinky promise is a pinky promise," Mack said, sticking out his pinky finger.

Renée gave Mack her finger and apologized again for the rude comment. She knew she would have to forget all about him in a few days, so she started preparing herself for the compartmentalization that would have to happen. The mission came first. "I'll see you around, Jarhead."

"Later, Pep," Mack said. "Does that mean I passed?"

"Passed what?" Renée replied.

"Did I make it to a second date?" Mack said and then tried his best to appear humbled.

"You did."

"Well, I hope I don't have to wait another three and a half years before I see you again."

"Me too," Renée said, and she meant it.

*****

Renée closed the back door of the Excursion as the first few drops of rain started hitting the windshield. She sat in the driver's seat, trying to process the phone call. She silently wondered if she had any friends awake at this time of night in the Middle East who could give her a situation report on what Mack was up against, but she knew it would only make things worse. She bowed her head, whispered a silent prayer for her husband, and then started the Excursion for the ten-minute ride home.

CHAPTER 3

Marco Bertoli pulled into the Foxxy nightclub and eased his brand new Porsche into the reserved parking space behind the building. He grabbed a comb from his jacket pocket and ran it through his hair as he looked into the rearview mirror. Combing his hair had always been a nervous habit, but lately, he was concerned that there seemed to be less of it every day. He examined the comb for any loose strands and when he didn't see any, he reassured himself that he had only been imagining it. The doctor had given him some medication to rub into his hair, but he could never remember to do it. He looked into the rear view mirror one more time and climbed out of the car.

He closed the door and pushed the button to activate the $3,000 anti-theft device he had just installed. He ran the comb through his greasy hair one more time and checked to make sure his TT-33 nickel-plated pistol was ready to go. Marco had no intention of using it tonight, but considering his meeting was with an unhappy customer, he figured he would be better safe than sorry. The young Eastern European girl he had sold to the man for $20,000 was not as hardy as he preferred. After his first experiment with her, the girl died, and Marco had to dispose of the body.

What he did with his women was no business of mine, Marco thought as he greeted the bouncer opening the door for him. He spotted the morbidly obese man the minute he walked through the door. The unhappy customer had a woman on his lap, and twenty-dollar bills flew out of his hand like he was printing them at home. *He may have been,* Marco thought and made a mental note to check a few of them as he walked to his table.

"Marco, so good to see you." The obese man slurred his words more than he spoke them.

"You too, my friend," Marco replied. "Are you enjoying yourself?"

"I need another one of your finest products from Croatia, and I am not going to pay the same price this time without some guarantees," the obese man said, only half paying attention to the woman sitting on his lap.

Marco took one look at the woman and nodded his head. She dutifully obeyed, climbed off his lap, and made her way to the back. Once she was behind the stage, Marco stared at the fat man and said, "We do not discuss business in their presence, and the price is the same, my friend. What you do with the product is none of my business. If you ruin the devices, you are responsible for replacing them, not me." Marco sat down in the chair opposite the morbidly obese man as another waitress brought him a small glass of his favorite vodka.

"I'll give you $15,000 this time, but I get to pick out my device before I pay for it. I want to make sure it looks durable."

"You know the way I do business. You look at my catalog, and you pick one. Next, you pay me $20,000, and then I deliver. It is too risky to let customers see the devices first, as you must understand."

There was a long pause, and then the obese man relented and finally said, "How long does it take to ship this time? I am really in a hurry for it, as you can see by my present situation."

"Two weeks, maybe less, depending on production time and shipping."

"Two weeks; what am I going to do for two weeks?" the obese man said, waving his fist full of twenty dollar bills.

"Spend your money at my club like you have been for the past five years. What else?" Marco said, waving his arm around the strip club. He liked to make people believe it belonged to him. It made him feel more important to tell his clients that he was in full control of the family business and that his younger brother, Matteo, was still learning the ropes. Marco owned none of it. In fact, he had a building suspicion that he would not be taking over anything except a back seat to his younger brother.

Several weeks ago, Marco had made a special deal with the obese man sitting across from him. The man was fairly important in the local government, and Marco knew his real name, but he never used it. If the public knew that he spent his nights in a strip club, his reputation would be destroyed. The obese man had helped Marco with a few legal problems over the past few years, so he did feel a slight sense of obligation toward the man, but business was business. The family business didn't usually involve selling the girls to clients so much as he just rented them out for $300 to $400 dollars an hour, depending on the quality, as he referred to it. Selling the girls outright was something that Marco had started entirely on his own through a contact he had made with some of his father's Russian friends.

Marco locally harvested most of his produce, but a cargo container with a few dozen products was shipped to a dock in Cleveland, Ohio, once every six or seven months. They came from Croatia, Moldova, Latvia, Slovakia, or some Eastern bloc country; Marco could never remember the names. They were shipped from Russia to the Alaskan coastline and then put into containers marked as Chinese-built riding lawnmowers. The girls were all packed into soundproof boxes until they made it through customs and were cleared. After a reasonable distance, one of the men would open all the containers and lock the girls down to the metal poll that ran along the container's inside until they reached the railroad.

Next, the containers were loaded onto a train and taken to Port Dover, Ontario. From there, they were once again jammed into the soundproof lawnmower containers for the late-night ride across Lake Erie on a fast-moving barge that could cover the distance in several hours. Once they arrived at the port, Marco and his men unpackaged them and then reloaded them into a small van for the short ride to his Westside Warehouse. By the time they got to Marco, they were so weak and pathetic that they gave virtually no resistance. Once in the warehouse, he fed them just enough to keep them alive, but he also got them hooked on heroin. Marco knew that a heroin addict was much easier to control so long as the heroin kept coming. It also had the desired effect of keeping them loyal to whoever provided it for them. As luck would have it, Marco was also a substantial supplier of heroin, so it worked out well for him. He also gained some free employment to help with his meth labs that he had started until the girls were re-homed, as he liked to put it. Marco had heard the expression used at the local animal shelter, and he thought he was being clever by using it. Marco may not have been fit to inherit the family business, but he had proved he knew how to make money.

Marco had just concluded his business with the obese man when Sal Rigo entered the club. Sal was wearing a black Armani suit with a crisp, white shirt unbuttoned to his chest and smoking a Toscano cigar.

"I thought I would find you here," Sal said. "We have some issues that need your expertise."

"Why didn't you just call me?"

Sal motioned to the back door, and Marco stood and followed him.

"What is this about?" Marco said, growing a little apprehensive.

"We have a new shipment coming in two hours," Sal whispered excitedly.

"How many?" Marco replied with every bit as much excitement. They were like two kids in a candy store.

Sal lifted his eyebrows and spoke softly for emphasis. "Twenty-five."

Marco quickly did the math and determined that he would make just a little over $350,000 that evening. Of course, he had to find buyers first, but that was the easy part.

"Do we have the purchase money?" Sal said casually, not wanting to offend Marco. It didn't work.

"What do you think?"

"Of course you have the money. Should we go and get ready?"

"Did you get a menu?" Marco asked.

"No, not yet," Sal responded quizzically. "Why?"

"We have a potential client in there right now, and he is eager to take delivery."

"Marco, you've seen what they look like when they get here; you may want to let the products ripen a little."

"You're right," Marco said. "Let's go."

*****

Special Agent Claire Larkin brought the Motorola Walkie-Talkie to her mouth and said, "Move in."

Instantly, twenty FBI agents were crawling all over the docks. Ontario Provincial Police Officers accompanied them from the drug task force, specifically recruited for the night's raid. Agent Larkin, from the Detroit FBI Field Office, was about to make the bust of her life. She had been investigating a group of sex traffickers for the past seven months. Her intel pointed to a shipment going down that night, at this port. Larkin strode confidently up to the delivery truck, pulled her weapon, and pointed it at the man behind the wheel.

"Get out of the truck and down on the ground. Now," she screamed as she pulled a little slack out of the trigger on her Glock 19. The commanding officer from the Ontario SWAT team said the same thing to the man seated in the passenger seat. The two men immediately climbed out of the van and hit the ground.

"Ne tire pas!" the older man screamed as he dropped to the ground.

"What did he say?" Larkin barked.

"He said don't shoot, but we can pretend we didn't hear them if that works for you," the Commanding Officer of the Ontario Provincial SWAT Team said, raising his Beretta 92FS pistol and pointing it at the back of the man's head.

"Alive, that was the deal," Larkin said. *These dirtbags were going to answer for their unspeakable atrocities*, she thought as she inched forward to the man on the ground. The two men were placed in handcuffs, and Agent Larkin ordered them to be taken into FBI custody. Something didn't seem right. Alarm bells were going off in her head since she first heard the men speaking in French. There was no intel about anybody speaking French. She knew she was in Canada, but this was supposed to be a Russian operation.

As she walked around the corner of the shipping container, she had her gun up and ready to fire. She clicked on her flashlight and pointed it toward the large metal door. Another agent stepped up to the door with a pair of bolt cutters and began working on the locks. Moments later, the shipping container's door began creaking loudly as it swung open. Special Agent Larkin pointed her flashlight into the container and wanted to scream. Inside there was nothing but two very fancy-looking sports cars. She didn't know the make or model but knew they were out of the budget for an FBI agent. Forty-seven more cargo containers were searched, but no sign of any girls.

Claire had hastily arranged the night's operation on a hunch, after a massive break in her case. The break had come when a man named Vasili Czernoski had been arrested in Fairbanks for drunk driving. He told the Alaska State Troopers that he was in Alaska as a tourist; his fingerprints, however, told a different story. Interpol had him on their list of wanted men in Russia for murder, so he was facing deportation. Facing a trial for murder in Russia had the unique effect of loosening Vasili's lips a little. He knew he was a dead man the moment he set foot in Russia. Deportation was just the bureaucratic term for it; he would never see a court of law in Russia.

Vasili was working for the Bratva when he crossed swords with the wrong people. He killed a relatively low-level lieutenant in a drunken brawl and was on the run. In exchange for remaining in United States custody, Vasili agreed to name names. He knew the Bratva could reach into the United States prison system and take care of business there as well, so in exchange for his loose lips, he requested witness protection. When the information he promised to divulge turned out to be worthless, the FBI began preparing him for extradition. The names he had named were pretty low-level immigrants with minor records.

Claire heard about the arrest in an email from one of her friends at the academy. He had sent it to her because he knew she had been working a case that involved Russians and a sex trafficking operation. Claire had Vasili in an interrogation room in the FBI office's basement two days later.

When she questioned him, Vasili made three mistakes. The first was to underestimate her abilities at witness interrogation. The second was underestimating her because she was a woman. The third and final mistake was overestimating his own intelligence. She eventually got him to confess to escaping Russia on a barge that had docked in Nome, Alaska, before making its way down to Anchorage. He also admitted to loading a shipping container full of girls from the same barge while it was docked in Nome to a different barge headed to Seward. The container had almost been dropped while it was being hoisted into the air by the enormous crane, and Vasili was close enough to hear panicked screams from inside. He said it sounded like a bunch of schoolgirls were inside, but he kept his mouth shut when the captain asked him if he had heard anything. Claire interrogated him until she plugged every gap in his story, including a very accurate description of the shipping container. She flew to Ontario the following day and began putting the operation together. Everything had gone according to the plan until it didn't.

Once the men were all brought to the headquarters' building, Agent Larkin ordered them to be placed in separate rooms for questioning. She had been up for more than twenty-four hours and was silently being ridiculed by the other FBI agents. The Ontario Provincial Police Department was also losing its enthusiasm for the operation. Nevertheless, she plowed ahead. She studied the faces and decided to start with the man she had ordered to the ground at gunpoint. He didn't look particularly menacing, but he did appear to be the most frightened in the group. She decided to go right at him as she entered the room. She slammed her fists down hard onto the table and looked him directly in the eyes. "What were you doing at the docks at three a.m.?"

"I work the night shift," he said, trembling.

"What were you unloading tonight?"

"I don't know; I don't open the containers. I just load them onto the barges," the man said as he broke into tears. "What am I being accused of, if I may ask, Agent Larkin?"

Claire knew that the man was telling the truth. She had spent hours honing her interrogation skills in front of the mirror in her bedroom. She went to every interrogation school the Bureau had and graduated everyone at the top of her class. She studied human reaction to stress and honed her skills at detecting lies until it had become gestalt. She even silently thought she could smell a lie, but she never said that out loud. She quickly changed her tactics and gave the man a little peek at her cards.

"You loaded a shipping container full of young girls onto a barge tonight that was headed somewhere in the United States." She continued to stare at his face as her words pounded him like hammers.

"I did what?" he said incredulously. "Ma'am, I just load barges. I never know what's inside them."

"Tell me about the barges you loaded tonight."

"There were three of them, but two are still in port."

"The barge that left tonight was headed where?" Larkin asked in a more civil tone.

"Cleveland," the man said, trying to wipe his eyes with his shoulder since his hands were cuffed behind his back.

Agent Larkin left the interrogation room and flipped open her phone. She rang the FBI switchboard at the Hoover Building in DC.

"Federal Bureau of …"

Larkin identified herself as she cut off the voice on the other end of the phone. She immediately asked to be transferred to the Cleveland Field Office's duty officer. Thirty minutes later, two FBI agents were on the docks in Cleveland, where the only thing they found out of the ordinary was a shipping container full of empty lawnmower crates.

Agent Larkin slapped her phone shut and threw it on the hotel room bed when the call came back. She knew that the special agent out of the Cleveland office was not happy with her at the moment, but she didn't care. She had been humiliated in front of twenty field agents tonight, but she didn't care. The case she thought would be her ticket up the FBI ladder was falling apart, but she still didn't care. The only thing she cared about was a hot shower and some sleep. The last thing she did before falling into a deep sleep was to book a flight to Cleveland for the following evening. There was a lot to do in Ontario, but she could delegate most of it. She pulled the covers up close to her chin and fell asleep.

*****

About the time that Special Agent Larkin was pointing her gun at completely innocent dockworkers in Ontario, Sal Rigo pulled the delivery truck to a stop just inside the port of Cleveland and killed the lights. Three of Marco's foot soldiers roved around the docks looking for any hint of surveillance. Marco flipped open his phone when the call came in and said, "Is the water rough?"

"It looks like a great night for a boat ride," came the reply.

Marco clapped the phone shut and nodded at Sal, who pulled the truck to the end of the pier. As they exited the truck, the waves from Lake Erie slammed into the rocks just twenty feet away. Marco knocked on the shipping container door and received a return knock from inside. He stepped back as Sal cut the deadbolts off the hinges. The door squealed open, and Sal made a mental note to have somebody grease the hinges before the next shipment. Inside were thirty-five riding lawnmower crates and one exhausted-looking man named Nikola. Sal handed Nikola the duffle bag that contained the purchase money. There was $150,000 in newly minted hundred-dollar bills which weighed more than Sal would have thought. The exhausted man took the duffle bag and walked toward the car parked at the end of the dock for his long road trip back to Seattle.

They unloaded the first row of lawnmowers with a large floor jack. Once they hit the second row, they began prying the tops off the crates only to find half-dead women curled up like caged animals. The stench in the container soon became overpowering. Feces, mixed with urine, sweat, and fear, permeated the container and almost made Sal vomit. The girls were too weak to stand and had to be carried to the truck by the men. Marco was very disappointed when he opened the last crate and found that one of the girls had died in transit. *I suppose that's the cost of doing business*, he thought and told one of his men to take care of the dead one. Two minutes later, the dead girl was on a small boat with the large floor jack attached to her ankle by a pair of handcuffs. As Marco closed the door to the truck, he smiled at Sal and clapped him on the back. "350,000 dollars ain't bad for two hours of work."

Sal just stood there smiling.

Two of Marco's men drove the boat about a mile out onto Lake Erie before killing the engine. Tito, the older man, began pulling the girl up from the floor as the other man struggled to lift the floor jack. Just as the guy with the floor jack hoisted it over the side of the boat, the girl's hand grasped Tito's shirt sleeve, and she tried to pull herself back onto the boat. Tito realized the girl wasn't dead and reached for her other arm to keep her whole body from going over the edge of the boat. Just as he grabbed her other arm, the one-hundred-pound floor jack splashed into the water and pulled the young girl from Moldova over with it. Tito stared at the black water in disbelief. He shot a glance at the other guy, who hadn't even noticed. He had already started walking back toward the engine. Tito stood there in disbelief and wondered if he should tell his partner or let it go.

Marco already thinks she's dead. I guess now she will be, he thought. He decided to let it go and sat down on the bench as the boat slowly turned around and headed back to the dock.

The cold water reinvigorated the young girl as her heart pumped adrenaline through her arteries. Pure fear invaded her mind as she pulled with her hands at the floor jack as it pulled her further down into the darkness. She reached the bottom seconds later, but her ankle wouldn't budge. With every ounce of strength left in her malnourished and frightened body she pulled against the restraint and felt the skin of her ankle tearing apart. She felt the crunching of the bones in her ankle as she tugged with a savageness that she didn't know she possessed. Her ankle finally gave way, but her oxygen had been spent. She floated effortlessly to the surface as the boat made its way to the shore.

CHAPTER 4

Mack cut the satellite connection and shoved the phone back into his rucksack. He also shoved the memory of his wife and baby girls from his mind with new found determination to make it home. He low crawled forward another twenty feet to get a better view of the valley floor. The insurgents were heading right for them. He clicked the mic on his vest and whispered, "Captain, I have eyes on fifty goat-humpers at approximately 900 meters. Requesting permission to send them some lead presents. How, copy?"

"Stand by, over," Apollo replied softly. He clicked the mic again and said, "G-Mar, what do you have on our six? Over."

"I have approximately seventy-five mobiles at approximately 800 meters.

They are moving slow but steady," G-Mar replied.

"Mack, how far out are the birds?" Apollo inquired as he stared at the topographical map spread out in front of him.

Mack mashed the button on his watch to illuminate the bezel. "Twelve mikes," he replied.

Apollo raised himself to a crouching position and slowly slid over to G-Mar's post. Apollo had operational command, but that didn't mean he couldn't get some advice. He chatted with G-Mar for several minutes and then keyed his mic.

"Mack," Apollo said.

"Go for Mack," he said, peering through his scope.

"Get some."

"Ooh-rah," Mack mumbled to himself. He calmly exhaled and began a slow, steady trigger pull. Mack lay motionless as the last of the oxygen exited his lungs. The slack was completely out of the trigger, and his mind was laser focused. The only thing moving was the electrical impulse from his brain to his trigger finger.

"Slow and steady," Mack could hear his grandfather's words echoing in his ears. Growing up in the small town of Browning, Montana, Mack had learned to hunt from his grandfather, a Cherokee Indian. He had given Mack his first rifle, a .22 Caliber with iron sights. He had Mack shooting at birds, squirrels, rabbits and other small creatures on the reservation before he was five. Browning was Blackfoot country, but when Mack's grandmother, Wawetseka White Horse, went to a pow-wow in Billings, Montana, in 1943, she was introduced to Mack's grandfather, Waya Kanati. The son of a Cherokee chief, Waya Kanati was impressive in every sense of the word. Standing just over six feet tall with muscles that seemed to go on for days, Waya Kanati was the very essence of a warrior. His long, raven-colored hair framed a face that looked like it had been chiseled out of granite. After many hours in the sweat house and long discussions into the late hours of the night, a marriage was arranged by the tribal elders. Waya was the third son of the Cherokee chief and would not be picked to lead the tribe any time soon. It was finally agreed that Waya would move to Browning and settle down with his new bride.

Waya had taught Mack that if he listened to the land, the land would speak to him. This was the same grandfather who had given him his name, Makoyii Kanati. It was an ancient tribal name that commanded great respect on the Blackfoot reservation, but when it came time to fill out the birth certificate, his mother insisted that he take his father's last name. The hospital registrar declared that the decision was not up to the child's grandfather, so the name Makoyii Kanati Murphy became official. Kanati was demoted to the insignificant middle name against Waya Kanati's wishes. It was the last thing Mack's mother had done for him before dying from complications of childbirth the following day.

Mack was jolted from his meditation by the recoil of the rifle. The sound hit his ears milliseconds later, and he breathed in. The green mist told him his aim was true, but before the mist had the chance to hit the dirt, he saw fifty muzzle flashes lighting up the night sky like another swarm of lightning bugs. He slowly started tracking targets by picking out the muzzle flashes as his profession's soundtrack played on the imaginative stereo system in his brain. Breathe in — breathe out — slow and steady — squeeze — recoil — re-aim — repeat. The words played over and over in his head, interrupted only by the need to reload. Breathe in — breathe out — slow and steady —squeeze — recoil — re-aim — repeat. Mack was sure that his pulse never jumped above seventy beats per minute. He had been training for this the last eight years of his life, and now it was go-time. Mack was firing on all cylinders as chests, necks, and heads exploded 900 meters downrange. He was in a trance-like state and didn't even hear the incoming hiss of mortar rounds until one exploded twenty meters from his position. It snapped him back into the moment.

He stopped looking for insurgents carrying guns and started searching for robed men kneeling next to mortar tubes, and he found one. Breathe in — breathe out — slow and steady — squeeze — recoil. The head of the Taliban soldier snapped back as the .300 Win Mag round slammed into his ethmoid bone, just under the bridge of his nose. Re-aim — repeat. The second he fell to the ground, another soldier lifted the projectile and got ready to place it into the tube. Breathe in — breathe out — slow and steady — squeeze — recoil. This time the mortar tube itself exploded into a thousand pieces of Soviet-made steel.

Mack somehow managed to hit the tube just as the mortar struck the firing pin. It knocked the tube backward, and the mortar round exploded when it couldn't exit the twisted steel. Mack started looking for more targets when he heard the unmistakable thumping of the Bell AH-1 Cobra attack helicopter in the distance. Re-aim — repeat.

The first missiles slammed into the ridge's backside where G-Mar, O'Malley, and Williams were. Mack turned his head, saw the fireball climbing into the night sky, and then felt the heat from it seconds later. The second Cobra flew low over their position and coughed out a stream of rockets and machine-gun fire. Mack couldn't find any more targets because the enemy had put their heads down when they heard the helicopter.

Apollo was looking through his NVGs to survey the damage from the Cobra's first pass. He saw several motionless men lying on the ground, but soon they were back up on their feet. He clicked on his Starlight scope and started squeezing the trigger. O'Malley was firing off short bursts from his M-249, and Apollo could see the barrel heating up.

"Change your barrel," Apollo screamed over the explosions. O'Malley stopped firing, popped the lid on the machine gun, and started the short process of replacing the barrel.

"Heads up, Mack. They're still coming," Sass shouted over the blasts. Mack went back to finding targets. He saw heads popping up over the rocks much closer than they had been. He was down to his last two magazines.

"We need to find the delivery," Mack shouted, and Sass began low crawling away from the sniper hide.

As soon as Sass cleared the ridge-line, he scanned the landscape for an infrared signal. He spotted it about a hundred yards to the North. The wind had picked up and blown the delivery further away than he had hoped. He keyed his mic to tell Apollo he was going to retrieve the package.

Apollo clicked his mic and said, "Cover Sass. He is retrieving the package. I say again, cover fire to the North. Friendly moving in to collect the package."

G-Mar and Echols pivoted and started looking for targets on their position's northernmost side. *Nobody yet,* G-Mar thought and sent Echols back to help on the eastern side before it got overrun. Sass made it to the package but realized it would take two trips to move it by himself. He cursed out loud and began cutting away the parachute chords from the thick, green duffle bags loaded with ammunition and grenades. He slung the first bag over his shoulder and quickly returned to the sound of small arms fire. The Cobras had finished unleashing their destruction; now it was the Harriers' turn. They certainly packed a much bigger punch as their first rocket slammed into the side of the mountain and caused the ground beneath Sass to move. He stumbled forward, but made it back in one piece. He dumped the bag behind the captain and yelled that he was going for the second one. Before he could turn to run, an RPG whistled past both men's heads and exploded into a pile of rocks thirty meters away.

The concussion left both men temporarily deaf, but no injuries.

"Williams, help me divide this up," Apollo said as he pulled his K-Bar from its leather holster and ripped the bag open. The vinyl bag had over one hundred fully loaded magazines of 5.56 mm ammo. Apollo reloaded his vest pockets with twelve new magazines, grabbed two cases of M249 ammo, and low crawled it over to O'Malley.

Mack was out of ammo, but the robed men kept coming. He pulled his Beretta from his drop-leg holster, but realized it would be no use. He keyed his mic and was about to yell into it when he saw Sass coming his way carrying a duffle bag. Sass dropped the bag next to Echols and started handing him magazines to stuff into his vest. Seconds later and he was next to Mack, repeating the same procedure. Mack refilled his own vest pockets and slammed a fresh magazine into his sniper rifle. Two seconds after that, he was back to hunting bad guys.

Sass looked into the bag and saw an entire box of 40 mm grenades. He loaded the pockets of his vest full of the projectiles and then loaded one into his M-203 grenade launcher. He took aim and squeezed the trigger; he was glad to be back in the fight. Soon he was knocking down bad guys every bit as fast as Mack. The characteristic thump and whistle were music to his ears as he started eliminating men two or three at a time.

The Harriers continued their barrage on the insurgents as Apollo and the rest of Charlie Team kept up the constant volley of small arms fire. The Harriers radioed that they were all spent, and Apollo called for a brief cease-fire.

"Sit-rep, over," Apollo said into his mic.

"Charlie Two, no visuals."

"Charlie Three, no visuals."

The rest of the team reported in, and everyone was unhurt. There were no reports of any foot mobiles, so Apollo decided to pull out.

"Charlie Team to Rally Point," he said and moved to the top of the ridge, keeping his head low to avoid creating a silhouette. Thirty seconds later, Apollo and G-Mar were studying the map.

"We didn't get any fire from the North Side right here," he said, jabbing his finger at the map. "Let's move out, head toward this valley right here, and regroup. This is a pretty exposed position, and if it weren't for the flyboys, we'd all be dead," Apollo said to the team. He knew they had all been thinking the same thing, but what's done is done—no use crying about it.

Forty-five minutes later, Charlie Team occupied the ridge-line overlooking a steep valley. The only way up the ridge was over the boulders, which wasn't easy. It made a much more defensible position, and the men were thankful. They had some boulders to crouch behind and a few precious trees to offer shadows. The moon had just decided to appear since the mission began over eight hours ago. Mack began creating a sniper hide in the rocks by building a small tunnel of stones to hide the muzzle flash. There was intermittent radio chatter as the team waited for the insurgents' next assault. Mack's thoughts went back to his phone call despite his best effort to keep his head in the game.

Mack's family had moved around a lot when he was a boy, but they always ended up back on the reservation. To young Makoyii, it seemed that everywhere he went, nobody could pronounce his name correctly. In the third grade, he decided to shorten it to Mak, but his teachers always inserted the letter C in his name for no particular reason, so Mak just went with it. Mack was the only name he could remember anybody calling him from then on. His brother, Kitchi Wohali, was two years older and had shortened his name to Kit for much the same reason.

Shortly after Mack started the fifth grade, his father Connor had been sent to jail. He was a violent man who would fly into fits of rage whenever he was drinking. He hadn't always been that way, but since his wife died shortly after childbirth, he had lost his way. He was fired from one job after another and soon fell into a lifestyle that put him on a collision course with the maximum security prison at Deer Lodge. He was sentenced to twenty years for attempted murder, but only served eight years before being released for good behavior, which was somewhat of a miracle. The lack of alcohol behind bars was the only reason Connor behaved, despite his endless promises to himself to be a better father. The day he was released from prison, Waya Kanati picked him up at Deer Lodge, and neither of them was ever heard from again.

Mack missed his grandparents dearly. Waya had taught him everything he knew, and his loss left a hole in Mack that had never been filled. Never, that is, until he saw those two little round faces wailing in the nursery. He loved those girls so much it hurt. He thought about his grandfather and how proud he would be. He thought about his wife and how worried she must be. He thought about the girls until the radio chatter brought him back to the moment.

"Charlie Team, this is Apollo. Sit-rep, over."

Sass was the last to check in. He had been staring through his night scope and couldn't decide if he had seen movement in the valley below. The team was spread out in a circle about twenty meters in diameter, and he had the best view of the valley floor.

You gotta be kidding me. These guys just don't know when they've been beaten, Sass thought and keyed his mic. "I have movement in the valley: ten-foot mobiles, carrying rifles, and one very annoying insurgent wearing NVGs. "*I should have shot that dude a long time ago*, Sass thought.

"I gotta say it lads; I'm downright impressed by these goat-humpers. Ain't a one of em wearing short-pants," O'Malley said.

"All right, listen up, men. I think O'Malley's right for a change," Apollo said. "These guys aren't typical Taliban. I'm pretty sure we stepped into a nest of insurgents. The NVGs, tactics, and accurate mortar fire all point to the fact that these guys have done this before. When the sun comes up in about an hour, our backsides will be flapping in the wind. I'm calling for a ride. We need to get this intel up the chain and come back another time, so be ready to move when I give the order." Apollo clicked off his mic, peered through his Starlight scope, and saw what Sass had seen earlier: several insurgents picking their way up the rocks. "Do not engage. I say again, *Do Not Engage!*"

Moments later, Apollo was lying next to Sass and Mack. "Let them come all the way to the top. I want to take one of them alive," Apollo whispered to Mack.

"Aye, aye, Captain. I hope you have a plan because that guy has NVGs just like we do," Sass said as he turned off his I.R. sight to avoid another mishap.

"No plan. Just let it play out. Punch their tickets if you have to, but let's try to take 'em alive," Apollo said and slapped Sass on the back. "I have total confidence in you."

"Hey Captain, I ain't fronting to be a Greek God. I'm just a creature. Know what I'm saying?" Sass said shaking his head.

"I have no idea what you are saying. I thought you were from

Chicago?" Apollo replied.

"Let me translate that for you Captain. He's speaking in Bronx. He said he is just a Yankees fan and not pretending to be a Greek God," Mack said trying to duplicate his Bronx accent.

"What do you want to do? Live forever?" Apollo said, quoting the famous Marine Dan Daly, who had earned not one but two Medals of Honor. Apollo let out a deep "oooh-rahhh," before making his way back to his position in a low-crouching shuffle. He made the rounds to tell the rest of the team he wanted the men alive, at least one of them anyway.

"Yeah, nah." Sass said to Mack when the captain was out of earshot. "How am I supposed to bag one of these bin Laden wannabes without punching their tickets?"

"If letting it just play out doesn't work, tell him he's under arrest," Mack said and gave Sass the thumbs-up right in front of his NVGs. "Besides, once a Marine Corps officer invokes the memory of Dan Daly, it might as well be a triple dog dare." They both chuckled quietly and went back to scanning the terrain ahead of them.

The two watched as the enemy picked their way up the boulders for ten more minutes. They were not moving as quickly in the rougher terrain, and soon they both heard the rotor blades in the distance.

"Apollo, this is Mack. Over."

"This is Apollo. Go."

"Sir, I am not sure we will be making any arrests tonight. The bad guys are still a few hundred meters away, and the birds are inbound."

"Affirmative. When I give the word, pull back to the South side of the ridge and get on the bird. They are landing on the ridge's backside, so we don't make ourselves targets. We've done enough for one night. We'll be back. Apollo out."

Two minutes later, the CH-53 Sea Stallion Helicopter was kicking up sand and small rocks as it attempted to set down on some uneven terrain.

"Charlie Team, fall back to my position. I say again, this is Apollo. Fall back to my position, over."

"Go, Sass, I'll cover you," Mack said as he pulled a fresh magazine out of his vest pocket and set it down next to his rifle. If things got hairy, he didn't want to waste any time fishing for fresh magazines.

Sass pushed himself to his knees just as the low thump of a mortar round echoed up the hill. He moved for a few more seconds until the sound got louder, and he realized it was coming his way. He dove for cover just as the 82 mm mortar impacted the rocky earth. The mortar detonated and sent a shower of hot lead in an arcing pattern toward the two men. Sass cried out in pain as a piece of shrapnel tore through his upper back. He was frantically pulling at his chest rig to get it off as Mack slid up next to him. Mack ripped the gear off as fast as he could, turning him over onto his stomach. He strained through the moonlit sky and saw a small gash on his shoulder blade.

As the air poured back into his lungs, Sass grunted a thanks to Mack and started looking for his rifle.

"Are you good to go?" Mack shouted.

Sass snatched up his rifle and grabbed his gear. "Ask me no questions ..."

I'll tell you no lies. Mack finished the sentence in his head and snatched up his own rifle. "Go, I'll cover you."

Sass was already bounding up the side of the rocky cliff as two more thumps were heard over the sound of small arms' fire. Mack pulled the trigger and dispatched another insurgent as the mortar rounds found their targets. Luckily, they were getting farther away.

Sass kept pumping his legs as lead slammed into the rocks around his feet. He heard the sharp cracks of bullets breaking the sound barrier as they hurled past his ears. Just as he crested the rise, he saw the helicopter spraying dust and debris in every direction. He lowered himself to the ground to cover Mack's retreat. He could see Mack crouching as he ran, but he didn't see anybody in pursuit at first; until a small metal reflection sent a shiver down his spine. He looked harder and froze for a second when he realized what he was looking at.

The man with the NVGs had obviously been able to climb the rise faster than anybody else, and he was only a few meters from Mack. He tried to shout, but the sound of mortars and the helicopter drowned his voice. Sass hit the Earth and tried to slow his breathing. He needed to take him out, but he didn't trust his aim in the off-hand position because if he missed too high, he would hit Mack. He peered through his Advanced Combat Optical Gunsight, or ACOG for short, and slowly pulled the trigger. Just as the spring was about to release and send the firing pin slamming home, the insurgent lunged forward and tackled Mack as he ran past him. Sass leaped to his feet and went bounding down the boulders as fast as his legs could carry him.

Mack was disoriented as he felt his body crashing to the earth. His first thought was he had been hit by a mortar. His head struck the rocky ground and sent a lightning bolt of pain down his back. The feeling of being tackled played at the back of his brain. He was the quarterback for the Browning Indians football team and had been tackled more times than he could count. It was a strange thing to be thinking about in the mountains of Afghanistan, but there it was. Mack tried to pull his legs up to stand, but he felt another blow to his face. *That was a fist* Mack thought. His NVGs had been knocked off when his head struck the rock, so his night vision was gone. Hot and sticky liquid was leaking into the corner of his right eye, but he could make out the figure of a man straddling his chest with his arms in the air. His vision suddenly came into perfect focus as he saw the man on his chest swinging a knife directly toward him. His arms were still over his head with the knife clutched tightly in his hands as Mack watched in horror. He tried to buck the man off him, but he wouldn't budge. The man's arms were now coming toward him in a downward motion. Mack tried one more attempt to dislodge the man from his torso, but it was no use. The knife was speeding toward his head as Mack spent the last of his energy.

Defeated, Mack stared directly at the man's face wearing the NVGs determined to meet his fate like a man. As he stared at the man, he realized that he was much older than he would have thought. His mouth was wide open, and he was obviously shouting something as the knife came closer and closer, but Mack couldn't make it out. Time was at a standstill. Mack even felt his body moving in slow motion to keep time with his brain. He was just about to close his eyes and accept his fate when the man's nose disappeared. Mack's brain was processing every detail. Part of the nose seemed to move to the left, while the other half just got pulled into his face. The scene unfolded faster and faster. The mouth snapped shut, and then the whole head seemed to move backwards as if it had been pulled from behind by an imaginary rope. The knife flipped forward and missed Mack's head by inches as the man's arms began falling to the side. The head snapped all the way back and Mack was left looking at the man's flowing beard and neck. The whole scene resumed at real time as though some imaginary finger had pushed the play button. The insurgent's head snapped completely back before the muscles, tendons and bones had met their anatomic barrier. The muscles of the neck fired reflexively with what little neurologic activity was left and pulled the head back into a normal position. As the insurgents head came forward, Mack could see the hole in the face where the nose used to be. He felt the man's legs go limp as the body balanced perfectly on top of him for a moment.

Mack was just about to heave the body off when a shadow flew directly over the top of him. The shadow had come from behind Mack, just out of his range of vision. It slammed into the insurgent who just milliseconds before was about to plunge a knife into his head. The shadow and the insurgent melded into one mass as they collided, sending them both toppling off of Mack's torso. The insurgent made no effort to repel the attack, and Mack knew that he was dead.

Sass wasn't convinced, so he pulled his own fighting knife and began plunging it into the man's chest. He had sunk the knife in several times before Mack tried to pull him off.

Farther down the embankment, the enemy was still firing wildly at nothing in particular. Sass was still trying to get one more thrust into the insurgent as he heard Mack screaming into his ear.

"We gotta move."

Sass felt his brain coming out of the blind rage that had just overtaken it. He stopped swinging and took a deep breath. It felt good to inhale. He realized that he had probably been holding his breath since he saw the man with the NVGs.

"Get on the bird. I'll cover you. Go! Go!" Mack shouted.

Sass bounded up the same rocky slope for what seemed like the tenth time that night before crouching at the top. He was back in the same position covering Mack's retreat. There were still muzzle flashes in the distance as Mack crested the hill. Sass slapped Mack's back when he ran past him and took one more look down the canyon before making his retreat. A tracer round whistled past his face, and he ducked instinctively.

"*That was ...*" he started saying to himself, but he was interrupted by another bullet tearing through his forehead and killing him right where he stood. His body fell backward toward the rocky terrain like a felled tree.

Mack heard the bullets ripping past his head, causing him to crouch down. He turned to see where Sass was just in time to see his limp body crashing to the ground. Pure terror invaded Mack's brain when he saw his friend lying limp on the rocky soil. He tried to convince himself that he had just tripped, but Sass didn't even attempt to break his fall. *No! No! No!* Mack was screaming inside of his head. He ran the ten meters back to Sass's position and slid to a stop next to his body. The small trickle of blood just above his right eye didn't look too bad, and Mack tried to convince himself that he was just unconscious, but he knew better. He slung his sniper rifle over his shoulder and grabbed Sass's arm. He pulled the limp body forward and heaved him to his shoulder.

Sass's rifle lay next to him, so he bent to retrieve it before running to the sound of the helicopter.

"Let's go. Let's go!" Apollo kept yelling.

"Sass is hit," Mack screamed as he neared the helicopter ramp. He ran past Apollo and into the belly of the helicopter before lowering Sass's limp body to the floor in front of Echols. "He's hit in the head!" Mack screamed again over the roar of the chopper.

Echols was on the ground kneeling next to Sass as the chopper lifted off. He saw the small hole just above the right eye, and his hand instinctively went to the back of his head to check for an exit wound. He pulled the strap, releasing his helmet with his left hand as his right hand felt the back of his skull. Echols' hand knew that Sass was dead before his brain could process the information. His hand felt a gigantic hole where it should have been feeling bone. He pulled his hand back, and the rest of the men saw the blood and brain matter sticking to it. Mack recoiled at the sight. He had seen dead bodies before, but they had never belonged to a friend so close. *That should have been me,* Mack thought to himself as he closed his eyes. He somehow knew that a large part of him had died right then and there.

CHAPTER 5

Marco and Sal had just finished getting their 'produce' settled in the warehouse. They were stripped naked, washed off with a garden hose, and assigned to a mattress on the warehouse floor. The warehouse was lit by a few fluorescent fixtures hanging from the ceiling. Once the girls were on the floor, they were given a few pieces of stale bread and some water in a dog bowl. The men were all carrying clubs, but none of the girls had the energy to resist. By 3:00 a.m., the two men were back at the Foxxy. Marco pulled a brand new bottle of vodka from behind the bar with two glasses.

"It's time to celebrate," Marco said as he twisted the cap off the Stoli Elit Vodka bottle and poured. They drank toasts to their ancestors, their fathers, and their friendship. They drank toasts to the newest shipment of faceless girls from some country on the other side of the world that would make them rich. They toasted the new cars they would purchase with their newly acquired wealth. They drank until they passed out on the elevated dance floor with the silver pole between them. They slept until the bartender showed up for work around four-thirty that afternoon. It wasn't the first time that Pete, the bartender, had arrived at the club only to find Marco's car parked in the rear lot. Today, however, a very lovely Mustang was parked next to it.

Pete started brewing a pot of coffee and offered to call a cab for the two men, but they stumbled into the parking lot before he could make the call. He followed them out the back door, told them they were in no condition to drive, and begged them to come back into the club. Vinny, Marco's father, had just gotten him off the hook for a DUI a month ago, and when Vinny heard that Pete had allowed his son to drive after serving him a pint of vodka, one of Vinny's men paid Pete a little visit. Under no circumstances was Marco allowed to drive home if he was too intoxicated. The message had been clear and the consequences even more explicit. Vincenzo Bertoli, or Vinny for short, was the boss, and nobody crossed Vinny.

Pete put his hand on the door of the Porsche and begged Marco not to drive. He said that his father would be pissed off if he got pulled over again after he had just gotten him off the hook for the last DUI. If there was one way to get to Marco, that was it. Marco discreetly brushed his wrist against his waistband to ensure that his Tokarev pistol was still there. He turned to face Pete and said, "You're right, Petey. Let's go back inside."

Relieved, Pete walked ahead to get the door for Marco and Sal. The second the three men walked into the club, Marco jerked out his nickel-plated Tokarev TT-33 and swung it toward Pete's head. Sal tried to react but he was too slow. Marco brought the gun crashing down onto the back of Pete's head. It was a fierce blow, but it only knocked him to the floor. Pete rolled onto his back and looked up at Marco, who was pointing the gun at his head.

"Marco, please, I was just trying to keep you out of trouble," Pete said as he grabbed the back of his head and felt the warm, sticky blood oozing into his hair.

"Marco, please," Marco said in a girl's voice. Then he found his own voice and yelled, "I don't need you or my father. Do you hear me?"

Pete was just about to say something when Marco squeezed the trigger. Pete's head erupted into a fountain of blood. Small parts of his brain were splattered on the hardwood dance floor in an arcing pattern.

"Marco," Sal said, suddenly sobering up. "What are you doing?"

"I'm tired of people telling me how my father keeps me out of trouble." His eyes were wild as he instinctively ran his hand through his hair. "Do you think the same thing?" Marco said as he brought the Tokarev up and placed his sights on Sal.

"No," Sal screamed, "I'm your friend, remember? Look, I hate your father every bit as much as you do, but he *is* the boss."

Marco lowered the pistol and was just about to say something when one of the dancers walked through the front door. She stopped in her tracks when she saw Pete and the bloody mess on the floor. Then she screamed. She looked at Marco holding the pistol and was about to cry out again when the Tokarev exploded.

One second she thought that something horrible was about to happen, and the next second it did. The bullet caught her right under the left eye. She was dead before she hit the floor.

"Marco, what the ..."

"Calm down, Sal," Marco shouted, cutting him off. He hated to see people let their emotions get the better of them. He lowered his pistol and told Sal to sit down.

"Marco, we need to come up with a plan and fast," Sal said, refusing to sit.

"Put some gloves on, and get all the cash out of the drawer," Marco said hurriedly. "We are going to make this look like a robbery. Don't touch anything behind the bar," Marco said flatly without a hint of remorse for what he had just done.

"I don't have any gloves," Sal cried out.

"Then use a rag. Just get the cash out of the drawer," Marco barked.

"Marco, this is stupid. We need to think," Sal said with spittle flying from his mouth.

"Shut up, Sal, and do what I tell you. Get the cash out of the drawer, and pick up the brass. I'm gonna get the film out of the surveillance cameras."

Twenty minutes later, they were five miles from the club in the parking lot of an abandoned car dealership. Marco pulled out his phone and called Matteo. He knew it would not go well, but he needed to do it. There was a lot of shouting and cursing, but Matteo finally agreed to help. The plan was to get to Detroit and lay low. Marco heard the condescension in Matteo's voice, but he decided to let it go. He knew the yelling and arguing was far from over, but Matteo would be a good ally. Not because Matteo felt any love for him, but because he would do what was best for the family.

Their alibi was far from solid, but they needed to act soon to make it work. Marco and Sal needed to get to Detroit and lay down some backstops. Matteo was in Detroit learning the money laundering aspect of the family business and would vouch that they showed up in the middle of the night. Marco knew he had to come clean with Matteo first. He had to tell Matteo what happened. Marco's younger brother held the same degree of hatred for their father, but Matteo was much better at concealing it. Set to take over the family business, Matteo was accustomed to making difficult decisions. Marco knew Matteo wouldn't throw him under the bus; he was family. Still, he had the nagging feeling that they were making mistakes. His concentration was clouded by too much vodka, mixed with an overwhelming fear of what his father would say when he found out.

Marco hung up the phone as he got out of his car, and he finished fleshing out the details of their plan. He brought Sal up to speed as the two leaned against his Mustang in the deserted parking lot. The plan included getting their vehicles off the road, picking up fresh wheels with a clean plate, and driving to Detroit. They both agreed that it was the best plan they could think of. Matteo would iron out all the details and make it sound more convincing. If he couldn't figure it out, he could keep them safe until the heat was off.

Marco sat down on the concrete in the shade of Sal's Mustang and tried to collect his thoughts. He needed to figure out how to get both of their cars off the road, and he needed to find new transportation. His phone rang, and he answered it instinctively without knowing who it was.

"It's Marco," he barked into the phone.

"Where are you at right now?" Matteo said without so much as a greeting.

"I'm on 130th at Johnnie's old car dealership. Why? What difference does it make?"

"I'm trying to help you, so just answer my questions without the attitude," Matteo shouted back. "Stay where you are for a few minutes. I am going to try to get you some clean wheels, but I am still working on it, so stay put. D'ya hear me?"

"Yeah, I hear ya," Marco replied and flipped his phone shut.

"Who was that?" Sal asked, concerned that Marco had just told somebody where they were.

"Matteo, he's trying to find us some clean wheels, so we can get to Detroit," Marco said stuffing his phone back into his shirt pocket. "I swear Sal, if he weren't my brother, I'd put a cap in him too."

Sal just shook his head. He knew Marco was on the verge of a complete meltdown, and he didn't want to trigger him any further.

Matteo flipped his phone shut and let out a long breath. He knew he had to call his father, but he was dreading it. Matteo cursed under his breath for still feeling such fear when he thought of his father. He clenched his jaw, closed his eyes, and steeled himself for the conversation that he knew was coming.

He dialed the numbers and waited. When Vinny picked up the phone, Matteo prepared himself for the torrent of curses. "Hey Pops, I know you said not to call, but I got an issue and I'm not sure what to do."

"What?" Was all Vinny said in return.

"It's Marco," Matteo said.

The conversation was much more pleasant than Matteo had planned on. What he didn't expect was Vinny's plan. "Are you sure Pops?"

"Yah, but don't do anything until I tell ya to. Is that understood?" Vinny said, exhaling a lung full of cigarette smoke.

"Sure Pops. Should I tell Marco to sit still until he hears from ya?" Matteo replied.

"Yeah, tell him he should be getting a call soon," Vinny said and hung up the phone.

Marco and Sal sat there in the lot for almost two hours. Marco called Matteo three times, but Matteo assured him that he was working on it and to sit tight. Twenty minutes after his last call to Matteo, Marco stood and decided to leave. He told Sal to get in his car and follow him.

"Marco, we are supposed to sit tight and wait for Matteo. I don't like sitting around either, but we both know that he is our best option right now," Sal said in a level-headed voice, trying his best not to throw fuel into the dumpster fire.

Marco was just about to respond when his phone rang. He scanned the caller ID and felt a quick chill run up his spine.

"Marco," he said, trying to sound as relaxed as he could.

"I have a job for you that needs to be done right now. Are you in Cleveland?" a Russian voice said softly.

"It's kind of a bad time right now. Can it wait?"

There was a silence on the other end of the line. It stretched on for almost a minute before Marco finally asked if he was still there.

"You have a very short memory, my friend. I was not asking. I am telling. Now pay attention, and do exactly as I say. I am aware of your current situation. I am trying to help you."

Marco listened for several more minutes before hanging up. He looked at Sal with a pained expression and told him that they had something they needed to do before they could go to Detroit.

"Marco, we have to get out of here. Do you really need to do this now?"

Marco glared at Sal and didn't say a word. He had just been put in his place by his younger brother and again by his Russian business associates; he wasn't about to take any grief from Sal.

Sal finally nodded his head in submission and said, "Whatever you say, Marco. I'm with you."

They both climbed back into their cars and fired them up. Marco pulled out first, and Sal fell in behind him. Marco opened the center console, took his earphones out, and plugged them into his phone. He rolled his window back up and pulled out onto the main road. He had only driven less than a mile when his phone rang again.

"Hello," Marco said into his earbud. The voice on the other end of the line was a bit garbled, but he comprehended everything. "Yes, I understand," he replied and then listened for another few minutes. He was being given turn-by-turn instructions and was only told what to do immediately before he had to do it. The hair on the back of Marco's neck was beginning to stand up as he realized that whoever he was talking to knew exactly where he was.

Marco drove on for a few minutes trying to figure out what could be so important to his Russian friend that he would have him followed. He kept checking his rearview mirror, but didn't see any cars even close to him. He kept making turns and eventually found himself on the interstate heading away from Detroit. Marco chanced a few questions, but he was given no information aside from the turns he was to make. After a few more turns, he was in a part of town he wasn't familiar with.

"The next vehicle that approaches you will be a large black SUV. I am going to tell you exactly how to do this, so pay attention. There can be no mistakes. This has to look like an accident, and the driver must be dead," the heavily accented voice said from what sounded like a million miles away. The man on the other end of the line finally finished speaking, and asked Marco if he understood. When Marco confirmed that he had understood the instructions, the man simply replied. "Then do it."

"OK," Marco said, but the line had gone dead.

The rain had just started falling as Marco looked at his phone. It was Sal calling on the other line, so he ignored it. Seconds later, Sal pulled out into the other lane to pass him and Marco's anger flared. He was just about to swerve to keep Sal from passing him when he saw the wisdom in the plan. Marco allowed Sal to pass and knew exactly what he had to do.

*****

Claire folded her phone and put it into her pocket. She had seen the look on the flight attendant's face and decided that it could wait until she got there. She had been on the phone with the same agent in Cleveland from the night before, filling him in on the operation she was conducting. Despite his abruptness the previous night, he seemed eager to help her and planned to pick her up at Hopkins International Airport at 8:30 that evening. She decided to use the time on the flight to think.

She liked flying because it gave her uninterrupted time to contemplate. She replayed the night in her head several times until she came to grips with the fact that Ontario was an unwitting accomplice in the trafficking industry, at least the particular operation she was trying to shut down. She racked her brain, but couldn't come up with a link to Cleveland. She knew there had to be a link, but couldn't make the pieces fit. Russian barges exchanging cargo in a tiny Alaskan port made sense, as it reduced any chance of being discovered in busier ports with more security. She slowly started piecing together a plan, but she was in the dark without an asset on the ground in Cleveland. Claire closed her eyes and silently hoped that this Cleveland field agent would be helpful.

Claire Larkin had grown up on the South End of Boston. The only daughter of a police officer and schoolteacher, her childhood had been pretty uneventful. Claire and her three older brothers were happy, despite growing up in one of the most violent towns on the East Coast. While she was growing up, her family never missed mass at the Cathedral of the Holy Cross until her father's funeral at the same church. That was the last time Claire darkened the door of any church, much less the one her entire family attended. Her father, Seamus Larkin, had been gunned down during his last night on the beat. He had been a Boston police officer for twenty-five years the night he was shot in the head while sitting at a traffic light. Claire's three older brothers were on the force as well, and two of them were working the night of the shooting, but the murder remained unsolved. Claire was certain it had to do with the last case her father worked as a detective before returning to the beat to finish his career.

Claire rolled her suitcase through the arrivals gate and headed toward the street to look for Special Agent Patrick Mulloy.

"You must be Special Agent Larkin," a deep baritone voice said from behind her.

As she turned, Mulloy extended his hand, and she took it.

"Come on. I'm parked just outside. Do you have any bags, Special Agent Larkin?"

"No, sir, and you can call me Claire."

"Only if you start calling me Pat," he said.

"It's a deal. Now, fill me in on the Cleveland scene."

"Well, we haven't seen much action in the flesh market," he said, but then apologized when he saw the way Claire grimaced at the words, "flesh market."

"Sorry, human trafficking. I'm forgetting myself. I didn't get much sleep last night," he said and sheepishly looked at Claire for forgiveness.

"Forgiven," Claire said and then changed the subject. "What about the Russians?"

"What about them?" Mulloy said stepping back so she could go through the sliding door first.

"Has the Russian Mob infected your quaint little town like they have mine?"

Mulloy shook his head. "No, our scumbags are from Italy, Mexico, Ireland, and a few from Jamaica, but not Russia. Where are you from?" Mulloy asked.

"Boston, South Side," Claire responded.

"Really? I didn't pick up on the Southie accent."

"I worked really hard to get rid of it, but when I get pissed off, it comes right back to me," Claire said, pronouncing the word hard as "haad."

They laughed and made small talk on the way to the Cleveland Field Office. Once inside, they got down to business.

"Coffee?" Mulloy asked as he showed her to the conference room.

"Water, please," Claire replied, dumping her briefcase on the desk and pulling out a file folder with at least thirty pages of notes.

"Well, what can Cleveland do for you, Claire?" Mulloy asked as he entered the room carrying two bottles.

Claire laid out the whole operation from start to finish. She filled him in on the Russian she had interrogated in Anchorage as well as the botched operation from the night before. She asked Mulloy dozens of questions, but played her cards close to her chest. The FBI was the premier law enforcement agency globally, but even the FBI had its moles. Mulloy struck her as a straight shooter. He seemed like the kind of guy that didn't go in for a lot of drama and avoided desk jobs like they were toxic waste. She was usually right on the money with her first impressions, and her first thought about Pat Mulloy was that he was a good man.

Pat Mulloy was Cleveland born and bred. He was a lifelong Browns and Indians fan and had the scars to prove it. He had been destroyed in 1987 when Earnest Byner fumbled on the 2-yard line in the AFC championship game. He chanted, "Belichik must go" in 1994 when Bernie Kosar was cut from the team. When the Indians best season was cut short by a major league strike, he vowed never to darken the doors of Jacob's Field again. His vows only lasted until opening day the following year. As painful as it was, Mulloy was Cleveland through and through. He had jumped at the chance to become the special agent in charge of the Cleveland Field Office three years ago. He had to admit he was a long shot for the job, but when it was offered, he didn't think twice. He had been with the Bureau for almost ten years when he received the job offer. His track record for taking down white-collar criminals had not gone unnoticed. He was with the Charlotte office when he took down a multi-billionaire who had been embezzling money through a maze of shell companies for over a decade. He was the agent in charge of the investigation when the indictment was made, putting his own career on the upward trajectory.

"Well, I gotta tell you, Claire, I've been in the Cleveland office now for almost three years, and you are the first to make mention of a Russian player. If there is any Russian involvement here, it is either very new or very well-concealed. My guess is that this is a new play for them. I actually had a pretty heavy caseload of Ivans when I was a rookie down in Atlanta, and they weren't really players in the trafficking game. They were more sophisticated, more ambitious than selling girls. I mean, they were in the prostitution business, but that was just a way to move their drugs. They were laundering and selling drugs and moving weapons for the most part. So I'm not sure where to start."

"Let's start with the players you do know. Who would be the most likely suspects in the trafficking industry here in Cleveland?"

"Assuming that Cleveland is the final destination," Mulloy said. "Moving cargo across Canada is fairly easy. Bringing anything illegal across the border is a different story. It is far easier to do that here than it is in New York, or Michigan for that matter. Cleveland makes sense as a stop along the way, but I doubt this is the final market."

"What if I told you that Cleveland is the final destination? Any players capable of moving that kind of cargo here?" Claire said, emphasizing the word *cargo* to indicate it was offensive.

"I'm sorry, Claire. I am a little set in my ways. You seem very passionate about this, and I want to help you. I just ask for a little grace with my word choices. If I am going to worry about offending you every time I open my mouth, I will just keep it shut."

"Fair enough," Claire conceded.

"Well, we definitely have our share of dirtbags here that could do something like that. I just haven't heard of anyone. I can ask my team and see if anybody has any suggestions."

"Let's not do that just yet. I'd like to keep the group as small as possible for a bit if that is all right with you."

"Sure," Mulloy said. "Where do you want to start?"

"Want to go to some strip clubs?"

Mulloy shrugged and said, "Which one? We have a few hundred of them here."

Claire took her turn at shrugging her shoulders. "Which one is your favorite?" she added.

Mulloy just laughed and told her that he hadn't been to one in over fifteen years. Not since his fraternity days at Ohio State.

"Well, I'm starving, and if memory serves me correctly, those types of establishments are not known for the five-star cuisine, so maybe we should grab a bite to eat first." She had noticed that Mulloy wasn't wearing a wedding ring, but many of the guys she worked with at the Bureau didn't. Not because they didn't love their wives but because they did. Being an FBI agent was a dangerous job; no sense bringing the family into the mix. When people saw wedding rings, they saw weakness. They read into the presence of a wedding ring an emotional tie that could be exploited. "Unless you already have dinner plans," she quickly added.

Mulloy caught her looking at his left ring finger, so he held it up. "My wife *is* the FBI, so she won't be disappointed if I get home late," he said with a fake smile.

There was a lot more to that story, Claire figured, but now was not the time for that kind of discussion.

CHAPTER 6

Renée Murphy pulled the Excursion out of the grocery store parking lot and headed toward her mother's home. Her mother had moved to a quiet suburb just outside Cleveland, Ohio, the year Renée finished at William & Mary to be closer to family. Renée's mother, Basmina Shaw, had been living in Newport News, where her husband had worked at the shipping yards. He had left Basmina when Renée was only seven, so there was nothing holding her in Newport News other than Renée's future. Renée had already shown great academic prowess, and combined with her athletic abilities, Basmina knew a quiet suburb in Ohio would not provide the same opportunities for her only daughter as life in the Ivy Belt. Technically, her husband left her long before Renée was seven, but that was the last time she heard from him. Once Renée had graduated college, though, Basmina put the East Coast in her rearview mirror and went to be with family.

Brianna had fallen asleep, and Aubrey was making adorable cooing noises. As she fought back the tears, Renée's mind was running wild with the possibility that she would never see her husband again. The CIA officer in her took over, and she began compartmentalizing. Mack had never resorted to the theater comment, so this must have been the real deal. He was far from home and in harm's way, so it was natural for a father to want to hear the voice of somebody he loved and to tell his babies that he loved them. Renée had met a lot of operators over her six years in intelligence, and if there was one man that could wade through a river of garbage and come out smelling like roses, it was Mack. He had made it through many of the fiercest battles in Afghanistan three years earlier with nothing but some scrapes, bruises, and dehydration.

Renée was a realist, though. She knew that if your time was up, it was up; it didn't matter how good you were. It was just beginning to rain, so she flipped on her wiper blades and settled in for the fifteen-minute ride home. She allowed her thoughts to wander back to the last time she saw Mack and smiled. It was just before he deployed to Afghanistan from Camp Lejeune.

*****

"Please do something for me, Mack Murphy," Renée had said as she hugged him goodbye.

"What's that, Pep?" Mack replied as he kissed her forehead.

"I want you to grab the first leaf you see fall from the first tree you find and put it in this." She handed him a small plastic sleeve. "Put it in here, and carry it with you in your left breast pocket next to your heart. Whenever you feel it or see it, I want you to think of me."

Mack had heard the order to move out, so he pulled her close to him one last time. He kissed her on the lips and then let her go. He held the plastic sleeve up and said, "I will." He knelt on the concrete tarmac and peered at the little girls, only four weeks old. They were both asleep and looked so innocent. It brought a tear to his eye, but he blinked it away. Remembering that day reminded her of everything that was good in the world. It reminded her of why Mack did what he did. Either men like him took the battle to the enemy, or the enemy brought it there. Either way, the war was happening. She was also reminded of the quote Mack used to repeat by Thomas Paine: "I prefer peace. But if trouble must come, let it come in my time so that my children can live in peace."

Mack had walked up the stairs and turned to look at Renée one more time before disappearing into the aircraft. She imagined what was going through Mack's head as he sat down on the plane for his third deployment to Afghanistan. She remembered the words she had written on the piece of paper inside the sleeve. It was an excerpt from Elizabeth Barrett Browning's Poem, "The Autumn."

> *How there you sat in summer-time,*
> *May yet be in your mind;*
> *And how you heard the green woods sing*
> *Beneath the freshening wind.*
> *Though the same wind now blows around,*
> *You would its blast recall;*
> *For every breath that stirs the trees,*
> *Doth cause a leaf to fall.*
> *Oh! Like that wind, is all the mirth*
> *That flesh and dust impart:*
> *We cannot bear its visitings,*
> *When change is on the heart.*
> *Gay words and jests may make us smile,*
> *When Sorrow is asleep;*
> *But other things must make us smile,*
> *When Sorrow bids us weep!*

*****

Renée recited the entire poem again in her head and gave into the wave of emotions washing over her. She knew it wasn't healthy to give into despair, but she had no strength left. She loved those precious twin babies in the back seat more than life itself. However, the thought of them never knowing the wonderful man that was their father made her lose her grasp on the present. She let the tears fall down the sides of her cheeks. She peeked into the rearview mirror and saw that both girls were sound asleep. She decided she would drive and cry for a while.

She was sitting at a traffic light with tears streaming down her face. She hadn't noticed that the light had turned green until the driver behind her honked the horn. She lifted her foot off the brake, stuck her hand up in the air as if to say 'I'm sorry,' and made a decision.

She decided to take the road through the Metroparks along the Rocky River. She loved driving that road as it wound in and out of the trees. The oaks and Canadian maple trees were already beginning to lose their brightly colored leaves, and it reminded her of being at William & Mary. She needed a little time to compose herself before she got home. As she turned onto Valley Parkway, the rain fell even harder. She peeked again at the rearview mirror and noticed a car had been following her since she left the grocery store. She was a trained CIA officer, and even though she was on maternity leave, she was incapable of letting her guard down. She instinctively lifted the center console to remove her personal Glock 19—more out of habit than concern. The fact that she had her babies in the back seat didn't allow her to take chances. She turned on her headlights and turned the intermittent nob on her windshield wipers up a few clicks to clean off her windows more frequently.

She meandered along the road for several miles, taking in the river's beauty and the colorful trees. Despite the rain, she was quickly engrossed in the beauty of the day. If nothing else, it made the trees look more alive. Her life at the agency revolved around information, intelligence, and observations, but her private life was all about imagination. It was a piece of herself that precious few people knew. She kept it hidden from her superiors at the agency as best as she could. It was her imagination that she cultivated as a young girl, losing herself in the world of books and poetry. She spent hours reading poems, literature, and whatever else she could find. It was her imagination that connected the dots in the briefing she had turned in a few weeks ago. She had a categorical memory and world events started becoming too random to ignore. One of her favorite classes at William & Mary had been "Game Theory." She was fascinated at how everything, no matter how random, seemed to have a pattern.

She had begun trying to explain world events using game theory and the information she was privy to as a CIA officer. After 9/11, she had begun making sense of it all. At first she just figured she was a rookie who was seeing connections where there weren't any. She had been warned in her training not to watch TV or read spy novels because that was not how the clandestine world operated. She had never been much of a conspiracy theorist, but too many pieces were starting to fit. She had never discussed any of her thoughts with anybody, not even Mack out of fear that everyone would label her a tinfoil hat-wearing nut job. Now, the culmination of seven years of mental gymnastics had been dismissed, and she had been ordered to flush it all. She admired her boss, George Siefert, but he was also a total mystery to her. He was far from perfect, but she always felt like she could trust him.

Growing up without a father, she would create the perfect man in her idealistic little head, and then she would imagine marrying him. They would walk down a flower-strewn aisle on the way out of the church and get on two white horses and ride off into the sunset. Sometimes the dream had them sailing on a small boat through crystal clear waters with the sun sinking low on the horizon. They would embrace each other as the waves rocked the tiny boat back and forth.

Her ideal man was always strong. That was the first requirement. Weak men were usually mean men in her limited life experiences. She remembered her father as very muscular with a fierce temperament. He was never abusive, though; she loved him for that. He did struggle with alcohol, but he never let his baby girl see that side of him. If he was on a bender, he never came home until he was sober. Her ideal man had to be smart too. He had to be somebody she could share her poetry with and who would read the same books, and discuss them with her.

Despite thinking her ideal man was a complete work of fiction, she had found him. He was a little paler than she had imagined in her dreams, but he was every bit as strong and intelligent. Oh, how she loved that man, and now he was in danger. All her CIA training, her intelligence, and her hard work could do nothing right now. All she could do was pray. The thought of praying brought back another funny memory, and she chuckled out loud when she remembered the first time she had taken Mack to her Baptist Church outside of Newport News.

"How come the priest isn't wearing any fancy clothes?" he had said after the service started.

"He's not a priest. He's a preacher," she whispered.

"What's the difference?" he whispered back.

Renée just smiled, patted him on the knee, and promised to tell him later.

A few moments later, Mack asked Renée, "Why is everybody smiling?"

She chuckled out loud but quickly contained herself and told Mack to shush. They could discuss everything afterward. "Just follow along in the Bible. I'll help you," she said, handing Mack a Bible from the small wooden shelf behind the pew in front of them.

Renée snapped out of her daydream as she saw an approaching car with no headlights. She flicked her own lights at the car and cursed under her breath. She was about to flick her lights again, but the car behind him pulled out into her lane. She immediately went for the brake and cursed the other car under her breath for driving so recklessly, especially since the rain was falling harder. The car in her lane overtook the other vehicle and quickly switched back to the correct lane with plenty of distance to avoid hitting her. Renée's heightened senses quieted, and her grip on the wheel loosened slightly. Just as she put her foot back on the gas pedal, the car with no headlights pulled out into her lane, and everything happened so fast she had nowhere to go.

The moment to slam on the brakes was gone, but she knew she had to do something. Time seemed to stand still for an impossibly long second as Renée reviewed her options. If she pulled the wheel hard to the left, she would plow directly into the oncoming car in the other lane. If she stayed straight, she would barrel into the sports car with no headlights that was almost on top of her. If she swerved to the right, she would go off the embankment and down who knows how far. In the blink of an eye, she made the only logical choice and spun the wheel as hard as she could to the right to avoid hitting the oncoming cars. She locked eyes with the man driving the little, black sports car for the briefest time. Renée thought the man who was about to drive into the grill of her husband's Ford Excursion looked like he had just walked off the set of a Quentin Tarantino movie. He looked like, for lack of a better word, a gangster. His eyes registered something just moments before impact that looked like fear, but it wasn't. The man appeared to be mad at Renée for getting in his way. The moment passed as she watched the man duck down into the vehicle's passenger side.

She pulled as hard as she could, but she was a millisecond too late as the driver's side of both cars collided head on, sending Renée and the two most beautiful baby girls up into the air. With its higher center of gravity, the Excursion ran over the Porsche 911 and used its front end like a ramp, catapulting itself into the air for a 360-degree flip before landing back down onto the left two tires. Renée tried to correct the wheels' direction as soon as they hit, but the momentum kept the Excursion rotating hard to the right. As the right two tires hit the ground, the vehicle's left side came off the pavement a good three feet before the Excursion slammed into the guard rail.

The massive SUV tore through the galvanized steel like tissue paper. The solid wooden post connected to the guard rail slammed into the SUV's transmission, but the forward momentum was too strong. The rear end came straight off of the pavement, causing Renée and the babies to go back into the air, this time end over end. The SUV landed on the roof before rolling sideways for three full turns down the steep embankment toward the river. When the colossal hunk of metal finally stopped moving, it was only meters from the river.

The Excursion was lying on the passenger side when it came to rest, and Renée was hanging from her seatbelt. She looked out the front windshield and saw a sports car a few hundred yards away. Renée stared at the red vehicle but couldn't tell what kind it was. All she could tell was that it was red, and it looked fast. The car was moving, but it looked like it was going backward. She figured it was an illusion since she was upside down. Then she realized the red sports car was backing up toward the vehicle that had hit her. She thought she saw the gangster still sitting in his car as she tasted bile in the back of her throat. Her fear and initial panic gave rise to anger.

Renée looked around the destroyed SUV and saw her phone lying on the dashboard. She tried to reach it, but came up short. She felt above the sun visor and located Mack's knife that was there in case of an emergency. That was just like Mack, always prepared. She jabbed the knife into the airbag, then sliced through the seatbelt. She dropped two feet onto the passenger seat like a sack of concrete. Her right side struck the armrest of the passenger seat, and she was sure that her ribs were broken. She wasn't sure if it was from the crash or the fall from the driver's seat, but it didn't matter. She had to get to her phone.

She finally reached her phone and flipped it open. She pushed a series of numbers, and it responded with several high-pitched noises. When the high-pitched noises stopped, she dropped the phone. It fell through the broken passenger-side window and hit the bare earth with a thud. As her world slowly began closing in on her, she heard the soft whimper of a baby directly behind her. Her breasts hurt, and Renée wasn't sure if it was from the airbag, or if it was a maternal instinct to feed and comfort her babies. The world continued to close in, and the pain slipped to the back of her mind. She had a strange metallic taste in her mouth as the rain landed softly on her face. *A Ford Mustang,* Renée said to herself as she finally remembered the make and model. The car that had followed her out of the grocery store parking lot rolled past the two sports cars but didn't stop. Renée saw a man driving that car too, but she couldn't stay focused on him as her world went dark. The next thing Renée recalled was waking up in the Emergency Room, riding a tidal wave of pain.

*****

Marco Bertoli had only minor injuries as he pulled his car to a stop along the right shoulder. It was making an awful racket, and steam was coming from under the hood. The front driver-side door and quarter panel were gone, and the front tire was in shreds, so that the Porsche was rolling forward on just the rim. If Marco hadn't ducked down when he did, the chassis of the Excursion would have ripped his head clean off his shoulders. Marco looked at the damage to his car and rapidly began altering his plan. His new Porsche was totaled, but whoever was in that colossal SUV was undoubtedly dead. "It needs to look like an accident," the man had said. Marco had done exactly what he had been told, but it didn't go the way he was hoping.

Marco had been thinking about his call with Matteo ever since he had left the parking lot. It was pretty ingenious, and Marco had to give his brother some props for coming up with the plan so quickly. He knew Matteo hated Sal, so the whole idea made sense. When his Russian contact called him and explained what needed to be done, Marco finally realized that he could pin the murders on Sal, and his life would go back to normal.

Marco was sure the SUV would swing the wheel to the left and plow directly into Sal Rigo, but it didn't. Marco was sure that Sal wouldn't have had time to react, but it didn't matter now. The only thing Marco was reasonably sure of at the moment was that the driver of the SUV was dead and Sal was very much alive.

He needed to get out of Cleveland, so drawing the whole thing out didn't make much sense. He needed to think a lot faster as the Porsche finally ground to a halt on the road's right-hand shoulder. *Maybe this was a good thing,* Marco thought to himself. This collision had the potential to fix all his problems at the same time. "Never let a good crisis go to waste," he had recently overheard somebody say. He just needed to figure out how to capitalize on the most *recent* crisis.

The Porsche was still making a terrible racket, and the smell of burnt and twisted steel hung thick in the air. Marco went to open the door but then realized the door was gone. He started to get out but changed his mind. He looked through the car and reached across the seat to grab the bottle of vodka he was saving for later that evening. He opened the bottle cap. Climbing out of the $90,000 hunk of metal, he poured the vodka onto the passenger seat and the floorboard. Next, he poured the rest of the bottle onto the driver's seat and dashboard. Marco pulled a book of matches with the Foxxy's logo from his pocket and struck one across the back. He used the first match to light the rest of the book on fire; then he tossed it into the front seat of his brand-new, wholly destroyed Porsche 911 Cabriolet Turbo.

The vodka caught fire immediately with a whoosh, causing Marco to stumble backward. As he turned to avoid the flames, Marco saw the black SUV lying on the passenger side and thought he could make out the Black woman's face hunched over the steering wheel. She wasn't dead yet. It looked like she was staring directly at him. Marco felt a chill run down his spine, but he shrugged it off. Judging by the damage to the vehicle, he was confident she would be dead soon.

He opened the door of Sal's Mustang and climbed in. The two drove off, looking over their shoulders to ensure no one saw what had just happened. Just as Marco was about to turn forward, he saw the Porsche explode. He assumed the gas tank had caught fire. They looked at each other, and Marco started to laugh. Sal couldn't believe Marco could laugh after what had just occurred, but soon he began laughing. They drove on laughing out loud, unable to contain themselves.

They didn't encounter another vehicle until they had driven well over a mile. It was a small Toyota with a group of teenagers inside, so they felt pretty good about the odds that they weren't paying attention. They drove out of the Metroparks and headed West. The car crash wasn't part of Marco's original plan, but he intended to capitalize on it. Thinking quicker now, with the adrenaline coursing through their veins and the alcohol wearing off, the two began fleshing out more and more details as they drove. Marco neglected to tell Sal that his original plan involved killing his best friend, but Marco figured what Sal didn't know wouldn't hurt him.

"OK, I drove to the club two nights ago by myself. You came in a half hour later and said you wanted to go to Detroit to see Matteo. I didn't want to put that many miles on my new Porsche, so we drove up in your car. Whoever killed Petey and Tiffany stole the Porsche and almost killed somebody with it in the Metroparks." Marco finished restating the plan for the fifth time as they drove along the back roads in the red Mustang. "Now you repeat it back to me. Sal, we need to be on the same page about every tiny detail in case we get questioned."

Sal was not as confident in their plan as Marco was, and he told him so.

"What's wrong with the plan?" Marco said.

"What if we got caught on a traffic camera? Every traffic camera from the club to the Metroparks took a picture of both our cars. What if they pull our cell phone records? I know they were burner phones, but what if somebody gives them the numbers? And another thing I just remembered: What about the car that passed us a few seconds after the collision? The guy driving it just rolled past without even looking at me."

"Don't worry about that car," Marco said calmly.

"Why, what are you not telling me?" Sal yelled banging his fist on the steering wheel.

"You don't want to know," Marco shouted back.

What if the woman doesn't die and can ID my car, and what if she can identify you in a lineup? What if somebody knows my car wasn't at the Foxxy last night while we were at the docks? This plan sucks, Marco. It's full of holes, and you know it," Sal said, banging his fist on the steering wheel again and again.

"Do you have a better idea?" Marco yelled.

"We can't go to Detroit in my car. We have to dump it. If they find my car, they can say it was the same car on the traffic cameras. I know a place where we can put it for a few weeks until the heat is off, and then we can dump it in Lake Erie if we need to. Let's just dump my car and get to Matteo's place and see what he says," Sal said, trying to calm Marco down.

Marco didn't respond; he knew that Sal was right. He played the events of the last five hours over and over in his head until he couldn't think anymore. Marco had no idea how drastically his life had changed that instant. He had no idea how violent the coming storm was going to be. He had no idea who the Black woman was, and he certainly had no idea who her husband was. If he had, he would have set the Porsche on fire while he was still inside. He finally reclined the seat and told Sal to wake him when they got there.

CHAPTER 7

The satellite image of the car crash was projected on the screen in the small underground bunker just outside Davos, Switzerland. The four men and one woman stared at it for a long moment.

"Clearly, nobody could have survived that crash," said the lone woman in the room. She spoke with an accent that would be hard for most people to place. It would have sounded like a German accent to the amateur linguist, but actually, it was Dutch. Native-born Dutch usually pick up German quite well, and speak it almost flawlessly. Johanna's mother was Dutch, but her father had been a high-ranking member of the SS.

The family fled Germany just after the war to avoid capture by the allies. Her parents escaped to her mother's native town of Amsterdam where her family's wealth could ensure that no questions were asked. It had been sixty years since they had fled Germany, but the rise of the Fourth Reich was indisputable after the fall of the Iron Curtain. Johanna's father returned to Berlin in late 1990, bringing his adult daughter with him. He died shortly after that, but he died a happy man in the place where it had all begun.

"Why did he flee? His orders were to ensure that she was dead," another voice added in an Eastern European accent.

"Because he is not to be trusted, just like I said before this whole thing began. I told you he is just a drug addict, and has no loyalty to anything other than himself. We need to put a contingency plan in place and do it immediately before this woman talks," the Middle Eastern man in the room said. "His father is a great man, but his son …" the man spat and then eased back into his leather chair.

"Gentlemen … and lady," a Russian voice said softly but loud enough to be heard. "Let me reassure you that multiple contingency plans are in place. This was just a hastily prepared operation to eliminate two birds with one stone. I can assure you that this is not a problem. He followed his orders precisely. If the woman is not dead, then maybe she will have learned her lesson. We need her to know that digging any further will be a very dangerous endeavor. Killing an American intelligence officer is a drastic step that will not be easily undone."

He didn't seem at all concerned by the scene unfolding on the large monitor. "We have assets in the United States, and I assure you this woman's briefing will never see the light of day," he lied. "Our roots are deep within the intelligence agencies of every major country in the world, and if this woman is not already dead, she will be out of commission long enough for us to make our next move. Now, let us adjourn and return to the festivities. I am sure that our absence has been noted by our esteemed colleagues in the press corps. We must all make every effort possible to distance ourselves from one another, especially in light of this new briefing. The odds of it leaking are very small, but still, we must remain vigilant," the man said as he pressed the security button on the desk.

The door opened, and five armed security guards entered the room. Each of the security guards waited for their respective charges to escort them back to the convention center. It was early in the morning, and the press, not to mention the conspiracy theorists, would go crazy if all five were spotted together.

The only man that didn't speak was younger than the other four in the room by about twenty years. He remained seated for another moment and watched his colleagues file out of the room. He was the only one who was at home so to speak. He was from Borne, but had spent most of his life at prestigious schools in America and England. His pale, white skin stood out in stark contrast to the black tuxedo that he wore. His thin, wispy blond hair did little to give his face any redeeming attributes. His lips were thin, and his nose turned up slightly at the tip. He looked as though he had a perpetual frown on his face.

His personal bodyguard whispered something into his ear and waited for a response. The thin, pale man simply rose to his feet and shook his head to indicate that he was not going to answer the question in that room. The body guard nodded in acquiescence and followed the man in the tuxedo out of the room toward the waiting limousine.

The man with the Russian accent had been the first man to leave the conference room. He was dressed in a dark gray, pin-striped suit with a neat Windsor-knotted, silk tie that matched his pocket square. His graying hair gave his regal face a note of authority, while his Russian accent made it clear that he was not from Switzerland. His face looked young, but his doddering gait revealed his years. Once he was out of the soundproof bunker, he punched a series of numbers into his cell phone.

"Hello," the man on the other side of the line said hurriedly.

"Please tell me this situation is under control," the man with the Russian accent hissed into the phone.

"I'm sorry, but I think you have the wrong number," Nathan Marchek, assistant deputy director of the CIA said into the phone and then disconnected the call. *How many times do I have to tell that idiot not to call me on my cell phone?* he thought as he dropped the encrypted government-issued cell phone on his desk and reached into his breast pocket. He thought for a moment about the insanity of what he had just done. He had just hung up on one of the wealthiest men on the planet. *We have rules in this game that need to be followed. I don't care how much money you have,* he thought again in a feeble attempt to justify his actions.

He pulled out another phone, slid the plastic covering off the back, and pulled a battery and SIM card from his other pocket. He fitted the new items into their respective places in the back of the phone and waited. Several moments elapsed before the burner phone sprang to life and played the brief jingle that indicated it was ready for use.

The man opened the text app and typed in the words, IT IS 2300-AS ALWAYS. He folded the phone and went through the same process in reverse, but after he pulled the SIM card out, he put it into a small box and pushed a few buttons. Within seconds, the SIM card was utterly useless. The small box heated the microscopic hardware to over 1000 degrees, rendering it useless. He waited for the SIM card to cool off before slipping it back into his suit coat pocket to be properly disposed of later.

A knock at his door startled him, but he didn't miss a beat. "Come in."

A young woman dressed impeccably in a business suit entered the room, followed by another young man who looked like he hadn't slept for the past three days.

"I'm sorry for the interruption, sir, but it's urgent," the woman said and stepped to the side, indicating that the young man had critical information to convey.

The young man stood there hesitantly, but then found his voice. "Sir, we just received a distress signal from an officer's phone."

"Who?" Marchek said.

"Renée Murphy," the young man replied.

Marchek sat back in his chair and stared out the window momentarily. "The pretty young colored girl, correct?"

"She is Black; yes sir," the woman said.

"Where did the signal come from?" Marchek said ignoring the young woman's attempt at political correctness. He was trying his best to sound as though all the information was new to him.

"Somewhere outside of Cleveland, Ohio," the young man replied. "Local authorities have been dispatched. There is nothing to indicate that she was in an ongoing operation, sir," the disheveled man added.

"She is actually on maternity leave," the young woman said hesitatingly. She knew that Marchek didn't like it when people spoke without being spoken to, but it was hard to keep that to herself.

"Maternity leave?" Marchek muttered with a hint of indignation. He recovered almost effortlessly as he saw the look on the young woman's face turn sour. "That's right. I remember," he added to conceal his disgust. The young woman standing in front of him shifted on her feet, and it was clear she had been offended by the comment.

"Should I let George Seifert know, sir?" she finally said.

"Hold off on that. I will personally get everyone together in about twenty minutes. I will let Siefert know when we have something to share. Right now, all we have is a distress signal. We don't even know if she is still alive." He reached for his desk phone as the two subordinates headed to the door, "and keep me up to date on any new developments," he added as his door closed.

The two looked at one another as they walked out of the office. The woman stopped a few meters later and glanced at the young man with a puzzled look on her face. "Do you get the impression that he already knew everything we told him, or was it just me?" she whispered.

"Keep your head down. We can talk about this later," he responded and then headed down the hallway in the opposite direction.

*****

Mack stared down at the lifeless body of Wayne Sass the entire way back to Bagram. He couldn't believe that his friend was really gone. The euphoria he had been feeling for the past nine hours was completely gone and replaced by a level of hatred for his enemies he didn't know he was capable of. It was dark inside the helicopter, and without his NVGs, he could see nothing other than the low glow of the electronic equipment in the cockpit sending a faint green shadow onto his dead friend. He instinctively went to flip down his NVGs, but when his hand hit his bare head, he remembered that he had lost them in the scuffle.

Mack sat in the darkness of the helicopter, trying to remember why he was 10,000 miles away from home killing men he had never met. He tried to think of a solid excuse that could explain the reason why one of his best friends was dead at his feet. He couldn't think of anything, but his mind did go back to the day the world changed forever.

*****

He had been about to take his first bite of steak at Shenanigans Irish Pub in Darwin, Australia, when Mohamed Atta vaporized himself in a cloud of jet fuel, concrete, and steel on the 97th floor of the World Trade Center. Mack was a Scout Sniper with STA Platoon (Surveillance Target Acquisition) as part of the 15th Marine Expeditionary Unit headed for the Gulf to enforce the no-fly zone in Southern Iraq. He was with his spotter and fellow Marine, Corporal Wayne Sass, when they saw the footage on the television over the bar.

They both went to the television, and Sass asked the bartender to turn up the volume. They went through the normal sequence of thoughts that just about everybody else did in the early minutes of the footage. The first thought was that it had been an accident, but when the footage was rewound and played back slower on CNN, the accident theory started to break down.

"That was a huge plane," Mack said.

"Dude, that was no accident. That looked intentional," Sass said, more to himself than anybody else.

The pub was crowded, but there was an eerie quiet in the building as everyone stared in disbelief. They both sat down but continued to watch the events unfold as they ate dinner. Seventeen minutes later, a second explosion was seen on the television. If he wasn't sure about the first plane, the second one made it all too clear.

"We better book it back to the ship," Sass said as he swallowed the last of his beer and started to stand. "Come on bro, we gotta go," he said again when Mack didn't seem to be moving fast enough.

"Come on, Duke, we've been cooped up on the Nickel for I don't know how long, and now you are in a hurry to get back to it? Mack said, using his nickname. When Mack learned his first name was Wayne, he asked him, like John Wayne? The name Duke had stuck. "I say we drink another beer for the people who just died,"

As Mack tried flagging down a waitress, a Marine with the shore patrol burst through the doors and began scanning the crowd. Mack met the eyes of the Marine and realized that another beer was going to be out of the question. The two made their way outside and started the short walk back to the ship. Sass asked the Lance Corporal if he had heard anything.

"All I know is that everybody's liberty pass just expired."

Sass was about to ask him another question, but he turned sharply away from him and headed down the street to search for the rest of First Battalion.

Once the two were back aboard, they made their way down to the bottom of the ship where the Marines were billeted. They were among the first Marines back, so they had the very crammed living space to themselves for a brief time. They learned there would be a briefing in one hour for all non-commissioned officers (NCOs), so to kill some time, they made their way to the cafeteria to see if the TVs were on. CNN was replaying the video feed of the second plane slamming into the South Tower over and over. It was apparent now that this was not an accident.

As more Marines began trickling back onto the ship in various states of drunkenness, the atmosphere became increasingly somber.

America was under attack, and those responsible were most likely from the Al-Qaeda terrorist network. Mack knew that they were headed to the Persian Gulf, but somehow he knew deep down that this was not going to be a routine six-month deployment.

The briefing was like all the others Mack had been in over his five-year Marine Corps career, with the notable exception that this one was the real deal. Mack had been deployed before, but he had never had an actual mission with real targets. He had been in countless briefings where the enemy was a paper tiger, created to make the training seem more realistic. Sometimes the enemy was just some fellow Marines, dressed in civilian attire and tasked with playing the role of terrorists or other hostiles. The briefings had always been a little artificial with endless details and what-if scenarios.

Major Keels walked into the area, and all Marines stood. "At ease, Marines," he said with a commanding voice. "I'm sure you all know why we are here and not out chasing Australian women and throwing back some Lagers. Let me just spare you all the suspense. We have been ordered back to the ship to await further orders. We are unsure what to think about this at the moment, but we know this was a coordinated terrorist attack. If you haven't heard, another plane just slammed into the Pentagon. That one isn't on the major news networks, but I just got confirmation that a lot of good men are dead.

The Marines groaned as they sat in disbelief.

"They died sitting at their desks," the Major said raising his voice. "We are not going to die sitting at our desks."

A loud burst of oohrahs and Semper Fi's rang out in the small briefing room before Major Keels was able to get the Marines under control again.

"We are going to get to work. We have tentative orders to pull anchor and head toward East Timor a little early. We had planned to get there in a week or two, but now it is imperative that we make it there as fast as our Navy brothers can move this Iron Nickel. It looks like we are the closest Marine Corps Unit to the area, and we are going to prepare for the worst. Australia poses no threat to our national security, so the only thing we are doing here is drinking beer and wasting time.

I want every one of you to watch the news as often as you can. I want you to burn into your minds those images of commercial airplanes flying into a building with thousands of civilians, and I want it to piss you off so bad that when I order you to jump, you will already be in the air. Am I understood?" The Major shouted the last three words so loud, his face turned red, and spit flew from his mouth.

"Yes, sir," the Marines echoed back so loudly it was heard topside.

The order came down from the Commanding General the next day to alter their current course and head full steam toward the North Arabian Sea to prepare for whatever came next. When the orders came down to alter course, there was a feeling of vengeance, although vengeance wasn't the right word. It was a reckoning; the balancing of the ledgers was about to begin. The September 11th attacks killed 2,977 Americans. Any terrorist who participated in the attack would be reckoned with. The President had made it clear that America would accept nothing less than total victory. The 600 Marines aboard the *USS Peleliu* would be among the first Americans to settle the score. The 15th and 26th MEU (Marine Expeditionary Units) were about to be the tip of the spear.

*****

Mack remembered that day as though it were yesterday. He remembered the look on Sass's face that told the whole story. Sass wasn't thinking about the dangers ahead, or about the revenge. He wasn't thinking about taking enemy fire for eight straight hours three years later. He wasn't thinking about taking a round to the forehead on some deserted ridge on the Pakistan border. He was only thinking about his brother, who had been a police officer for the New York Police Department. Sass didn't know it at the time, but his brother was at Ground Zero when the first tower fell, killing him instantly as he was running up sixty flights of stairs to get to the wounded.

Mack couldn't help but think of Sass' parents, who had now lost two sons in the war on terror. How would they take the news? He was sure that his parents were proud of him for taking the fight to the Taliban, but he was also confident they would have preferred a living coward to a dead hero.

The helicopter ride back to Bagram should have been full of high fives and slaps on the back. Mack knew in the darkness of the helicopter that every man was processing his death in their own way. Mack wasn't sure exactly what his way was, but it didn't feel like it was working. He wondered if his fellow warriors were feeling the guilt that he was feeling. He wondered if Apollo was feeling guilty for not calling for a ride home sooner. He wondered if G-Mar was feeling guilty for getting on the chopper before the rest of his men.

Mack knew all of the reasons to feel guilty, but they all paled in comparison to his own. Sass had just saved his life only to have his own taken away a moment later. If he had seen the man with the NVGs a second sooner, Sass would be alive. If he had fought the man harder, then he would still be alive. The next haunting thought for Mack was that if he had been killed, then Sass would still be alive. He wouldn't have had to stop on that ridge to cover his retreat. He most definitely would have carried him back to the helicopter just as Mack had done for him, but it would have been him on the floor, not Sass.

Mack remembered hearing the commanding General's briefing just before going to Afghanistan for the first time. His briefing was about pain and loss at the death of friends. He had warned the Marines that losing friends was going to happen. He warned that the shock of death would never get easier. Just before he finished his briefing, he explained the worst type of grief. He said it was the overwhelming euphoria you felt when you were not the one killed. He said the feeling of relief to know that it wasn't you who died, but rather a comrade, was a guilty grief that would never fade.

The most haunting fact of all was that Mack had felt that rush of adrenaline that the General had warned them about many years ago. Mack indeed felt relieved that it had not been him that was killed on that ridge, but the relief turned into a dagger and it drove itself straight into his heart.

None of it made sense as the turbulence snapped Mack out of his memory. He felt the helicopter dropping altitude for the second time that night as the sun began to peak out from the horizon, sending a million shades of red over the beautiful Afghanistan mountains, also known as the Graveyard of Empires.

CHAPTER 8

Mack got off the chopper and filed into headquarters for the debrief. He was met by Alpha Team and a few slaps on the back. He stared back at his brothers-in-arms as he took a seat on top of a stack of MRE boxes. Mack was still stunned about what had happened, but couldn't blame the other Marines. They probably didn't know. Just as he sat down, the Major entered the room, forcing him back to his feet. He was slow to rise, and when the Major said, "As you were," Mack slumped back down onto the boxes. The Major started clicking some buttons on his laptop, and an image began taking shape on the overhead projector screen.

"Before I begin, I'd like to take a moment to let you all know that Sergeant Wayne Sass was killed in action last night." There were several curses, and a few new dents were punched into desks and lockers. Mack looked around the room and saw a lot of anger-filled eyes on weary faces. "I'm asking for strict radio silence on this one until his family can be notified. You all know the drill, and I expect everyone to comply." Major Hanlon shook his head to indicate that he felt the men's pain. "Sergeant Sass was a good man, and he will be missed. I want to remind you that Sergeant Sass did not die because of any politician. He died protecting his friends. He was covering Staff Sergeant Murphy's withdrawal when he was shot by enemy fire." The Major asked for a moment of silence before moving forward with his briefing.

Mack closed his eyes and remembered the entire event. He lamented as he remembered good times with Sass in previous months. He was a good man. He was a good friend. He was a good Marine. No, he was the best.

"'Til Valhalla," a Marine in the back of the room shouted. "Semper Fi," came another voice.

Mack just listened and fought back the emotions that were swirling around inside his head.

The Major cleared his throat and clicked a few more buttons on the laptop. After several moments, a grainy image sprang to life. It became obvious they were all looking at a satellite image of the battlefield that night. As the Major pushed more buttons, the picture zoomed in until Mack was looking at what the Major wanted Charlie Team to see. The sun continued peaking up over the horizon, sending rays of light onto the projector screen as Mack stared at the images.

"What you are looking at, Marines, is a live picture of your work last night. This is the most magnificent thing I have seen since this miserable war started," Major Hanlon said. "Battalion S-2 estimates that there are over seventy dead Taliban in these images. The amount of intelligence we gleaned from last night's mission is priceless. Charlie Team," the Major said in a clear, commanding voice, "outstanding job, Marines."

A round of applause would have normally erupted from the command building, but the response was more subdued in light of the loss of one of their own. There were a few more oorahs and some slaps on the back, but Mack stayed glued to his seat. He wasn't sure what he felt. *Am I upset because my friends aren't? Is it right to be even remotely enthusiastic when a fellow Marine gets killed? What is wrong with me?* All these thoughts and a dozen more ran through Mack's mind as he stared at the images of the battlefield.

"There are going to be some medals hanging around necks for the work that happened last night. A Purple Heart for Sergeant Sass, and a Navy Cross if I have anything to say about it. Purple Hearts for Staff Sergeant Murphy and Staff Sergeant Williams for sure. Now, Alpha Team is heading back out there in about fifteen mikes to clean up the mess, to pull as much intel off these dead bodies as possible, and destroy the weapons. Bravo will be on standby should the mission go south. Charlie can hit the rack. You earned it," the Major said.

As Charlie Team headed out the door, Major Hanlon stopped Mack to shake his hand. Mack offered him his hand and shook it firmly. When Major Hanlon didn't let go, Mack was unsure what to do. Just then, Major Hanlon leaned forward and said directly into Mack's ear, "Tell your wife how the movie ended. I'm sure she's pretty worried about you."

Mack looked Major Hanlon in the eyes. Mack knew that the Major had heard the entire phone call from the night before. But when the Major winked at him, he just nodded and said, "Aye-aye, sir," and headed for the door.

"I'm sorry about Sass. I know he was a good friend," the Major added over his shoulder.

"Yes, sir, he was."

Mack stopped short of his team's building before going inside. He dropped his pack and started fishing through the outside pocket to retrieve the satellite phone. He powered it on and walked behind the building for some early morning shade. He pushed the buttons and waited for the series of pings and pauses until he heard the phone ringing 10,000 miles away. The phone went right into a prerecorded message saying that the phone number he was trying to call was inactive. Mack dialed again and got the same response. He dialed a third time, pushing the buttons slowly as he watched the numbers appearing on the screen. Same result. He powered the device down and headed around the building to grab his pack and get some shut-eye. He knew there had to be a reasonable explanation for the recorded message, so he wouldn't worry about it now. When he woke up, he would call Renée from the Battalion H.Q. landline and find out what had gone wrong with her phone.

He didn't lie down so much as he fell into bed. He was exhausted, and the adrenaline from the last eight hours was wearing off. He closed his eyes and tried to sleep, but all he thought about was his friend's lifeless body lying in a bag somewhere. He looked around at the rest of the team, who were undoubtedly thinking the same thing. Mack pulled his poncho liner over his head and fought the tears as they ran quietly down his face and onto the floor to mix with the rest of the tears from the warriors surrounding him. The last thing Mack heard was the CH-53 Sea Stallions taking off and banking low over his barracks.

*****

Once the pretty woman in the business suit and the guy who looked half asleep left his office, Nathan Marchek pulled out his personal cell phone. He made a few phone calls from his desk rather than using his landline. He had been with the agency for over 30 years, and at no point during that time had he ever trusted a landline telephone. He trusted cell phones even less, but the calls he was making could all be explained. To the casual listener, his phone calls seemed innocent enough. "How was your weekend? What golf course did you play last week? How are the wife and kids doing?" All of the phrases seemed like small talk, but they were all part of a secret language that had been cleverly designed over years of careful operational planning. He had been a part of a very select group of individuals most of his adult life. In fact, his entire career at the agency had been made possible by the men he was casually conversing with over the phone.

The answers he received were as innocuous as the language he was using, but when he finished his last call, he had an entirely new set of marching orders. The organization did not say a single word that would blow their cover over the phone. They didn't use email either as it was becoming ever more difficult to avoid being hacked. The only acceptable form of communication that didn't involve a face-to-face encounter was placing ads in local newspapers. It was as old school as you could get, but it worked. No sense fixing it if it wasn't broken. The following day Marchek would be reading the *Wall Street Journal* to see where he was to meet with his superiors.

He put his cell phone down and pulled out the briefing Renée Murphy had written and started reading it for the tenth time. He had to admit that it was nothing short of incredible. She had figured out that a select group of the world's wealthiest people were working together to bring about a new world order. This group of the world's wealthiest people made the Bilderberger group seem like an insignificant group of business owners. The fact that Renée had been able to uncover the inner workings of this group was astonishing.

The CIA had been building files on these individuals for more than fifty years, but were never able to connect any two of them, much less draft a manifesto that pulled the cover off the entire operation. The fact that she had named names in her briefing was enough to ensure that the briefing would never see the light of day. Marchek knew that the briefing was explosive and agreed with Maxwell Kaine, the director of the CIA, when he decided to bury it. He had been ordered to destroy any record of the briefing and to delete any electronic files that had been shared between the four employees of the CIA who were privy to it. He had obeyed by deleting the files from his laptop as well as deleting any record of the email from the CIA servers. The only remaining copy of the briefing Marchek was aware of was the one he was holding in his hands—except for the copy he had sent by official government courier to Moscow.

Renée Murphy had been ordered to delete it as well, and when the CIA computer gurus tapped into her laptop, they reported that it had been destroyed as ordered. She had been given a stern talking to after turning in the briefing just weeks earlier. The fact that she had just become a new mother seemed to take the edge off her disappointment at having her briefing dismissed, but Marchek could tell she wasn't happy about it.

What nobody knew, including Nathan Marchek, was that she left a digital copy of the briefing in a very secret location. She had reasoned that if her briefing was just a bunch of hogwash, they would not have ordered her to delete it. It would have simply been filed away in the basement of the CIA building, never to be heard of again. She realized it had struck a nerve somewhere, with somebody, so she had complied to protect her career. Secretly though, she knew it would be a significant piece of information that could be leveraged in her favor someday, so she put it on a small jump drive and buried it where only she and one other man knew where to find it.

Marchek arose from his desk and headed toward the elevator of the CIA headquarters building. He punched the button and then swiped his CIA badge across the card reader. Moments later, he was in the basement of the building and making his way across the sea of cubicles that were mostly deserted at this time of day. It was just after 8:00 p.m., and the day shift was being slowly replaced by their night-time counterparts. As Marchek made his way toward a bank of monitors, he made eye contact with the young woman sitting behind her desk. He simply nodded at her and continued walking toward the opposite side of the room.

The young woman saw Marchek and then nonchalantly pulled up the window on her computer that had been minimized for the past two hours to keep prying eyes off her screen. The satellite image flickered to life as it was scanning the coast of the United States. It had just been surveilling a small winding road outside of Cleveland, Ohio. At 7,000 kilometers above the earth, the satellite was screaming along at 10 kilometers per second. She punched a sequence of numbers and letters and then pushed the enter button. The screen flickered again before the feed was cut.

The low-earth-orbiting satellite had gone offline for the past two hours due to mechanical issues. At least, that was the official story. Once the young woman punched in the code, it was back online. She was not happy about what she had been doing, but Marchek's orders had been specific. She knew full well that if she were to be caught, she would be charged with high treason and spend the rest of her life in a prison cell. She knew that Marchek was not a man to cross, but the money he had been giving her was worth the risk. Her government salary was decent, but it didn't afford her the finer things in life that she felt a woman of her intelligence and achievements deserved. Not only had she sold out her country for a nicer apartment in Georgetown, but she had sold her soul for a few extra purses and a few extra dollars in her bank account.

Nathan Marchek made his way back to the top floor over the next five minutes. He stopped at several different locations on various floors to check in with his network of agents. He smiled to himself as he thought about how different this place would be once he took over. The current director was getting older, and the political winds were shifting. The new direction of the wind left Marchek in a very good position to take the wheel, while it left the current director on a certain path toward retirement and life in a seniors-only village in Florida. The current director was a useful idiot, in Marchek's opinion. He could be counted on to do the right thing when it mattered, but his hesitancy in many situations gave Marchek the time he needed to move his chess pieces around the board to prepare for his next moves.

His patriotism and devotion to the conservative views of the country could be relied on when anticipating his course of action, but his outdated way of looking at world events made him a true dinosaur in the clandestine world. He was the director of the CIA more for his name and popularity among the Beltway types. He was a patriot no doubt, but not the type that would rock any boats. Marchek knocked on the director's door and waited for his response.

"Come in," the voice of an old man said loud enough to be heard.

Marchek entered the room slowly and offered a greeting once he had seen the old man behind his desk. "Do you have a minute, sir?"

"Of course, Nathan. What can I do for you?"

Nathan walked confidently across the room and took a seat on one of the leather-backed chairs across from Maxwell Kaine's desk. He drew in a long breath before he asked his question. He was careful to create a look of discouragement and defeat before he asked Maxwell if he had heard anything further about Renée Murphy. The director shook his head as he studied Marchek's face. The two sat in silence for a moment staring at each other before Marchek interrupted. He hated it when Maxwell stared at him like that. He knew he had not made any mistakes, but it always felt like Maxwell was reading his mind when he stared at him so intently. It used to unnerve him whenever Maxwell stared at him, but over the years, he had learned not to break the stare too soon. If he broke his stare too soon, he would appear guilty; if he held it too long, he would appear defiant. After the correct amount of time, Nathan finally said, "I hope this has nothing to do with the briefing."

"Why would it?" Maxwell shot back.

"Sir, I know you like the Murphy girl, but can we really trust her to keep a lid on this thing?"

"We've been over this before, Nathan. If John Smith and George Seifert say she can be trusted, she can be trusted." Maxwell Kaine sat back in his chair, but he kept his eyes locked on Marchek. He decided it was not the right time to let him know the briefing had surfaced at the US Embassy in Russia. It had been delivered via diplomatic courier the day before. Maxwell wasn't sure yet who the intended recipient was, but he had to assume it had been delivered. His Mossad counterpart, Yonah Levin, informed him a few hours ago that the briefing had been found in the burn bin at the US Embassy in Moscow. Maxwell knew better than to ask Yonah how he had heard that, but he did make several mental notes.

The fact that it was in the burn bin was clear evidence that it was intended to be leaked. Maxwell didn't say anything because he didn't trust Marchek—he didn't trust anybody. He just sat there patiently and ran the entire conversation with Levin through his head while he stared at the man across from him.

"That doesn't mean she wasn't compromised," Marchek snapped back. "Anybody could have hacked her computer and stolen those files. You know the risks better than anybody. What if her briefing was accurate? What if the FBI gets ahold of it and wants to start sticking their noses in our business? You know we have open cases that involve every single person on that list. They have all made political donations to just about every Congressman and Senator on the hill. When that kind of information gets disseminated on the internet, the conspiracy theorists will never let it go. The chaos a briefing like that would unleash is more than any country on the planet is ready for."

Maxwell Kaine held up his hands to signal Nathan to be quiet. He shifted in his chair and stared at Nathan for an uncomfortable amount of time before he finally spoke. "If everybody does the right thing, then this little problem goes away. Right now, there is nothing to indicate that this briefing is in the wrong hands," he lied. Maxwell leaned back in his chair and started thinking again. He tried untangling the knot, but he just couldn't quite get ahold of the ends of the rope. He knew Seifert wouldn't have mishandled a report like that. In fact, he was surprised that George had come to him with it at all. It was just too explosive. It didn't matter that the entire report was almost dead-on accurate; it wasn't ready to see the light of day.

He had to give Renée Murphy credit for putting all the pieces together and seeing the connections where most people would not have. The fact that the report was out there now sent a shiver down his spine. They had all been so careful. The only thing more worrisome than the intended consequences would be the unintended ones. The Murphy Report, as he had begun referring to it, was a veritable list of the most powerful men and women on the planet. The list itself wasn't what worried Maxwell. Anybody could figure that out. What worried him was that Renée Murphy had deciphered plans that were centuries old and involved everyone on that list. The Murphy Report had laid out in stunning detail every significant event of the past fifty years that tied every one of those names together.

Marchek squirmed in his seat. He had the feeling Maxwell was holding something back, but he couldn't prove it. Oh, how he despised the older man on the other side of the desk. *Why doesn't he just retire and play golf like every other eighty-year-old man? He is standing in the way of real progress in the world and doesn't even know it,* he thought to himself. "OK, sir. I trust you," he finally managed to say and then stood to leave.

"Sit down for a second. You're always in such a hurry. I have a few questions for you," Maxwell said in a collegial tone. "Let's say this briefing does get out there on the internet," he said with a crumpled-up face, indicating that the internet was just a passing phase that would soon be gone. "Who stands to benefit from this type of information? The agency has plausible deniability. We say it was a tabletop exercise that was meant to spur creative thinking. Or we say it was just a work of fiction by one of our officers, and we leave it at that. Who stands to benefit from this?" Maxwell said, folding his hands on the desk in front of him indicating that Marchek now had the floor.

Marchek knew instinctively that Maxwell was setting a trap. He had watched him do it to countless others over the course of his thirty-year career. He knew it so definitively that it shot a bolt of panic through his spine. He knew he would have to choose his words carefully, and he had to do it quickly, or he would be tipping his hand. "I don't know," he replied trying to buy time. He had rehearsed this conversation in his head a hundred times over the past several days, and he was sticking to the script. "The Russians and the Saudis, if I had to guess. We know that Russia is looking to expand across Eastern Europe, and the Saudis are always looking for ways to blackmail us. If this briefing gets out, it will totally hamstring our standing with NATO, and it will drive up petroleum prices to a level that nobody could afford."

"Be more specific, Nathan. I want well-thought-out responses, not just off-the-top-of-your-head speculations."

Marchek had been expecting that question as well, and he was prepared. "If Vladimir Rusilko knows we are suspicious of his activities in the Balkans, he will shuffle the board, and thirty years of infiltration will have been for nothing. If he does go through with his invasion into the Balkans, oil prices will skyrocket, and the only people who will be able to afford a full tank of gas will be working at the Kremlin. If the Crown Prince knows we can connect the dots between himself and Osama bin Laden, then the public will want us to invade Saudi Arabia and we will never leave Afghanistan. He will bog us down with more terrorist attacks than the American public has the patience for, and we will find ourselves at war against the entire Middle East. A war we can't win, and we both know it. What if Anders Remberg decides to cancel his bank's loans and collect the debts that most countries can't pay. I could go into more details, but suffice it to say, that briefing cannot see the light of day."

When Marchek was done speaking, Maxwell simply nodded his head in agreement. He had been listening attentively, but inside his head, he was trying to decide if Marchek was the one who had leaked the information. He was all but sure he had, but he didn't let on. He was trying to decide whether he would give the man a little more rope or let him hang himself right then and there. He eventually decided to give him more rope.

"What do we do if the briefing does get out?" Maxwell said when the room got quiet.

"We put as much distance between Renée Murphy and the agency as we can. We do exactly what you said earlier, and we downplay it on the surface. Under the surface, we need to find out who leaked it and what their motivation was. If it was Renée Murphy, she needs to be dealt with. If it was Seifert, we have bigger problems."

"How so?"

"Because digging through Seifert's past will be much more complicated than Murphy's. He has been in every major conflict since Vietnam, so the list of accomplices and possible motivations is much longer. Seifert has friends in half of the intelligence agencies around the world, and enemies in the other half. He is impossible to read, and he is very good at covering his tracks."

"True," Maxwell said somberly.

"I am going to let Seifert know about Murphy unless you can think of any reason not to just yet," Marchek said, rising from his chair.

Why wouldn't we tell Seifert? Maxwell wanted to say, but he didn't. "Why don't we both do it? I think his initial reaction will be telling, don't you?"

"Great idea," Nathan said and pulled out his phone. Just as he was about to dial, there was another knock at the door. The same young woman from earlier walked into the office to give Director Kaine an update on the distress signal.

"Sirs," she said, seeing Marchek looking over his shoulder at her, "We just heard from the Cleveland Metroparks Police Department that Renée Murphy was involved in a hit-and-run accident. Murphy's SUV was off the road and severely damaged when the police arrived. It took a while to cut her out of the car, but she is en route to the local hospital. Her twin daughters were in the car at the time of the accident, and they are being transported by helicopter to the local children's hospital. Local authorities say a Porsche collided with her SUV, but the driver of the Porsche fled the scene. The only witnesses are a group of teenagers who happened upon the wreck several minutes afterward. According to the first responders on the scene, they didn't think there would be any survivors."

Maxwell let his head drop a little at the news, and Marchek affected a grieved look that he was not feeling. In fact, he was becoming more optimistic by the moment.

"Has anybody thought to contact her husband? He is deployed to Afghanistan currently. He's a Marine if memory serves me correctly," Maxwell Kaine said somberly.

"No, sir. I will contact the Red Cross as soon as I have more details if you want me to," she replied.

"Please do."

The young woman said that was all she knew and quietly excused herself from the room. Once she was gone, Maxwell and Nathan's eyes met as they both tried to figure out what it meant. Nathan was the first to speak, as usual, and he suggested that it was a deliberate attempt on her life. Maxwell Kaine agreed, and he even said so before dropping his head into his hands. "Those poor little girls," he said more for himself than for Nathan.

The two men sat there discussing the ramifications of the new information for close to an hour before Maxwell suggested that they contact George Siefert. "We don't want him to hear about it from somebody else."

Nathan dialed the number and then put his phone on speaker as they both sat waiting for George to pick up the phone.

CHAPTER 9

It was 10 p.m. in Chevy Chase, MD, and the Director of the Near East and South Asian division at the Central Intelligence Agency, George Siefert, had just finished pouring himself a shot of Maker's Mark whiskey as he settled into his recliner. He pushed the play button on the Bose remote, and soon the music of Chopin filled the room. He was his favorite composer. Not because of the music itself but because it reminded him of his daughter. The years of piano lessons had paid off as she played Chopin's ballade no. 1 in G minor to audition at the Juilliard School. She had been accepted a week later, which was a bittersweet moment for the man who held some of the world's best-kept secrets.

She was his world, and his world would be moving away soon. His wife died of ovarian cancer eleven months earlier after a three-year battle that slowly destroyed her mind as well as her body. He and his daughter both grieved the loss, but his daughter was much stronger than he ever dreamed of being. She grieved for her mother for almost six months before she snapped out of it one day. She came to terms with the finality of death and decided that it would no longer prevent her from living her life. George wished that his grief only lasted six months, but he still wore it on his chest like a medal hanging above his old Army uniform pocket.

Just as the music started getting louder, *forte* was the word for it, if he remembered his daughter correctly, his cell phone rang. He silently cursed the interruption as he fished the phone out of his pocket. He muted the stereo and answered the phone abruptly.

"Seifert," he barked into the phone.

"George, this is Nathan Marchek. I'm here with the director; you're on speaker. I'm afraid I have some bad news for you." Nathan was George's immediate superior and the only man between himself and the director.

"There is no easy way to tell you this, but it looks like somebody tried to kill Renée Murphy tonight. From what we can tell, it was a hit-and-run about two hours ago. The local PD says she isn't expected to make it."

George was in shock. His first instinct was to correct Nathan and let him know that wasn't possible. She was on maternity leave here in the States somewhere. *Ohio, somewhere outside of Cleveland,* he thought. She wasn't involved with some ongoing clandestine mission. *That was preposterous*, he thought to himself, but the auditory complex in George's temporal lobes was still firing, indicating that Nathan was still talking. He hadn't heard a thing after the words, "kill Renée Murphy."

"I'm sorry, did you say Renée Murphy?" he finally blurted out.

"Yes, George, I'm sorry," and he meant it. He actually liked Renée. Who didn't like Renée? She was intelligent, energetic, and drop-dead gorgeous, but that didn't change the fact that she needed to be dealt with. Nathan explained that an alert from Renée's cell phone went out just moments after the crash. "She apparently had the presence of mind to send out a distress call. It was actually our people who called the police to the scene."

"Thanks, Nathan," George mumbled and closed his eyes.

He heard Nathan say something about calling him when he had more information, but his head was still swimming from the news.

Director Kaine looked hard at Nathan and leaned forward to offer his condolences as well. "She is a talented young lady, and it's a shame. We will be doing everything we can to get to the bottom of this," he said respectfully.

"Thank you, sir," George said and then heard the line go dead. George flipped the phone shut and turned the stereo off as his thoughts carried him away. Chopin would have to wait; he needed to think. His daughter Kelly was at her grandmother's house in North Carolina for the weekend, so George grabbed his coat, set the home alarm, holstered his Beretta, and walked into the garage. He pushed the large button that activated the overhead garage door and then slipped into his Lexus SUV. He had thirty seconds to leave the garage before the alarm tripped. The garage door finished closing behind him with seven seconds to spare.

George didn't need to be told to get to Langley. It was expected when an officer went down. Twenty minutes later, he was pulling up to the gate at the CIA headquarters in Langley, VA. He rolled down his window and flashed his badge as he looked at the security guard and the camera behind him. The facial recognition software was doing all the work; the guard was just there to push the button that raised the gate. A green light only visible to the guard meant the face was cleared for admission. A red light meant the face was not. It was a simple job, really; the hard part was wearing the scowl on their face for eight hours every day. The gate wouldn't go up if the light was red, but it wasn't.

Two seconds later, George pulled his foot off the brake and began rolling through the gate. He swerved around the concrete barricades erected after 9/11 and found a spot close to the building. He was high enough up on the totem pole to warrant his own space, but George was an operator at heart. He never took what was offered, and he never did the same thing twice. There weren't that many cars in the parking lot at this hour, so he picked a random space, got out of his car, and made his way inside.

After two more security checkpoints, he was finally in his office.

He fired up the computer at his desk and pulled a different bottle of Maker's Mark from a drawer. It was contraband inside Langley. Not because you couldn't bring alcohol into the building, but because he didn't get the proper clearance. He knew he had been drinking more lately, and he quietly resolved to do better.

As the first sip of the liquid burned a trail down his esophagus, he tapped the buttons on his keyboard to bring up the program he was wanting to access. As he waited for the security software to scan his device, he looked around his office at the pictures on the wall. His favorite was of his daughter, Kelly, standing next to the President in the Oval Office the day he presented him the Distinguished Intelligence Medal for his work in Afghanistan two years ago. Standing next to his daughter was his wife, Priscilla. She was frail looking from her chemotherapy but was adamant about being there for such a monumental accomplishment.

The computer program finally sprang to life, and he entered the fourteen-digit alphanumeric password that he was required to change every forty-eight hours. He pulled up Renée's file and read it for the millionth time. On the way to the office, he had come up with a shortlist of the people who would want to kill Renée. After a lot of thinking, he discarded almost every name as he tried to whittle down the list of people who would even know how to find her. The thought had crossed his mind that it was an accident, and nobody was to blame. But ordinary people didn't drive off after an accident; only people with something to hide did that. He entered the names of a few people who had risen to the top of the list, but none were in the country. One came back as location unknown, but he couldn't make the pieces fit.

He picked up the phone and dialed Renée's encrypted CIA phone number, but it went into a digital recording without ringing. He smiled briefly to himself when he realized that Renée had had the presence of mind to disable her cell phone after being struck head on in a collision. Marchek told him that Renée's vehicle was forced off the road, and her

SUV had flipped several times down an embankment before coming to a stop just meters from the river. According to the police report, she was badly injured, as were the two children in the back seat, yet she had the presence of mind to destroy her phone.

If it had been an accident, Renée would not have needed to destroy her phone. It would have been impossible for anybody just to pick up her phone and log into it. She disabled it for a reason. It was a distress call. Or, maybe it was just a total coincidence, George said to himself, but then dismissed the thought as quickly as it came.

George Seifert did not believe in coincidence; he learned a long time ago if something smelled bad, it was bad. He had attempted to get some information from the Cleveland Police Department, but they were not forthcoming. The ongoing investigation, jurisdiction, subpoena, blah, blah, blah. Seifert knew the drill.

He made another call to an old friend at the Bureau and was surprised when it was answered on the first ring.

"Aguayo," came the very sleepy voice on the other end of the line.

"Hey, old friend," George said.

"What's up, amigo?" Julian Aguayo said. "Is everything OK?" he blurted out, realizing what time it was.

"I'm good," George said. "I need a favor from you if you have a second."

"Anything for you, Gringo." Julian said in an overly dramatic Mexican accent.

"One of my officers may have been killed in a hit-and-run outside of Cleveland, Ohio. The local PD isn't very forthcoming with details, and they didn't seem to care when I told her she was an agency employee. I was wondering if one of the nation's top law enforcement officers were to call if he might have a little more pull?"

"Consider it done. Anything else?"

"Let's get together soon; I miss that wet back of yours," George said in jest.

"Let's make it happen; only let's do it in private. Being seen with a Gringo may ruin my reputation," Julian said and then clicked off the phone.

George sat in the quiet office for a while thinking back over the years since he had met Renée. He thought about how she had come to be a part of the agency.

A CIA recruiter named John Smith was at William & Mary looking at one of Renée's classmates, who was quite the computer hacker. He had just happened to be walking across campus when Renée and the rest of the cross-country team ran by him during practice one day. He looked at Renée and made a mental note to figure out who the beautiful woman was. She was black, but there was something else. Her eyes were piercing green with the hint of an Asian brow line. Her hair looked naturally curly and silky, too. She was tall and muscular but still very feminine. At five feet ten inches, she was supermodel tall, and as she ran past him, her stride seemed effortless.

Later that night, when the recruiter learned about her ability to speak Pashto and Russian, he forgot about the computer hacker. George remembered specifically requesting her after 9/11. At that time, she had been with the agency for just a little shy of three years. She was amazing in every sense of the word. She spoke Pashto fluently, thanks to her maternal grandmother and grandfather while growing up in Newport News, Virginia. Her paternal grandmother had taught her Korean, and it was as much a natural language for her as English. In high school, she had realized she had a natural talent for learning languages, so she taught herself Russian. It wasn't long before she was carrying on conversations with one of her mother's colleagues at work who had just emigrated from Russia the year she started high school.

By the time she entered college at William & Mary, she was already fluent in Pashto, Korean, Russian, English, and Spanish. She had scored in the top ninety-ninth percentile on her SAT, and when she combined her academic scholarship with her sports scholarship for cross-country running, she was getting paid to go to school. At William & Mary, she double majored in Global Studies and Computer Science. She was an impressive student, to say the least, and eventually graduated Summa Cum Laude. Her junior year at William & Mary was when the Central Intelligence Agency first noticed her. By that time she had added Arabic and Dari to her impressive list of languages.

George finally decided it was time to see Nathan Marchek. He was still in his office and probably would be for several more hours. Whenever an officer went missing or had an attempt on his or her life, nobody got any sleep. He was just about to knock softly on his door when he heard voices on the other side. It was the director himself. He was in Nathan's office; that was odd. The boss usually summoned people to his office. It never went the other way around.

He quickly remembered the surveillance cameras in the hallway, so he acted like he had forgotten something. He patted his pockets for effect and then turned around to go back to his office. He retrieved a recording device that would slip neatly into his shirt pocket, and another quick shot of the hot liquid before walking back to the office. He immediately knocked twice.

"Come in," Nathan said.

George pushed the door open and walked into the room.

"Have a seat, George," Nathan said somberly.

"Good evening, Director," George said as he took his seat.

Maxwell nodded to George and adjusted his position in the seat. He drew in a deep breath and sighed. Maxwell Kaine started to speak and then stopped. He looked at the file in his lap and handed it to George. "Listen, George. I know this will be hard for you, but we need to make some quick decisions. We need to act immediately to keep this from blowing up in our faces."

George started to look at the file, but he stopped. "Blow up? How, sir?"

Maxwell nodded to the file and sat patiently while George read it.

Moments later, he held up his hand as he saw George getting upset. "I know this is hard for you to read, but we just learned this information a few hours ago."

"This is ridiculous," George said, sitting forward in his seat. He looked at Nathan Marchek sitting behind his desk with a strained look on his face. "Nobody believes this, do they?"

"I'm sorry, George, but we have every reason to believe that Renée Murphy was compromised. We know that she authored this briefing, and we just learned that it turned up in the hands of one of our agents in Moscow. Renée Murphy holds one of the CIA's greatest secrets, and we cannot afford to have somebody out there who does not have the discipline to know when to keep quiet," Marchek said somberly.

Maxwell shot a glance across the desk at Marchek. He had decided it would be better to confront Marchek in his own office to make him more comfortable. He had just shown him the memo about the briefing being found in Moscow twenty minutes earlier, and they had renewed their previous conversation about the ramifications. Maxwell was just about to ask Marchek if he had leaked the file, but the small voice in the back of his head told him it was a bad idea. Marchek had been trying to convince him that Renée Murphy had just become a liability, but Maxwell wasn't sure.

George had seen the briefing a few weeks ago, just after Renée had emailed it to him and copied Marchek. They had both quietly urged her to let it go, and for all George knew, she had done just that. To hear that she had quietly leaked the report was preposterous. The thought that she had sold it to Russian agents was impossible.

All three men sat staring at one another for a long moment. Nobody moved, nobody spoke. It was a stand-off until Marchek breathed out a sigh and said how sorry he was. Maxwell continued the staring contest, and he let his eyes land on Seifert. He could read George's body language and saw that he was getting ready to explode. He quietly urged him to calm down.

George felt his blood pressure going up, and he took a deep breath trying to remain calm. He didn't feel calm; he felt anything but calm. *Nobody ever calmed down when somebody told them to calm down,* George thought. He was a seasoned CIA agent, so he quickly started compartmentalizing. Standard operating procedure required that he deal with the here and now; put the emotional issues in a box, and open them up later. The rest of the discussion didn't go very well, and George was dismissed with Nathan and Maxwell's most profound sympathy.

Maxwell Kaine quietly excused himself after George had left and walked briskly back to his office. Sitting down behind his desk, he reached into his top drawer, pulled out the encrypted cell phone, and punched in the numbers. When the phone picked up, he simply said, "Are we still hiring?"

"Da," came the reply in a heavily accented Russian voice.

"I will send you the resume," Maxwell said and hung up the phone without saying another word.

Maxwell stowed the phone back in the top drawer and sat back in his chair. He needed to strategize, and he needed to do it quickly. He made a few more phone calls and then headed to his couch to try and catch a few hours of sleep before his long plane ride in the morning. He lay there quietly when the answer to his problems presented itself. He had seen the frustration on George's face and knew that he was a man of profound integrity and honor.

A new burst of energy filled him with excitement as he climbed off the couch and walked back to his desk. He sat there in the dark for several more minutes, forcing his brain to think of every angle before he dialed the phone number. As the phone rang, he felt at peace with his decision, even though it would end the career of a promising young CIA officer.

Back in his office, George began making mental lists in his head. Phone calls he needed to make, people he needed to see, and the most important one, a Moscow report he needed to verify. It just didn't make sense. Renée Murphy was, for lack of a better word, perfect. He knew she would not sell out her country. Hell, she had the presence of mind to destroy her phone ten seconds after rolling her car down an embankment. That proved that Renée Murphy had more courage than either of the men he had just been speaking with.

What was the endgame with this one? he wondered. He had never liked Maxwell Kaine, much less Nathan Marchek, but he had never known either of them to have anything against Renée. This whole thing stunk, and George was going to get to the bottom of it. He logged onto his computer, booked a flight to Cleveland at 8:00 a.m., and then shut his computer down. He went through all the same checkpoints on the way back to his car, but just as he was about to put the key into the ignition, his cell phone rang.

"George, are you still here in the building?" It was Maxwell Kaine.

"I was just about to pull away. Is there something I can do for you, sir?"

"Yes, I was wondering if I could speak to you for a second in my office."

"I'll be right up," George said and then disconnected the phone.

Going back through all the checkpoints for the third time that night, made George's mind race. Maxwell Kaine was not the type of man who forgot to tell you something. Making him come back was intentional. George had played this game long enough to know when he was being played. Just before knocking on the director's door, he steeled himself for another round of inter-agency chess. Kaine had made the first move by making him come back to his office. Now it was George's turn. He knocked softly on the door and waited for Kaine to call him in.

"Come on in and close the door," Kaine said.

George pushed the door open and then closed it quietly behind him. He sat on the sofa Kaine had offered him and turned down the brandy.

"George, how long have we known each other?"

"I haven't been keeping track, sir. I guess since Iran, back in eighty-one."

"Ah, yes. Those were different times for sure. If we had just listened to our men on the ground then ..." Kaine trailed off as if he had just remembered that Seifert was the man on the ground. The patronization was obvious, and Maxwell knew it didn't have the desired impact as he took a long pull on his brandy snifter.

"I suppose you are right, sir, but I was just a rookie and nobody seemed to care what I thought," George said, giving Maxwell his best fake smile.

"George, I'm going to read you in on something that will never leave the four walls of this office. Is that understood?" Kaine said as he leaned backward into his seat.

George had been down this road before. This was patronization 101. Make somebody feel important and special, and then tell them something they don't want to hear. Do it right, and you will have them eating out of your hand. Do it wrong, and a thirty-five-year veteran of the CIA will call you out for the obvious crap that it was.

"I'm not sure I want to be read in on this if it concerns that report you handed me an hour ago."

"Well, it does, and I am sorry to be the one to give you that news."

"Permission to speak freely, Director?" George said.

"Of course."

"That report was ridiculous, and you know it. Marchek knows it, and I know it. So, whatever you are about to read me in on had better have something to do with you telling me that Renée Murphy is not on trial here, or I am going to have to respectfully decline."

Maxwell Kaine sat back in his seat, analyzing George's candor. He stared at George for an uncomfortably long time before speaking again. "George, I have always admired you. You may think I am just patronizing you again, but I can assure you I am not."

George shifted in his seat a little, indicating to Maxwell that he had indeed felt patronized earlier. George felt a trap coming, but he didn't know how to avoid it, so he decided to spring it instead. "OK, I'll bite.

Why have you admired me?"

"Because you are so damn noble all the time. I wish I had your unswerving devotion to my people like you do for yours." Maxwell placed his hands down on the desk and took a deep breath. "OK, all the cards are on the table now. Yes, the report was leaked. Yes, it is completely ridiculous that Renée Murphy was the one who leaked it. But, I need Marchek to think it isn't."

"Why?" George blurted out with more sarcasm than he had intended.

Maxwell Kaine leaned back in his seat again and slowly drained his brandy snifter. He took a deep breath in and let it out slowly. He began from the beginning and told George everything he could. Two hours later, he finished reading George in.

It took George several minutes to digest what he had just been told. It was so crazy that he kept waiting for Maxwell to break into laughter as though it were all some big joke. The ramifications of what he had just been told were catastrophic. There was no way that it could be true. If it were true, nothing could be done about it. If there were no way to do anything about it, then why tell it? None of it made sense, but when Maxwell finished speaking, George had made up his mind. "Count me in."

Maxwell sighed and nodded to let George know that he had understood him. "I know it is a lot to take in, but I need your help if we are going to fight this battle together. Everything I just told you is known to only two other people in the entire agency. You, Renée Murphy, and myself."

"And Marchek," George corrected.

"He knows a completely different version of the story, but *yes*," Kaine said.

George thought the world of Renée, but he agreed with Maxwell Kaine about all of it, and he couldn't possibly see how to win the fight without sacrificing her. It was all so hard to believe. The one thing

George did know was this: If it were true, then Renée would willingly sacrifice herself. If it weren't true, then he would kill Maxwell Kaine himself.

CHAPTER 10

The Life Flight helicopter touched down at the University Children's Hospital just after 8:00 p.m. The two small car seats were unloaded and brought into individual trauma bays right next to each other. The flight team worked efficiently as they transferred the tubes and IV lines from their transport machines to the room's equipment. There was a flurry of activity in the trauma bays, and the Emergency Department doctor taking care of Brianna declared that she was stable enough to be transported to the CAT scanner. Brianna was gently removed from the car seat and placed into a vacuum-sealed mattress that would hold her little head and body in perfect alignment. The purple blanket with little teddy bears embroidered on one side went with her into the vacuum mattress. The endotracheal tube was sticking out of her little mouth, and the tape used to secure it all but covered the little girl's face. Her small arms were covered with blood and hung limply at her sides with two IV lines protruding from them.

In the next room over, Aubrey was receiving the exact same care from a completely different team of doctors and nurses. The other ER doctor worked furiously assessing Aubrey. She ordered a blood transfusion and barked out several other orders for medications and blood tests as well. When she was satisfied that Aubrey was stable, she indicated that she should also go to the scanner. The same process unfolded with Aubrey with the vacuum mattress. Her little blanket had not reached the hospital and was undoubtedly still inside the Excursion. There was, however, a tiny, pink teething rattle wedged between her and the car seat. The charge nurse took it and slipped it into her pocket. She knew little things like that were priceless and would mean the world to somebody. Two nurses wheeled Aubrey off to the CAT scanner, and the rest of the medical personnel all filed out to continue the work that never seemed to end.

Brianna's tiny stretcher was rolled out of the radiology department to the Pediatric Intensive Care Unit twenty minutes later. Dr. Howard, the radiologist, muttered a curse under her breath as the reformatted images began appearing on the screen. She was not a neurosurgeon, but she knew in her heart that this precious little girl would not make it. Brianna's little head was filled with blood, and the small bones of her cervical spine were contorted in a way that even an eighth-grader could tell was unnatural. The cervical bones of a three-month-old hadn't calcified yet and were still just little pieces of cartilage. They were specifically designed to withstand the stress of a vaginal delivery, but what Brianna had just been through was more than the little pieces of cartilage could take. Dr. Howard knew the little girl's twin sister would be next, so she silently prayed that the sister would have drastically better results.

As Aubrey came out of the CAT scanner and the images started appearing on the screen, Dr. Howard's heart sank even further. Although the head seemed to be undamaged, Aubrey had a much worse injury. Brianna was almost certainly brain-dead and would be spared any further trauma. Aubrey had a severed spinal cord and would be paralyzed for the rest of her life, however long that may be. More problematic, though, was the internal damage to her little organs. Aubrey was on her way to the operating room to have her small spleen removed and to repair the laceration to her liver, while Brianna was awaiting the decision to remove life support. Dr. Howard picked up her phone and called the surgeon. After the discussion with the Pediatric Neurosurgeon was complete, Dr. Howard hung her head a little at her desk and whispered a silent thank you that it had not been her own little girl. She finished scrolling through the images to write her official report. Aubrey's journey was just beginning, whereas Brianna's was already over, she thought as she began speaking into the dictaphone.

*****

"How are my babies?" Renée wanted to scream, but the tube in her throat made it impossible to speak. She was at a community hospital in the Emergency Department, only a few minutes away from the crash. The babies had been life-flighted to the Children's Hospital on the East side of town, but nobody had told Renée. The nurse hadn't even noticed that she was awake until Renée began trying to pull the tube out of her throat, setting off a host of alarms. She pleaded with her eyes as the young nurse was speaking to her. She was becoming frantic with pain and uncertainty. She desperately wanted the answer to a question she couldn't even ask. It was an answer that would either make her pain bearable and give her a reason to fight or succumb to the pain and be swept away with it forever.

As she begged with her eyes for the nurse to tell her about Brianna and Aubrey, a young man in a white coat entered the room. *He must be the doctor*, Renée thought. The man in the white coat was speaking to the nurse and giving orders for medicines. Renée heard the word fentanyl for sure and another word that sounded like Versed, but she couldn't be sure. Renée knew what the drugs were for, but she shook her head as if to tell the doctor *no*. She wouldn't go back to sleep without finding out how her babies were.

Renée mustered all the strength she could summon and yanked her hand toward her mouth to pull out the tube again, but she was not strong enough. The doctor grabbed her arm and said something soothing as the nurse began fidgeting with her I.V.

"Brianna, Aubrey, I love you," she wanted to scream in case the babies were close by, but the medicine robbed her of a clear mind. She tried to fight the drug's effects, but she was losing. The pain slowly faded away, and Renée felt light. She was thankful she couldn't feel the tubes or the pain. She tried to focus on the ceiling to keep herself from drifting away. She started counting the tiles on the ceiling. She was taken back to her interrogation training at the farm. "Pick something and focus on it so intently that nothing can intercede," she heard her instructors saying. "Pain can be mastered just like anything else with the right motivation," they told her. She felt like she was losing as the pain faded and the ceiling tiles seemed to be getting farther away. She forced her brain to concentrate, but it was no use. The medications made her eyelids feel like they were made of iron. She didn't have the strength to keep them open any longer, and she let them close. Her last thought was of Mack, Brianna, and Aubrey.

*****

"Staff Sergeant Murphy," a voice called from the doorway of Charlie Team's barracks.

Mack opened one eye and saw Lance Corporal Witter standing in the doorway. He worked in the company office, but that was all Mack knew about him. "Yeah," Mack finally blurted out as he rubbed his eyes.

"You have a phone call at the CQ," Lance Corporal Witter said hesitantly.

"Be right there," Mack said, feeling a knot forming in his gut. He hadn't been able to reach Renée a few hours earlier, and he knew that was unlike her. She never let her phone ring more than two times before picking up. He had only been asleep for two hours, and his body was still exhausted from the night before.

Thirty seconds later, Mack pushed through the command quarter's door.

"She said she was from the Red Cross," Lance Corporal Witter said as he handed the phone to Mack.

"This is Staff Sergeant Murphy, and this is an unsecured line; how can I help you?"

It was a Red Cross call from the States, which usually meant that somebody's loved one had passed away. His first thought was that Sass's parents had heard the news and were calling to talk to him. He had met them several times before they had deployed, and he considered them friends. Millions of thoughts simultaneously went through Mack's mind, but the one that overwhelmed them all belonged to Renée. Mack noticed Major Hanlon sitting quietly at his desk, looking at Mack as he entered the building. He saw Apollo, who had locked eyes on him as well.

"Sir, I'm Rebecca Haines with the American Red Cross in Washington, DC, and I am calling to let you know that your wife and children were involved in a terrible car accident. We are currently arranging transportation to have you return to the US as soon as possible."

"I'm sorry, ma'am, but who is this message for exactly?" Mack said, but his mind had already clicked all the tumblers into place. *Your wife and children,* he had heard the woman say. Mack held his breath as he waited for the reply. A three-second delay could seem like an hour when you are getting shot at, but it could seem like a lifetime when you are waiting to be told the ones you love are dead.

"It is for you, sir," she said hesitantly.

Mack's knees went limp, and he almost crashed to the ground, but was able to catch himself on the desk. The blood drained from his head as Lance Corporal Witter tried to break his fall. Mack managed to hold onto the phone and keep himself vertical long enough to recover slightly. All those millions of thoughts that had just run through his head were gone; the only thing left was emptiness.

The line was silent for several moments, and she quietly said, "Sir, are you still there?"

"I'm here," Mack said, wishing it were all a dream.

"Sir, I'm so sorry to inform you that your daughter Brianna is brain-dead. The doctors said there was nothing to be done. She is on life support, and the team there said they would keep her alive as long as possible. Your wife is in the ICU and is in a coma, and your daughter Aubrey is in critical condition as well."

All Mack heard was that Brianna was brain-dead. That was his baby girl. She looked just like Renee with piercing green eyes and caramel colored skin. There was no doubt it was Renee's daughter. The tears couldn't stay locked up any longer, and Mack walked out of the CQ as they slowly started dripping off his chin and making tiny splashes on the collar of his battle dress uniform. One drop landed on his left breast pocket, so he instinctively pulled out the clear plastic envelope and reread the poem for the thousandth time. He returned to Hotel Charlie, as his team referred to their barracks, and was relieved to find that everyone was still asleep. Mack sat down on his bunk and tried to keep his hands from shaking. He looked around the room for something to punch and finally settled on the plywood wall next to his bunk. He punched it several times before Corporal O'Malley woke up and grabbed him from behind to keep him from hurting himself.

"What's wrong, Mack?" O'Malley shouted, more to let the others know he needed help than for Mack's sake.

Williams and Echols were awake now and jumped out of bed to help subdue Mack. They piled onto him and grabbed at his arms and legs to keep him from thrashing any further.

Mack calmed down a little, and his friends let him go slowly in case it was a ruse. He stood to his feet and then pushed his way past the three men with confused looks on their faces. He knew they assumed he had snapped because of Sass, but he didn't feel like sharing the latest tragedy with them. Somehow, he reasoned within himself that if he said the words out loud, it would give them legitimacy. His head swirled with the news, and his hands were shaking again. He collapsed back into his bunk and buried his face in his hands. He was aware of the men asking questions, but he couldn't form the words to answer them.

"I just need to be alone for a while," he finally said. He apologized to O'Malley when he saw him rubbing his shoulder and then did the same for Echols.

They all went back to their bunks, and Mack was alone again. He didn't feel like punching anything anymore, but he didn't know what to do. He finally pulled out Renée's picture again and stared at it. Two minutes later, Apollo walked through the door. Mack was still sitting on the edge of his bunk, staring at the picture of Renée. Her hair was wet, and water dripped down the corner of her mouth. Her perfect set of white teeth contrasted with her dark skin.

"I got you on a bird out in thirty mikes, Mack. Get out of here. Go be with your family," he said and started to leave, but he stopped. He began to speak, but was surprised by his own emotions. He tried again, but all he could manage to say was, "I'm sorry."

All the guys were wide awake and pressing Apollo for answers, but all he said was, "You'll have to ask Mack," before pushing the door open and stepping out into the sun.

*****

Special Agent Mulloy pulled the phone from his jacket pocket and flipped it open. "Mulloy," he said as he set his soft drink on the restaurant table.

"Hey, it's Aguayo. I have a favor to ask you."

"Aguayo, how are you doing, my friend?"

"I'm good, amigo. Are you still in Cleveland?" Aguayo said sympathetically.

"I like it here; the Browns are going all the way this year. Just wait and see," Mulloy said.

"Yeah, OK." Aguayo laughed. "Let's get back to reality my friend. I need a favor from you."

"Can it wait twenty minutes? I am having dinner with my wife."

Claire looked at Mulloy and was about to give him an irritated look when she remembered his comment earlier.

"Cold pizza in your office again?" Aguayo laughed. He knew who Mulloy was married to. "Married and stuck in Cleveland. It doesn't get much worse, my friend. Come on down to the Lone Star state. We need people with your talents down here."

"Exactly what talents are you referring to?"

"Your talent for working overtime, which allows people like me to have a life."

Mulloy just laughed and said, "What can I help you with?"

Aguayo filled him in on the hit and run and the double homicide at the Foxxy. Aguayo had spoken with the detective in charge of the double murder at the strip club a few moments before he had called Mulloy. He left out the part about the CIA wanting to know; he knew that Mulloy was no friend of the agency.

"How did you hear about this all the way down in Texas? Seems like I should have found out about this first," Mulloy said, raising his eyebrows.

"I have always been a few steps ahead of you, my friend. Can you dig around and tell me what you come up with? It might pertain to an ongoing operation I have down here in El Paso."

"I'll look into it and get back to you." He flipped his phone shut and went back to the soft drink as he looked at Claire and smiled.

"Are you just gonna sit there and eat or tell me what that was all about?" Claire said, clearly irritated Mulloy wasn't saying anything.

"If I tell you now, you will be like every other cop I have ever met. You'll stop eating and insist we leave right now. I hate that. I love these gyros, and I'm not gonna leave it here half-finished," Mulloy said, taking another bite.

"OK, I promise I will let you finish eating," Claire said, like she was talking to a teenager.

"Turns out we have had quite a crime spree today in our quiet little hamlet. A few hours ago, there was a hit-and-run accident in the Cleveland Metroparks; an SUV with two babies in the back collided with a Porsche 911. The SUV and the Porsche were both totaled, but whoever was driving the Porsche is in the wind." Mulloy took another bite of his gyro and looked at Claire again.

"I'm confused; what does this have to do with my case?"

"Well, it just so happens that the Porsche belongs to one Vincenzo Bertoli," Mulloy said and waited for Claire to put the pieces together.

"Is that supposed to mean something to me?" Claire replied, growing angry.

"No, but he is our friendly neighborhood Mob boss, and one of the strip joints he owns up on Brookpark Road has two dead bodies in it right now, yet to be identified. So, it looks like we are going to the Foxxy tonight. It may be completely unrelated to your case, but if we had to randomly pick a strip club, it might make sense to start where the dead bodies are," Mulloy said as he pushed the last piece of his gyro into his mouth.

A minute later, Mulloy finished chewing his last bite and flipped open his phone. He made a few quick calls and mostly listened. He grunted uh-huhs several times and a few OKs and then flipped it shut.

"I hope you weren't looking forward to the entertainment. My contact at the PD assures me that everyone in the Foxxy is fully clothed tonight," Mulloy said.

"I will try not to be disappointed," Claire said and motioned for the waitress to bring the tab. "This meal is on the Detroit Bureau."

"I guess it doesn't matter who pays; Uncle Sam will eventually get the bill," Mulloy said, tossing his napkin onto the table. "Let's go clubbing."

Twenty minutes later, Larkin and Mulloy walked into the Foxxy nightclub and saw the coroners and forensic agents snapping pictures and dusting the entire place for fingerprints. *Good luck sorting out all the DNA samples in this joint*, Mulloy thought.

"Claire, over here," Mulloy said, introducing her to Lieutenant David Daniels of the Cleveland Police Department.

"Nice to meet you; what do you have so far?" she said.

"Well, it looks like a small caliber to the side of the face on this poor guy. This pretty woman here definitely had it a little better with a shot straight through the left eye. She probably felt a little pain on the way down, but it was over pretty quick, for her anyway. The other guy likely had a few seconds to contemplate his poor career choices before he checked out. He has a separate wound to the back of the head, so he was probably knocked to the ground before he was shot. It was basically an execution from what I can tell."

"You said small caliber, but from the looks of the blood spatter, it doesn't exactly look like a small caliber did this," Claire said.

"Small caliber doesn't necessarily imply poor ballistics. If you look closely, the entrance wounds are pretty small, but the damage is significant."

"What type of small caliber bullet leaves a small hole but a lot of damage," Claire asked, but she already knew the answer. She wanted to see if Detective Daniels knew his stuff, or if he was just blowing hot air.

Daniels shot Claire an irritated look. "Well, Special Agent," he said with sarcastic emphasis on the word *special*, "why don't you just get to the point and spare me the drama?"

"OK, fair enough," she said. "What caliber would you say if you had to guess?"

"Now, that wasn't so hard, was it?" Daniels looked back at the bodies for a long moment before finishing his thought. "I would say it was a rifle round, based on the damage, but we are inside. Nobody uses a rifle to kill somebody at point-blank range. So, either this was all done by a handgun that is chambered with a small, highly powerful bullet, or the perp used a shortened rifle like an AR pistol. My best guess is it was something along the lines of a .223 based on the small entrance wounds." Daniels knelt next to the woman and looked closely at her face before speaking again. "She's no more than twenty-five. What a shame."

"Do we know who they are?" Claire said, staring at the hole in the young woman's face.

"Neither one of them had an ID on them," Daniels said sarcastically, looking at Claire to see her reaction.

"Most criminals in Detroit don't carry ID either. Are you saying Cleveland criminals are more or less intelligent?"

"Are you implying that they are both criminals because they work at a strip club?" Daniels replied.

"I'm saying shady places are where you find shady people," she shot back.

Detective Daniels decided to let the last comment go. "It's Friday night, and when my guys showed up, there was a closed sign on the door, and the building was locked. A customer apparently saw the young woman's legs from the window and called 9-1-1. I listened to the tape, and it is pretty interesting."

"Pretty interesting how?" Claire said.

"Well, the call came from the pay phone across the street at the gas station. The guy said he wasn't going to testify; he said he knew his rights and didn't have to make a statement. He was just passing on an anonymous tip. He didn't stick around to speak to anybody."

"Why is that interesting? He probably didn't want anybody to know he was at a strip club," Mulloy said, shrugging his shoulders.

"Probably," Daniels said and left it at that.

Claire made a mental note to listen to the 9-1-1 call anyway. She wondered what Detective Daniels was thinking. She thought that old salty detectives knew more than they ever let on.

"Whoever did this obviously had the key to the building because it is a keyed lock inside and out," Claire said as she pointed to the locks. Before anybody could respond, she pressed on. "It looks like this guy was trying to confront whoever came in through the back door before he got knocked to the floor. The young lady had obviously just come in the front door since she still had her coat on. The guy wasn't wearing a coat, so he was obviously already in the building when the perps made their way through the back door."

"That doesn't explain the blow to the back of the head," Mulloy said pointing at the man lying supine on the ground.

"No, it doesn't. It would imply that the victim knew the assailant. You wouldn't turn your back on somebody you didn't know, would you?" she replied.

Mulloy looked back at the bodies lying on the floor before nodding his head in agreement. "Good observation."

"No employees showed up for work tonight, so either they all got sick, or they were instructed to take the night off. The club belongs to a Vincenzo Bertoli, one of Cleveland's finest citizens, to be sure." Daniels said. "Two of my guys are trying to track him down now, but the accident in the Metroparks fits the timeframe. The car from the Metroparks was registered to Vincenzo, but everyone seemed to think it was Marco's car. We pulled the surveillance cameras, but it's a dead end. It's like they knew we were coming. It's just a twenty-second Keystone Cop clip over and over again for six hours."

"Any ideas on where Marco is right now?" Claire said, staring at Daniels, who was obviously no stranger to the sight of dead bodies.

"He isn't in any hospital for a 200-mile radius, but that doesn't mean he isn't farther than that. Forensics estimate it went down around 4 p.m., so he could be halfway to North Carolina by now. Too big of a range to throw a net on the Emergency Departments. We will have to wait and see if anything gets called in. His apartment down on the lake is empty, just a bunch of empty Vodka bottles. The surveillance camera there hasn't had him in the place for two days. He does have a brother, but his wife says he's in Detroit on business."

Claire perked up when he said *Detroit*. "What does he do in Detroit?"

"Probably the same thing he does here. Sells drugs, runs rackets, and whatever else the old man tells him to do," Daniels snorted.

Claire shook her head and started walking around the place to see if anything jumped out at her. She looked at the sign on the door stating the club's hours of 5:00 p.m. to 4:00 a.m., and she did some fast calculations. She walked behind the bar and saw the register was open, and the only thing in it was coins. *That's odd*, she thought. Who pays with coins at a strip club? There were two empty vodka bottles on the bar, and she made another mental note. She had never worked in a bar, but she thought empty bottles in a club were a lousy idea as tempers regularly flared in places like this. She knew that any good bartender wouldn't leave an empty bottle lying on the bar at closing time.

She pulled out her cell phone and dialed the Detroit office. After a few moments, she asked one of her colleagues if he had ever heard Bertoli's name, and he assured her he hadn't. He clicked a few keys on the computer and reported that Marco Bertoli had a few traffic citations that were all settled out of court with all charges dropped. No other charges or investigations. Pretty clean for the most part.

"I've got a Vincenzo Bertoli here. He seems to be more of the type of guy you are looking for. Well-known Mafia guy out of Cleveland, not sure if it's a relative or not?"

"It's his father. Keep digging and let me know if you get anything on him," she said, clapping her phone closed and sliding it into her jacket pocket. She wandered around the club before entering the back parking lot and found a bunch of cigarette butts lying on the ground. She told Mulloy, and he had a cop pick them up as evidence.

The two were just about to leave when one of the police officers yelled for Detective Daniels. "I've got a shell casing here."

Claire and Mulloy spun on their heels, and headed toward the officer who was crouching behind the leg of a table by the rear door. A few seconds later, the officer brought the shell casing out, hanging on the tip of his pen so as not to contaminate the fingerprints.

"I can't say I have ever seen a shell casing like this one before," the police officer mumbled to Detective Daniels.

"It's a 7.62 x 25 mm," Claire said.

"That's not a 7.62 round. A 7.62 is a rifle cartridge like the .308, and this is not a rifle cartridge," the officer said.

"She's right. I saw those rounds a lot in Atlanta," Mulloy interjected. The market got flooded with them after the Iron Curtain fell. They were made in Russia and other block countries. They're the caliber of choice for most special forces, Spetznaz in particular."

"Spetz what?" the police officer said.

"Spetznaz, they are the Russian equivalent of our Delta Force. These bullets are illegal here in the States because they are considered armor piercing," Mulloy said, grinning at Claire. *The girl knew her stuff,* he thought.

Twenty minutes later, they were back in Mulloy's car heading back to the Cleveland Field Office.

"So, how do we find Marco Bertoli?" she said as she pulled on her seatbelt.

"I'm gonna go down to the office and make some phone calls. I'll see what I can turn up. Have you got a place to stay tonight?"

"Yeah, I booked a room at the Hilton downtown."

"Hilton, the Detroit office budget must be a little bit bigger than Cleveland's. We usually have to stay at motels in the low-rent district."

"Well, then you're clearly doing something wrong in Cleveland," she said.

"Yeah, to be honest with you, though, I'm more of a cheap motel kind of a guy anyway."

"Do you need a vehicle? I can get you one out of the motor pool, or I can drop you off. It's up to you."

"A car would be nice, but it can wait until tomorrow. Thank you."

"I'll have one of my guys pick you up in the morning, and you can keep the car. I have an 8:00 a.m. appointment. Otherwise, I'd pick you up myself. Get some sleep, Special Agent Larkin. It's late," Mulloy said.

"Thanks, Special Agent Mulloy," Claire said, mimicking Mulloy's use of their official title.

"I'll call you if I hear anything," he replied and then offered to help with her bags.

"I can get the bag. I'm a big girl," she said with a smile creeping over her face.

"I wouldn't exactly call you big, but you do appear more than capable of handling a carry-on with wheels. My father beat a lot of things into me growing up. Some are easier to forget than others."

Claire just smiled and got out of the car. She pulled her suitcase out of the back seat and closed the door. "See you tomorrow, Mulloy."

"Yes, ma'am," he replied.

CHAPTER 11

The neurosurgeon was exhausted after the six-hour surgery, but that was just the first surgery scheduled for Renée. Orthopedics still had several fractures to deal with once she was stable enough. She went through four units of blood before the neurosurgeon could clamp the three bleeding vessels in her brain. The surgical tech changed the bandages on her head and chest as the doctor looked for a family member to update. The burns on the chest and face were minor, but the bleeding into her head was another story. The surgeon left her with an intracranial pressure monitor in place, or a 'bolt' as it was commonly referred to. It monitored the pressure inside the head and kept Renée's brain from herniating into the foramen magnum at the base of her skull. It made her look like Frankenstein, but it was keeping her alive.

Renée's eyes fluttered open, and the light was overpowering. To her half-conscious mind, it looked like a spaceship was flying directly toward her. She tried to move her head away from the light but couldn't, so she closed her eyes again and hoped the spaceship didn't land on her face. She heard several people talking, but they seemed so far away. Somebody was adjusting something on her right wrist while another was adjusting something between her legs.

She tried to speak, but nothing came out. "Where am I?" Renée's brain ordered her mouth to speak, but the tube in her throat made it impossible. She remembered the car crash; she remembered the gangster driving the sports car; she remembered the red car driving backward. She remembered a black sedan that she thought had been following her. Despite everything, she could not recall how she had gotten to this bright room where everything felt strange.

The heaviness on Renée's chest wasn't painful, but it was uncomfortable. She couldn't think what could cause the pressure, but she felt hands pushing on her chest as though they were trying to keep something from moving. It felt like somebody was applying a bandage to her breasts and the bottom of her neck. Her breasts felt like they were swollen, and she ached to hold her babies to them. Renée began experimenting with various body parts. She could move her feet but couldn't bend her knees. Her left leg seemed to be higher off the bed than her right leg, and it was sticking off the bed at a funny angle. She realized it was sticking up into the air. Her left arm was freely mobile, so she lifted it off the bed, but the strength it took to do that left her drained again and with a newfound pressure in her chest. She tried to move her right arm, but it felt like it had been strapped to the bed. She felt something heavy against her face but couldn't tell what that was either. She risked another glance, and as she opened her eyes, she saw a gloved hand fidgeting with the tube that was sticking out of her throat.

Renée's brain finally cleared enough for her to remember where she was. The realization came to her slowly at first, but when she finally figured it out, she wanted to scream. She desperately needed to know how her babies were doing.

The drugs were wearing off as slow, steady waves of pain began rolling over her entire body. She fought the urge to vomit when the pain reached its peak, but she was losing the fight. The wrenching started low in her stomach, and in seconds, her mouth was full of bile. She tried to bring her left arm to her face to remove the tube, but it was being held by a very strong arm. Panic filled her mind as she continued to struggle for air. *Just let me go so I can save myself,* she wanted to scream.

The alarm bells went off on the monitors as her mouth and nose filled with the acidic fluid. Now she was choking on it. A second later, a man wearing a surgical mask appeared, hovering over her, pushing a tube into her mouth and plunging it deep into her throat. It must have been a suction tube she realized as the bile and what little air was left in her lungs was sucked out. Finally, the tube came out, and the air began pouring back into her lungs. She heard more muffled voices and saw faces hovering over her chest.

"She's coding," she heard a female voice yell.

"Get the surgeon back. She's still bleeding," another voice yelled. It sounded like it was coming from just behind her head. The anesthesiologist, *I never could pronounce that word correctly,* Renée thought. Faces hovered around her as she heard a small buzzer going off from a short distance away. They were all wearing surgical masks, and then she felt a burning sensation in her arm just below the bicep. She recalled the burning sensation in her arm that led to her sedation earlier, and she was determined not to lose the fight again. *You gotta fight like you're the third monkey outside the ark, and it's starting to rain,* she heard her father's voice telling her.

Strange, she thought to herself, remembering her father's voice amid all this chaos. Before the crash, she could go years without giving the man so much as a thought. Now, she could see her father standing on the front yard of their home in Newport News attempting to teach her how to box. She was wearing boxing gloves that seemed ridiculously large on her five-year-old hands. Her father held a big foam pad that he waved around as a target for Renée to punch. The obnoxiously bright light in the room faded slowly as the voices began sounding more and more distant. She tried to keep her eyes on the foam pad as she fought for every second of consciousness. Suddenly, the foam pad was gone;

all she could see was her father's face. He had tears running down his cheeks as he put his hands on her face. She was a little girl again, and her father was big and strong. Renée felt the darkness creeping in again, and she knew that she was losing the fight.

"I was a horrible father, NeeNee, and I'm sorry."

Renée looked at his face for a long moment as she played the words over in her head. NeeNee. That was the name her father had called her when she was just a little girl. It had been so long since she heard that name that she had forgotten it. Hearing it again didn't bring back painful memories like it used to when she was growing up. She had gotten over her father leaving her many years ago, but she was surprised when she felt sorry for the man crying in front of her. She tried to reach up to his face and wipe away the tears, but her arms wouldn't move. She spent the next few moments slipping in and out of her dreams. One second, she could hear the machines buzzing and strong voices yelling words like, 'epinephrine,' and 'all clear,' and 'continue chest compressions,' and the next, she could see her father's face with the tears streaming down.

"I was a horrible father, NeeNee, and I'm sorry."

Renée tried to tell him it was OK, but he put his hands on her mouth. She opened her eyes and saw the gloved hand pushing the tubing in and out of her mouth again, and she was confused. She closed her eyes again and saw her father holding a small child in his arms, and his tears were gone. Renée assumed that one of her earliest memories had surfaced from deep within the part of the brain that stored those images. Maybe the neurosurgeon had rattled old memories loose when he was poking all the sharp instruments into her brain. Curiously, Renée looked closer at the tiny baby wrapped in a hospital blanket. She wanted her father to hand the baby to her, but he said he couldn't.

"I was a horrible father, NeeNee, but I'm going to take real good care of Brianna until you get here. I promise." Just as he finished speaking, he began moving further away from her. The realization that her father was holding her little Brianna didn't fully dawn on Renée. She felt warm and peaceful watching her father hold her child the way any parent would. Her past resentment toward her father dissipated as she watched him placing gentle kisses on Brianna's forehead. When the two began getting further and further away, the gravity of the moment hit Renée. She tried to scream, but the world around her had gone silent. She willed her father to come back and let her see her baby one more time, but a tiny voice in the back of her head registered defeat again. She was certain that one of her questions had been answered, and it tore a hole into her soul, but she was at peace with it. The burning in her arm grew more intense, and it finally gave way to a warm feeling throughout her entire body. Then, mercifully, she went back to sleep.

A few blocks away, Aubrey was being wheeled out of surgery as well. Hers had been every bit as complicated as her mother's, and the surgeon was not very hopeful that she would live through the night. Her spleen had been removed, and her liver had been deeply lacerated. Her poor little body had lost so much blood that it was doubtful she had any of her own blood left. The anesthesiologist had to keep giving her more and more blood to keep her blood pressure stable, and by the time the surgeon had begun closing the incision, little Aubrey had been through five units of blood—an amount equal to three times her original blood volume. She was wheeled back to the Pediatric Intensive Care Unit, where Renée's mother, Mina, awaited her.

*****

Mina was short for Basmina, and she was exhausted. Her night had started at the community hospital when she heard about the accident from the police department. When she was told that Renée was being transferred to the University Trauma Center for a surgery that would probably last five to six hours, she drove across town to check on her precious grand-babies. She had wept for hours sitting at Brianna's bed.

Seeing the three-month-old baby hooked up to monitors and IVs was more than she could bear. She knew that Mack was on his way, and she couldn't imagine the pain he must be feeling. She loved Mack. She couldn't have asked for a better son-in-law, and her heart broke for him as much as for her daughter.

When Mina was finally able to see Aubrey, she was unrecognizable. Her little face had been so swollen from the accident that Mina could barely see her eyes. She was hooked up to as many tubes as Brianna, but she seemed worse off. Brianna had already been declared brain dead, so there was no more struggle for her. Aubrey was being watched over by at least three nurses and a host of other people, so Mina didn't even know who to talk to. As the surgeon entered the room, he shook her hand sincerely and introduced himself.

"Mrs. Shaw, I'm Dr. Asher, and I'm a pediatric surgeon. I tried to speak to you or any family member before the surgery, but the nurses told me nobody had arrived yet, and time was critical."

Mina just shook her head, trying to speak, but no words came out. Finally, she managed to say, "I got here as quickly as I could."

"Of course," Dr. Asher said. "I was also told that her mother is in critical condition as well, and I am so sorry."

Mina mouthed the words *thank you,* but no sound came out.

"Aubrey here is a little fighter. I thought we were going to lose her several times during the surgery, but she really hung in there. I had to remove her entire spleen, as it had been lacerated deeply during the accident, and I was not able to save it. Her liver had a bad laceration to it as well, and that is why she lost so much blood. The liver is a very difficult organ to operate on, and it is even more difficult when it is an infant's. She lost a lot of blood, but we were able to replace it with donor blood. The problem is that almost her entire blood supply is foreign to her now, so she will be fighting against her new blood. My biggest fear at the moment is infection. Children are resilient to infections, but her little body does not have much reserve to fight anything right now.

If you don't already know, her spinal cord was severed high up in her neck, so she will never breathe on her own again." Dr. Asher paused as he saw tears filling the woman's eyes and spilling onto her cheeks. "I'm so sorry."

"Thank you, Doctor, and God bless you for everything you have done. I truly mean that, but I don't think I can take any more right now," Mina said, patting the doctor's arm gently.

"I understand," he said, squeezing her hand. "Please don't hesitate to reach out if you have any questions."

Mina turned back to Aubrey and watched her little chest rising and falling much quicker than she would have thought was normal. The ventilator was like a metronome, keeping a steady rhythm for Aubrey's lungs to match.

*****

Mack was on board the C-130 Hercules Air Force plane thirty minutes later, as promised. He had given the guys a quick rundown on the phone call before he packed his things, and they all did their best to help. They didn't know what to say any more than Mack knew what he wanted to hear. He threw his pack onto the floor and then slumped down in the cargo netting that was to be his seat for the duration. They were wheels up a few minutes later and over Turkmenistan an hour later. Fifteen more hours and they would be wheels down in North Carolina. Only one stop at Ramstein Air Force Base for fuel and to pick up some wounded soldiers heading to Walter Reed before arriving stateside. After that, a commercial flight to Hopkins International Airport would have him in Cleveland in less than twenty-two hours from the initial phone call. Sitting in a cargo net seat for twenty minutes was uncomfortable; twenty-two hours was pure torture, but Mack didn't give it a minute's thought. Every second was one second closer to Renée and his baby girls.

Three hours into the flight, he was jolted awake by turbulence. He was surprised by how fast the pain came right back to him. *Why?* he thought to himself. Mack was never one to reflect on the things he had done in his life. He knew he had just killed men the night before, a lot of men, but they were terrorists; they were the ones responsible for killing thousands of Americans. It was a war, and that made it OK. *Didn't it?*

He couldn't step off the path his mind had wandered down. He remembered the night before, seeing the green mist splashing up into the night sky as round after round found their mark, and new souls were hurled out into eternity. Whether or not they found their seventy-seven virgins or a fiery hell, Mack couldn't say for sure. His next thought was for Sass. How could he enthusiastically kill dozens of enemy fighters and have the nerve to weep for one of his own?

What was nagging at him? Something from the night before weighed on him more heavily than usual, and he didn't know what it was. Wrapped up in the emotion of his babies and wife, he couldn't shake the feeling that there was a definite cause and effect. Somewhere over Germany, the disturbing thought began to materialize. *Is this my punishment?* Mack wondered. *Punishment for what, killing?* That wasn't it. He felt his body temperature drop a few degrees when it finally dawned on him. It wasn't the killing he was being punished for; it was for the enjoyment of killing.

He remembered his excitement as he watched the green mist spraying into the moonless sky. He remembered the euphoria when the bodies dropped limply to the ground. *One more bad guy out of the fight,* he had said to himself. He also felt a wave of guilt rise up in his heart when he remembered his body count. He was actually counting the number of men he had killed like he was the main character in a twisted video game. Twenty-seven was his number. He knew that snipers didn't care about their kill count, but he knew his, and for that, he felt ashamed.

One thought seemed to give birth to ten more. Mack remembered feeling relieved when he realized he had only received a laceration to his arm. It made him feel invincible. He was killing people at will, and all they could do was scratch his arm. The feeling of immortality was like a drug to him. He realized that he had spent the last year trying to get another fix of the adrenaline rush he had first experienced in Afghanistan almost three years earlier. He spent eight years learning how to kill people, and he was good at it. No, he was *exceptional* at it. Not until that very moment did Mack realize the same cruel game he had been playing could be played on him. First, Sass dying in combat and then his own family. Now he knew what it was like to lose a battle in the killing game. Overall, it wasn't the killing that hurt him the most. It wasn't the accident that had happened to his family that hurt him the most. What hurt the most is that through all the killing, all he could think about was more killing. He realized he was planning on killing whoever had just played the game against his wife and two babies. He tried to control his rage, but it started to boil over.

The rage inside Mack had settled to a low boil just after wheels up from Ramstein AFB in Germany. During the refueling, a dozen wounded soldiers were loaded onto the C-130. They were casualties from the second battle of Fallujah, which had started just a few weeks before. Mack couldn't help but wonder what life was like in Iraq. Several of Mack's friends were deployed there right now. He didn't see any familiar faces being loaded onto the plane, but he did see several Marines. He nodded to them in silent recognition—one warrior to another.

Eight hours later the C-130 taxied to a stop, and Mack grabbed his backpack. On the tarmac to meet him was Sergeant Major Lenahan. He was the Senior Enlisted man in Force Reconnaissance and Mack's former Company First Sergeant before he was promoted to Sergeant Major. When Lenahan heard the news of Mack's family, he knew he had to extend his condolences personally. Sergeant Major Lenahan yelled over the noise of the propellers that a van was waiting to take him to Jacksonville. He handed him a large backpack and an envelope, then shook his hand.

"I'm sorry Mack, but I want you to know that you have the entire Marine Corps family at your disposal. Call on me or any one of us if you need anything. Is that understood?"

"Yes, Sergeant Major, thank you," Mack said, looking at the backpack.

"It's some fresh civilian clothes and a few things you will probably need," the Sergeant Major said and pointed to the van.

Mack thanked him again, headed toward the van, and climbed in the passenger seat. He stowed the two backpacks on the van floor and opened the envelope. It had $2,000 in it and a note from the Sergeant Major.

Staff Sergeant Murphy,

I can't imagine what you are going through right now, but I want you to know that the Marine Corps is a family. We take care of each other and lean on each other when times get hard. I keep a little money set aside for rainy days. You have some difficult times ahead of you, and I know that you are probably not prepared for the little things that are going to come up. I have arranged for you to have a government vehicle in Cleveland, Ohio, when you get there this morning. Sergeant Rice is the recruiter in that neck of the woods and will pick you up at the curb. Use the vehicle for as long as you need it, and use the money. That's an order!

You are in my prayers. Semper Fi

Sergeant Major Sean Lenahan

Mack put the money back into the envelope with the letter and closed his eyes. The tears were threatening again, but he refused to give into grief just yet. As hard as he tried, a little moisture had accumulated at the corner of his eyes, so he was glad for the cover of darkness to hide his grief. The private first class driving the van didn't say a word and just drove South to get Mack to his plane.

*****

Just after midnight, Marco and Sal pulled a minivan into the Motor City Casino parking lot. Marco went to the casino and asked to see Matteo. Minutes later, one of Matteo's foot soldiers came strolling through the casino wearing a sweatsuit and smoking a cigar. He didn't approach Marco and Sal but motioned for them to follow him off the casino floor. The man took them to a large office in the basement of the hotel. The three sat there in silence for almost twenty minutes before Matteo entered the room. Marco went to hug Matteo, but Matteo stopped him by holding up his hand.

Marco started to speak, but Matteo slapped Marco's face. "What is wrong with you?"

Marco's anger flared at being slapped, but he realized Matteo was the only one who could help him. His father was out of the country and had left strict orders that he was not to be disturbed. Marco and Sal filled Matteo in on all the events from the past twenty-four hours, leaving out the part about the shipment of girls from their Russian contacts. Matteo listened with growing irritation as they recounted the story.

After a long pause, Matteo sat on the edge of the desk and looked hard at Marco. "Are you certain this woman in the SUV cannot identify you?"

"No, not certain, but I am sure she is dead by now," Marco said, grinning.

"Well, she isn't dead," Matteo screamed. He stood back up and wanted to hit Marco again but held off. He paced the room for a few long moments and then looked at the two in disgust. "And there were two babies in the back seat, you morons."

Sal started to speak, but Matteo cut him off.

"The only reason I don't kill you myself and pin this whole thing on you is because your father is a good man. You are as worthless as this one," Matteo said, pointing his finger at Marco.

"Sorry Matteo," Sal said, defeated.

"You have made enough mistakes for one day, Marco, so please try to stay where I put you and stop making this situation worse. Is that understood?"

Marco just nodded, but inside, his blood was boiling. Who did Matteo think he was, talking to him like that? If he hadn't needed Matteo's help, he would have walked out of the room and gone to the casino.

Matteo walked out of the office and made his way to the penthouse suite where he had been living for the past three months. He used the key card to open the door and pushed it open. He had forgotten about the women in his room until he saw them lying on the bed together, and he got irritated. "Come on, out. Not tonight. I have a lot of work to do," he said, tossing clothes at the women and hurrying them out of the room. When the room was quiet, he sat down at the desk and pulled out his cell phone. He took a deep breath, pushed the number five button, and held it down until the phone began dialing the number. The phone rang ten times before it was answered by a very irritated Vincenzo Bertoli. Matteo had been silently hoping that his father wouldn't answer the phone, but he did.

"Hey, Pops, sorry to bother you right now, but I need to update you on the situation. I know you said no interruptions, but things are getting a little out of my control right now." He started filling Vinny in on things, but he cut him off.

"Is this a burner?" Vinny hissed.

"Of course, Pops, I know what I'm doing."

"OK, well, at least I have one son who isn't a total idiot," Vinny said with as much disgust as he could muster. Vinny was always amazed at how stupid his oldest son was. How Marco never figured out that Sal was on his payroll was beyond explanation.

Matteo filled his father in on the fact that Sal was still alive and how Marco had blown it. He told him about everything that he had learned from the Cleveland Police Department as well as from their informants at the FBI. Matteo could tell that his father was getting more upset every second by the sound of his breathing. He could hear his father lighting one cigarette after another as he recounted the events from the past twenty-four hours. More than once, Vinny asked him to repeat a part of the story, not because he didn't hear Matteo but because he couldn't believe how incredibly stupid Marco was. Several minutes later, Matteo finished explaining and waited for his father to respond.

"I swear, I'm gonna kill that asino myself." There was a long pause before Vinny said anything more.

Matteo knew better than to force his father into saying something. He was the boss, and he responded when he was good and ready, not a moment before. He had a notebook out, and he was twirling a pen between his fingers as he waited for his father to give him instructions. He would never let the paper out of the bedroom, but he knew that Vinny was not a man that liked to repeat himself. He scribbled furiously when Vinny began barking orders, and he kept his mouth shut until he was done speaking.

"Is that understood?" Vinny finally said.

"Yes sir, I will make sure it gets done," Matteo replied with more confidence than he was feeling at the moment.

"Call me when it's done," Vinny said and cut the connection.

Matteo knew better than to say goodbye. He had learned that his father wasn't much for telephone etiquette, and when Vinny was done talking, he simply hung up the phone.

CHAPTER 12

Anatoly Kuznetsov pushed the intercom button to answer the phone sitting on the edge of his beautifully ornate desk. It was made during the eighteenth century from Karelian birch imported from Finland. It was his prize possession, and he loved to stare at the curly wood grains. He was about to leave for his dacha in Minsk when the phone had rung. He had thought of ignoring it, but when he saw that the call was coming from inside the Kremlin, he decided he had better take it.

"Kuznetsov," he said confidently into the phone.

"I hope you are enjoying your vodka, Anatoly. I was hoping we could go for a walk in Gorky Park this morning. Can I meet you there around 9:00 a.m.?"

Anatoly's heart skipped a beat as he listened to the voice on the other end of the line. It was the exact phrase that he used when he was a field agent with the KGB, only he hadn't used it in almost ten years.

"I would love to, but I am afraid I am not going to be able to break away today," he said with a regretful tone. Although it sounded like rejection, it was a response in the affirmative. There would be no stroll through Gorky Park today, but there would be a meeting. He hung up the phone and looked at his watch. He didn't have much time. He had to make it from his humble 20,000-square-foot home in Rublevka to Novo-Ogaryovo in less than an hour. It was less than twenty miles, but traffic would be pretty thick at this time of the morning. He pushed the intercom button and informed his driver about his change of plans before heading to the bedroom to change his clothes. His jogging suit would not be appropriate where he was heading.

Anatoly had come from Bratsk, a tiny town on the Angara River. Anatoly's father had been a prison guard at the Gulag Angara until 1955 when he went to work building the hydroelectric dam. His father had died a year later in a freak accident during construction, leaving behind a wife and three children. Anatoly was just six and the oldest of the siblings when his father passed away. His three-year-old sister Galina died one month later of tuberculosis. Anatoly's younger brother was only two months old when their father died, and he never knew what became of him. Anatoly remembered his mother taking the young baby to a massive house on the Angara River one morning on her way to the factory. That night his mother came home alone. She never talked about it.

When Anatoly asked his mother about his baby brother, she beat him with a metal ladle until he finally managed to escape through a small window in the back room. He never asked again. His mother died shortly after that in an accident at the wood mill, where she worked long hours after her husband's death. Anatoly was seven years old when he was sent to the Irkutsk orphanage to remain for the next eleven years.

Anatoly had a remarkable talent for cruelty that went mostly unnoticed at the orphanage. The only thing about Anatoly more disturbing than his cruelty was his intelligence. He wasn't just smart; he was a genius. His intelligence caught the attention of Moscow State University when he sat for the ninth-grade exams. The school system in Bratsk was not precisely a center for educational excellence, but when young Anatoly scored an almost perfect score, many heads turned.

His scholarship to Moscow University was sealed when he matched the perfect score on his college admission test in the eleventh grade. Upon graduating from Moscow State University in 1978, he was recruited by the Russian military. They didn't have to try very hard; he had been planning to join the military his entire life. He had quickly landed in the Russian Special Forces. After the war in Afghanistan ended, his services with the KGB were quite marketable.

At thirty-five, he had risen through the KGB ranks with impressive speed. The KGB regrouped into two branches when the Iron Curtain fell in 1991. One group became known as the Federal Security Service, and the other became the Foreign Intelligence Service of the new Russian Federation. Anatoly became part of neither group. Instead, he branched out on his own with his unique talent set. As the Union of Soviet Socialists collapsed, a pseudo-capitalist Polit Bureau arose, and Russia was set to become an extremely lucrative place. Anatoly made some decisions, took some risks, and became fabulously wealthy in ten years. He had made so much money that he was confident he would never spend it all in twenty lifetimes. So, he did what all filthy rich people do; he spent his time trying to protect his wealth while keeping his eye on opportunities to make even more.

The Russians knew the Baltic states would descend into chaos. They had spent fifty years behind the curtain, so they had no idea how to govern themselves; nor were they prepared. The old guard would never let the younger people embrace capitalism, and the young people would never forgive their elders for their lot in life. Mix in some ethnic disputes that had been evident for a millennium, and the Baltic states were on a collision course toward civil war. There to make money on the war-torn states' depravity were people like Anatoly—people who had spent their lives skulking around in places like Yugoslavia and Chechnya doing the dirty work. Anatoly had seen the opportunities ripe for the picking when Ronald Reagan made his famous speech in Berlin. He had cast his lot with the old guard, and his decisions were paying off in spades.

As wealthy as he was, though, he was just a pawn in the bigger game. Anatoly was still just the muscle of the operation. He had come up from the streets, so the true aristocracy and Polit Bureau types would never look on him as their equal. Anatoly was OK with that—as long as the money kept pouring in, the vodka continued to flow, and the endless supply of young girls from the Balkans never dwindled.

It didn't matter how wealthy Anatoly was; he had been summoned. He began making a mental list of everything that had to be done in short order, and then he opened his drawer, pulled out his favorite 45-caliber pistol, and tucked it into his briefcase.

Anatoly closed the door to the limousine that had dropped him off in front of the very Russian-looking dacha about twenty minutes outside Moscow. Staring up at the front of the mansion made him realize that he was out of his league. Despite his tremendous wealth, Anatoly knew he was just a pawn to the man he was about to meet with. Anatoly's information made him valuable, but his lack of scruples and brutality made him indispensable. He was what most people in polite society would refer to as a sociopath. He committed rape for the first time when he was just twelve years old; he had killed for the first time just months later, and his conscience never scolded him for either act since. He was a magnificent actor when it came to blending in with the socialites whose company he kept lately, but Anatoly always longed for the days when he could let his thirst for blood be sated.

He walked through the marble edifice into the mansion's great hall and was instructed to have a seat by the fireplace. Two minutes later, he was offered coffee. The butler rebuked him when he asked for vodka, telling him it was too early for such beverages. Even the hired help seemed to have an aristocratic air that he despised, but he just acted sheepish and consented to the coffee. Three hours later, he was ushered into another room deep inside the house. It had no windows, no wall decorations, no marble floors, and no occupants. He took a seat in a metal, folding chair as he steeled himself for another long wait. He knew the game. It wasn't his first trip to the mansion, and he prayed it would not be his last. He had heard the rumors about the very room he was sitting in. He couldn't help but smile when he realized he had helped perpetuate the myths about this place.

The house belonged to Vladimir Rusilko; he *was* the Russian Mafia, the man at the top of the pile. A filthy pile, to be sure. The Polit Bureau was said to be in total subjection to the man. His money had been made mostly by legal means in the oil industry, but like most wealthy men, that was the sign on the store front. The sign on the back of the store read like a list of the seven deadly sins.

A full two hours after he had been shown to the sparse room, a door opened in the back behind the metal desk, and a diminutive woman entered the room carrying a pewter tray with Anatoly's favorite vodka and two small glasses. Anatoly knew it would be rude to pour a drink before his host entered, so he sat patiently. A few minutes later, Vladimir appeared through the door. Anatoly rose quickly to his feet, but Vladimir motioned for him to sit back down.

"I am so sorry to keep you waiting," Vladimir said without a hint of sincerity. He was simply reciting the next line of the script, a script that had been acted out many times before in the small room. He had just arrived at his home after the long flight home from Switzerland, and he was exhausted. He had a few more things to do before he could sleep, but this was the most important.

Like the actor Anatoly was, he accepted the words with more deference than they had been offered.

"We have a situation that has recently come to my attention, and I need your services once again, comrade."

"I am your humble servant, comrade."

"It seems we have a business associate who cannot keep his mouth shut, and he has put us in a very delicate situation. He is a fairly low-level associate, but he has very loose lips. He was arrested in America—Alaska, to be specific. Interpol has identified him as Vasili Czernoski and requested the FBI return him to Mother Russia. It appears he did not want to return home and has made a deal with the FBI to continue his stay abroad. I am not concerned about him; I am quite sure you know what needs to be done about that, correct?"

"Of course, comrade; it shall be done." Anatoly knew he had just been given a kill order, and nothing else needed to be said.

"The real problem is that he seems to have put certain events into motion that require your services as well. Our Italian business associates in the US are asking for our help in dealing with the FBI. It appears our associate Czernoski has compromised our operations." Vladimir opened one of the metal drawers, pulled out a skinny envelope, and slid it across the desk to Anatoly. "The son of one of our associates has failed to complete a task given to him by myself. As much as I would like you to deal with him personally, it would put tremendous strain on some very delicate relationships. I do, however, need you to complete his task with much haste."

Anatoly didn't reach for it right away; he didn't want to seem too eager for a new assignment, but he didn't wait too long either. He finally pulled the envelope off the desk and assured Vladimir that he would not fail him.

Vladimir motioned for Anatoly to open the envelope and then sat back in his chair.

Anatoly took a sip of his vodka and opened the envelope. The file contained three photos, six passports, and three names. The three photos were of Vasili Czernoski, Marco Bertoli and Renee Murphy. Their names matched the photos and the six passports were to help him in and out of the United States should matters deteriorate. After the names and faces were burned into his memory, he inserted them back into the envelope. He slid the six passports into his jacket pocket as his mind began making plans for how to proceed. He would have preferred to go to his vacation home for some much-needed relaxation and entertainment before he left for the US, but the 'much haste' comment from

Vladimir made that a very bad idea. He had his marching orders, and he was a soldier.

Vladimir extended his hand across the desk and shook Anatoly's more firmly than Anatoly thought he was capable of. At eighty-two, Vladimir Rusilko's face maintained a youthful appearance, but his body was having trouble keeping up. Once Anatoly was dismissed, he shuffled his way back to his office on the main floor of the mansion. He slowly lowered his tired bones into the overstuffed leather chair and stoked the fire behind him. He was irritated by the fact that he felt cold all the time. He knew that his doctor had put him on blood thinners and had even explained that they would make him feel cold, but he didn't have to like it. After he got the fire roaring, and the warmth had returned to his hands, he spun the chair around and opened the top drawer of his desk. He pulled a small phone from the drawer and dialed a number from memory. His body might have been failing, but his brain was as sharp as ever.

When the voice on the other end picked up, he greeted the man warmly and began making the necessary small talk before diving into the business at hand. Once the correct words had been spoken in precisely the correct order, Vladimir was certain that the connection was secure. Without further pleasantries, he finally got down to business. "One of your employees is poking her nose into business that does not concern her."

Peter Markenson listened intently to the older man before responding. "If you could give me a name, I will ensure that this does not continue, my friend."

"The name is Larkin, and I am not your friend," Vladimir added. The pleasantries had already been dispensed with, and he hated small talk. "I trust you will handle this expeditiously," Vladimir said as though he were talking about a minor traffic violation and not a murder investigation.

"You can be assured I will," Markenson said, but the line had gone dead.

Peter Markenson hung up the phone and started tapping keys on his computer. Moments later, he had the information he needed. Then he pushed the intercom button on his desk. A young woman pushed through the door of his office and stood in front of his desk, waiting for instructions.

"I need to see Roberto Clarke. He's the special agent in charge of the Detroit Field Office. I need him here tomorrow morning at the latest. Send the jet for him if you can't get him here commercially. That's all," Markenson said with a wave of his hand.

The woman didn't make any sign of moving, which irritated Peter. "Was I not clear?"

"You were very clear, sir. May I tell him what this is regarding?"

"Do you know what this is regarding?" Markenson said sarcastically.

"No, sir," she replied.

"Well, if you don't know what this is about, how are you going to tell him what this is about?" Markenson said in what he hoped was the most condescending voice he could muster. "If I *wanted* to tell you, I *would* have told you," he shouted as the young woman backed up toward the door. "Tomorrow by 9:00 a.m., no later," he added at the top of his voice as the door closed.

*****

Mack walked down the jetway to his connecting flight to Cleveland only half paying attention to the men and women around him. He heard several people thank him for his service, so he just tried his best at a smile and a nod before continuing down the ramp. He had taken his seat toward the rear of the plane when the middle-aged stewardess leaned over to whisper something in his ear. They were about to close the door, but the captain of the plane had given the OK to move the young serviceman to first class for the two-hour flight to Cleveland.

Mack thanked the stewardess and fell into the window seat. He was grateful that it was the lone seat on the port side of the aircraft, so he would not be forced to engage in any small talk with curious passengers. He stared out the window at the tarmac and couldn't believe that less than twenty-four hours ago, he was killing insurgents on the other side of the globe. He was still keyed up, but the comfortable seat and low humming of the engines gave him the peace and quiet to get a few moments of rest.

He had just fallen asleep when the memory roared back to life. He was staring at a young Afghani girl lying on her back in the little brick house near the Arghandab River Valley about eighty miles West of Kandahar. Mack had been picked to join Bravo Company, the First Light Armored Reconnaissance Battalion for the push West toward Lashkar Gah on his second tour to Afghanistan. He, along with a Marine Cook who hadn't seen a stove since the war began because he spoke Pashto, and several Reconnaissance Marines had begun going house-to-house looking for any Taliban soldiers hiding in the tiny village.

Just as one of the Recon Marines was about to kick open the poorly constructed wooden door, it exploded outward. Mack instinctively dove for cover and brought his rifle up to his shoulder. He saw what looked like AK-47 barrels sticking out of the tiny window at the rear of the building, so he squeezed the trigger. The Marine on the ground was rolling around in obvious pain, so Mack jumped to his feet and sprinted toward the door. He was almost to the wounded Marine when he saw the small grenade tumble out of the gaping hole where the door used to be, and he dove to the ground. He clenched his teeth, waiting for the detonation, but it never came.

A few moments later, he saw that the grenade still had not gone off and he was up moving again. He didn't wait for orders. He just plunged into the small hut with his weapon at the ready. He wasn't prepared for the sudden darkness and cursed himself for not thinking about that before he plowed through the doorway. His eyes took a second to adjust, but his trigger finger didn't wait. Seeing something moving toward the back of the house, he squeezed the trigger four times, sending a total of twelve bullets into the small room before everything went quiet.

As the smoke cleared and daylight began pouring into the room through the bullet holes, Mack could see two men lying on the floor and a shalwar kameez hanging from a make shift clothes line. The men were dead, and he realized that it had been the shalwar kameez that had caught his eye. It was a woman's dress in Afghanistan, and it was hanging there to dry. He wasn't sure if his earlier bullets had killed them both or if his latest barrage had done the damage, but it didn't matter. The Lieutenant was the next man through the door, but he lowered his rifle when he saw Mack standing there.

"You OK?" the Lieutenant shouted.

Mack hadn't been injured, but the sound of his own weapon had temporarily rendered him deaf, so he didn't answer. His gaze fell just a few feet past the men on the floor to a small bed in the corner of the building. Lying on the bed was a small girl who wasn't moving. Mack silently willed the child to stir, thinking she was sleeping, but before his eyes could process the scene, his brain knew the child was dead. He walked slowly toward the bed staring at the lifeless body more intently with every step. He vaguely heard the Lieutenant saying something about a booby trap, but it sounded like it was coming from a mile away. He had reached the bed and was peering down at the lifeless child despite the Lieutenant's protest.

He knelt at the side of the bed and slowly turned the child over as his life began changing forever. When the body was facing him, Mack could see the bullet hole in her head, and he just knew in his heart that he had killed her. She wasn't quite a year old, he guessed. He wanted to cry, but the Lieutenant was dragging him away from the site, and he didn't have the strength to resist. Just as the sound returned to Mack's ears, he saw the peaceful look on the child's face.

Mack had been seeing that little face for the past two years in his dreams. He had never told Renée about it. She didn't need to know. He had never told anybody from his own unit either. All they knew was that he had taken out a few Taliban on a daring assault on an occupied structure. He had even won a medal for it, but he never wore it. Nobody had ever noticed that the medal was conspicuously absent whenever he was in dress uniform. He had never mentioned the scene again, but he knew he would carry that little girl's face with him the rest of his life. Mack stared at the face so intently, wondering why it didn't look upset. There was no hatred in the young girl's face; no thoughts of revenge or retaliation; just a peaceful, calm look that rose above the violence surrounding her.

Mack had frozen his mind in time as he stared at the little girl's face. He wanted her to wake up, so he could apologize, but she never did. As Mack stood there staring at the little girl, her eyes popped wide open, and Mack sat straight up in his seat. He looked around and saw several faces, including the middle-aged stewardess, staring at him from the aisle. He offered a quick apology for who knows what he had just done and then sat forward and put his hands to his face. So that was it. *An eye for an eye*, he thought as he forced down the emotions that had begun bubbling over the surface.

CHAPTER 13

Mack burst through the doors of the Intensive Care Unit and began walking directly toward the nurses' station. The nursing staff had been anticipating his arrival, so when the handsome yet weary-looking young man in Marine Corps digital fatigues walked through the door, the receptionist immediately knew who he was. Mack hadn't even bothered to change into the civilian clothes that the Sergeant Major had given to him.

The ICU secretary tried her best to smile as she quickly stood up and escorted Mack to Renée's room. As he entered the room, he saw Renée's mother with her back to him, looking down at the bed. He was not prepared for what he saw. Her entire head was covered in bandages, and a large tube protracted from her mouth. Her left eye was visible under the bandages and was swollen to the point that her eyelashes were obscured. Her right eye was completely covered with bruises. An odd-looking piece of equipment seemed to be stuck into the bandages directly over her left temple. Mack stared down at her for what seemed like hours. He was afraid to move. He didn't know what to say. For the first time in twenty-eight years, Mack was paralyzed by fear. He wanted to scoop her off the bed and hold her, but something inside his head told him it was not a good idea. He was doing everything he could to stem the tears amassing at the corners of his eyes.

"Hello, Mack," Basmina whispered.

Mack had forgotten she was even in the room after he saw his beautiful Pep lying there in the bed, almost entirely unrecognizable. He turned and saw her walking toward him, and he reached out his arms to hug her. Mack had never taken to calling Renée's mother anything but Mina. He liked the Afghani names. Not only did her full name mean beautiful, but the nickname he called her meant to love. Mack had never known his own mother, but he couldn't imagine anybody taking over that role.

"How long have you been here? Mack asked Mina.

"I don't even know. When I got to the hospital on the west side after the accident, I couldn't see her because they were transferring her here for surgery. I went to see the babies while she was in surgery. I was so tired I had to go home and sleep before I could make it back here. The surgeon told me he needed to transfer her here because they had a burn center and more capabilities than they have at the community hospital."

Mack had been strong for almost twenty-four hours around other people as he traveled home from Afghanistan, but when he saw Renée lying there, he lost all control of his emotions and gave up trying to be strong. Mack cried, and Mina hugged him even tighter. The ICU nurse pulled up a chair for Mack to sit in and hold Renée's hand.

"I love you, baby. Pep, can you hear me? Can she hear me?" Mack said a little louder than he intended at the nurse who had offered him the chair.

"She can definitely hear you, but she is unable to respond." Just then, a Middle Eastern-looking doctor entered the room and introduced himself as Dr. Alin Pravin. Mack was instantly wary of the young man standing before him because he didn't look much different than the men he had been hunting for the past two months. Mack kept his mistrust in check and decided to give Dr. Pravin a fair shake.

The doctor explained that he was taking care of Renée in conjunction with a host of other specialists. He briefly gave Mack the rundown on her condition using words like hemorrhage, edema, coma, hypotensive, and a host of others and Mack had no idea what he meant.

"I have no idea what you are talking about, sir. I just want to know how she's doing," Mack finally blurted out.

"I'm so sorry. I'm not explaining myself well," Dr. Pravin said with more than enough sincerity to be believed by Mack." She is stable, but her chances of making a full recovery are fairly small."

Mack started to say something, but Dr. Pravin was determined to explain himself.

"The pressure on her brain is too high, and we will have to take her back to surgery if it doesn't start coming back down. Her heart quit beating after the first surgery here, and she had to be resuscitated several times before going back for the second surgery.

"You said first surgery here," Mack interrupted.

Mina reminded Mack about the transfer from the west side and then turned back to Dr. Pravin for him to continue.

"That tube you see coming out of her head measures the pressure building up inside her brain. It is very high due to the swelling and ongoing bleeding she is experiencing following the trauma. If the bleeding does not stop or if the swelling does not go down, we will have to operate again."

"Well, do it now if it's too high," Mack shot back.

"That is dangerous too. She has been through a lot, and the neurosurgeon and I are concerned that she will not be strong enough to undergo another lengthy procedure. She has been to the operating room three times now since the accident and has lost a lot of blood. We are doing everything we can to bring down the pressure in her head, but that also lowers her blood pressure. Having low blood pressure makes her heart pump faster. It's a precarious position," Dr. Pravin said, closing his eyes to emphasize the gravity of the situation.

"What are you telling me?" Mack said impatiently. "And why does she have these bandages all over her?"

"I'm saying that it does not look good for her to pull through this. If she does, she will most likely have severe neurological deficits. This means anything from never walking again to never breathing on her own again. I'm so very sorry. I am doing everything I can; I hope you know that. To answer your last question, she suffered several burns in the accident; the bandages are to prevent her burned skin from getting infected."

There was a noticeable amount of emotion and empathy in Dr. Pravin's voice, and Mack felt a little ashamed of how he was acting. "I'm sorry, Doctor, but this has …" Mack didn't finish the sentence as the lump in his throat choked off his words.

"It's OK. I understand this is extremely difficult. I will be here all day, so if you need me, just ask the nurse, and I can talk to you again. I know that your daughters are at Children's Hospital, and their prognosis is not good either. Again, I'm so sorry," Dr. Pravin said as his own voice caught in his throat. Dr. Alin Pravin was a good man who truly cared for his patients. What's more, his wife had just given birth to their second daughter, and he was trying to imagine the horrific pain Mack was going through, and it overwhelmed him as well. He wiped a tear from his eye as he turned and headed toward the door.

"Basmina, I'm so sorry," Dr. Pravin whispered as he left the room.

Mack knew what he had to do next was going to be impossible. He put it off but then felt guilty for procrastinating, so he stood. He bent over, kissed Renée on the forehead, and whispered, "I'm gonna go check on our girls, Pep; I'll be back soon."

"Take my car. I will stay here until you get back," Mina said, handing Mack the keys.

"I have a car, but I think I will just walk," Mack said and hugged her again.

Twenty minutes later, Mack walked up to the cradle that held Aubrey. He looked down at the pitiful sight, and an entirely new wave of emotion washed over him as his body began to tense. This new emotion was rage. Who could do something like this to a little baby? But he felt the hypocrisy of his own words before he could speak them. The tears were threatening to break through again, but the anger overpowered them, and he felt his temper starting to flare. Tubes were sticking out of her mouth and nose. She had little IVs coming from both arms, and she looked so beautiful despite all the equipment. Right next to her was Brianna in another space-age-looking tent called an *isolette*, only ten feet away. Mack was doing everything he could think of to control the rage he was feeling as the neonatologist walked into the room.

"Mr. Murphy, I'm Doctor Puckett, and I am so sorry."

Mack looked at the doctor's face and shook his head up and down, but he couldn't form the words to respond.

"I can come back in a few minutes if you'd rather be alone with the girls for a bit," the doctor said.

Mack just shook his head and between deep breaths, he managed to ask how the girls were.

The doctor started with Brianna as he walked to the crib farthest away. "Well, Brianna sustained an injury we call an epidural hematoma. It is when the brain bleeds, and nothing can stop it. She is brain-dead, meaning the only thing keeping her alive is the machine. Once it is removed ..." His voice trailed off as Mack raised his hands to say he had heard enough.

Mack turned to look at the other crib and just pointed, unable to speak.

"Unfortunately, Aubrey's spinal cord was severed at the level of her third cervical vertebra, so she is paralyzed. She suffered a liver laceration during the accident, and the surgeon had to operate. Her spleen was lacerated, too, and it had to be removed. I don't think she will ever breathe again on her own, but it is still too soon to say."

Mack stood over the crib and stared at her for a long moment before finding his voice. "So, what you're telling me is that Brianna is essentially dead, and Aubrey will never leave this machine," he said, pointing to the box that connected the tube going into her throat.

"Yes ... I'm sorry," the doctor said.

Mack looked down at Brianna and then at the doctor. "Can I take her to her mother?" Mack said, barely able to finish the sentence before a new wave of emotion rolled over his chest.

"Yes, sir, I have arranged transport to the ICU if that is what you want."

Mack just nodded.

"I will let the nurses know, and we can get started," Dr. Puckett said somberly and exited the room.

Ten minutes later, the nurse came into the room, followed by several other people. Mack had no idea who they were. He just stood back as the Pediatric Intensive Care Unit (PICU) nurses began attaching all the tubes and wires to a portable cart for transport to the main campus about a block and a half away.

"Can I hold her?" Mack asked.

"Of course," the Charge Nurse said.

Mack reached into the crib with trembling hands. He gently lifted Brianna, brought her to his chest, and kissed her on the forehead. "I love you so much," Mack whispered and began shaking as he sat down in a wheelchair for the ride over to Renée. He didn't notice the stares from the employees and visitors as the entourage rolled through the children's hospital on the way to the ICU. He stared down at his beautiful baby girl the whole way and forced himself to see Brianna and not the faceless little girl in the Arghandab river valley.

Twenty-five minutes later, the entourage rolled through the main doors of the ICU. With Brianna in his arms, Mack stood up and carefully placed the tiny bundle on Renée's chest. The monitors were beeping and alarming, but the nurse reassured Mack everything was OK. Mack gently grabbed Renée's arms and folded her hands around Brianna in a cradle hold. The beeping on the monitors escalated even further, but this time it was Renée's and Mack knew that she was aware of what was happening.

"Is she OK?" Mack said to the nurse, who was busy adjusting the ventilator.

She just nodded her head.

Once everything was situated, Mack signaled to the nurse to disconnect the machines keeping their three-month-old Brianna alive. The nurses turned off the ventilator, disconnected the IV, and quietly stepped away from the bed. Mack leaned over the bed and placed his left arm around Brianna and his right arm on Renée's left shoulder with his hand draped across her forehead.

"I'm so sorry, Pep. I'm so sorry," he said, shaking uncontrollably and sobbing loud enough to be heard at the nurses' station. He didn't care who heard him, and he didn't care what any of them thought. He knew he should sit before he fell to the ground with grief, but the Marine in him stubbornly locked his legs and willed himself to stay right where he was. He didn't even notice when Mina joined the group and began weeping silently as well.

Instinctively, Mack knew when Brianna took her last breath. He looked down at the baby he had held with one hand only three months earlier. He remembered how impossibly tiny she looked in his callused hand. A fresh wave of grief washed over him, and his anguish was unbearable. He had no idea where the tears were coming from, but they poured down his face like a hot Mississippi rainstorm. He gently stroked Brianna's little cheek and felt the sickening cooling of her skin. He was shocked at how quickly the life drained from her tiny body. When he could bear it no longer, he looked to Renée. She was still in a coma, but her breathing seemed more ragged, and her face seemed to be grimacing a little more than before. Could she be aware that her baby was dead? Had she finally received the answer to the question she had been silently trying to ask? The unknown answer that had been keeping her alive and fighting?

Mack looked from Renée down to the little bundle lying on her chest and knew in his heart that Renée was not going to make it. He had seen the love that Renée showered on those two beautiful baby girls, and he knew that she would want to follow them wherever they went. Mack knew in the pit of his stomach that he was alone once again in the world. He resisted the thought that Renée was going to die, but he knew it. He knew it just as sure as he knew he was standing there weeping like a man who had lost it all. When he could no longer hold himself up, he collapsed into the chair next to Renée's bed as Mina took her turn at the bed to kiss and hold Brianna one last time.

Finally, Mack looked up at the nurse standing outside the ICU room and just nodded his head. They wouldn't let Brianna stay in the room forever. As the nurse came quietly to the bed, though, Mack couldn't do it. "I need to hold her again if that's OK?" he said through quiet sobs.

"Of course it is." The nurse lifted the tiny bundle off Renée and handed her to Mack. He shivered as he remembered that day three months ago when a different nurse gave him his baby girl for the first time. He remembered the feeling of overwhelming joy and happiness. He couldn't fight the irony as he realized that he had experienced the complete spectrum of human emotion within the span of three months. He realized that he had experienced the fullness of life and the contentment when he held Brianna for the first time. Now, he experienced the emptiness of death and the restless feelings that accompanied it.

Mack felt so many emotions flooding his heart in rapid succession. He thought about the monster who had done this. He thought about revenge, and he thought about murder. The worst thought yet was regret for spending the time he had left with his precious little girl dwelling on the previous thoughts. He brought Brianna's little ear to his mouth and whispered, "I love you so much, baby girl. I love you so …" The last words got hung up in his throat as fresh sobs burst through. Mack cried out in pain and agony. He was sobbing and trembling, and he couldn't stop. His Marine bearing was gone. His situational awareness was gone, and all that was left was a man who had indeed lost it all. He kissed her tiny nose and saw one of his tears spill onto her little cheek. He kissed the cheek and tasted his own tear as his chest heaved up and down in agony.

Mina had quietly excused herself from the room, telling the nurse she would sit with Aubrey for a little while. She knew Mack needed this, or he could never move forward.

When Brianna's little lips turned a pale blue shade, Mack called for the nurse. Seconds later, the nurse was standing next to him. "You are just going to have to take her; I'm not going to be able to hand her over," Mack said between sobs. Mack also knew that he didn't want his last memory of Brianna to be one where she looked dead. He had been quietly trying to convince himself that she was just asleep and that it was all a nightmare, but the blue tint to her little lips had robbed the last of his hopes. The nurse left the room, and Mack let his shoulders slump forward as his head fell limply to his chest. The nurse was at his side two minutes later, offering him the little purple blanket with the teddy bears. Mack took the blanket and was overwhelmed by the fresh set of emotions that accompanied the blanket's softness.

Mack wasn't sure how long he sat there sobbing and clutching that little purple blanket. He had heard the nurses quietly going about the job of caring for Renée. He listened to the machines making the beeping noises and watched Renée's chest rise and fall with the sound of the ventilator. The tears dried, and he was left with a sense of emptiness. Several hours later, Mack heard the nurses talking about Renée and realized that the shift was changing. The day nurse let Mack know she was leaving for the night and would be back in the morning. He thanked her for everything she had been doing and introduced himself to the nightshift nurse. He quietly returned to his chair with brand new respect for nurses.

*****

Maxwell Kaine hung up the phone and stood. He was so tired from the events of the past twenty-four hours that he could barely think straight. He knew he needed sleep, but he had a few more things to do before he could make the thirty-minute ride to his home. He returned from the washroom feeling a little more invigorated than he had earlier. He went through the same sequence with the burner phone and the anti-bugging equipment and settled in as he waited for his call to be answered.

When Yonah Levin answered the phone, it was almost 5:00 a.m. in Tel Aviv, but he sounded like he had been awake for hours. Maxwell knew Yonah was an early riser, which is why he liked him so much.

"I have an idea, Yonah, but I must act now. Are you secure?"

"Of course, tell me."

Maxwell laid out his plans in intricate detail as Yonah listened quietly on the other side of the world.

"It is risky, but I do see the benefits," Yonah finally replied.

"Do you believe the others will think the same? I don't have time to establish a quorum," Maxwell said with trepidation.

"I think it will be favorably received. If this Murphy Report is as volatile as you say it is, then keeping a lid on it is the best course of action. I don't see any other way forward, do you?"

Maxwell sighed as he answered. He hated these decisions more than anything else, but they had to be made … and they had to be made now.

CHAPTER 14

It had been four days since Mack burst through the doors of the ICU. Brianna was dead; Aubrey was in critical condition; and Renée was in a coma. The pressure remained steady on Renée's brain, but Dr. Pravin told Mack not to get his hopes up. He explained that the chances of a complete recovery dwindled every day. The entire host of specialists coming and going from the room made Mack's head spin. Neurologists, neurosurgeons, cardiologists, pulmonologists, respiratory therapists, physical therapists, nurses, lab techs, and an entire army of medical students and residents filled Mack's days with half-hearted apologies and medical jargon that he didn't understand. He knew they were all just doing their jobs, so he listened respectfully. In his heart, Mack knew that his Pep was gone for good.

He caught himself wishing that she would stop fighting and go be with Brianna. Seeing his beautiful Pep like this killed him, but his conscience always screamed at him for such thoughts. He didn't dare put a voice to his thoughts in fear that they might come true. He desperately wanted his Pep back. He remembered the fun times they had shared and the memories they had made, and it left him exhausted. He used the shower in Pep's room and never wandered far from her side. Mina had taken to sitting with Aubrey most days, but Mack always walked the two blocks to check in on her twice a day.

Mack listened to the machines' quiet hum and prepared for another restless night in the chair beside Renée's bed. His stomach was telling him to eat, but his brain was playing cruel tricks on him. The thought that something would happen while he was gone was too much for Mack. Usually, Mina brought him some food to eat in the room, but she was planning to go home for the night at Mack's insistence to get a good night's sleep. Mack thought about going down to the cafeteria to grab a bite when Dr. Pravin entered the room.

"Mr. Murphy, I just got off the phone with Dr. Cleavant at Walter Reed. He is a neurosurgeon, and he is one of the best. He is sending a team here to escort Renée to Bethesda," Dr. Pravin said with a hint of optimism.

Mack looked at the doctor and asked, "Is that how this normally works? Why can't he do the surgery here?" Mack was just about to ask another question when Dr. Pravin interrupted him.

"No, sir. I was surprised to hear that as well. Normally, there isn't much we can't do here, so transfers to other hospitals are pretty rare. Dr. Cleavant has been doing amazing things with traumatic brain injuries since the war started in Afghanistan. Most of the literature about TBIs, as we call them, has come out of Walter Reed. I have been informed that your wife works for the Central Intelligence Agency," Dr. Pravin said clearly taken aback by the fact that nobody had mentioned that earlier.

"That's right; she's on maternity leave for another month."

"It seems to me there have been a lot of strings pulled to make this happen. Your wife must have many friends," Dr. Pravin said as he gestured toward the bed. "Dr. Cleavant is requesting that we do another CAT scan of her brain before the team arrives tonight. He will want to know the results before they arrive at Walter Reed. I will go down to the CAT scanner with her to ensure that she is stable through the entire procedure," Dr. Pravin said as he stared at the monitor on the ventilator. He punched a few buttons and watched the monitor for a few more seconds until he was satisfied with the results.

"When will they be here?" Mack said hesitantly.

"They should be leaving Walter Reed now. So that puts them here in about two hours, best guess," Dr. Pravin said.

"Will I be able to go with them?" Mack said, becoming more and more uneasy with the plan.

"No, sir, I'm sorry."

Mack stared down at Renée and squeezed her hand. "If this were your wife, what would you do?" Mack asked without looking up at the young doctor.

The question took Dr. Pravin by surprise. He hadn't thought about it until that very second. He didn't answer right away, but when he did, the emotion in his voice surprised Mack. "I would do whatever it took if it were my wife. Dr. Cleavant is the best there is. If it were between me and Dr. Cleavant, I would pick Dr. Cleavant any day of the week."

Mack stood to his feet, walked slowly to Dr. Parvin, and extended his hand. "I am not sure if I have said this yet, but if I haven't, I'm saying it now. Thank you."

Dr. Pravin shook Mack's hand and felt the burning tear at the corner of his eye. "I haven't told you this before, but I have two daughters at home as well, and I can't imagine the depth of your pain right now. It has been a great honor to care for your wife, and I want to thank you for your service," Dr. Pravin said, swiping at the tear that had broken through the crevice.

"You're welcome," Mack said and then resumed his post at Renée's side. He remembered his first opinion of Dr. Pravin, and he felt bad. He had obviously been born and raised in the United States. He was actually of Indian descent and Mack knew that he was as much of an American as he was. He was the last person to get distracted by skin color, but war had clearly changed him somehow.

"We will be heading down to the CAT scanner here shortly. I will be with her the whole time," Dr. Pravin said.

"Why don't you go home to your own family? I'm sure the night Doc is more than capable of pushing a stretcher," Mack said, smiling for the first time in over a week.

"My girls are all in New York this week. I can't stand the big empty house," Dr. Pravin said and instantly regretted it. "I'm sorry, that was a very selfish thing to say."

"It's OK, Doc. I understand," Mack said. "I'm glad you're here.

Three hours later, the time had come for Mack to say goodbye. The CAT scan had gone off without a hitch, and the team had arrived from Walter Reed. Mack leaned over the stretcher, kissed Renée's forehead, and placed the little purple blanket under her left arm. He wrapped the blanket around her arm so Brianna's name was visible under the teddy bear. "I will see you soon, Pep. Don't worry about Aubrey; Mina is going to take good care of her while we are gone." Mack could tell the team was getting a little impatient, so he stepped back and watched the two young men push her toward the Emergency Room to the awaiting ambulance.

Mack felt a chill as the stretcher disappeared behind the automatic door. He couldn't put his finger on the new emotion that had overwhelmed him in the first seconds after saying goodbye. It was a mix of great pain, regret, sorrow, and loss. Mack didn't have the hint of optimism that Dr. Pravin had shown earlier. The closest emotion he could name for sure was loneliness, but that didn't quite fit either. As Mack returned to the ICU to gather his few belongings, his mind began putting it all together. When the answer struck him, Mack forced it back down. He wouldn't say it out loud. He wouldn't give it a name. He would leave the thought in his mind and keep it from escaping.

Mack pulled the big government-owned Crown Victoria out of the garage and drove toward the Emergency Department to pick up Basmina. He had called Mina right after the discussion with Dr. Pravin to fill her in on the new plan. She had decided to stay with Aubrey until they came for Renée and then ride back to the suburbs with Mack.

Basmina slid into the passenger seat and pulled on her seat belt. "Mack, I really think you should sleep tonight and drive to Bethesda in the morning. You are completely exhausted, and it is supposed to rain all night," Basmina pleaded.

He planned on going to the Children's Hospital for another visit with Aubrey before making the eight-hour car ride to Walter Reed, but he was anxious to get going. When Mina told him there was no change in Aubrey's condition, they drove home. Mack thought about arguing, but he saw the concern on Basmina's brow, and he changed his mind. Twenty-five minutes later, Basmina and Mack pulled into her home with a sack full of fast food.

Mack had only been inside Basmina Shaw's home a few times in the three years he and Pep had been married. He shoveled in the food and set about looking around at the pictures that hung on the walls. Pictures of Renée no older than Aubrey brought a fresh wave of pain over him. It wasn't until then had he understood that Basmina had just lost a child the way he had.

Basmina pulled the image from the wall and held it. "This was my favorite picture of her as a baby. She was so curious. Even when she was a baby, I felt like she spent her days trying to figure things out. She was such a good baby."

Mack heard the word "was," and it drove a new bolt of pain through his chest. He knew that Basmina didn't mean to say it like that, but it didn't matter. He knew that she was right. He knew that Renée was gone, and he had a reasonable suspicion that Basmina knew it too.

Mack curled up into a ball on Renée's old bed, smelled the clean sheets, and drifted off into a restless sleep. He dreamed of their wedding day three years ago and the honeymoon that followed. He dreamed of the day that he had proposed to Renée. He dreamed of a tiny, pink baby rattle. He dreamed of the green mist in Afghanistan. He tried his best not to see the little Afghani girl's face, but she floated into his dreams anyway. He smiled at the little child lying limply on the bed, but this time he noticed that her face was different. This time, the face belonged to Brianna, and Mack thrashed under the covers. He fought the images for what seemed like days until it all mercifully slipped away, and then he didn't dream at all as the exhaustion dragged him down to a level of sleep he hadn't experienced in months,

*****

The paramedics pushed Renée's stretcher off the elevator and stopped at the nurse's station.

"Where do you want her?" the lead paramedic said.

"Does 'her' have a name?" the nurse replied.

"Renée Murphy, twenty-eight-year-old black female. We just got here from Cleveland, Ohio."

"She's going to ward seventy-one, so I will call them," the nurse said, relieved that she would not have to do the new admission. She disappeared into a back room, leaving the two paramedics standing in front of the desk. The lead paramedic began adjusting the oxygen tubing while the other pushed buttons on the ventilator. Thirty seconds later, the charge nurse emerged from the back office. "They will be here shortly to get her from you," the nurse said.

"We can take her there. It's no big deal," the paramedic said, trying to be friendly.

"That's the presidential suite. Nobody in or out without authorization. Thank you for the offer, though," the nurse said very matter-of-factly. "This is a military hospital, gentlemen. We do things a bit differently than they do in Cleveland."

"Whatever you say, Captain," the paramedic said and offered a mock salute.

"I'm a Major," the woman replied.

"I'm sorry?"

"I'm not a Captain. I'm a Major."

"Sorry ... Major!" The paramedic tried to apologize again, but the nurse wasn't having any of it.

Just as the paramedic was starting to say something else, two women in scrubs and a man wearing a white coat exited the elevator pushing a hospital bed. When they got to the nursing station, they introduced themselves.

"I'm Dr. Cleavant. Thank you for bringing her to us. We can take her from here. Do you have some paperwork for me to sign?" The two nurses didn't bother to introduce themselves and got to work transferring Renée from the portable stretcher to the ICU bed.

The paramedic held up the clipboard, and Dr. Cleavant scribbled a quick signature. "Thanks again," he said and handed back the clipboard as the nurses from Ward 71 finished the transfer.

Ten minutes later, Renée Murphy was being hooked up to the monitors in the presidential suite. Dr. Cleavant was examining her when Maxwell Kaine entered the private ICU suite.

"Can I help you, sir?" Dr. Cleavant said not looking up from his patient. He had been flashing a light into Renée's eyes.

"My name is Maxwell Kaine. I am the director of ..."

"I know who you are. What can I do for you?" Dr. Cleavant said without taking his eyes off of Renée's pupils.

"I was hoping you could give me your prognosis. This is a very distinguished employee."

"I was planning to take her to the operating room in the morning. After that, I will have a better idea. I'm sorry I don't have a better answer. She just arrived," Dr. Cleavant said looking at the many bandages on her face and neck. *Dr. Pravin didn't mention these burns to the scalp, and I thought the bolt was on the other side,* he thought as he began doing his secondary survey of the young woman he had been asked to consult on.

"I am sure you will do your best," Maxwell said and started to leave the room. "Oh, I brought a few friends with me. They are going to look after Mrs. Murphy while she is here. I'm sure you understand that we value her security."

"Yes, that is fine with me. As long as they stay out of my way," Dr. Cleavant said, sounding a bit irritated. He hated working on the presidential suite. Politicians, world leaders, billionaires, congressmen; they were all the same.

Maxwell Kaine was about to walk out of the room, but he stopped. "Do we have a contingency plan to get Mrs. Murphy out of here quickly in case the president needs to use the room?"

"The same plan that is always in place when princes and billionaires want to stay here," Dr. Cleavant said with obvious irritation.

Maxwell Kaine just stared at Dr. Cleavant for several moments, trying to decide if he liked him or not, but it didn't matter either way. He needed the most secure hospital bed in the world if his plan was to succeed. The plan was simple, had very few moving parts, but ultimately depended on the intelligence of the men he had selected for the job. The best plan is always the simplest, he said to himself. He was hoping the two men in the hallway were smart enough to keep their mouths shut, but if they were not, he was sure they were greedy enough to accept promotions in exchange for their silence. Maxwell finally decided that he didn't like Dr. Cleavant as he turned toward the exit.

Just outside the door, the two men in black suits stood tall and menacing. They had been given their orders, and they were very specific.

Maxwell paused for a moment and then spoke. "Make it convincing," he whispered to the taller of the two men and then headed down the hall.

Once Kaine was inside the parking garage, he pulled his encrypted cell phone from his pocket and dialed the numbers from heart. A few seconds later, the line picked up.

"Is it done?" came the voice of Yohan Levin from the other end of the line.

"It will be very soon. Everything is on track," he said and ended the call. Maxwell closed the burner phone and slid it back into his pocket. He pulled out his official CIA phone next and punched another phone number. When George Seifert answered the phone, he sounded half asleep. It took him a second to realize who was on the other end of the line. "George, I am at Walter Reed," he said into the phone. "Renée Murphy is here and seems to be doing fine. I just left her room, and the doctor assured me she is doing very well. He is taking her to the operating room in the morning, but he seems to think things will go smoothly. I just wanted to give you an update. I know how close the two of you were and that I have been praying for you."

The last part was gratuitous. It was just what people said. Kind of like, have a great day or how are you doing? I am praying for you contained just the right amount of sympathy mixed with what sounded like general concern, and Maxwell delivered the line perfectly. He cut the connection and dialed a few more phone numbers before instructing his driver to take him back to Langley.

*****

Anatoly Kuznetsov pushed the laundry cart to the elevator, punched the up arrow, and hunched over on the cart to wait. He wore a solid blue baseball hat pulled down over his eyes. His housekeeping uniform was a bit small through the shoulders, but he wouldn't be wearing it for long. His shoes were the only thing out of place. They were tough, durable-looking, black leather boots that looked like they belonged on a Russian soldier about to kick in a door. Anatoly always looked the part, but nobody ever noticed a man's shoes. They were the only part of the wardrobe that didn't permit variation. The right shoes were always the best way to prepare for any situation.

When the elevator reached the bottom floor, he shoved the

housekeeping cart into the elevator and pushed the button with the number six on it. A few moments later, the door opened on the sixth floor. Anatoly grabbed the cart handle and pushed it off the elevator. He froze momentarily when he noticed that the man waiting to get onto the elevator looked like a federal agent. The bulge over his hip was not concealing his side arm very well. Anatoly didn't make eye contact but just shoved the large cart past and nodded his head.

He continued to push the cart toward the presidential suite as he pulled his ID badge from his shirt pocket. He stopped the cart just before the main doors, held the ID badge to the proximity wall access port, and saw the green light illuminate. A split second later, the bulletproof door let out a loud click as the doors began swinging inward. Anatoly checked his peripheral vision before proceeding to the most secure hospital suite on the planet. There were no guards at the door, but he could see several men in suits sitting in folding chairs at various points on the ward. He pulled a fresh laundry bag from his cart on the way down the hall. It was 3:00 a.m., and the ICU staff looked like they were all about to fall asleep. The endless beeping and humming noises became like background noise to all but the most vigilant of nurses.

As he entered Renée's room, he hesitated for another split second when he saw a man slumped over in a chair, snoring quietly. His first thought was that it was the woman's husband, but the cheap suit and bulge above his ankle left no doubt to his identity. Anatoly decided that his snoring was going to work to his advantage. He entered the room, grabbed the laundry bag from the metal hamper, and tossed it into his cart. He was doing his best to be quiet, without making it look like he was *trying* to be quiet. He took a fresh bag from the stack and placed it into the empty laundry hamper.

After securing the new bag around the metal hopper, he quietly removed a 50 ml syringe. He pulled the plunger to load it with nothing but air. He twisted the syringe into the plastic tubing just before it entered the black woman's arm and pushed the contents in as quickly as the 22-gauge catheter would allow. He slid the syringe back into his pocket and pushed his cart to the end of the hallway. He swiped his badge one more time and walked briskly out in the hallway, heading toward the elevator. He pushed the down button on the elevator and quietly fought the urge to run.

Just as the door opened, his heart stopped beating momentarily as he was staring at the same agent from earlier. He regained his composure and averted his eyes as he pushed the cart onto the elevator once the man had exited. He hit the button for the basement, pulled the Beretta pistol out of his waistband, and wrapped it in a pillowcase so that it was more accessible should he need to get out of the building faster, and breathed a sigh of relief. Two more minutes, and he would be back in the van and on his way to the airport, where he could return to his country aboard the very impressive Gulfstream that Vladimir Rusilko had allowed him to use for his brief but very necessary assignment. As Anatoly exited the loading dock, he heard the distinct bell signaling a code blue and smiled to himself. Another successful mission behind enemy lines. Long live Spetsnaz.

*****

On the way back to Langley, Maxwell received a text message on his agency phone that simply said, "Done." He rolled the window down a crack and let the night air fill the back of the limousine. It was a gruesome line of work, but keeping America's secrets had to be done. One more move on the chess board, and he was closer to fulfilling his life's work. He knew that it had to be done, he knew that Renée would have wanted it that way; he knew Renée's family would take it very badly, but it didn't matter. The only thing that mattered was getting things done and making the world a better place to live. The hard work was just getting started though, as he closed his eyes for a brief nap.

*****

The dream returned as Mack's sleeping body faded in and out of the distinct phases of the sleep cycle. He watched the baby girl clutching the worn-out blanket between her two little hands as the bullet tore through her little body. He couldn't tell if it was Brianna he had just shot or the girl from the Arghandab River Valley. The bullet made a loud, knocking noise as it hit the wall behind the girl. Mack heard the knock, but it didn't seem to fit. It wasn't the sound a bullet made when it hit a plaster wall. He heard another knock, and somewhere in Mack's brainstem something was urging him to wake up. Mack was up and moving in a second when he heard another knock coming from the bedroom door. He was disoriented and badly shaken from the dream, but he moved to the door quickly. He pulled open the door and saw Basmina standing there in the glow of the light with tears streaming down her face.

"What's wrong, Mina?" he said as he grabbed her shoulders. "She's dead," she cried.

Who's dead? Mack thought. She had to be talking about Aubrey, but then he realized it had been a dream.

"Renée."

He had just seen Renée a few hours ago, and she was alive. He cursed at himself for not going to see Aubrey again that night before they returned to Mina's house. He felt his knees starting to buckle, and it didn't even register that Mina had just said *Renée*.

Mack directed Mina into the living room and helped her sit down on the couch. He was just about to ask her to repeat it all when it hit him. "Did you say Renée?"

Mina nodded as her shoulders began heaving up and down with uncontrollable sobs. Mack pulled her to him and hugged her hard. The full weight of it was still landing on him as he felt his own tears start to fall. "How?"

"A woman from Bethesda called and said that she coded just an hour after she arrived there," Mina said between sobs.

Mack stood to his feet. His fists were clenched, and he began pacing back and forth through the living room and hallway. He was trying to keep the pieces of his world together by sheer determination. He kept shaking his head and telling himself that it wasn't true. He cursed at himself for silently wishing that Mina had said Aubrey, not Renée. It was an impossible situation. He didn't want anybody to die, but if he had to choose, he would have chosen for Renée to live. Just as he had those thoughts, the disgust he felt for himself began bubbling up, and he just made it to the sink before throwing up violently. The bile tasted acidic and it smelled awful. He had smelled his own vomit before, after many of his adrenaline rushes in Afghanistan. He stared down and saw the meal he had just eaten running down the sides of the steel sink. He lost his equilibrium and the room started to spin. This time it was Mina's turn to offer comfort.

Mack clutched the kitchen sink, but his legs would not hold him up a second longer. He fell to the kitchen floor and crashed onto the linoleum in a heap of anguish. He wasn't just crying; he was wailing. He was screaming in between sobs and pounding his fists on the floor like a three-year-old throwing a temper tantrum. He didn't care. He had no idea the human body was capable of such pain and suffering. Saying goodbye to a three-month-old daughter was tough, but he had never spoken to her meaningfully. He had never heard her say she loved him back. Brianna had never called him *Daddy*, had never crawled up onto his lap and run her hands along his face. The baby girl had never even uttered a coherent word; yet his whole world shattered at the loss. Renée was a totally different type of pain.

Where Brianna had never confessed her undying love for Mack, Renée had. Without her, Mack felt like he was driving in traffic with his eyes closed. The sense of direction was gone. Up was down, and in was out. Nothing made sense to Mack at the moment. If somebody had to die, why couldn't it have been him? Mack had felt that feeling before leaving Afghanistan when Sass was killed, but this was totally different. He wondered where this would rank on the General's types and stages of grief. He just lay on the kitchen floor, clutching his fists and forcing the painful thoughts as far down into his soul as he could reach. The feelings of revenge and murder were rising to the surface faster than Mack could process them. The next thing he knew, Mina was lying on the floor stroking his head as if to soothe a small child who had just scraped his knee. Mack had no words to describe the love he felt for Mina at that moment. She had just become somebody Mack thought he would never have. She became his mother too.

CHAPTER 15

A loud knock at the hotel door startled Marco, who was just waking up from a long night of drinking vodka and gambling at the casino. Sal was in the room next to him and was still fast asleep. It had been four days since they had arrived in Detroit, and they were getting restless.

"Wake up, Marco!" the voice said as the door opened.

"What do you think you are doing?" Marco said as he grabbed his pants from the floor.

"For God's sake, Marco. It's two o'clock in the afternoon. Are you going to do anything today or just sit there while Dad and I bail your ass out again?" Matteo said, slamming the door closed behind him.

Marco just tuned him out, grabbed his cigarettes out of his pocket, and started to light one.

"This is a no-smoking room, moron," Matteo said as he grabbed the cigarette out of his mouth and tossed it into the garbage can. "You have ten minutes to clean up and be ready to go. If you are not downstairs in ten minutes, so help me, Marco, I will turn you in myself."

"Go where?" Marco mumbled.

"I will tell you on the way," Matteo said, shaking his head in disgust. "Tell your worthless friend Sal he has ten minutes too, not a second more."

"Is he going with us?" Marco said with a bit of apprehension in his voice.

"I don't see that we have a choice," Matteo snarled. He walked back to the door and yanked it open. Just before slamming the door shut, he yelled, "Ten minutes. Please be late, so I have a reason to throw you to the wolves."

Eight minutes later, Marco and Sal were sitting in the hotel lobby. The previous night had really sobered them up to the trouble they were both in, so they reluctantly took Matteo's tongue lashings.

Warrants had been issued that morning for Marco and Sal, so Matteo needed to get them out of the country for a while. Matteo pulled up to the front door of the hotel, driving a brand-new, fully-loaded, black Cadillac. It couldn't have been more than a few weeks old. It still had the new car smell. Two minutes later, they were driving toward a private airstrip just outside of Detroit. Sal was sitting in the front seat, and Marco picked the rear seat, so he could sprawl out. He also liked the thought of being chauffeured around by his little brother. Sal pulled a pack of cigarettes from his pocket and shook one out into his fingers.

"If you light that thing, I will drop you off at the local precinct and leave you. Is that understood?"

"Yeah, sure," Sal said, shoving the cigarette back into the pack. He had forgotten how much Matteo hated cigarette smoke.

"Where are we going?" Marco finally said from the back seat.

"I don't know, and I don't want to know. So don't call me when you get wherever it is Pops is sending you."

"Pops? You told him?" Marco said, sitting up straight in his seat. Just as he was about to say something else, Matteo cut him off.

"Of course, I told him everything. He's not just our father; he's the boss. I know you think you are the boss, but let me just set your little pathetic brain at ease. You're *not*. I don't take orders from you, and I damn sure don't take orders from this one," Matteo yelled, jabbing his finger toward Sal. "If Pops says put their dumb asses on a plane, then I put your dumb asses on a plane, and I don't ask any questions."

"I gotta get back to Cleveland. We just had a shipment come in, and nobody there knows how to move the cargo."

"Shut up, Marco. Just talk normally and forget all the ridiculous cargo business. They are girls, and I am going to take care of everything while you are gone. As far as I am concerned, you both can stay gone forever. I'm tired of cleaning up your messes, and so is Pops. You know he isn't turning the business over to you now; that's for damn sure. In fact, I'll be surprised if he even keeps you in the business after this fiasco."

Marco had enough and pulled his Tokarev from his waistband and pointed it right at Matteo's head. "Give me one reason not to pull this trigger right now, you arrogant ..."

Sal cut him off, "Don't do it, Marco. Not again. Just put the gun down, OK?" Sal screamed.

Marco pivoted the gun and pointed it directly at Sal. "You don't tell me what to do, Sal," Marco said in a surprisingly calm tone.

"That might actually be the best thing you have done in the past ten years," Matteo said sarcastically. "Might save me the job later on."

Marco swung the gun back to Matteo's head and squeezed the trigger. Click.

"Did you really think I would let you get into my car with a loaded gun? You are even dumber than I thought," Matteo said as he yanked his gun out of his shoulder holster. He pulled the car to the side of the road and got out. He barked orders at Sal, and seconds later, he exited the vehicle. Sal walked around the side of the car and got behind the driver's wheel. Matteo got into the back seat and pressed the barrel of his own pistol into Marco's temple.

"Now drive, Sal. I'm going to have a little conversation with my stupid big brother on the way to the airport."

The rest of the ride to the airport was uneventful, and Sal pulled the Cadillac alongside the private jet parked on the runway. When the car came to a stop, the door to the jet opened, and steps folded out. Two minutes later, Marco and Sal were screaming over Lake Michigan, headed to an undisclosed location in Central America.

*****

"This is Special Agent Claire Murphy with the Federal Bureau of Investigations, and I am trying to reach Nathan Marchek," she said into the phone on her desk.

"Mr. Marchek is in a meeting right now. Can I tell him what this is concerning?" the young woman replied.

"I am conducting the investigation into the death of one of his employees, and I need to see the autopsy report. I called Walter Reed, but they said the report had been sealed and that I would need director-level approval to see it," Claire said trying to sound as intimidating as she could.

"I will give him the message ma'am," the woman replied again. After the exchange of phone numbers, she hung up.

Claire sat at her desk for a few more moments before she picked up the phone and dialed again. *Why not? she thought to herself as she listened to the phone ring.*

"Central Intelligence Agency, how may I direct your call?"

Claire introduced herself again, but this time she asked to speak to Maxwell Kaine. She knew he would never answer the phone, but she hoped that if she rattled enough cages somebody would take notice.

"He is in a ..." the woman on the other line started to say, but Claire cut her off.

"Meeting. Yes, I have been hearing that all day today. Well, could you pass on a message for me please?" Claire said, repeating the same message to the new secretary, and then she hung up the phone.

An hour later, Claire was called into Roberto Clarke's office. It was nothing out of the ordinary; she was in his office most days for various reasons, so she didn't give it much thought on the short walk down the hall. She knocked on the door and stole a glance at his secretary who seemed to know something that she didn't.

"Come in Claire," the voice on the other side of the door said softly. Roberto Clarke was a nice man, but he was clearly occupying a seat that he had no business sitting in. He was a good agent she had been told, but he had taken to politicking rather than investigating midway through his career. For reasons nobody could remember, he had been promoted to the top job in the building.

"Good afternoon," Claire said and stepped inside.

"Close the door," Clarke said and pulled out a file.

She was growing apprehensive as she watched Clarke fumble with the pages before finally setting them on his desk. *It was like he was arranging his notes before a speech so that he didn't stumble through it,* she thought to herself as he finally had them arranged correctly.

"I'm pulling you off of the case in Cleveland," Clarke said and then held his hands up as he saw Claire starting to protest. "We have enough work to do here, and Mulloy is more than capable of working this on his own."

"Sir, it isn't a Cleveland case. This is a trafficking ring that just happens to have some ties to Cleveland," she said when she was sure that Clarke had finished talking. He was an annoying man who just kept talking and talking. It was almost impossible to interrupt him without being insubordinate, but this was her case. She had been working it for months, and she wasn't going to just drop it.

"I meant the CIA agent case, but I need you to stand down on the trafficking case as well," Clarke retorted and then braced for the impact.

"What?" Claire said not even trying to pretend she wasn't being insubordinate.

"I know, I know. Those orders didn't come from me; they came from the top," Clarke said raising his voice an octave above Claire's.

"What?" She finally managed to say again, "What are you talking about?"

"You are dangerously close to a letter of reprimand Special Agent Larkin. I suggest you start choosing your words more carefully. Turn over all of your notes and stand down. You will have a new assignment on Monday. Now go home and clear your head. This discussion is done. Is that understood Agent Larkin?"

"Yes ... Sir," Claire said and stood to leave.

"It was fantastic work," Clarke said as she left the office, but she didn't respond.

*****

Mack was sitting next to Aubrey's little spaceship, as he liked to call it. Bells, whistles, oxygen, buttons, and dials. It looked like something out of Star Wars. It had been forty-eight hours since Renée's body had been brought back from Walter Reed. He had been at the funeral home all morning making arrangements. He was almost inconsolable when the CIA agent that had accompanied the body back from Walter Reed, told Mack that the coffin had been sealed.

He started trying to open the coffin anyway, but Mina and the CIA agent had talked him down. They had told Mack that an autopsy had been done, and with all the surgeries, it just wasn't possible to have an open casket. It was how the government worked. Once Uncle Sam sealed that coffin, it would take an act of Congress to open it up again. Mack knew the drill. He had been down this road with his fellow Marines many times before. He knew the coffins were not allowed to be opened, but it made him more grief-stricken. He remembered saying goodbye to her just after her CAT scan, before being sent to Walter Reed. He remembered that feeling that he would never see her again, and now he realized he had been right.

He couldn't bear the thought of returning to Mina's house after being at the funeral home, so he drove back to the hospital to sit with Aubrey. Mina's house was just one giant shrine to her only daughter. Pictures of her were everywhere. He knew it helped Mina to be surrounded by all the memorabilia, but it made his pain more intense. Mack had been allowed to hold Aubrey for a short time right after he had arrived at her room. He sat there, feeling her little lungs inflate every time the machine whirled. He played with the little curls that had grown on the temples of her head. One of the nurses had put a tiny pink bow in her hair, and she was wearing a hospital gown that said, "I love my daddy." The nurse gently lifted Aubrey from his arms when it was time to change her diaper.

"Unless you want to do it?" the nurse said playfully.

Mack nodded his head and stood to change the tiny little diaper. Just as he placed the tiny baby back in the crib, he heard a tone he had never heard from all the machines that were helping keep Aubrey alive. It was not the staccato beeping of the ventilator alarm when the pressure had built up on the circuit that he had grown accustomed to, and it wasn't the high-pitched beep that an IV medication had finished infusing. This one was different, and he didn't like the sound of it. Neither did the two nurses who were sitting just outside the room as they came hurrying in and flipped on the lights. The one nurse went directly to the wall and pushed the code blue button, then she immediately began pushing on Aubrey's diminutive chest.

"What's going on?" Mack said as he jumped out of the way.

"She's coding," the nurse said, and she pushed on Aubrey's chest with a force that surprised Mack.

Moments later, the neonatologist on call was in the room giving medication orders. He quickly detached the breathing tube from the ventilator and used the bag to deliver breaths to Aubrey.

"What's happening, Doc?" Mack said, growing more and more frightened by the second.

"Mr. Murphy, I need to focus on what I am doing here, but as soon as other people arrive, I can take a moment to explain things to you, OK?" Dr. Hartwell said in an impossibly polite voice, given the situation.

"Don't let her go. Do whatever you have to do. I can't lose her too," Mack said more to himself than anybody else in the room.

One hour later, Mack barely heard Dr. Hartwell sit down beside him. He explained that Aubrey's lungs had given out. The pressure in her little lungs got too high, and it caused a pneumothorax. It meant that the lung had popped like a balloon, and now there was air on the wrong side of the lung tissue. The lack of oxygen caused her little heart to quit beating, and she never regained a heartbeat. He asked Mack if he wanted to hold her, and Mack said he would.

The beeping and buzzing noises were gone, and Mack was left with the ten-pound baby girl all wrapped up in a pink blanket with monkeys on it. She was nestled in the crook of his arm, and he was singing softly to her as he rocked her back and forth in the rocking chair. Her little chest heaved a few times, but the nurses had prepared him for that. It still unnerved him, and he almost cried out for the nurse when her whole body shook. He held her tightly and watched the life drain from his little girl. Aubrey was definitely his baby. While Brianna had the caramel skin of her mother, Aubrey's skin was a very Irish shade of white.

Mack cried for the millionth time in the last two weeks. Renée's body was at the funeral home preparing for the burial with Brianna, and now he would have to go through the same process for the third time in as many weeks for his little Aubrey. Mina was at home when Aubrey passed, but he didn't have the heart to tell her what had happened over the phone.

Mack knew Aubrey was gone, but his arms clung to the little bundle. He quietly willed the child to start breathing again. It had been five minutes, but it felt like a blink. He tried to finish the song he had been singing, but he couldn't. His jaw was tense and sore. He thought it was the first time in his life that he had sore muscles from crying. He just sat there for what seemed like forever, staring at the little pink monkies on the blanket. He had never been one for praying, but today he made an exception. The first thing he prayed for was the strength to go on, all while knowing that he would rather be praying for his own death. The next thing he prayed for was a name. The name of the man who was driving the Porsche, who had unleashed this desolation.

He didn't hear the nurse when she asked him if it would be OK to take the baby. He just nodded and watched the little pink bundle disappear from the room. Moments later, the nurse handed him the little pink blanket and the matching rattle before quietly leaving the room. Mack stared down at the little pink blanket and remembered the day he bought it in the hospital gift shop. It was the day that Aubrey and Brianna were born. The blankets came with matching rattles. Aubrey's blanket came with a little pink monkey holding a miniature version of the blanket. He quietly wondered what Aubrey would have called the little monkey if she had lived long enough to give it a name. He thought about the little purple blanket with the Teddy bears that belonged to Brianna.

Mack didn't know what time it was when the nurse came in to ask if there was anything she could do for him. He knew it was a polite way of saying it was time to go, so he stood up and thanked her. The tears were dry, but the pain still seared a hole straight through his heart. He walked out of the hospital for the last time and got into the government sedan for the twenty-minute-drive home.

All the way home, Mack thought about his girls. How cruel life could be. He knew that death was final. He knew that there was a God; he just wasn't sure he wanted to meet a God who could put one of his children through the kind of pain he had just endured. It would have been one thing if all three girls had been killed instantly in the crash. He would have had one tragedy to endure. The fact that all three of his girls had died at different times was like going through hell three times. He knew it was just an expression, but he figured if hell were real, it would probably feel a lot like how he felt at that moment.

Mack decided that he couldn't go home just yet. He knew he had to tell Mina about Aubrey, but he also knew there was a limit to what you could ask a person to endure. He had really come to love Mina over the past two weeks, and the thought of seeing her face when he broke the news was too much for him right now. Mack drove for an hour before turning the big sedan toward Mina's home.

CHAPTER 16

The day of the funeral was cold and rainy. There were over 500 people in the small church in Olmsted Falls, and most of them accompanied the two coffins to the cemetery. Maxwell Kaine and George Seifert from the Central Intelligence Agency were there to pay their respects. Besides them, Mack only recognized a few faces. One close cousin of Renée's, one of her high school friends he had only met once, and one very tired-looking Marine who had traveled all the way from Afghanistan to be with him. Spencer Williams had been given two weeks of leave, and he brought letters from every member of Charlie Company. He had brought a cashier's check as well for over $10,000. Everyone in the entire company had pitched in to help with the funeral costs. Mack told him the agency had covered all the expenses, but Spencer refused to refund the money. "Use it for yourself then, brother. It's the guys' way of saying *sorry*, and to hand it back would be a slap in the face."

Mack agreed and then slipped the check into his pocket.

The pastor of the Baptist Church that Renée had grown up in had traveled from Newport News and gave the eulogy at a very moving service. He asked Mack if he wanted to say anything at the graveside, but Mack was pretty sure he would just turn into a blubbering fool, so he declined.

Twelve Marines from the local reserve unit showed up for the funeral and did an amazing job of carrying the caskets. Their dress blue uniforms were crisp, and the 21-gun salute was perfectly timed. The first volley of gunfire startled Mack and brought back a lot of memories from Afghanistan. He shot Spencer a quick glance and realized that he had jumped a little too.

The graveside service was very moving as well; Maxwell Kaine gave a very patriotic speech. George Seifert recounted meeting Renée and how much he admired her. He spoke about her service to the country and how sad he was that she was gone. He did his best to say some comforting words about the two girls, but there wasn't much to say. They were only three months old. Mack decided on a whim to say something about his babies, but he was pretty sure nobody could make out any of his words over his sobs.

Finally, Mina moved forward and placed flowers on the coffins, and everybody fell in behind her to do the same. When everyone had filed away, Mack was left alone, sitting in a metal, folding chair two feet from the coffins. He knew he should be with Mina, but his stubborn pride kept him anchored to the coffins. It would be all over once those coffins went into the ground, and the only thing left of his girls would be the memories. An hour had slowly ticked by, and Mack noticed another car in the parking lot with somebody sitting behind the wheel. He squinted through the fog and realized it was Spencer. Mack knew that Spencer would sit there for a year and a half if Mack needed him to, but he began to feel guilty.

Mack thought back to the last mission he was on in Afghanistan with Spencer, and it made him long to return to his unit. He knew the Corps wouldn't let him return to combat duty, but he missed his brothers. He was so grateful for Spencer being there, but that was Spencer. Mack's brother didn't fly in for the funeral and only sent a sympathy card after Brianna's death. He doubted if he even knew that Renée was dead. He knew the phone operated both ways, but he was good with the arrangement.

The last time he saw his brother Kit, was moments after punching him in the face on the front porch of his house. His brother took to booze after their father passed, and Mack had had enough one night. It was just before he was set to leave for college in Missoula, and his brother accused him of killing their mother. Mack had heard the accusation from his father before, but that night it didn't go over well. Mack pulled back and knocked him right off the porch and into the front yard. He was down the three steps and in the front yard when Kit stood to his feet, so Mack put him back down. He told him what a lousy brother he was for blaming his mother's death on a newborn baby, and he got into his truck and never saw his brother again.

He had gone home a few days later to retrieve his belongings, but his brother was out working on the ranch and didn't see him. He had only talked to him on the phone twice since that day. The first time was when Kit called to tell them that the ranch was being foreclosed on, and the second was when he called for bail money. Some brothers are picked out for you, and some brothers you pick out for yourself. Spencer was the latter.

The night of the funeral, Mack and Spencer were throwing back a few beers in Mina's basement. They talked about the guys and a few of the missions that they had been on in Mack's absence. They talked about the latest arguments between O'Malley and Apollo. The conversation even wound its way back to Sass and how badly the guys were taking it. It was after they finished talking about Sass that Spencer turned somber.

"Hey, brother, I just want you to know I'm sorry for what you've been through. Nobody should have to go through what you just did."

Mack started to reply, but Spencer cut him off.

"I didn't say that to get a thank you. I didn't say that to console you.

I said it because I meant it. I think that a part of you died right along with your wife and daughters, and I'm worried about you."

Mack started to reply again, but Spencer put his hand up in a gesture to tell him to be quiet.

"I don't want you to say a thing. I know you are grateful that I am here. I know you know how sorry I am, but I need to tell you this before I go back. When Lara was killed on 9/11, I went to a dark place. I mean, it wasn't just a dark place; it was a horrible place. I spent the first few months contemplating suicide. Anything just to see her again; it didn't matter. I started trying to figure out the easiest way to go. Shooting myself seemed easiest, but I didn't want anybody to find my body. I thought about pills, but I figured that was how women did it. I figured I would just head out into the mountains and disappear, and eventually, I would succumb to the elements.

I finally got past those feelings when a new set of emotions started taking root. I spent most nights trying to come up with a plan to kill everyone even remotely involved in the attacks. I plotted my revenge slowly and methodically, and when we got to Afghanistan, I was like a coyote in a henhouse. I wanted to kill every single one of them, and I damn sure tried. The more of them I killed, the deeper my pain got.

Revenge is like cancer, Mack. It is going to eat you up, and I just don't want you to go there. I have been watching you today, and you are acting exactly the way I did when Lara died. I know you better than you think I do, and I see the wheels turning in there," Spencer said, pointing at Mack's head. "I don't have any answers. I don't have any advice other than this. I want you to hear me when I tell you this, and I want your word that you will think about what I have to say long and hard. Don't go there! Don't let your brain start plotting your suicide or fantasizing about *your* revenge, or it will grab ahold of your soul, and it won't let go until it is too late.

The night you left Afghanistan, I hurt for you like I haven't hurt in a long time. When I found out that they had all died, I died too. A part of me died right along with the part of you that died. You are my best friend, and I am telling you this right now. If you have any thoughts of getting even, of seeking revenge, please, please, please just let it go."

Mack shifted in his chair as he watched the emotions on Spencer's face. He felt his own emotions swirling around again. His first emotion when Spencer started talking was anger. How dare he tell me what to do and what not to do? What does he know about this pain? But then he realized that Spencer knew exactly what he was going through. Mack's next emotion was regret. Regret for being upset with the one man who came to help him bury his family. Regret that he had never seen how much Spencer was hurting. Regret that he had never reached out to Spencer the way he had just reached out to him.

Mack's last thought was guilt. Spencer had laid bare every thought he had for the past three weeks, and he was right. Mack had been dreaming of revenge; he had been plotting. He thought that the word *plotting* was too innocent. He had been fantasizing about his *revenge*. Spencer had nailed it.

"Spence, I don't know what to say. You're right; it's exactly what I have been doing. It is exactly what I have been planning, and I don't know how to stop. I don't know how to turn that part of me off, and it scares me. How did you turn it off?"

"I haven't. I just learned to hide it better than most people. I still dream of killing these people. I fantasize about it too. It has ruined me. I used to be a happy-go-lucky guy who spent his time drinking beer and having fun. I don't care about that stuff anymore. All I care about anymore is killing. It occupies my every thought, and I can't stop. That is why I am telling you not to even start. It's like crack, man. You kill one of them, and suddenly, no amount of killing will satisfy you."

"So, what do I do?" Mack finally said.

"I don't know, but I have a few suggestions. Don't go back to the Corps. They will be more than happy to indulge your lust for blood. Get out of the Corps. Go be a dog sledder, a charter fisherman captain, a circus clown. Hell, I don't care what you do. Just do something else. Mack, you are a good man, but I know how this ends for people like us. It gets in our heads, and nothing will get it out."

"I have three years left on my contract. I can't get out," Mack said.

"Yes, you can. I spoke with Apollo, and he said he could get you an honorable discharge with no strings attached. Just say the word."

Mack stood in the basement and looked at the pictures hanging on the wall. He thought about what Spencer just said, and it made sense. Spencer was right on. "I don't know, Spence. I love the Corps. I love what I do. I don't know if I would even be good at anything else."

"You will be the best at whatever you decide to do. Just decide to do it, and the rest will fall in place."

The two sat in silence for another ten minutes before Spencer stood and said, "Come on, I have something for you."

Mack followed him up the stairs and out to his car. He popped the trunk lid and pulled out Mack's gear from Afghanistan. "It's all here. More than enough to keep you warm and comfortable for a few months. Put it all on your back, and get out of here for a few months. I have a buddy who runs a guide trip down the Pacific Crest Trail. It is 2,653 miles of the most beautiful scenery you have ever seen. This is the best time to start it if you are heading North. It starts in Southern California and goes all the way to Canada. You may not remember this, but you and I talked about doing it when we were in SCUBA school."

"I do remember that," Mack said, smiling. "We were so tired of being in the water, we thought it would be nice to walk for a few thousand miles." The two of them stood in the driveway, laughing about it.

"I'd go with you, but I feel like this might be something you need to do on your own," Spencer said, and then they both returned to the basement. "I have one more thing to say to you, and this is the most important, so keep your mouth shut until I'm done."

Mack gave Spencer a mock salute, sat back in his chair, and opened another beer. "I know all the feelings that are going to be running through your head in the coming weeks and months. I have been there, brother, and trust me when I say that people like you and I are not good with this stuff. We don't take stuff like this lying down. We don't go and cry on some headshrinker's couch and swallow pills to make the pain go away. We take the pain head on, and we feel every ounce of it because we think we need to. We think that shouldering all the grief will make it just a little easier. We guilt ourselves into thinking that happiness is over, and a normal life is a thing of the past."

Spencer knew he was getting through to Mack as he watched him shifting uncomfortably in his chair. "This is the last thing I want to say to you, and I need you to hear me Lima Charlie brother. It isn't a matter of *if* you get to feeling that eating a bullet would make things better; it's a matter of *when*. So, *when* that time comes for you, I want you to remember one thing. If you pull that trigger, then they win. If you whack yourself, then all the dirtbags who have ever lived will be the winners that day. You are one of the good guys, and don't ever forget that. If you decide that you are going to go after them and kill them all, I need you to know that you can call me, and I'll be there faster than you can hang up the phone. And when I get there, we'll kill em all together. Do you hear me, Mack? Do you hear me?" Spencer said louder.

Mack just sat there staring at Spencer for a few minutes before he stuck out his fist. "I hear ya, brother."

Spencer bumped his fist with his own, and they sat in silence for a few more minutes before turning in for the night.

Spencer spent a few days with Mack after the funeral before heading back to Texas to see his parents with his remaining leave time. Mack saw him off at the airport and thanked him again. They hugged just before the security checkpoint, and Spencer made him promise to think about what they had discussed. Mack agreed and said, "I'll see you when I see you."

Mack left the airport feeling restless. He had started going through Renée's things with Spencer's help, but he eventually had to ask Mina to keep them all in storage. He couldn't do it, not yet.

Mack had nowhere to go when he left the airport. He couldn't go back to Mina's. Seeing all Renée's and the babies' things lying around was too painful. He needed to think, and the best way to do that was to drive. He had grown up in Montana, and there was no shortage of open road to process his thoughts. He called Mina on his cell phone and told her that he had to head back to Camp Lejeune, but he would be back in a few days. He checked into a room at a small, out-of-the-way hotel just outside downtown Cleveland close to the bus stop. He ordered a pizza from a local restaurant and sat on the bed waiting for it. He pulled on a set of headphones to tune out the rap music playing in the room next to him and conducted a mental inventory of his life.

Many of his friends from the service had gotten out only to find that life on the outside was more than they could take. He liked Spencer's idea of hiking the Pacific Crest Trail, but he was pretty sure he wouldn't be doing that anytime soon. He had kept in touch with a few of his friends who had processed out, and every one of them told him they missed their friends, the camaraderie, and the adrenaline. Mack missed these things, but in Mack's case, he missed so much more. He would be lying if he didn't admit to himself that suicide looked like the only way out. He knew where his guns were, and he knew he could get to them. He knew that if he got drunk enough, he could pull the trigger, and that was precisely what he had been planning to do.

The following morning, he brought the government car back to the recruiter's station. Next, he went to the bank and cashed the check Spencer had given him and withdrew the rest of his savings account for a total of $14,000. He bought a one-way ticket to Jacksonville, NC, and settled in for the twelve-hour ride. He watched the countryside flash past him on his way down I-77 until it got dark, crossing into North Carolina. At a little past ten in the evening, he arrived at the small apartment he and Renée had rented just off the base.

He wasn't prepared for the emotions that hit him the second he walked into the kitchen. There was a picture of the girls' ultrasounds hanging on the refrigerator and a copy of the same picture that he had carried in his helmet. Mack opened the refrigerator and remembered exactly why he loved Renée so much. Inside was a box of Arm and Hammer baking soda and nothing else. The woman was a meticulous planner and never forgot a thing. She went to her mother's house a week before the girls were born and left the apartment spotless. He wasn't sure where she got the energy to clean just a week away from having twins, but it didn't surprise him.

He was returning from Okinawa and planned on flying into Cleveland directly before the birth. His flight from Japan was delayed. Luckily, Renée didn't go into labor for another two days. He made it home with just a few hours to spare before his beautiful twins made their grand appearance.

The next day, he retrieved the three fake passports and the two Beretta 92FS 9mm pistols that Renée had given him, just in case he decided to go through with his plan. They were in a safe deposit box at a Credit Union in Jacksonville. Renée had explained that she might have to get out of the country in a hurry and that most agents had cash and passports in safe deposit boxes just like this one. She told him that she couldn't disappear without him, so she made sure he had the same means of escape.

Along with the passports was an encrypted message that only Mack and Renée could decipher. The note had three locations on it and an email address they could each access if necessary. It all seemed so pointless now. The time they had spent plotting their someday escape seemed like a foolish endeavor.

He caught a cab and went back to the base to retrieve his few belongings from his wall locker. His old pickup truck was still in the Lemon Lot, so he pulled the keys out from underneath the bumper and hopped in. It fired up on the first crank. *Man, I love this truck,* he thought to himself. When he bought his Excursion, he just couldn't part with the truck, so he left it on base. He had told Renée he would try to sell it while he was in Afghanistan, but he didn't try really hard.

His unit was still in Afghanistan, so the barracks were pretty deserted. Mack wanted to see a few of his friends before he headed back to Cleveland, but when he knocked on their doors, he didn't get an answer. It was almost 2100 hours, so he knew where they would most likely be found.

Mack walked through the front door of the Driftwood to see if he could find any old friends. The Driftwood needed no explanation to any Marine who had ever served time at Camp Lejeune. Mack had only been there once, and he vowed never to return. The place was nice in a seedy way, but he had gone to celebrate his promotion to staff sergeant at the urging of his friends, who had rented a private room for the event. Much to the disappointment of his fellow Marines, he simply drank several beers and was courteous to the ladies. He made eye contact with them as he talked to them and never let his eyes wander elsewhere. He had been engaged to Renée at the time, and it just didn't feel right to him, but friends were friends. He felt embarrassed the entire night, but knew his friends were enjoying themselves, so he tried to relax.

To Mack's surprise, the bar was deserted. He was about to leave when the waitress asked him if he wanted anything to drink. He didn't feel particularly thirsty, but didn't feel like returning to the apartment either, so he sat down. He sat at the bar with his back to the stage the entire night, checking the faces of everyone who entered the bar, but he didn't see anyone he recognized. He had a long discussion with Brittany, the bartender. Turned out she was in law school and was about to finish. What did Mack know about this world? He assumed everyone in there had a sob story or a hard luck life landing them in such a place, but he liked the young girl. At 2:00 a.m., he asked Brittany to call him a cab, and he grabbed his sweatshirt and headed for the door. Just as he was about to get into the cab, he heard a familiar voice behind him telling him to wait.

"You forgot your hat," Brittany said, holding it out for Mack.

He took his hat and said, "Thank you," and then turned to get into the cab when Brittany spoke again. "I know who you are, by the way, and I just wanted to say how sorry I am for what happened to you. I wasn't going to tell you. I just assumed you were here to forget about all that for a while." There were moments of awkward silence until Brittany finally said, "Well, good night, Mack. If you ever need to talk again, you know where to find me."

"Thank you, Brittany. I would love to see you again, but maybe you could put more clothes on next time." They both smiled, and Mack got into the cab. He went to put his University of Montana camouflaged trucker hat on as the cab pulled away from the curb when he realized that there was a bar napkin inside his hat. On the napkin was a phone number and the name Julie. Under the name, she wrote, "If you ever need to talk." Mack smiled to himself and realized that Brittany was just her stage name, and he had just been hit on by a stripper.

It wasn't until he crawled into bed that he realized that the young lady at the bar said she knew him. She had called him by name, and he knew he had not given it to her. How did she know him? He had only been there one time. He didn't remember that she was the one who had danced for him. She was just doing her job, but she knew there was something different about this one. He wasn't there to look at naked girls. She could tell it made him uncomfortable, and it made her feel even worse for what she was doing. He had given her his name, and she didn't forget it. When the local news aired the story of what had happened to his wife and children, Julie had been crushed.

CHAPTER 17

Two months after the funeral, Mack was sitting on Renée's grave, staring at the headstone. It was a peaceful place in the western suburbs of Cleveland, Ohio. He had meticulously maintained the grave over the past two months. He had spent nearly every day there since he had returned from North Carolina. The cemetery was deserted, except for a few groundskeepers. He was surrounded by Canadian maples and giant birch trees. The grass that had been cut away to dig the grave had been laid back over the caskets after the funeral, but it didn't have time to grow before the snow fell.

Mack stared up through the leafless tree that cast a meager shadow over Renée's headstone and saw the mostly cloudy sky through the bare branches. He glanced off and on at the stone next to Renée's as well for the past three hours. His heart was heavy as he stared at the names that brought him so much joy a few short months ago.

Brianna Browning Murphy - August 11, 2004, to November 21, 2004.
Aubrey Barrett Murphy - August 11, 2004, to November 29, 2004.
Renée Zaafirah Murphy - April 20, 1976, to November 25, 2004.

They had all been buried together. Both babies in the same coffin directly above Renée's. That was the way Mack had wanted it. The funeral home initially balked at the idea, but the manager quickly relented when they saw the look on Mack's face. It was an unusually warm day in early February, and the sun had just started to dip below the horizon. Mack felt the first shiver as the temperature began dropping with the sun. For the past three hours, Mack had been sipping the bottle of Jameson he had brought with him, and he was finally feeling the warmth radiating out from his abdomen. He hadn't drunk enough for what he was about to do, but he figured it wouldn't matter.

The flood of memories returned to him in a way he hadn't been ready for. He remembered giving Renée the nickname Pep on the *USS Peleliu*. He remembered the day he proposed to her in Okinawa, Japan. He remembered how beautiful she looked, nursing two beautiful baby girls. As the first hint of night fell on the deserted cemetery, he pulled the gun from his jacket pocket and stared down at it for a long moment. He started talking out loud to Renée as if she were standing right there.

"Pep, I'm hurting pretty good right now. I feel lost in a storm. I don't know where to go from here, and I need you to help me. I want to see you and the babies again so bad it makes me physically hurt inside." Mack held the gun up against his chin and went on. "I could come see you right now, Pep. Believe me, I want to come see you." He lowered the gun and let the emotion sweep over him, sending his body into a small convulsion of anguish. His chest started to heave up and down again as the sobs overtook him. He cried out loud enough to be heard from a mile away. "*Why?* Why did this have to happen to me?" he screamed so loud his voice gave out.

Mack stuck the gun to the side of his head with his chest heaving up and down. He clenched his teeth and closed his eyes as he started to let the slack out of the trigger. He squeezed a little more and felt the spring begin to move. He had been hoping that this would be easy, but it wasn't. He had been hoping he would have the courage to pull the trigger when the time came, but he didn't. The trigger was a hair's breadth from releasing the firing pin, and Mack's tears were flowing like a faucet. Just as he thought he had pulled the trigger as far as he could, he felt something brush his hand. He let the tension off the trigger and lowered the gun to find that a leaf had fallen onto his hand. It sat there perfectly balanced as a fresh wave of raw emotion coursed through him.

Mack instinctively looked back up at the tree, and it was what he didn't see that troubled him. There wasn't a single leaf on the entire Canadian maple tree. The harsh Midwest Ohio winter had stripped from it every semblance of life. He couldn't help but realize that he felt much like that tree. Ohio had stripped away everything that had meant something to him as well. He remembered the poem, and he remembered the leaf that he had taken from the Kashmir elm tree he was sitting beneath on his first patrol in Afghanistan. He remembered putting the leaf into the small clear envelope that Renée had given him.

Mack realized that the leaf had been a survivor. That leaf had hung in there through the harshest winds that blew off the Great Lake and stubbornly refused to fall. For the first time in three months, Mack knew what he needed to do. No, it wasn't a need. Mack knew what he had to do. He felt it as sure as he felt the chilly February wind on his neck.

Mack wasn't sure if he could name what had to be done. It wasn't revenge on that scumbag Marco Bertoli, although he felt it was his responsibility to prevent him from doing it again. It was more like ... a settling of the accounts. It was ... a reckoning. Mack's next thought was about what Spencer had told him the night of the funeral. He realized Spencer knew all too well the emotions that he would be going through, and he was spot on. He recalled something else Spencer told him that night. He remembered Spencer telling him that the feelings never went away, that he had learned to conceal his emotions from everyone. Mack knew that he would have to do exactly what Spencer had done.

His life was over. Never again would he have the effortless smile and good-natured humor about him. Something was dead in his soul, buried alive. Mack decided that suicide was an option he could leave on the table if he needed it, but right now, what he wanted more than anything in the world was to see Marco Bertoli's head explode an instant after he pulled the trigger of his Beretta 92 FS service pistol. Mack put the tiny Canadian maple leaf into his coat pocket. He flipped the safety switch on his pistol and stood to leave.

"Pep, you know what I'm thinking, and it makes me feel ashamed. I know you would never approve of what I am about to do, but I can't stop it any more than I could stop what happened to you. Forgive me, Pep. I love you so much. I know you would not be proud of the man I am about to become, but it's taken ahold of me and won't let me go. I'll see you again someday. Maybe when this is over, I'll do something to make you proud of me again." Mack knelt in the snow, pulled the built-in bronze vase out from the headstone, and dropped his dog tags into it. He put the piece of paper that he had laminated into the vase as well before closing it back up. On the piece of paper was the Elizabeth Barrett Browning poem that had made him think of Renée in the past two months.

> *"I tell you, hopeless grief is passionless—*
> *That only men incredulous of despair,*
> *Half-taught in anguish, through the midnight air,*
> *Beat upward to God's throne in loud access*
> *Of shrieking and reproach. Full desertness*
> *In souls, as countries, lieth silent-bare*
> *Under the blenching, vertical eye-glare*
> *Of the absolute Heavens. Deep-hearted man,*
> *Express Grief for thy Dead in silence like to death;*
> *Most like a monumental statue set*
> *In everlasting watch and moveless woe,*
> *Till itself crumble to the dust beneath!*

Touch it! The marble eyelids are not wet—
If it could weep, it could arise and go."

Mack peeled himself away from the headstones and started to walk back toward the truck. He got a few steps away from the truck and stopped. He turned around and took one last look. His tears had dried, and he remembered his favorite line from Homer's Iliad. "He grieves, he weeps, but then his tears are through. The Fates have given mortals hearts that can endure."

Who was doing the weeping? Was it Priam weeping for Hector or Achilles weeping for Patroclus? Mack tried to remember. His brain finally told him that it didn't matter. The point was that no amount of killing in Homer's books ever made things right. It didn't stop the man gods from trying, though. Mack had the thought of dragging the body of whoever killed his girls behind his truck for twelve days, just like Achilles had. His next thought was that he should feel ashamed of himself for that. His third thought was that he didn't feel ashamed at all, *Marco Bertoli needed killing.* "This must be what Spencer was talking about," Mack thought. He finally turned again and climbed into his truck. He had the overwhelming sensation that his tears were through. He couldn't imagine shedding another one. Surely whatever part of the body that produced tears had to have broken down by now.

Mack knew the day was fast approaching when he would have to return to the Corps. He had been given three months of hardship leave after Renée and his children were killed. It was almost up. Mack considered going back early, but his unit was set to rotate back from Afghanistan anyway, and he knew they wouldn't send him back to combat. He knew the Marine Corps didn't trust him to be ready for the high stakes of combat so soon after burying his wife and children, but they didn't say it outright. It didn't bother him; he had nowhere else to go. The police had indicted Marco Bertoli, but rumor had it that he had fled the country. Mack hadn't heard from the police department, so justice seemed like it would never happen anyway. He had read the papers incessantly, searching for leads into the investigation but came up empty.

Mack had been reassigned to a training battalion at Camp Lejeune for a few weeks until Charlie Company returned from Afghanistan. In the Marine Corps' infinite wisdom, they assumed a new unit would make the stress easier. He just accepted his new orders and began preparing for the long drive back to Jacksonville, NC.

When the day finally came, Mina walked him to his truck to see him off, and to make sure he knew he was still her son, even if Renée was gone. Mina cried a little as Mack climbed into the truck. He rolled the window down and promised to call from time to time to let her know how he was doing. Mina watched him go with the suspicion that she was seeing him for the last time.

Mina was a tough woman and knew better than to hope for things beyond her control. She just watched from the curb until Mack was out of sight and walked back inside to resume her life of quiet anguish. She knew a new chapter in her life was unfolding; she just didn't feel like reading it yet. At fifty-eight years of age, Mina was not in the habit of making life-changing decisions. However, over the next several months, she did just that. She sold everything she had, placed her precious belongings in a storage shed, and booked a flight to Islamabad, Pakistan. She had found a job with a nongovernmental agency working as a translator. Her ultimate goal was to be able to walk into Afghanistan when the war ended and reconnect with her Afghani roots.

She had been to Afghanistan once when Renée was just a child after the war with Russia had ended. She accompanied her mother and father to their homeland in Afghanistan and fell in love with Kabul. She vividly remembered her father picking berries from a mulberry tree and handing them to her by the handfuls. The smells on the streets of Kabul were intoxicating. She couldn't imagine what the city looked like today after years of war, but she longed to return. It wasn't something tangible; it wasn't a sense of patriotism to a country she didn't belong to anymore. It was the need to belong to something. She had always felt like a foreigner in the United States. She just looked too different, behaved too differently, and believed differently. She was a Christian, no doubt, but she remembered her grandparents telling her that Christians were common in Afghanistan in the fifties and sixties. She wanted to bring her faith to her people, but more than anything, she just wanted to have a people.

Mack drove down I-77, heading toward Camp Lejeune with the radio silent. He used to let the radio blare whenever he got into the truck, but since the death of the girls, driving had become an escape for him. He would stare out the window and think. Mostly he thought of the many ways he would kill Marco Bertoli, the man who had brought such grief upon his family. He couldn't shake the feeling that he was turning into a totally different man. If he were honest with himself, there was no real turning involved. It was more like a switch had been flipped. As he remembered hearing Mina's words that night telling him that Renée was gone, he was certain he knew exactly when the switch had been flipped.

Mack drove for hours with nothing but the rumbling of the old engine and the whine of the tires on the road to keep him company. Driving always brought back memories of growing up in Montana. He remembered his grandfather, Waya Kanati, driving the old '57 Chevy pickup into town with him and his brother Kit, sitting in the bed of the truck with Waya's dog, Raven. She was half wolf, half husky and fiercely loyal and protective of the two young boys. He could feel the dog's hair whipping around his eyes as he hugged him. He watched the mountains of Glacier Park disappearing behind him as they drove down the highway toward the little town of Browning.

Mack remembered hunting with Waya Kanati on the reservation with the long bow and arrow that Waya had made for Mack's tenth birthday. He felt the tension in his chest as he drew the arrow back, staring the big bull elk in the eyes. When he let the arrow fly, it struck the elk right through the heart, and Waya Kanati shouted with excitement. It was Mack's first kill.

Mack remembered Waya Kanati telling him about his mother and how beautiful she was. His mother, Ahyoka Kanati was Waya's and Wawetseka's only child. Her name meant, "She brings happiness," and Waya loved her more than anything else in the world. He explained to Mack and Kit that someday they would understand the depths of a father's love—when they had children of their own. Mack smiled at the memory as the old Ford truck rumbled down the highway.

*****

Mulloy picked up the report that had been thrown on his desk earlier that day and saw that it was from the ballistics lab. He started reading it but knew what it was going to say. The shell casing had indeed been a 7.62 x 25, but there were no fingerprints on the brass casing. He called the evidence room to ensure that it would be tagged for the trial if he were ever to get his hands on Marco Bertoli. The officer in charge of the Cleveland evidence locker answered the phone when Mulloy called and promised to tag the bullet casing as soon as it came back from the ballistics lab. Next, Mulloy checked his email to see if he had any leads from the BOLO (be on the lookout) he had issued a few months earlier, but nothing. He had planned to make a trip to see Vinny Bertoli later that day since customs had just informed him that he was back in the country. He was hoping to have something to go on before the meeting in case Vinny decided to be cooperative, which he doubted would be the case, but better to be prepared.

Mulloy rang the bell and waited a moment before a young woman in a maid's uniform answered the door. "My name is Special Agent Patrick Mulloy with the FBI, and this is Special Agent Adam Millson. Is Vincenzo Bertoli here?" Mulloy could see the woman was frightened, so he went on to say, "He is not in trouble, ma'am, but I do need to speak to him."

"Mr. Bertoli does not live here, sirs. This is the home of Giuseppe Rigo." The woman held up her finger, "I will go get him for you," she finally said with a thick Spanish accent.

Ten to one, she's here illegally, Millson thought as he unlatched the holster under his suit coat. *Better safe than sorry,* he thought.

Thirty seconds later, the woman returned to the door, followed by a middle-aged man in a business suit. "Mr. Bertoli does not live here, as I'm sure Rosario just told you," the big man said, pointing at the maid. "But I am pretty sure you already knew that. What do you want?" Giuseppe Rigo said.

"Is your son Salvatore Rigo?" Millson said.

"You know he is. What do you want?"

"We are looking…"

"It was a rhetorical question. I don't care what you want?" Giuseppe said, raising his voice.

"We need to speak to your son. Can you tell me where I can find him and what is a good time to pay him a visit?" Millson said, stepping closer to the door.

"How does *never* work for you?" Giuseppe said, staring at Millson, almost daring him to take another step forward.

Mulloy tried to defuse the situation and asked Giuseppe if he had seen his son lately.

"None of your business," he said and closed the door.

"Well, that went better than we expected," Millson said sarcastically. "Now what?"

Mulloy started to head back to the car but stopped. He spun around and went back to the door and knocked again. He waited a few moments and then knocked again. He was about to knock a third time, but the door flew open, and there stood Giuseppe in the doorway, looking irritated. "What do you want to know now? My favorite color?"

"No, I just didn't get a chance to tell you something. It's the reason I came here," Mulloy replied.

"What?"

"I wanted to tell you that I know where your son is," Mulloy said.

"And where is that?" The big man said shifting on his feet.

"About to be standing on death row," Mulloy said and scraped the bottom of his chin with his fingers extended at the man in the doorway. Giuseppe let loose a steady stream of curses, but Mulloy had already turned to leave. The door slammed shut as Millson turned to catch up to him.

"What was all that about?" Millson said, chuckling.

"I wanted to see if he really knew where his son was."

"And does he?"

"He does. His body language was screaming it, even if his filthy mouth didn't say it."

"How do you know?"

"Did you see the way he started shifting on his feet when I told him I knew where Sal was?"

"Yeah."

"He was worried. He tried to cover it up by asking a rhetorical question. 'And where is that?'" Mulloy mimicked. "He tried to sound surprised, but he already knew where he was."

"Now what?" Millson said.

"Now we wait for them to mess up. I guarantee you he is on the phone right now, telling Marco and Sal to get in the wind. He had to assume we were closing in on them. Now he knows we are."

"I don't think it is going to be that easy," Millson said. "The two of them are probably out of the country, hiding in some little town in Mexico where we will never find them. Are we still going to pay a visit to Bertoli?"

"We don't need to," Mulloy said as he clapped Millson on the back. "If Larkin is right, and I don't see any reason why she isn't, they will be chomping at the bit to get back here. If he is running a flesh market, he will want to get back to work soon. Besides, he isn't exactly on the way up the ladder. His younger brother is going to be taking over for the old man, so he needs to carve out his own little niche, and he can't do it from the other side of the border."

Millson and Mulloy got back in the car and drove a few blocks away. The plan had worked perfectly. They had stalled the old man long enough for the other agents to get the surveillance equipment in place. The phone had been tapped, and the directional microphone was pointed directly at the front window of Giuseppe's house. Giuseppe Rigo may have been high up on the Mafia food chain, but he didn't have the resources to install a very good security system. The listening devices were up and running, and Mulloy called the other agents for an update.

"He's making a phone call now. I'll put it on speaker."

"Vinny, hey. I just had two feds at my house. How are the boys?"

"I have no idea, you fool. Hang up the phone," Vinny cursed before the line went dead.

"Well, at least one of them has some common sense," Millson said.

The plan was still going well as Vincenzo opened a new burner phone and started dialing some numbers. The triangulation software was crunching the signal and doing its best to locate where the call was going. After several minutes, the computer screen flashed a location in Guadalajara.

"It's just that easy," Mulloy said as Millson shook his head. Millson was a rookie, but he had great potential. Mulloy liked him too, so that made his job much easier. "Now we just have to send somebody down there to spook him, and we can sit back and watch him run."

"Why don't we just pick him up in Mexico?" Millson said.

"Because it will take months to get him extradited here. His father is a very powerful man, and the second he lands in Mexican custody, he will be gone for good. He will be back, and I don't think it will take long."

CHAPTER 18

Marietta closed the door behind her and slid the four padlocks into place. She put the key into the deadbolt from the inside and locked it too. Security was her number one concern. She dropped her backpack on the small table by the door and then hung her keys on the hook. She was from Moldova where summers could be brutally hot, but she had never experienced humidity like this. The wind blowing off of the lake seemed like a sheet of hot water, and it drenched her T-shirt and jeans the moment she left the apartment. She shuddered for a second and let the relative cool of the apartment complex wash over her.

She left the lights off as she checked the thermostat and turned it down a few clicks. The air conditioning was part of her rent, so she took full advantage of it. She pulled her soaking T-shirt off and dropped it into the hamper. The bra came next before she grabbed a new T-Shirt from her closet and pulled it over her head. She lit the gas stove and put a kettle of water on for tea. When she finally managed to stop sweating, she sat down on the worn bar stool and peered through the telescope. It wasn't a very nice telescope, but it got the job done. Once she had the front door of the Foxxy nightclub in focus, she attached the camcorder and started recording. She didn't want to miss a single person going in or out.

Where are you Collette? Where are you my sweet little sister? Marietta said to herself for the millionth time. It was more of a prayer than a thought. She thought if she could say it enough, she would be able to find her. She felt like the millions around the world chanting ridiculous prayers while fumbling around with beads. She didn't believe in God. If God were real, then she had no desire to know somebody who could allow the type of cruelty she had endured. She closed her eyes and drifted back to that fateful day in Chișinău, Moldova.

*****

Marietta and Collette had been walking down the Strada Bucuresti after leaving Moldova's National Museum of History. Marietta worked in the gift shop while Collette worked with the curator. Collette loved the history of Moldova. She would always correct Marietta and say, "It is Moldavia, not Moldova." Moldavia was the name of her beloved country before the Ottomans and the Russians, and the communists, and all of the other wretches that took a once peaceful country, and turned it into a hell hole.

Collette had managed to keep her faith in God throughout their childhood. Marietta had lost her faith the day their father died and left the two girls in the care of their alcoholic mother. How many times had she asked God, "Why did you take my father and not my mother?" Why take the one person in the world she could trust and leave her with the last. The coffin had been in the ground for only two days when her mother took her and Collette out of school and forced them to look for work.

It wasn't the school or her friends that Marietta missed; it was her safety. She saw the way men looked at her and her sister when they walked down the street. She could feel the eyes of the men boring into her as they pretended to pick out souvenirs at the museum. How many times had she been propositioned by disgusting old men after her father had passed away. Schools had rules; schools had codes of conduct; and schedules had to be kept. There was protection within the confines of the building, and it was her only way out of the ghetto. If she was going to go anywhere in the world, it would have been through school. Now it was gone.

The last of the afternoon sun was gone, and dusk was setting in as the two girls walked down the marble stairs of the museum on their way to the street. It was a nice September night, and neither were in a hurry to get home. Their mother had been drinking again, and they knew the evening would be the same as it had always been since their father died. Collette decided to take the long way home through Central Park. She loved looking at the monument to Stephen the Great. Not because it was beautiful, but because of what it represented. To Collette, the monument stood for everything that Moldova had once been, a powerful country feared by its neighbors. A religious country with roots that stretched back to the fifth century.

The two strolled through Central Park arm-in-arm as the sun finally fell below the horizon. Their shadows danced as they walked under the street lamps past the monument to Alexander Pushkin.

"I don't know why he gets a monument. I never did like his poems," Marietta said as she wrinkled up her nose.

"That's because you don't understand them," Collette replied in a pleading tone of voice.

"Well then you will have to help me understand them. You have always been the smart one Collette."

"Stop saying that. You are smart too," she replied.

It was getting late, and they knew they could not put off the inevitable. They joined hands and started the long walk home. The street lamps ended, and the night sky was lit by only a few bare light bulbs in their neighborhood. A dog barked loudly behind them, and it sent a shiver down Marietta's spine. She hated dogs ever since she had been bitten as a child.

"It's just a dog barking," Collette said, feeling Marietta's body tense. "I will protect you big sister."

One dog barking turned into two and then four. The whole neighborhood turned into a cacophony of barking dogs. It was almost as if they were trying to scare Marietta, or warn her. She gripped Collette's arm tightly and increased her pace. Two blocks from their home, a headlight flickered in the night. Marietta thought it was a motorbike at first, but the soft shadow it cast was too wide. It had a burned out bulb on the right side of the vehicle, and it was driving very slowly. The two moved to the very edge of the cobblestone road and did their best to ignore the vehicle. It was getting closer, and they could both see that it was a van. It was only about ten yards away, and Marietta heard the sliding door open, and she saw a faint glow spill out onto the road.

Just then she heard footsteps behind her, but when she turned, her world went dark. She felt the stinging pain on the top of her head just as the faint glow of the van faded into nothing. She was vaguely aware that Collette had tightened her grip on her as she collapsed to the ground.

They both awoke a few moments later, and Marietta could tell she was moving. She tried to open her eyes, but everything was still dark. She ordered her eyes to focus, but it was no use. She turned her head and felt the coarse fabric brush against her nose, and then it dawned on her that she was covered. The covering smelled like cigarette smoke, and it was tight against her mouth. Marietta tried to move her mouth to push the material away, but it didn't budge. She felt the saliva backing up in her throat as she tried to swallow. She couldn't move her tongue, and the corners of her mouth began to ache. She bit down hard and realized that there was something in her mouth too.

Next to her on the floor of the panel van, her sister was trying to scream, but it sounded muffled. *They must have done the same to her,* Marietta thought and then panic set in. She had heard the stories from her friends about the abductions that happened all over Eastern Europe. She had seen the news reports about young girls being abducted and never heard from again. She struggled to free her hands, but it was no use; they were tied so tight, she could barely feel them. The blood was being cut off, and her fingers tingled. Pure fear began washing over her, and she tried to cry out, but her own voice sounded muffled.

The next two months were pure hell. Her hood was never removed for more than two minutes—enough time to shovel a few handfuls of food into her mouth. She never saw a single face in two months. She could hear the other girls voices whenever they screamed out, but they were usually silenced immediately with a thud. She felt the swaying of a small boat and then the gentle rocking off a larger one. She got seasick and vomited more than once and had to sit in it for days. Her own bowel movements landed on her feet and collected at the bottom of the crate. The smell gave her such nausea that she vomited over and over again. While at sea she was brought topside, so that her crate could be cleaned. The icy blast of the Bering Sea tore at her flesh so badly that she yearned for the relative safety and warmth of the crate. She had no way of keeping time. It was all a blur as she recalled the horrors she had endured. It wasn't until the night she escaped and saw a date on a newspaper that she realized it had been a full two months since she and Collette had been abducted.

*****

Marietta sensed movement a few hundred yards away, so she spun and put her eye to the telescope. Her eye adjusted, and she saw a man and a young woman walking toward the front door. The distance between them made it clear that they weren't together. The girl was wearing high heels and a dress that barely covered her. She zoomed in with the telescopic lens and was disappointed when she realized that the woman was not Collette, and the man was not that greasy animal she saw in her nightmares. Then girl was a dancer at the club and Marietta's heart silently ached for her. She had seen the man many times before but could never get a recording of him in focus. She kept trying to focus the telescope as the obese man waddled in through the front door. At the last moment he looked to his left.

"Gotcha." Marietta whispered.

Marietta rewound the video but was disappointed when she saw the Man's face. He was just a pudgy faced old man. A dirty old man for sure based on where he was heading. She had been hoping that the man was Marco Bertoli, but when she zoomed in, she realized it wasn't. She filed the picture of the pudgy-faced man away in her memory and went back to the telescope. A few more men approached the door, but they were not him. It had been six months, and Marietta was beginning to lose hope. She had seen the indictment in the newspaper a few months earlier along with a grainy photo of Marco Bertoli. When she saw the face in the newspaper a bolt of panic ran down her spine. It was him. She had done her homework. She had found the Foxxy nightclub out by the airport and had rented a sleazy apartment with a view of the entrance. It wasn't a perfect view, but she could always make out the faces when they were on the way out better than the way in.

She had been working every day for the past six months at the adult bookstore. It was a degrading job, but it paid well. It gave her the chance to scan the faces of the men who walked in. She hoped she would find Marco Bertoli, and then she hoped she never would all in the same thought. She figured the best place to look for an evil man was in an evil store. She was thankful that she never had to touch any of the filth that walked into the place, but just having their eyes on her was torment enough. Her English was good, and the owner of the Adult Book Store didn't care about work permits or visas. In fact, he didn't care about much at all as long as she showed up to work and did what she was told.

Marietta opened the blinds just enough to let the street light in. It gave her just enough light to read the collected poems of Alexander Pushkin. Reading the poetry somehow made her feel closer to Collette. Marietta didn't have time for poetry when she lived in Moldova, but remembering their last night of normal life, she felt drawn to it. She opened the old paperback book to her favorite poem and read it aloud.

> *Don't ask me why, alone in dismal thought,*
> *In times of mirth, I'm often filled with strife,*
> *And why my weary stare is so distraught,*
> *And why I don't enjoy the dream of life;*
> *Don't ask me why my happiness has perished,*
> *Why I don't love the love that pleased me then,*
> *No longer can I call someone my cherished--*
> *Who once felt love will never love again;*
> *Who once felt bliss, no more will feel its essence,*
> *A moment's happiness is all that we receive:*
> *From youth, prosperity and joyful pleasantry,*
> *All that is left is apathy and grief ...*

"I understand him now Collette," Marietta said as a tear rolled down her cheek. "I understand him." Marietta wiped her tear and when she looked back through her telescope one more time, her heart froze. She had seen the back of a man wearing a very expensive suit, but she had only been able to glimpse him from behind. She watched as he disappeared into the club, and then she snatched the video recorder. She began rewinding and then stopped the video. She played it back and strained to see the face of the man who had just entered the club. It was grainy as always, but her voice caught in her throat when the man's face came into view. "That's him." She heard herself say out loud. She had only seen his face for a brief moment six months ago, but she would never forget it. The face she was looking at was Marco Bertoli.

Marietta bounded off the small wooden stool in front of the window and ran to her bedroom. She grabbed the gun from her nightstand, slipped it into her waistband and ran back to the door. She shoved her arms into a jacket and started unlatching the bolts. It was still ridiculously hot outside, but she needed the light jacket to conceal the gun. In a moment she was on the street walking toward the Foxxy nightclub as the wind blew hot air across Lake Erie slapping her face like a hot towel. She made it to the parking lot, pulled the knife from her pocket and plunged it into the front tire of the car the disgusting animal had just exited. She walked back to the safety of the gas station across the street and waited. She had rehearsed the plan in her head so many times, imagining her movements. She hoped it wouldn't be a long wait, but none of her hopes ever came true.

Two hours later the man stumbled from the club, and Marietta steeled her nerves. She pulled the revolver from her waistband and checked it for the thirtieth time that evening. She thumbed the safety switch off, pushed off the wall, and started heading across the street. The wind had died down, but the heat was still intense, and her shirt clung to her chest. She was vaguely aware that she had forgotten her bra, but she didn't care. She watched in her peripheral vision as another car approached from the east and began to slow. Her brain was trying to sort out the details as the events unfolded in front of her. The slowly approaching car reminded her of her last night in Moldova. Seeing the animal again only meters from her brought back the pain and the fear that she had endured. Just as Marco Bertoli reached his own vehicle the other car pulled into the parking lot. It was a Cadillac and it looked new. The windows were tinted so darkly that she couldn't make out the occupants, but she instinctively knew they were up to no good. When Marco saw his own car leaning to the right, he started cursing loudly. Marietta watched in confusion as the Cadillac pulled alongside of Marco's car and the back door flew open.

She could hear Marco yelling something at the car as he pulled his hands out of his pockets and held them in the air. He stood with his hands out and palms facing upward in a gesture that appeared to say, "You found me."

A man jumped out of the back seat of the Cadillac before it came to a stop. "Get in Marco," he said calmly. "Pops wants to see you."

"I ain't going anywhere with you. The last time I saw you, you put a gun to my *head*," Marco said emphasizing the word *head*.

"After you tried to shoot me in the back of *mine*?" The other man replied.

Marietta had the gun out and didn't even care if the men saw her. She had only shot it once before, and she was not looking forward to it. She had missed wildly the first time she shot it, so she told herself to get as close as she possibly could before pulling the trigger. She heard the men shouting loudly now and they sounded upset. She heard the new guy yell something about turning yourself in and the animal replying that he wouldn't. Three other men exited the vehicle and surrounded Marco with guns drawn.

Marietta stopped. She knew full well that she could put a bullet into that animal, but she also knew she couldn't win a gunfight. Not with only six bullets and five men. She gently slipped the gun into her pocket and turned slightly as she crossed the street. A few more feet, and the men would see her and realize that she didn't belong there. She started to panic and realized that she had waited for so long to fail now, and it made her heart sink. *I'm sorry Collette, I tried,* she said to herself and turned on her heels.

The five men were still shouting as she turned to look over her shoulder. She could just make out the license plate so she etched it into her memory. She took a quick look at the other men, but didn't recognize any of them. She heard doors slam and then the squeal of tires as she made it safely to the other side of the street. She was heading for the gas station when the car pulled out of the Foxxy and raced past her up the street.

Back in her apartment, Marietta sat on the linoleum kitchen floor sobbing and shaking violently. She had failed Collette, and now she would have to live with her failure again. She failed to protect her baby sister in Chişinău and she failed to find her here. She thought of pulling the gun back out of her pocket and ending her misery. One thought led to another, and soon she had the barrel of the revolver sticking into her left ear. She moaned and rocked back and forth letting the sobs overwhelm her. She started squeezing the trigger many times, but never could bring herself to pull it. She saw that animal's face again tonight, and it somehow lit a flame in her that burned even hotter. She wanted to quit, but her sweet sister's face kept urging her forward.

Marietta was a sweaty mess lying on the floor. She realized that her plan had been pretty pathetic. She had spent the past six months waiting to walk across the street and demand that a man tell her where her sister was. How foolish she had been. She needed a new plan. She couldn't rely on timing and an ancient revolver to get Collette back. She needed to take control of everything. She needed to think; she needed to outsmart the man, and she needed more firepower.

The beginning of a plan was forming in her mind as she drew a bath. Her sweaty hair hung on her shoulders like seaweed as she slowly undressed. She finally eased herself into the cold water and felt a new burst of energy. The plan was coming to life, and it brought a flicker of hope. She would start a new life in the morning. She would begin implementing the plan in the morning. She would be a new person in the morning, and she would really start trying to find Collette in the morning.

She let the cool water rinse the sweat off of her as she lathered the bar of soap. She washed her hair twice before moving down her body. She washed her breasts and her stomach as the tears finally quit falling. She washed her legs and finally made it to her ankles. She stared at the scar on her ankle for a moment and remembered the pain. She remembered twisting and pulling with all her might, and then she remembered the pain of her ankle being broken and then sliced open by the metal handcuffs. In her mind's eye she could see the handcuffs that had been clasped around her ankle falling to the bottom of the frigid lake and coming to rest on top of the large floor jack as she swam frantically toward the surface.

CHAPTER 19

"Special Agent Larkin, this is Detective Abrams. I am the field training officer for the sheriff's department. How are you today?"

"I'm fine," Clair said, staring at her computer screen. She was only half paying attention when Detective Abrams said the name Marco Bertoli.

"I'm sorry, did you say Marco Bertoli?"

"Yes, ma'am. He just strolled into the sheriff's department a few hours ago and said he was turning himself in. We ran his name through the system, and he is wanted on a murder rap in Cleveland, Ohio. He said he just found out about the warrant a few days ago when he was talking to his father on the phone. Claims he's been in Mexico since a few days before the murders, and he just wanted to clear his name."

"Well, he's full of it. We have him for five murders now, and he's going to prison," Claire said excitedly. Is he still in custody?"

"Yes, ma'am."

"Here in Detroit?"

"Yes ma'am."

"I want him in federal custody. He is wanted on murder and human trafficking. He is a federal prisoner at this point." Clair was preparing for a turf battle but was pleasantly surprised when Detective Abrams said, "Sure thing, where can I drop this dirtbag off?"

"Take him to the Federal Building. I will meet you there and sign for him," Claire said and began scrolling through her phone.

"Yes, ma'am. I will see you shortly."

Claire hung up and dialed Mulloy's cell phone. He picked up on the first ring, but before he could say hello, Claire started talking.

"Hey, it's Claire Larkin. Guess who I have?"

"A boyfriend, I hope," Mulloy said sarcastically.

"Very funny. I have Marco Bertoli in custody. How soon can you get here?"

"I'm on my way. See you in three hours."

Claire drove to the Federal Building and parked her car in the gated lot next to the building. She handed the FBI agent her car keys before crossing the street. Once inside the building, she walked directly to a nondescript door just before the metal detectors and swiped her badge. The door buzzed, and she pushed into the long hallway leading to the interrogation rooms. She swiped her badge twice more before she made it to the room where Marco Bertoli was seated behind a two-way pane of glass.

She signed a few forms taking custody of Marco Bertoli and thanked the detective for his good work. She watched from the other side of the glass as two agents fingerprinted him and searched him again for contraband. When the two agents left the room, Claire pulled a chair up in front of the glass and sat staring at him. She was studying his every move and formulating a plan in her head for the interrogation that was sure to follow. She knew he would never confess to anything. Narcissists like Marco Bertoli did not have it in their DNA to admit to any wrongdoing, so she knew that she was going to have to outsmart him.

She pulled his file from her briefcase again and started rereading it as she settled in to wait for Special Agent Mulloy. This was technically *his* collar since Bertoli was being charged with a murder in his jurisdiction. Even though she suspected him of being behind the sex trafficking, she didn't have enough evidence to charge him and besides, she had been pulled from the case. She knew that he would be extradited to Cleveland once Mulloy arrived. She couldn't figure why he would surrender in Detroit and not in Cleveland where the crimes had been committed, but she could sort that out later. Mulloy was about two hours away, which gave her time to think, but she needed to think fast. She tried to think of an excuse to give to her boss, but decided it could wait. For now, she had a crack at the man she had been hunting for almost nine months.

She finally decided to take the subtle approach as she pushed through the door into the interrogation room. Marco had been sitting there for almost an hour when Claire entered. She made sure the door didn't lock when it closed behind her. She had made that mistake early on in her career, and if it hadn't been for the guards watching the monitors, she would most certainly have been killed. Marco had been yelling at nobody in particular for over an hour, saying he wanted to make a phone call. He had been demanding his lawyer. He had been demanding a cigarette and a cup of coffee. Claire had sat watching him the whole time.

"Mr. Bertoli, my name is Special Agent Larkin. Do you mind if I ask you a few questions?"

"Yeah, I mind. I've been sitting here for four hours, and I haven't been offered a phone call. I haven't been offered a cigarette or anything. So I ain't saying nothing until my lawyer gets here."

"It's only been one hour," Claire said sarcastically. "Did you graduate from high school?"

The question was so crazy that it took Marco by surprise. "Yeah, did you?" Marco fired back.

"Did you ever go to college?"

"No, and what the hell does that have to do with the fact that I am sitting here being held against my rights? Look, I turned myself in, but I have proof that I am not responsible for whatever it is you think I did."

"It has everything to do with it. You see, most of the criminals I deal with are very educated. The criminals I investigate do not make stupid mistakes like you. In fact, I think you are probably the dumbest criminal I have ever investigated."

"Well, why don't you tell me about all these mistakes that I have made?"

"I can't do that, but what I can tell you is that you are going to jail for a very long time. You may be heading to death row. Ohio is a capital punishment state, and they electrocute people for double homicides. I can't imagine what they will do with a dirtbag that committed five murders, two of them children."

"I didn't do anything, and if you don't let me talk to my lawyer, then you will be the one behind bars. When my father hears about this, you won't even be able to carry a library card, much less an FBI badge."

"Is that so?" Claire said with fake interest. "Tell me, tough guy, who is your father, and why do you think he has the power to get you off the hook for five murders?"

"Vinny Bertoli," Marco said with a grin. "He makes a lot of problems go away."

"I know. That's why he sent you to Mexico. You see, I think you are his biggest problem. In fact, I think you should be more worried about your father than I am. If I'm not mistaken, his instructions for you were to stay put and not try to get back into the country for at least a year or two. It turns out you could only handle tequila and tacos for nine months before you and your buddy drove back across the border a few days ago."

Marco was about to say something but thought better of it. *How did she know all of that?* he wondered, but he knew better than to ask. "We'll see," Marco finally said before asking to speak to his lawyer again.

"You see, I knew you weren't very intelligent. I accused you of five murders, and you denied it. I threw out a completely plausible story about where you have been for the past nine months, and you clam up like a muzzled dog. It's all in the eyes. Turns out you can tell when a man is lying by his eyes. I have no idea where you have been these past nine months, but my instincts were correct. Your eyes tell a much different story than your mouth. I think you are scared of your daddy. I think you are scared to death of your daddy because he may be planning on how to make his biggest problem go away."

Marco turned his eyes toward the door and started yelling for his lawyer again.

"I'll get your lawyer, don't worry. In fact, I will call him in just a few moments if you want me to. I just have one more question for you."

"I'm not answering any questions without my lawyer."

"That's OK. I can read your facial expressions much better than I can understand your fifth-grade English. Are you familiar with call tracing software?"

When Marco stared at the door, Clair pressed on.

"You see, most thugs buy burner phones because they think that they are being sneaky. They use them for a few days and then get a new one. Seems pretty reasonable until you realize that every cell signal emits a frequency that bounces off the cell towers that are the closest to it. The FBI has been using software that can literally track every single phone call and pinpoint the exact location of that call down to an area of about six square meters.

I know this is all over your head, but try your best to keep up. If you make a phone call from your apartment in Cleveland, we see a certain phone number, and we can track you right down to your fancy balcony overlooking Lake Erie. The next time you make a phone call from your sleazy nightclub, that same number comes up, and we can pinpoint your location right down to the silver pole in the middle of the room. It is only ironic that two people are killed in that nightclub the next day. I can tell you are fascinated, so I will keep going," Claire said, staring at every wrinkle around Marco's eyes.

"The next time you make a phone call from your very shiny sports car while traveling through the Metroparks about a mile from where three innocent people were killed, it comes up as the same number. Now here is where you can help us. Can you give me a solid reason why somebody would be hanging out at your apartment, your nightclub on the night two people were killed, and driving your car through the Metroparks two minutes before three more people were killed, and yet that certain somebody isn't you?"

Claire could feel the tension rising in the room, so she backed off a bit. She didn't want him to panic yet, and she needed the tiny wheels in his brain to keep moving. "Where you and Sal went wrong was using the same burner phone more than once. You see, we can check every cell phone number that pings a certain tower. We find the three closest towers to all three locations and see if any number pops up more than once. Your number popped up three times. I wouldn't feel bad, though, if I were you. It's where everybody messes up. You get a little lazy, and the next thing you know, you are facing a death sentence," Claire said sarcastically.

Marco shifted in his chair. He just stared at Larkin as he leaned forward. "I want to see my lawyer."

"Sure thing, dirtbag. You have already answered all my questions. If I were you, though, when the agent from Cleveland gets here, I'd start working on a plea deal," Claire said as she stood to leave.

"If I were you, I'd be looking for a new identity and a plane ticket somewhere far from here where you can hide the rest of your life," Marco said with a grin.

"I might just do that, but first, I'll add threatening a federal agent to your list of charges. Although, that is going to be the least of your concerns. I'll see you when they are strapping you into the chair at the federal prison in Mansfield," Claire said and walked out the door.

She stood in front of the two-way mirror and watched Marco's reaction. She had been making up most of what she had just said, but it paid off. She was glad she had turned the microphones and video recorder off, or her little stunt wouldn't have worked. Marco's facial expressions had told her everything she needed to know. She saw the way his eyes darted back and forth as she laid out the evidence against him. She knew it would be a long shot, but she played him like a fiddle. This was going to be the easiest prosecution she had ever had a part in. Even if she couldn't link him to the shipment from Canada, she could still shut his business down, and shut it down she would.

Special Agents Mulloy and Millson walked into the Federal Building and made their way to the interrogation room. Mulloy hadn't seen Claire in three months. He was a little apprehensive about seeing her again, but he was a little excited too. They exchanged pleasantries, and Claire filled them in on the discussion she had just had with Marco. Mulloy shook his head. She was amazing, he had to admit.

"Well, we have an uphill battle on this one, and it's proof that money can buy just about anything."

"What are you talking about?" Claire snapped back.

"He has a valid visa that was stamped in Nogales, New Mexico, the day before the murders. I called our evidence room on the way up here, and nobody can seem to find the bullet casing we found that night at the club." Claire was just about to start firing off questions when Mulloy held up his hand. "I haven't even told you the best part. Turns out there was a stolen vehicle report filed for one Porsche 911 Cabriolet the day before the murders."

"What the ..."

"I know," Mulloy said, cutting her off again. The case is pretty flimsy, but we do have the eyewitnesses at the crash scene, and we will find the shell casing. We also have traffic cameras that show Marco's car and a man fitting his description the day of the murders, so, it's not a lost cause just yet."

Claire sat down on the desk and closed her eyes. She let out a long breath and then looked at Mulloy, who had been staring at her and said. "You know what this means, don't you?"

"Means we have our work cut out for us." Mulloy replied.

Claire shook her head. "It means that Daddy has been pulling strings since the murders and finally has all his ducks in a row. When you and the rookie here spooked him, he decided that now was the perfect time to come back home. He figured that the heat was on, and better to come clean, turn yourself in, and avoid a very public extradition."

"He never would have made it to extradition," Mulloy said.

"Of course not, but that's not the point. The point is, Vinny felt the heat and brought him back to face the music so it didn't appear that he was running. Do you have any idea how difficult it is to get a backdated passport stamp?" Claire said.

"Yeah, I know it is hard, but it isn't impossible. Not with the right amount of money."

"Exactly," she answered, "It took time to get everybody involved in this, and when his plans were finally ready, he brings him back to play the role of the wrongly accused." Claire just shook her head, closed her eyes and spoke softly. "This scumbag is gonna walk."

Mulloy walked into the interrogation room very slowly. He pretended to read a report as he sat across from Marco. He sat down and just continued to read. When he finally looked up, he locked eyes with Marco and stared for a few long moments.

"Is this supposed to intimidate me?" Marco finally said, breaking eye contact.

Mulloy stared at the side of his head for a few more moments. "Mr. Bertoli, can you please tell me something," Mulloy finally said.

"I'm not telling you a thing without my lawyer present," Marco said, growing irritated.

"You do know that you are about to be charged with five murders?" Mulloy said with a hint of disgust.

"I didn't do anything," Marco said again, staring right back at Mulloy. "Am I supposed to be intimidated by this little staring game of yours?"

Mulloy leaned in close and spoke in a whisper. "What if I told you that I have two eyewitnesses across the street from your nightclub the night two people died, and three eyewitnesses that put you and your friend Sal Rigo at the site of the car accident that left three more people dead? What would you say to all that?"

Marco sat in relative silence. Inside his head, though, alarm bells were sounding all over. His father had said that he had taken care of all that. He said it was safe to come home, but he had to play this thing exactly the way he told him to. There was no mention of witnesses at the Foxxy. The noise inside Marco's head was deafening as he desperately tried to figure out what this FBI agent was talking about.

"Sworn statements, character sketches, absolutely confident they can identify you both in a lineup. What would you say to that?"

Marco's lips pursed together, and he let out a smile. Finally, the silence in the room was becoming overpowering, and Marco whispered, "We'll see."

Mulloy just stared at Marco and didn't flinch. He knew the case would be an uphill battle, but he never let the dirtbags know what cards he was holding. Always better to let the dirtbags assume you were holding all the cards.

A few seconds later, Mulloy stood and walked out of the room. On the other side of the two-way glass, Claire stood watching. She was certain Marco had been driving the car that evening, and she was sure he was behind the murders at his own club. She wasn't sure because of any evidence; she was sure because watching the man squirm on the other side of the glass spoke louder than any amount of evidence.

*****

"Staff Sergeant Murphy, there is a telephone call for you. It's an unsecured line," the company clerk Corporal Lasoya said.

Mack followed the corporal into the quonset hut and picked up the phone. "This is Staff Sergeant Murphy, and this is an unsecured line. How may I help you?"

"Staff Sergeant Murphy, this is Patrick Mulloy from the Cleveland, Ohio, FBI office."

"I hope you are calling with some good news for me," Mack said with an edge of irritation he wasn't trying very hard to conceal. It had been almost ten months since Renée and the babies had been murdered, and the only lead was a stolen car registered to a dirtbag who ran a strip club and was the son of a local Mob boss.

"Well, I am not sure that anything I say will bring you comfort, but we have secured a grand jury indictment for Marco Bertoli. We believe he was driving the car the day your wife and children were killed. The trial will begin in approximately eight weeks. We are up against a lot of obstacles, though. Our eyewitnesses may not be very credible; his car was reported stolen two days before the accident, and his father seems to have an army of lawyers working on his behalf. I know I promised to let you know if there were any breaks in the case, so that is what I am doing."

Mack felt a little embarrassed at how he responded to Mulloy, so he offered a quick apology and thanked him for his call. He told him he planned to be at the trial; thanked him one more time, and then hung up the phone.

Mack walked out of the air-conditioned company command building and squinted his eyes at the noonday sun. The Iraqi air was dry and hot, and it sapped his strength. He was surprised at how quickly the emotions came flooding back to him. His Force Reconnaissance Unit had been in Iraq for the past two months, and they were slated to be there for another two. Mack knew that it would be tight, but he was pretty sure the deployment would be over before the trial started.

Mack pushed through the plywood door that led to the battalion headquarters quonset hut and removed his University of Montana truckers hat instinctively. He was a Force Reconnaissance Marine, so uniform standards were pretty relaxed, but some habits were ingrained. Major McMullen was staring at a map in the center of the room, and when he heard the door slam, he looked up.

"Hey, Mack," he said and then returned to staring at the map.

"Sir, can I get a moment of your time?"

"Sure thing. What's up?"

"I just heard from the FBI agent working my wife's case, and he says that they have a suspect in custody, and they have indicted him. The trial starts in two months."

Major McMullen was quiet for a few moments before speaking. "I'm not sure what to say. I guess that's a good thing. What do you think?" McMullen stared at Mack waiting for his reply.

"Well, sir, I think it is a good thing. He seems to think he is responsible for the death of my wife and kids."

McMullen didn't say a word. He was a wise man and knew that fewer words were always better than the wrong words at times like this.

Mack took a deep breath and went for it. "Sir, I was hoping to be there for the trial."

"When did you say it was supposed to start?"

"He said two months from now. Most likely after we rotate back to the States."

"Well, if we are back stateside, then I am sure I can spare you for a few weeks. How long did they say the trial will take?"

"I'm not sure. Why, sir?"

"I was going to wait until after this op is over with to tell you, but I don't see any reason to keep it from you any longer."

Mack cocked his head to the side and stared at the Major curiously.

"You were selected for Gunnery Sergeant. It will be effective in three months. Congratulations, Gunnery Sergeant Murphy," the Major said sticking out his hand.

Mack stood there stunned for a few seconds before shaking his hand and thanking Major McMullen.

"Team assignments stay the same for the remainder of deployment. I am sure you understand; now is not the time to rearrange the team."

"Of course, sir."

"I have you slotted to attend Staff NCO school six weeks after we rotate back to the States."

"Thank you, sir. I don't know how long the trial will last, but I feel like I need to be there at least for the verdict."

Major McCullen looked at Mack for a long moment and then finally asked, "Why?"

Mack just shrugged his shoulders. The question irritated him, but he was the Major, and he was entitled to an answer. "I guess I just need to look him in the eye and let him know that he didn't get away with it."

"What if he does? What if they don't find him guilty? What then?"

"I don't know. I have never had to deal with something like this before," Mack replied.

"Let's make plans. Staff NCO school, and if it works out for you to make it to the trial, then I will do what I can to make it happen. Fair enough?"

"Yes, sir. More than fair."

"OK, now get your head back in the game. You roll out in four hours," Major McCullen said as he winked at Mack.

CHAPTER 20

Judge Neely walked into the courtroom, and everyone stood. The trial was about to get underway, and Mack and Mina sat directly behind the two district attorneys that had been assigned the case. Mack stared at the faces of the seven men and five women that had been selected for the jury. All five women were mothers, and three of the seven men had children of their own. That was all a good thing, the lead DA had told him. It meant that when they showed pictures of Aubrey and Brianna, the parents on the jury would be moved as they thought of their own children.

Two of the jurors were Hispanic; four were Black, and the rest were White. Mack wasn't sure why the DA was excited about that, but he didn't press the issue. The lead DA was a diminutive looking man, who looked like he had not been out of law school for more than a year or two. Mack couldn't help but think that he was out of his league, playing with the big kids on a federal murder case, but he decided to give him a chance. His name was Albert Michaelson, and he was definitely more at home in a courtroom than a battlefield, but Mack decided that he may just surprise everyone. Besides, there was nothing for Mack to do during the trial other than watch, since he wasn't a witness to the crime. He decided to let the young attorney prosecute criminals; his job would be to kill them if they didn't get convicted.

Mack had asked the DA to let him take the stand to talk about the whole ordeal in the hospital, but he refused. He wasn't sure how Mack would stand up to cross-examination and felt it was a risk they didn't need to take. The evidence would be enough to secure a conviction, he assured Mack.

The district attorney stood to make his opening statement just as the back door of the courtroom opened. Claire spotted Mulloy in a seat on the prosecution side at the back of the courtroom and quietly slid into the seat next to him.

"Here we go," Mulloy said.

"I hope they hang his greasy neck from the rafters," Claire replied.

The lead prosecutor ignored the sound of the door closing behind Claire and plowed on with his opening statement.

"Ladies and gentlemen of the jury, you are all here to uphold one of the most precious rights we have as Americans. The right to a speedy trial. This man," he said, pointing at Marco Bertoli, "is entitled to a speedy trial by a jury of his peers. You are here to serve as peers to this man that has been accused of murdering five people in cold blood. While you are all here to carry out this most sacred office, I would not go so far as to consider any of you his peers. Most people, yourselves included, have what is referred to as a conscience. This man, as I am about to prove to you, does not seem to be burdened by a conscience. That is why you must protect your true peers from men like this. As the state is ready to bring evidence against this man for the senseless murder of five individuals, your job will be clear. To hear the evidence, decide its validity, and make the best judgment that you are capable of, to prevent this type of atrocity from ever happening again."

The district attorney went on to explain the nature and means of the five murders, including the use of a vehicle as a murder weapon. He went on to lay out why the jury could do nothing short of convicting

Marco Bertoli guilty of first degree murder on two counts and vehicular homicide on three separate counts. He was interrupted by the judge at that point to strike the previous information from the opening statement. The defense was on their feet at the exact moment as the judge, and the noise level rose dramatically in the courtroom.

Judge Neely's voice screeched across the room, asking for order in the court. "Mr. Michaelson, I am convinced that they taught you law at law school, and you know certainly well that leading statements like that are not permitted at any point in this process and definitely not in an opening statement. If this is the type of case you are planning to try, I suggest you recuse yourself immediately so that the state can appoint new counsel."

Claire had never been to law school, but she did know enough of the law to know that he was on pretty thin ice for a while before the judge finally interrupted him. As the judge went on berating the prosecutor, Claire began feeling uneasy. She couldn't figure out what was eating at her until the judge had finished scolding the attorney. His last words to the young prosecutor were "my rights." He was referring to his own rights to ensure that Marco Bertoli had a fair trial, but the word "rights" sparked a memory in Claire that she couldn't quite grasp.

Claire's amygdala, the part of the brain that attached emotional significance to a memory, began spinning through the archives. She wasn't sure why the judge's voice was triggering it, but it had definitely triggered it. She closed her eyes and forced her mind to put the pieces together. She whispered the word, "rights" over and over again in her head. When she finally had the answer, she almost jumped out of her chair.

Mulloy could tell that something was bothering her, so he leaned close and said, "You OK?'

"I'll tell you later," she said with a growing sense of impending doom.

The defense decided to waive the opening statement, which

surprised Mack a little, but he figured the most expensive lawyers money could buy didn't make rookie mistakes the way a young wet behind the ears prosecutor would.

The first witness the prosecution called was the driver of the car that came upon the accident first. It was a nineteen-year-old kid, and when he took the stand, he acted like he was the one on trial. When it came time to place his hand on the Bible though, he didn't hesitate.

"Mr. Greene, is it true that you were driving your car through the Metroparks on November 19, 2004?" the DA said.

"Yes, sir."

"Is it true that you came upon a bad car accident that prompted you to call 9-1-1 on your personal cell phone?"

"Yes, sir."

"Is it true that just before you saw the car accident, you saw a red Ford Mustang pass you in the opposite direction traveling at a high rate of speed with two men in the front seat?"

"No, sir," the kid replied with a voice that seemed much less confident than it had a second earlier.

The DA stopped his pacing and stared up at the young man on the stand. "I'm sorry?"

"No, sir," the witness repeated.

The DA went back to the table and pulled a sheet of paper from a stack and began reading. "Just before I saw the SUV on the side of the road, I saw a red Ford Mustang racing past me going super-fast with two men in the front seat."

The DA looked directly at the young man before speaking again. "Are those not your exact words in the sworn statement you provided to police just two hours after you witnessed the scene of the accident?"

"Yes, sir."

"So, you did see a Red Ford Mustang that day?"

"No, sir."

"I'm sorry, Mr. Greene, I am having difficulty understanding you.

Are you saying, under oath, after placing your hand on the Bible and swearing to tell the truth, the whole truth, and nothing but the truth, that this statement that you made was false?" the DA said, holding up the piece of paper for the whole court to see.

"Yes, sir."

"Your Honor, can I request a brief moment to consult with my witness?"

"No you may not. Proceed with your witness."

The DA looked at the young kid incredulously and asked him again. "I'm sorry, Mr. Greene, would you care to tell the court why you have changed your story regarding what you saw on the 19th of November?"

"I was mistaken."

"You were mistaken?" the DA repeated quizzically.

"Yes, sir."

Mack looked across the courtroom at Marco Bertoli, sitting at the defense table grinning from ear to ear. The young DA started to say something, but thought better of it.

"Are there any further questions," Judge Neely said.

"No, sir."

The cross-examination went quickly as the defense attorney simply asked the teenager about the Red Ford Mustang. When the teenager replied for the third time that he did not see a Red Ford Mustang that day, the defense attorney took his seat.

The DA called the other two teenagers who had been in the car that day to the stand, and they both retracted their statements as well.

When the third teenager, a young woman, retracted her initial statement, the DA became visibly angry. He approached the witness stand and put his hands on the railing in front of the young woman. "Who convinced you to change your story? Have you been approached by any member of the defense? Have you spoken with …"

He was cut off by the sound of the gavel, and the judge ordering him to approach the bench.

"Your Honor, it is obvious that these witnesses have been tampered with, and I demand …"

"You may demand nothing. Now either ask your witness a question, or the defense may cross-examine."

The DA took his seat defeated. The defense cross-examined the young woman quickly, and the judge released her from the witness stand. Mack was staring at Marco as the witness walked past the defense table on the way to her seat. He was almost certain he saw Marco wink at her as she walked past him, but he couldn't be sure. When the young woman took her seat, the judge ordered a recess for lunch and the court watchers stood. Mack continued staring at Marco as he went to the back of the courtroom.

"I'm going to kill that dirtbag someday if it's the last thing I do," he muttered, but Mina didn't hear him.

As the crowd shuffled out of the courtroom, Claire grabbed Mulloy's arm and pulled him aside. "We need to talk."

"If this is still about the fact that I never called you back, I can explain everything," Mulloy said with a sheepish grin on his face.

"Shut up, moron, and listen to me. I don't care if you never call me again, but you will be very interested in what I have learned today. So much so that you will probably wish that you had never called me in the first place."

"I don't know about …"

Claire shushed him again and pulled him to a seat in the hallway. "Listen to me and listen very closely because what I am about to tell you changes the entire dynamic of this case."

Mulloy looked at her and realized that she was scared. Looking closer at her hands, he saw that she was trembling too. He put his hand on her shoulder and asked "Are you OK?"

"Stop patronizing me and listen. Do you remember Detective Daniels telling you that somebody had called in an anonymous tip after the murders at the nightclub?"

"Yeah, some drunk saying he knew his rights, and he wasn't going to testify."

"My rights, he said I know *my rights*," Claire corrected him.

"OK, so what does that have to do with the trial?"

Claire leaned in to whisper in Mulloy's ear so that nobody passing by would hear her. "The caller was Judge Neely."

"What the ..."

"I know you think I am losing my mind, but I guarantee you that it was him. I played that call over and over in my head so many times that I have the entire thing memorized right down to the inflection in his voice. He was very drunk, but the man on the pay phone was Judge Neely."

Mulloy had to shake his head a few times to fully grasp what he was hearing. He had learned a long time ago to trust Claire implicitly, but this was too much to wrap his head around. He started to speak, but Claire put her hand to his mouth to make sure he didn't say a thing.

"I know you think I am crazy, but you are going to have to trust me on this one."

"We have an hour before the trial resumes. I need to hear this for myself," Mulloy said.

The two made their way to Mulloy's car. Once they were inside, Claire flipped open her phone.

"Hello Detective Daniels, this is Claire Larkin. You probably don't remember me, but I was at the nightclub investigating with Special Agent Mulloy the night of the murders."

"Tall drink of water with chestnut hair and a smile that could launch a million ships, and blue eyes the shade of a Carolina sky after a thunderstorm. Chances are that I could pick you out of a lineup long before you could pick me out. Yeah, I remember you. What can I do for you?"

Claire was impressed and a little embarrassed, but she pressed on. "Do you remember the anonymous call that alerted the police to the murders that happened that night?"

"Yeah, some drunk guy who kept insisting he knew his rights, if I remember correctly."

"Exactly. Something about that voice made you a little curious, and I want to know why."

"I don't remember," Daniels said hesitantly.

"I think you do," Claire responded.

"Am I in trouble with America's finest, Special Agent Larkin? Do I need to get a lawyer?" he said sarcastically.

"No, Detective, I promise you are not in trouble. I think you heard that call, and it triggered something that you didn't want to say out loud."

"Could have been. It was a while ago. I have slept a few times since that night, and I am not as young as I used to be. Memory is a bit slower these days."

"Look, I am not trying to frame you, corner you, or make you do anything that you do not want to do. My father was a detective in Boston before he was killed, so believe me when I say that I respect the hunches of veteran detectives more than you think. There was something to that call, and I am asking for your help."

"OK, ma'am. I guess I do remember a little bit about that call. How can I help you?"

"Why did you think it was interesting?"

"Maybe I had heard that voice before and thought it sounded familiar?"

I knew it, Claire said to herself. "If you still want to help me, I am at the federal courthouse in Cleveland right now. Could you bring that recorded message to the courthouse, please?"

Special Agent Mulloy was the next one to take the stand for the prosecution, and he made a compelling argument that Marco had indeed been in the nightclub that night. Fingerprints and some grainy surveillance videos taken from a nearby building seemed to prove Mulloy correct. Still, the facial recognition software gave only a 38 percent possibility that the face in the car was Marco Bertoli's, and his father owned the club, so the fingerprints meant nothing. The shell casing was found, but the chain of evidence had been broken, so it was thrown out of the case. The young DA argued that it was photographed at the scene, and there was a report indicating it was indeed a 7.62 x 25mm, but Judge Neely didn't budge.

Mulloy had been on the stand many times in his career, but he had never felt as nervous as he was that afternoon. He had heard the recording after Detective Daniels had played it for him, and he was as convinced as Claire. The nasally voice was hard to forget after you spent the day listening to it. The problem was not trying to prove that the judge had made the phone call; it was trying to figure out what that had to do with the case against Marco Bertoli.

The trial reached the sixth day when the prosecution rested. The defense called numerous witnesses to the stand, and everyone swore under oath that Marco Bertoli had been in Mexico City for over twenty-four hours before any of the murders had taken place. The next two days were filled with various employees of the strip club being called to the witness stand. The waitress who had been working the night prior gave sworn testimony that Marco and Sal had not been in the club the night before. The next three employees all said the same thing. A hotel clerk from some casino in Mexico City also gave sworn testimony that Marco and Sal had arrived at the casino the night before the murders took place. Just two days later, the defense rested, and all that remained were the closing arguments. The judge smashed his gavel and called a recess until the following day when closing arguments would be heard.

*****

Mack opened the door for Mina, and the two walked into the restaurant together. They found a quiet booth at the back where they could talk undisturbed. Mina had sold her house a few months after the funeral and was working between Peshawar, Pakistan and Washington, DC, when the trial started. They were both staying in a hotel in downtown Cleveland and were eating dinners out every night together. The stress of the past two weeks was clearly getting to them as they collapsed into their seats across from one another.

"Did you see the jury today?" Mina asked.

"I did," he replied.

"I feel so bad for them," Mina said.

Mack was confused as he looked at her face across the dimly lit table. "Why?"

"Because they have the weight of the world on their shoulders. They have to decide if they follow the evidence or listen to their hearts. Mack, the evidence is all circumstantial. We know the defense is lying, but the jury has to follow the facts. They clearly want to convict that man, but the evidence isn't enough."

Mack closed his eyes and realized exactly why he loved Mina so much. She was almost always right. He looked at her face intently, and for a moment, he saw Renée. She had Mina's eyes and her brains. He had never met Renée's father, but he was sure she got her stubbornness and athleticism from him. He loved Mina for her compassion for others. Even when every ounce of his being told him to object, he couldn't. She was right. She had summed up in one sentence what his brain had been telling him all week. Mack let out a long breath and finally nodded his head in agreement.

"I want you to listen to me, Mack, because I have something important to tell you."

She reached across the table and grabbed Mack's hands in hers.

Mack sat up straight in his chair and raised his eyebrows as if to say, "I'm listening."

"Tomorrow, when we walk into that courtroom, I want you to know one thing. It doesn't matter what that jury says. Nothing will bring Renée or those precious girls back to us. Nothing a judge does or doesn't do will make any of this right. Revenge is not an emotion, it is a poison, and if you drink from that cup, it will consume you. I don't want anything the jury does tomorrow to steal the love you have for my baby girl, and I don't want anything that happens to take you away from me too. I know you have your own life to live, and we will go our separate ways after the trial, but you will always be my son. That is what I want you to remember. That is what I wanted to tell you." Mina had tears in her eyes when she finished speaking, and all she could do was squeeze Mack's hand in hers.

They ate their meal quietly, and when they were done, they headed back to the hotel. Mack walked Mina to her room before hugging her good night. He didn't feel tired and was sick of his hotel room. He walked back to the parking garage and got into his truck. He fired it up and pulled out onto the road, unsure where he was headed, but he needed to drive. As he drove through Cleveland, he found himself thinking of Renée. His thoughts went back to Tsuken Island off the coast of Okinawa, the day he asked Renée to be his wife.

*****

Twenty minutes after Mack had signed his leave papers, he and Renée were driving like mad south to San Diego. They would have to hurry if they wanted to make their flight. He had spent the better part of three months making his plans, and he was pissed off at the company clerk for taking so long. If all went smoothly, he would be relaxing with Renée on white, sandy beaches in less than twenty-four hours. They managed to make it to their flight just as the flight attendant was closing the doors. When the attendant saw his Marine uniform, she stopped and pulled the door back open and said something into the phone on the console.

Since the war on terror had started, the airlines were making every effort to accommodate servicemen. Five and a half hours later, their plane touched down in Honolulu. As much as Mack loved Hawaii, it was just a layover. Renée protested as he led her to a cab for the short ride to Hickam Air Force Base for their next flight. As they got out of the cab at the front gate of Hickam Air Force Base, a white panel van pulled up alongside them. A man Renée had never met before hopped out of the van and bear hugged Mack, lifting him off the ground.

"Mack Murphy," the Marine said in a booming voice.

"How are you, old buddy?" Mack said, fighting for air. The man was gigantic and made Mack look like a midget in his embrace.

He put Mack down and stared at Renée for a long moment before he dropped to one knee. "You must be the angel Mack has been droning on about for the past three months. I am pleased to make your acquaintance, Your Highness."

"Get up, you big oaf," Mack said, laughing.

Renée giggled out loud as the giant stood, taking her hand in his. He gently leaned over and kissed Renée's hand softly.

"My name is Douglas Callahan, and I am truly honored to be in your presence."

Renée giggled again as she introduced herself.

Mack clapped Callahan on the back and said, "Sorry, buddy, but we are in a hurry. You are going to have to drool some other time. We will catch up on our way back. Is everything set?"

Callahan gave Mack a disappointed look and said, "Have I ever let you down?"

"No, you haven't," Mack said and started putting their bags into the back of the van.

"You can ride up front, my queen," Callahan said, taking her by the hand again and opening the passenger door.

All Renée could do was laugh as she climbed into the van. Callahan drove straight past the Air Force guard and made for the airstrip.

Ten minutes later, they had said their goodbyes, and Mack promised to spend more time with Callahan on their way back through Hawaii.

They boarded the C-130 and settled into the seats in the front of the plane—usually reserved for officers—and buckled their seat belts. They had almost the entire plane to themselves for the ten-hour flight to Okinawa.

When the flight touched down at Kadena Air Force Base in Okinawa, Japan, they both felt rested. Renée had been pestering Mack for details of the trip since they had left, but all Mack would tell her was his name, rank, and Social Security Number. When Renée's interrogations got particularly intense, Mack would recite the Marine Code of Conduct.

"I am an American, fighting in the forces which guard my country and our way of life. I am prepared to give my life in their defense. I will never surrender of my own free will. If in command, I will never surrender the members of my command while they still have the means to resist."

When she realized that Mack was not going to say a word, Renée finally gave up and decided to enjoy the suspense.

As they walked down the ramp of the C-130, another van materialized onto the tarmac, and another Marine stepped out. There was no end to the surprises that Mack Murphy was capable of. The welcome this time was not quite as boisterous, but it was evident that the young Marine clearly held Mack in high esteem.

"Everything is on schedule," the young Marine said to Mack as he accelerated away from the plane. They drove off of Kadena and merged onto the Okinawa Expressway for the forty-five-minute ride to Camp Hansen.

Mack had arranged for a pilot friend of his to take him and Renée out to the island of Tsuken-Jima that was about twenty miles west of Okinawa. There was a small Marine Corps training area on the north side of the island that was just perfect for what he wanted to do. His old STA Platoon commander was the officer in charge of the training facility and had heartily agreed to Mack's request. As they strapped into the web seats on the bulkhead of the helicopter, Renée looked concerned. The last time she was on a helicopter with Mack, they were headed into combat.

"Where are you taking me?" she screamed over the sound of the rotor.

"Don't worry. There won't be anybody shooting at us this time," Mack said, reading her thought. "Just enjoy the scenery," he shouted.

Five minutes later, they banked hard over the island's north end. Mack had put his hand over Renée's eyes and told her not to look. He unbuckled his seatbelt and stood to look through the window on the port side of the chopper. Looking down at the beautiful, white sandy beach just a few thousand feet below, Mack grinned like a schoolboy. Captain Halsey had pulled it off. He took his hand away from Renée's eyes and yelled over the rotors, "Look at that beach."

Renée craned her neck but couldn't see out the window, so she unbuckled her seatbelt and stood. As she looked out the porthole, she started to cry. Below on the beach, written in letters that had to be twenty feet long were the words, *"Will you marry me?"* She turned to face Mack, who had already made it down onto one knee, and with tears in her eyes, she threw her arms around him. He hugged her back but stayed on one knee. When Renée pulled away, she saw him holding a green block of clay in his hand. She looked puzzled for a moment, but quickly realized what it was. It was a block of C4 explosive.

"I couldn't afford a diamond," Mack yelled over the helicopter's noise, "but I figure we can use this to break into a real nice jewelry store and find one you like."

Renée laughed at first but quickly started to cry as Mack pulled his other hand out from behind his back and showed her a small, felt box with a neat bow wrapped around it.

Renée fought back more tears as she began opening the box. She had somehow not noticed that the helicopter crew chief was recording her with a small camcorder. She opened the felt box and saw a perfect diamond on the C scale. The only thing it lacked was the carat. It was small, but it was perfect, and Renée had said *yes*. She didn't know that Mack had arranged with the commanding officer on the tiny island of Tsuken-Jima to use the entire training facility for the week. They were the only two people on the 16,000 square meter base with more than one-quarter of a mile of white sandy beach for five days.

*****

Mack drove through the streets of Cleveland as he recounted one of the greatest days of his life. Before he knew it, he was on the same road where Renée and his baby girls had been forced off the road. He had been to the spot many times before but felt compelled to return one more time. He knew it was stupid, but he just felt closer to her there than he did in the hotel room. He closed the door to his truck and slid down the embankment that led to the river where his Excursion stopped on that tragic day. He sat on the bank of the river, throwing stones into the water as he wrestled with his thoughts. He knew Mina was right, but he couldn't shake the feeling that it didn't matter. Mack somehow knew in the back of his mind that what happened tomorrow in that courtroom would change the course of his life as much as what had happened almost a year ago.

He closed his eyes for the millionth time and thought of Renée and his girls. He tried to convince himself to listen to Mina, but he knew that he never would. He was wired differently than most people. Injustice was not something he could endure; it was something he had to correct. It didn't matter if the jury convicted Marco Bertoli for the murder of his wife and children; he had already done that. If the judge didn't sentence Marco to death, then he would. Mack reached for Renée's worn-out copy of Elizabeth Barrett Browning's poems and allowed it to flop open in his lap. By the light of the moon, Mack saw that the book had fallen open to the twentieth sonnet. He squinted in the moonlight to make out the words:

> *Beloved, my Beloved, when I think*
> *That thou wast in the world a year ago,*
> *What time I sat alone here in the snow*
> *And saw no footprint, heard the silence sink*
> *No moment at thy voice ... but, link by link,*
> *Went counting all my chains, as if that so*
> *They never could fall off at any blow*
> *Struck by thy possible hand ... why,*
> *Thus I drink Of life's great cup of wonder!*
> *Wonderful, Never to feel thee thrill the day or night*
> *With personal act or speech,—nor ever cull*
> *Some prescience of thee with the blossoms white*
> *Thou sawest growing! Atheists are as dull,*
> *Who cannot guess God's presence out of sight."*

Mack closed the book and fought back a tear from his eye and realized that the memory of Renée and his baby girls had made him cry again. He had promised himself that he would never cry again, but it was an impossible promise to keep.

CHAPTER 21

The DA tried to stir the jury into recognizing the obvious. He tried to clarify that the defense had clearly tampered with three of his witnesses, but the judge cut him off again. He implored the jury to look beyond the obvious intimidation tactics that had been employed with the defenses witnesses. They all worked for the Bertoli family, so of course they were going to say those things. He brought up all of Marco's prior arrests to not only convince the jury that he was indeed a sociopath but also a murderer. The jury hung on his every word and seemed to be in silent agreement. He tried to conceal his disgust for the judge as he finished making his case. He closed with a reminder to the jury that the lives of five people had been taken, and he urged them to take everything that they had heard into account before reaching a decision. It was clearly a shot at the judge who had instructed the jury to strike his earlier comments about witness tampering. He was about to sit down but at the last minute he changed his mind. It appeared to Mack that he was trying to make a decision. He turned around and walked slowly back to the jury box.

"Let me say one more thing," holding his index finger up in the air. "If justice is not served here today, then the next dead body will be on each and every one of you."

Mack wasn't an attorney, but he had studied people his entire life. He watched every member of the jury intently, and a few days into the trial, something became abundantly clear. The jury was clearly disgusted by Marco Bertoli. When the pictures of his babies were put on the podium, Mack saw the mothers wiping their eyes. He saw the fathers' jaws clench, and he knew in his heart that they would convict Marco Bertoli despite the witness tampering. He watched the individual members who almost refused to look at Marco, afraid that he would somehow infect their own lives if they looked at him too long.

The defense attorney stood to make his closing arguments.

"Ladies and gentleman of the jury, at the risk of being condescending, let me state the obvious. There is absolutely no evidence that would lead a reasonable person to conclude that my client has done anything wrong. He was in Mexico the day the murders happened. His car had been reported stolen by his father two days before the murders. There is absolutely nothing that links my client to these tragic murders. The DA, who has clearly not been doing this for very long, has made childish attempts to convince you that you are not required to follow the law. He has made accusations against my client that have clearly been proven false. He has made accusations against a prominent member of this community in an attempt to sway you emotionally so that you will overlook the law. When you adjourn here in a few moments, you will be provided with a folder containing all of the evidence against my client. It will be up to you to decide his fate. That is not a responsibility to be taken lightly. When you open the evidence folder and see that it has absolutely nothing in it, then you can all breathe a sigh of relief. When you see that empty folder, you will not have to worry about your conscience, your bias, or your duty. When you see that empty folder, you will know that there is nothing left to be done. I want to thank you all for putting your lives on hold this past week to fulfill the duty of every free citizen.

To Mack it seemed they were just waiting to find the dirtbag guilty on all counts, but they were clearly in a bind. Everything the defense attorney had just said was true. Mack felt the thermostat in his brain being turned up a few degrees. He glanced at Mina, and her face had the verdict written all over it. The jury adjourned, and the courtroom emptied as trial watchers filed out to await the verdict.

Mack was sitting on one of the benches outside the courtroom with Mina when the older district attorney came to tell him that the jury had reached a verdict. He was a middle-aged man with a permanently tired expression on his face. He was the same guy who had just told him less than an hour ago to prepare for a long deliberation. Mack had been wondering all week why he was letting the younger man do all the talking and asking all the questions. Surely the most experienced man should have been in charge, but the court system operated much differently than a Marine platoon.

"Is that a good sign or a bad sign?" Mack asked on the way back into the courtroom.

"You never can tell," the assistant DA replied with the same tired expression Mack had been watching for the past week and a half.

Mack watched as the last of the jury shuffled back into the courtroom. They had only been in deliberation for just under an hour. It seemed to Mack like it was a good sign. He felt like the district attorney made a compelling argument. His car was at the scene; the teenager testified that he had seen the Mustang shortly after the accident, even if he did redact the statement. Surely the jury couldn't forget about that evidence. The defense attorney had tried to make it look like the teenagers didn't even know what a Mustang was, much less be able to identify one in the rain.

"What teenage boy didn't know what a Mustang looked like," Mack had wanted to yell out during the testimony. He had just taken his seat when he heard the bailiff raise his voice.

The Honorable Judge Bartholomew T. Neely entered the courtroom from a door behind the bench, and when everyone was standing, he took a seat. He shuffled some papers and looked toward the jury box. "Has the jury reached a verdict?" he finally said.

"We have, Your Honor," said the young woman who had been elected to be the chairman of the jury.

The bailiff took the piece of paper the young lady handed to her and gave it to the judge. He unfolded the piece of paper and adjusted his reading glasses. Once the judge had read the paper, he handed it back to the bailiff, and the process was reversed.

After the young girl stood again, the judge called for silence. He ordered Marco Bertoli to stand and nodded to the woman, indicating the floor was hers.

"We, the people, find the defendant, Marco Bertoli, not guilty of homicide on two counts."

The courtroom erupted with cheers, and the judge slammed down his gavel.

"There will be silence in the courtroom until the forewoman has finished reading the verdict."

Marco and the rest of the Bertolis were all smiling and slapping each other on the back, but Mack was laser focused on the jury.

"We further find the defendant Marco Bertoli not guilty of reckless driving. We find the defendant, Marco Bertoli, not guilty of vehicular homicide on all three counts. We find the defendant, Marco Bertoli, not guilty of making threatening statements to a federal police officer."

The woman sat down, and the entire courtroom erupted again. Loud whistling and cheers could be heard all the way down the hall. Camera flashes popped, and the bailiff tried to restore order, but the chaos was incredible. The judge finally got the courtroom back under control and informed Marco he was free to go.

Mack sat in stunned silence. He looked at the district attorney, who offered some apologetic words, but Mack didn't hear them. Mack looked at the jury, who looked relieved as they began filing out of the courtroom. He looked to his right at the crowd cheering and applauding. He looked to the judge, who was shuffling papers, and then to the jury one more time, who seemed to be deliberately refusing to make eye contact with him. He looked back at the judge saying something to the bailiff that he couldn't make out. The world closed in on Mack in an instant. The walls of the courtroom were contracting down, and the voices turned into muffled sounds. Time stood still as the bile began rising in his throat. The pulse in his head began pounding, and he felt that familiar surge of adrenaline—the same excited feeling he got when his life was in jeopardy, only it wasn't. Or was it? His peripheral vision was fading, and he felt the way he had just before kicking down a door in the Kandahar province in Afghanistan. Mack closed his eyes briefly and saw little Aubrey cooing up at him and Renée holding Brianna on her breast as she fed the one-week-old infant. Mack wasn't sure what was making him move, but it wasn't common sense. Common sense said to sit down while the judge is still sitting on the bench. An outside force had invaded his body, but rather than fight it, he let it take control, and it felt … right.

Mack knocked over his chair as he climbed up to stand on the plaintiff's table that morning, but as he felt his boots connect with the wooden tabletop, he knew he had something to say. Mack heard the gavel drop and the judge saying something, but he tuned him out. Mack turned on his heels and yelled loud enough to be heard.

"Hey, Guido," Mack yelled over the crowd. "Your daddy may have gotten you off the hook, but Daddy isn't going to save you when I find you. Do you hear me?" Mack screamed. "You may have gotten away with this in the court of law, but I make you one promise here today. Right now, as sure as I stand here on this table, I will kill you! And not just you. I will kill everybody who made this kangaroo court possible. If I find out that the jury was involved in this kangaroo court, I will kill them, and if I find that the district attorney was involved, I will kill him too," Mack pointed at the DA with spittle flying from his mouth.

The judge was banging his gavel, yelling at Mack for order in the court. The judge warned him that any further speech would be considered active threats and that he would be arrested.

"I am going to kill you all. It may not be tomorrow, it may not be next week, but I will kill every single one of you." Mack was now screaming over the noise. As the bailiff began running towards the plaintiffs table, Mack locked eyes with the judge and over the roar of the crowd said, "If I find out that you're involved, then make no mistake, I will kill you too."

"You're under arrest. Bailiff, arrest this man and put him in detention. There will be no bail until your hearing."

Mack didn't fight with the bailiff who yanked him off the table. He didn't fight as the handcuffs clicked into place; nor did he fight the shoving from the bailiff as he pushed him toward the door. Mack never broke his stare on Marco Bertoli. As the bailiff was leading Mack out of the courtroom, all he could do was stare into the cowardly eyes of Marco Bertoli and mouth the words ..."I'm going to *kill you*."

Marco laughed at Mack as they dragged him from the courtroom. He was about to yell something to Mack when Matteo grabbed him and said something quietly in his ear. Marco caught Mack's eyes as he was going through the door, and he blew him a kiss.

Mack lunged back through the door, but the bailiff was ready. He was taken to the ground, and the next thing Mack felt was a knee in his back. Several other bailiffs from nearby courtrooms poured into the room and overwhelmed Mack. He knew he was beaten. He let his body go limp, and he turned his attention inward. He needed to play along; get out of the building, find that scumbag, and drill a 9 mm hole through his temple.

Mack saw the judge hurrying out of the chambers like he had seen a ghost. He saw Vincenzo slapping Matteo on the back, and he saw everyone staring at him. If Mack didn't have the wild look in his eye, he would have noticed a thin, young Moldovan woman with thick, curly black hair and a very determined face standing by the door. She had a scar on her left ankle and a hatred in her eye's that matched his own. The last thing Mack did see on the way out of the courtroom were the tears in Mina's eyes.

*****

Claire Larkin strolled through the front door of the steakhouse and saw Mulloy in the corner booth. She made her way through the maze of tables, and just as she was about to sit down, Mulloy stood to greet her.

"Sit down, you Neanderthal. Spare me the chivalry. What the hell was that all about today?" She was firing off questions faster than Mulloy could respond.

He threw up his hands and just stared at her. "Man, she is beautiful," he thought. It took a few more seconds for him to find his voice. "First, I have no idea what happened today. Second, do not insult my chivalry. It is how I was raised, and if it insults you, then that is your problem, not mine. It is called *respect*, and it is who I am. If your father didn't raise you correctly, that is not my fault."

Claire could tell that she had wounded him. Her first reaction was to pounce, but she thought better of it and just offered a polite apology. "I'm sorry. I am just still in shock about what happened today."

"So am I."

"The evidence was overwhelming. Half the jury was in tears when they showed the pictures of those two beautiful babies. His car was placed at the scene of not only the nightclub killings but also the car accident. Same for his dirtbag friend and his car. Why they didn't indict him too is still a mystery," Claire said fidgeting with her purse.

"Take a breath, and keep your voice down," Mulloy said clearly embarrassed for Claire.

Claire didn't bother to look around, but she did lower her voice. "I'm sorry, I just can't believe that dirtbag is going to walk."

"I can't either."

"The shell casing was from a 7.62 x 25 mm handgun, which are almost exclusively found in Soviet pistols. He had a previous arrest for carrying a concealed Tokarev pistol, which just happens to be chambered in 7.62. The jury would have heard all of that too, but it was thrown out of court as well four years ago. Something smells."

"I know, I was there too. I agree, but there is absolutely nothing you can do about it now. Sometimes the story doesn't have a happy ending. Life isn't like a best-selling novel. You can't tie up all the ends with a pretty bow. Just because the case is over doesn't mean the story is. I have a pretty good feeling that there will be a sequel to this story, but it isn't coming out any time soon. It's not like it was a hung jury or a mistrial. He was acquitted. Game over. You can't try him again."

Claire just glared at Mulloy and gave him her best 'no kidding' face and picked up the menu. "To top it all off, I get a call from my station chief this afternoon. Get this, he doesn't call me to say that he was sorry about the trial today. He calls to tell me that even being there was an act of insubordination, and that he is going to write me up for it. Not only did he pull me off the trafficking case for absolutely no reason; now he is telling me that I shouldn't even have come to the trial. It's like he doesn't even want to solve crimes. I had to remind him that I am on vacation."

Mulloy looked at Claire with a puzzled look on his face. "You took vacation to come to this trial?"

"So, what if I did?" she said defensively.

"You have got to learn how to stop taking this job home. If you don't, you are going to end up …"

"Like you?" Claire cut him off.

"Yes … like me," Mulloy said letting his head fall into his hands.

"I'm sorry, that was uncalled for," she said, and she meant it. *Why can't I keep my thoughts to myself?* Claire thought under her breath.

"No, you're absolutely right," he said and peaked through his fingers at her. "Claire, you are undoubtedly one of the best field agents I have ever met. In fact, I would be willing to say that you are the best I have ever met. He dropped his hands to the table and met her eyes.

"But?" she said anticipating what he was about to say.

"But, you have got to learn how to turn it off. When was the last time you did anything that didn't involve work?"

Claire started to speak, but stopped. She started to speak again and realized the fact that she had hesitated in the first place spoke louder than anything she could say. Her bottom lip began to quiver, and Mulloy could tell she was close to tears.

"Now I'm the one that is sorry," he said. "I just can't stand to see you this disappointed."

The waiter arrived at the table and they both plastered fake grins on their face as he introduced himself. They both placed their orders and sat back in the booth. They stared at each other for a few moments, but neither wanted to break the silence.

Mulloy finally looked at her and smiled.

"What was that for?" Claire said grinning.

"I think that was the first time I looked at you, and you didn't have something you wanted to tell me."

Claire started to say something sarcastic but was interrupted by a genuine laughter that she hadn't felt in months. She just let herself laugh a few moments and then she eventually snorted which made her laugh even harder. The snort got Mulloy laughing and the two just sat there like two high school kids. A few moments later, Mulloy remembered that he was going to tell her something, but he thought better of it.

"Are you going to tell me what is on your mind or do I have to drag it out of you?" she said still giggling a little.

Dang, she is so intuitive, Mulloy thought. "Well, I got a phone call today as well, from the director himself. It was a gag order essentially. I am not allowed to discuss the case with anybody, and if the press wants my opinion, I am simply to state that the judicial system has done its job and that we are continuing our efforts to find the person responsible," he said mimicking the director's high-pitched voice.

Claire giggled again at the impersonation of the FBI Director's voice. "OK, big deal. That's SOP. What else did he tell you?"

"He basically told me to drop the entire case. Not to investigate any further and to just let it all go."

"Stop investigating five murders? Are you serious?" Before Mulloy could respond, she added. "So, what are you going to do?"

"What I'm told to do. What else can I do? If I start poking my nose around, I'll be out of a job at best, maybe dead," he said shaking his head in disgust.

"Well we can't just drop it. Five people are dead, and the local PD isn't going to figure this out," she said.

"I'm not saying we drop it; I am just saying that we can't broadcast what we are doing. In fact, just you and I having dinner together is probably a bad idea. We need to make them think we are in full compliance. Hand over all our notes, and move on to the next case. Any digging we do from here on out must be done discreetly."

"What does your gut tell you about all of this?" Claire said after the waiter dropped their food off.

"It tells me that money can't buy happiness, but it can buy an acquittal," he replied.

"You think this all comes down to money?"

"Doesn't it always?" he said cutting into his steak.

"I'll tell you what I think," Claire said swirling spaghetti into her spoon with her fork. "I think that the human trafficking industry is not just for creepy old guys who live in their mother's basement. I think it infects our government, law enforcement agencies, and politicians. I think that this poor CIA agent uncovered something that our government doesn't want uncovered. I think that the Bertoli family is more than just a two-bit crime family. I think a lot of things, but I admittedly can't prove a damned one of them. What I think mostly is that the director himself is in on this. Let me ask you this," she said taking a bite of her spaghetti. She covered her mouth with her hand as she chewed and talked at the same time. "When was the last case you worked that warranted a call from the Director?"

"I've only spoken to the last Director one time. This was my first interaction with the new guy," Mulloy said shaking his head.

"Exactly," Claire said pointing her finger at Mulloy for emphasis. "It just doesn't happen. The Director spends his days rubbing elbows with politicians and testifying on the hill. He doesn't get involved in the day-to-day operations of a Cleveland field agent."

"I agree with everything you just said, but let me remind you that what you are implying is dangerous. You can't go off halfcocked on this."

"What do you suggest I do then?" she asked.

"Patience."

"Patience, that's all you got. Am I supposed to climb a hill, sit with my legs crossed, and wait for the stars to align too?"

"It would probably be more productive than what you want to do. It might also keep you alive longer."

"Mulloy, I am asking for your help. I have a lot of respect for you, and I know that you are not drinking the company Kool-Aid. I just need to hear you say that I am not crazy."

"You're not crazy."

"What do I do? And don't say drop it. You know I can't just drop this, but I need to know how to keep this case going, off the books. Have you ever done that?"

"Yes. As a matter of fact I have several cases I am still investigating off the books. It is a dangerous game, though. You can't slip up even once. You can't let your emotions cloud your judgment. I know you want to nail this scumbag, but if what happened today doesn't give you pause, then you're a fool. People like this will kill you and then go cheer at their kids' soccer game twenty minutes later. You are the enemy to these people, and they do not fight fair. If what you say is true, and this goes all the way to the top of the Bureau, you will have to decide if your life is worth the risk. Is whatever you hope to gain, whatever justice you would like to serve, worth your life? Because, if you go down this road, you may get to a point where you will have to make that choice."

"Will you help me?"

Mulloy let out a long sigh. He poked at the steak on his plate before putting his fork down. He stared at Claire for a long moment and asked himself silently if he was contemplating helping her because he believed she was right or because he was head over heels in love with her. He wasn't one to get all weak-kneed around beautiful women. He had dated some truly gorgeous women in his day. They all paled when it came to Claire. It wasn't just her beauty that drove him nuts; it was her passion. Beautiful women were a dime a dozen, but a beautiful woman with the kind of drive and determination Claire had were diamonds in the rough. "I'll help you on one condition," he finally blurted out.

"What is that?"

"We do this on my terms, not yours. You are too emotionally wrapped up in this to see straight, and I am not going to risk my life and yours on your emotions."

Claire let out her own sigh and sat back in the booth. "Deal. Now what is the plan?"

"I already told you, patience. You go back to Detroit, jump into whatever cases you have on your plate right now, and you make every attempt to portray the fact that you are moving on. Don't even mention the trial unless somebody asks. Hand over everything you have. I'm sure you have copies of it all for yourself. Most importantly, you keep your mouth shut and your eyes and ears open. Guys like this don't fly straight after a near miss. In fact, I guarantee you that this has done nothing but embolden this piece of crap to dream up even bigger schemes. Bertoli is going to mess up again, and you just need to make sure you are where you need to be when he does. This is not going to be a two-week fix. This may go on your entire career, but if you blow your stack and get bounced out of the Bureau, you will have lost any chance of bringing this guy to justice."

Claire nodded her head. She liked Mulloy, and for some reason that she couldn't quite wrap her finger around, she trusted him too. That was saying an awful lot in her line of work. If Claire were honest with herself, the list of people she trusted would fit on a fortune cookie message in 20-point font.

"One more question; then I will drop it. How does the judge fit into this whole crazy circus? I mean, what are the chances that the judge who calls in an anonymous tip about two murders ends up being the judge hearing the same case?"

"Zero. The chances are zero, Claire, but you have a little piece of the pie that he doesn't know you have. Nobody would have put that together, and you did. Nobody would have even thought to put those pieces together, and yet here we are. I need you to hear me when I say this, and I need you to do what I tell you to do. Tuck it away and leave it there. We will pull that piece of the puzzle back out when we need it, but that kind of information is not just dangerous. It's deadly. If you think for one second that the people you are dealing with would not have you killed, you are not ready for this game."

Claire shook her head slowly, letting what Mulloy said sink in. She knew he was right. They ate the rest of their meal in relative silence. They didn't talk much more about the case or what the plan was going forward. Mulloy was adamant that she take a few months and not think about it, starting right then and there when the dessert came. *The cheesecake was above average,* Claire thought, *but Mulloy clearly thought it was perfection on a plate.* He drove her back to the airport in time to catch her flight. Out of habit he opened the trunk and retrieved her luggage, but this time Claire let him. His corny chivalry was starting to grow on her. She wasn't sure if she was unconsciously letting her feminist guard down, or if he was consciously trying to tear it down. It didn't matter either way. He lived in Cleveland, and she lived in Detroit. He was married to the FBI, and she was still trying to rise to the top. It would never work out.

She said goodbye, shook his hand, and headed inside. As she got to the ticket counter, she felt somebody staring at her, so she turned around to see Mulloy still at the curb. He was leaning on the Crown Victoria, staring at her. She waved again, and Mulloy waved back but didn't make any sign of getting into the car. Claire let out a little smile and turned back to the ticket agent. She took the ticket and started walking toward security but noticed that Mulloy was still watching her.

Ugh, men can be so annoying, she thought and walked back toward the exit. "What?" she said as she got closer to Mulloy, who was still leaning on the car.

"Nothing," he said genuinely. "I just hate seeing you go, that's all."

She was about to say something sarcastic, but she stopped herself. She started to speak again but stopped short. *What is wrong with me?* she thought. She finally found her voice and said, "Well, maybe you can come visit me sometime in Detroit. If your wife is OK with that?"

"I'd like that."

"See you soon, Mulloy. Now run along. You're starting to creep me out."

Mulloy laughed, pushed away from the car, and walked the few steps toward Claire. He didn't give any hint of his intentions until he was just inches from her face. He grabbed her shoulders and planted a gentle kiss on her cheek. "I'll see you around, Special Agent Larkin."

Claire stood there speechless, wondering what had just happened, but as Mulloy turned to go, she grabbed him and kissed him long on the mouth. When she was done, she turned and walked into the terminal and directly to the security gate without looking back.

CHAPTER 22

Mack heard the metallic clank as the cell door slammed into place. He wondered if the excess noise was on purpose. It was like adding insult to injury. Being put into a cage was an assault on the senses. His eyes darted back and forth as his brain tried to size up the dimensions. His sense of smell had already been violated when the main door was opened to the general population of prisoners. It was a smell that Mack had smelled before, only in different buildings. The smell of more than a hundred men living in close quarters was one he was quite used to. His nose was at home, but his eyes and ears were anywhere but. Another loud, clanging noise assaulted his ears, and he realized the outer door was slamming shut. He had counted seven doors and three flights of stairs since he was dragged through the courtroom.

Mack looked down on the bed and found an orange jumpsuit, and he remembered hearing the jailor's orders to put it on and to stick all of his personal belongings through the door onto the floor outside of his cell. He reluctantly obeyed and found the jumpsuit to be quite soft, and it fit fairly well. *Well, at least I have that going for me,* Mack thought. He slipped on the shower shoes and turned his back to the door. Six feet wide and eight feet deep was the size of his new home. Mack fought back the emotions as he slowly slid to the floor. He sat with his back against the bars and stared into the cell. He couldn't bear to see the bars as it was a constant reminder that the man who killed his family was not behind them ... he was.

Mack's head hung low as he listened to the other inmates yelling things at him. He ignored it as he tried to figure out what had happened. One moment, he was watching the trial of the man who killed his family, and the next, he was being thrown in jail. Mack had never felt the way he did earlier in that courtroom. He wasn't sure what had come over him, but he was pretty certain that it had come to stay. When he heard the words "not guilty," a part of his brain that he didn't know he possessed sprang to life. It was a primitive part of the brain, no doubt. It was the part of the brain that civilized societies had suppressed for so long that it became anathema. It was primitive in the sense that it was simple, but it felt like a more advanced way of thinking than Mack thought he was capable of.

This new way of thinking that had sprung to life inside him was calculating and patient. It was incapable of remorse or fear. Up until that moment in the courtroom, Mack had thought of revenge, but it didn't consume him. He knew that people died and that accidents happened. He might have moved on with his life as difficult as it would be if justice had been served. If Bertoli had been sentenced to jail time, it would have been justice. If Bertoli had been sentenced to jail time, it would have allowed Mack some closure. If Bertoli had been sentenced to jail time, it would have allowed Mack to pick up the shattered pieces of his life and make a new start. But Bertoli was declared to be not guilty; therefore, nobody would pay for the murders of Renée, Aubrey, and Brianna.

Mack tried to convince himself that he was surprised. Truth was, he was going to kill Bertoli regardless. He tried to pretend that he was outraged by the judge's decision, but he wasn't. He tried to steer the ship of his emotions back out to sea, but it was too big and the harbor didn't have enough room. His life had been put on a collision course, and no amount of righteous anger, convictions, jail sentences, or grief would alter its trajectory.

Mack sat on the floor with his knees to his chest as he felt the winds of change blowing through his soul. His first instincts were to fight off the changes that were coming. He fought back the waves of darkness rising inside him as he sat on that cold concrete. The more he fought, the harder the waves came. He felt like he was back on the North Shore of Oahu, trying to catch waves at Sunset Beach. Every time he caught a wave, the thirty feet of solid water slammed him under. He would be rolled around for almost a minute in the violent turbulence before his head finally popped up, gasping for air. The harder he had fought those rip currents, the angrier they had become. He thought of the lessons the waves had taught him, and he just let the violent water carry his body until it spit him out.

Sitting there on the floor with the tears forming in the corners of his eyes, Mack let go. He gave in and let the waves take him where they wanted him. They carried him to darker and darker places until the only thing left inside Mack's soul was the darkness. He sat there for hours just letting the darkness consume him. When the door clanged again, he slowly stood. His legs had cramped from sitting so long, and the pins and needles were stinging his muscles. He breathed in and let the pain consume him in a way he never had. The pain was welcome inside Mack's new primitive brain, but more than that, it was necessary.

As he turned to face the bars, something played at the corners of his mouth. It was a gesture that he hadn't needed in a very long time. In fact, he couldn't remember the last time that simple facial expression had made an appearance. He figured the last time he had allowed it to creep across his visage would have been before Renée and the babies were killed. The sensation at the corners of his mouth kept moving, and before Mack knew what to think, it had spread across his entire face. Mack stood there in the prison door, smiling from ear to ear. It wasn't a fake smile either; it wasn't a plastered-on expression to confuse the world into thinking that everything was all right. It was a genuine, honest-to-goodness smile, and it scared Mack to the depth of his soul.

When the guard wheeled the cart with dinner in front of Mack's door, he still smiled. The guard looked at Mack and then did a double take.

"Well, you look different than you did a few hours ago."

"I have a new purpose in life," Mack said, without letting the smile fade.

"Well, that's good, I guess. As long as it doesn't have anything to do with what just happened in that courtroom."

"It has everything to do with what just happened in the courtroom."

"Revenge is a dead-end street, young man."

"I know, but it will not be my death at the end of the street," Mack said and winked at the guard.

The guard just shrugged his shoulders and slid the tray into the cell. Mack took the tray to his bed and devoured the entire thing. Twenty minutes later, Mack was doing push-ups, sit-ups, and jogging in place. The training started today, and the training was not going to be fun. It was going to be painful, miserable, and totally necessary for Mack's new purpose in life.

Not guilty! Those two words had catapulted Mack toward a future of pain and suffering. More than Mack would ever think possible. He might have had second thoughts if he had known just how much pain and suffering his primitive brain was about to unleash. He might have tried to do something different; he might have given up completely. But he didn't. He just smiled.

For the next two days, when he wasn't punishing his muscles, he sat quietly in his tiny cell. He let his brain run wild with possibilities. He quietly began carving out a future that would allow his body and brain to become deadly weapons. He drew the blueprints and laid the foundation for the deadliest warrior the world would ever know.

Three days after the trial, Mack stood in front of a different judge. This time he was on the opposite side of the courtroom. He only half paid attention to the proceedings as his public defender assured him that it was all a formality. The court would drop all charges and consider the time spent in the county detention center as payment in full for his actions. He heard the gavel drop and only vaguely realized that it had all gone exactly as he was told it would. Three days in the county jail had been a reawakening for Mack Murphy. With the notable exception of a visit from Mina before she had to be back in DC, Mack had spent the last three days in quiet solitude. He found that he wasn't in a hurry to leave; he wasn't even in a hurry to get a decent meal. He had actually come to enjoy the solitude with nothing except his thoughts and plans. The near future was going to be the most difficult time for him to endure.

He didn't have to think about what he would do next. He was assured that the Marine Corps would not be filing additional charges for conduct unbecoming of a Marine, but he knew that his career was over. He knew that the Marine Corps was honoring a warrior who had lost it all but would never be promoted. Gunnery Sergeant was where his career would end. There would be no re-enlistment ceremonies, and there would be no platoon sergeant billets coming his way. He knew that the next three years would be spent spinning his wheels and waiting for the honorable discharge at the end. But that was all part of the plan.

Surprisingly, Mack didn't care. His newfound purpose in life came complete with a patience that he had never possessed. His beloved Marine Corps was only doing what was best for her. He knew it wasn't personal. He knew there would be no hard feelings. No one Marine is bigger than the Corps, not even Mack Murphy. Overall, Mack was grateful that he would be allowed to finish off his enlistment. He was ready to get back into the fight on terror. He had never made plans for life after the Marine Corps, and now it didn't matter. He didn't even feel like giving it a second thought. He just picked up his belongings and made his way to the street.

The sun was bright when he pushed through the big glass doors of the County Jail. He squinted in the sunlight and looked to the curb, where he saw a familiar face leaning up against his pickup truck. Spencer leaned forward and pushed himself off the fender and stood straight. He took a few steps, and when he was close enough, he threw his arms around Mack's shoulders and hugged him tightly.

"I'm sorry brother," he whispered into his ear.

"Yeah, me too," Mack said and hugged Spencer even harder. "I guess I don't listen very well."

"Don't say another word. Just get in the truck, and let's go eat. What's done is done, and there is no sense dwelling on it."

"Did you hear?" Mack said.

"About what?" Spencer replied.

"The Captain called me yesterday to tell me the Corps wasn't pressing charges."

"I'm glad to hear that, brother. I'm in town for a few days. Maybe we can just drive back to Lejeune together and have some fun along the way."

Mack got into the car and leaned his head against the window as Spencer pulled away from the curb. He thanked him for coming to get him and told him how much he meant to him. The two drove in silence for a while before Spencer pulled into Mack's favorite fast-food restaurant and killed the engine.

"There's something I want to tell you," Mack said.

"You got raped while you were in there? I promise I won't tell the other guys," Spencer said, mocking a serious face.

"You're an idiot, and no, that's not it."

"I know you don't have any money. This one is on me. Besides, I forgot to tell you that I got promoted to Gunnery Sergeant while you were in the slammer."

Mack started to protest when it dawned on him that Spencer got promoted. He congratulated him, and he was honestly very happy for him. They talked about Marine Corps stuff for the next hour and a half sitting in the restaurant. When they got back into the truck Spencer finally remembered to ask Mack what he wanted to tell him earlier.

"You're my brother, right?" Mack said, staring out the window.

"Of course, what's up?"

"Something happened to me that day in the courtroom, and I just want to say that no matter what happens to me …"

"What the heck are you …"

"I mean it, Spence." Mack cut him off, and his tone of voice rose a few octaves." I am not the same person I was before, but I just want you to know that I will always have your back, and you will always be my brother."

"Of course, bro. I know that."

"Good, then that's all I'm going to say about that."

"We cool?" Spencer said, raising an eyebrow. He had spent the last few days trying to figure out where Mack's head would go after this latest setback, but not even he could figure out where Mack was.

"We're cool, Gunnery Sergeant," Mack finally said and gave him a smile.

Spencer had offered to help Mack go through the storage unit, but Mack said it was something he needed to do on his own.

The next day he began the task of going through Renée's and the babies' things. He had hired a company to pack up the entire apartment and put it in a storage facility by Mina's old house; he'd paid for a year in advance. As he began pulling out baby blankets and car seats, Mack noticed the tears were not quite hiding at the corners of his eyes like they used to. What Mack felt when he saw the girls' little rattles and Renée's old T-shirts was becoming less about grief and more about anger. He was sure he had been through however many phases of grief the head shrinkers were claiming there were nowadays. He didn't put much stock in people who had never done something trying to teach somebody who had. He put a box on the pickup truck bed filled with stuff he was determined to keep. The rest he would leave in the storage unit and let Renée's cousin go through and do with whatever she wanted.

He found Renée's old flip phone. It was the one that she had called him on the day she was killed. He was surprised the agency hadn't asked for it. He flipped it open and wasn't surprised to find that it was completely dead. He plugged it into the charging cord in the front seat of his truck and went back to work. Six hours later, he had gone through the entire storage shed and had filled up three boxes. He had two little blankets that the girls were wrapped up in when they went home from the hospital and the matching pink and purple rattle toys that he had bought for the girls at the hospital gift store.

He had Renée's favorite Elizabeth Barrett Browning book of poems. He grabbed a few of Renée's old T-shirts and a handful of his own clothes. He found a shoebox with pictures of the mother he had never met and the father he never pleased. He sifted through the pictures, grabbed a handful, and threw the rest into the dumpster next to the storage shed. He grabbed the letters he had written to Renée from Afghanistan as well as the letters she had written to him. He took their wedding album as well as another box of pictures from the few vacations that they had taken to Hawaii and Topsail Island. There was one thing he just couldn't allow himself to think about. The C4 engagement ring he had bought her. He had no use for it, and he couldn't even imagine giving it to another woman. Selling it seemed wrong too, but for some reason, keeping it seemed too painful. He slipped it into his pocket and decided to think about it later.

He took the GLOCK 19 that he had bought for Renée for Christmas the first year they were married with the inscription on the slide that read ... "What shall we add now? He is dead." The opening line of Elizabeth Barrett Browning's Poem "Died." He grabbed the two spare magazines and the paddle holster and put them in his glove box. As he rolled down the overhead door to the storage shed, his mind was locked in a battle for his heart. The past year had brought him unimaginable grief. The past year had stolen from him a normal life that most people took for granted. The past year had transformed him somehow from a patriot who loved his God, his country, his family, and left him with three boxes of mementos and a thirty-year-old pickup truck.

He smiled to himself and decided that somebody really ought to write a song about him. He was sure it would be a billboard hit on the country music charts someday. As he pulled away from the storage shed, he allowed a little smile to creep over his face. The memories of Renée were all good. His babies had set up permanent residence in his heart, and his newfound focus on life was razor-sharp. The plan was essentially complete; all he had left to do was implement it.

Mack and Spencer made it to Lejeune a few days later, and the whole unit expressed their condolences. First and Second Recon companies had been disbanded and all the Recon Marines got shuffled around. Mack ended up back in First Force Recon Battalion with Spencer and G-Mar. It was great to be back among some familiar faces, but it didn't feel like it had before. G-Mar was about to be promoted to Master Sergeant, which meant his operating days were coming to an end. He would be holding down a desk in the battalion office from here on out. Spencer had been promoted to Gunnery Sergeant and had taken G-Mar's place. Mack learned that his promotion was canceled, which put him underneath Spencer for the first time in their careers. Mack didn't care. He was happy for Spencer. He couldn't have picked a better team leader.

After the shuffling, First Force Reconnaissance was first up on the deployment schedule, and everyone was upset. The guys who had been planning to deploy were put back in training status, and a few of the guys including Mack, G-Mar, and Spencer, who had just returned, were heading back out. Mack had been down range more than most of the other guys in the new unit, so that gave him a lot of respect. Everyone in his new platoon knew what had happened to his family, but nobody asked him about it.

He had met several of the other Marines at various schools, but Spencer was his only real friend when he showed up. G-Mar was so busy getting acquainted with his new leadership role that he had no time to reminisce. Mack wanted to make new friends, but it became more difficult after a while. He had heard all the stupid cliches about not wanting to get close to anybody for fear of being hurt, but that was just psychobabble to Mack. He didn't make friends anymore because he had nothing to offer a friend. His heart was just a giant lump of petrified tissue that beat only to keep him alive, not to enjoy being alive. His new focus in life didn't allow for friend-making. Even Spencer grew a little distant from Mack, but he didn't blame him at all. Mack knew that it was his own fault. Being around people for too long tired him out. He felt like he had to put a sign around his neck whenever he was with others that said, "Yes, my wife and kids were killed, but I have not turned into a psychopath."

Maybe he *had* turned into a psychopath. In fact, that was probably the best way he could explain what had happened to him. He had clearly undergone some type of metamorphosis. He knew who he had been when he started, but who he was when he finished was anybody's guess. Mack had read about serial killers in college and knew they all had borderline personality disorders. He knew enough to know that you didn't just develop a borderline personality disorder. It was something you were either born with or you weren't. What Mack had experienced was more like a complete psychotic break. The break was like a reset button that erased everything that used to make you who you were and replaced it with a slightly or drastically different version of your former self. Mack finally decided that psychopath was probably the closest thing to the truth. Sociopaths were born, and psychopaths were created, he remembered reading somewhere. *Well, call me what you will,* Mack thought. *I am who I am.*

CHAPTER 23

Mack could hear gunfire getting closer as the Humvee roared into the outskirts of Ramadi. The heat would have been unbearable if he hadn't been used to it after three months in Iraq. Spencer was yelling something about earning their paychecks, and Mack grinned to himself. He stole that line from Apollo, but he didn't call him on it. To the junior men on the team, Spencer was the seasoned warfighter now. Mack closed his eyes in preparation for the battle to come, but he didn't need to calm his nerves as he had previously. In fact, he was almost too calm. *The fear of dying must be inversely proportional to the joy of living*, Mack thought, as he racked the slide on his Beretta 9 mm sidearm before slamming it back into his drop-leg holster. "Just another day at the office," Mack yelled to nobody in particular.

Spencer looked at Mack across the bed of the Humvee and made a mental note to keep a close eye on his best friend. False bravado had never been Mack's style. It usually meant that a warfighter was getting reckless. He had seen the signs when they arrived in Iraq, but so far, Mack had kept everything together when it counted. He had seen him charge the enemy who were flanking their position outside of Baghdad a few weeks earlier, but it had paid off. It had saved the life of a Navy SEAL, who would have almost certainly been killed. The SEAL team leader had put Mack up for the Bronze Star, so everybody chalked it up to a hard-charging Marine just doing his job. Spencer knew better, though. He had tried to talk to Mack about his recklessness, but Mack just brushed him off. The worst part of the whole thing was Spencer didn't blame him one bit. He knew the depths of grief a man was capable of when an injustice stole everything from him. He felt the same way on September 11, and if he were honest with himself, he felt every bit of Mack's pain.

The Humvee screeched to a stop just outside the five-story building. Gunfire was raging from across the street, and the entire city of Ramadi was in total chaos. They had been brought in to set up overwatch for Third Battalion Eighth Marines as they pushed their way into the center of Ramadi. The six Marines crashed through the front door and started climbing stairs. The building had been cleared by Lima Company a few hours before, but the enemy had dug into the apartment complex across the street. Fire was erupting from both buildings as Spencer went looking for the man in charge. The building was one of the tallest in Ramadi, and it afforded the best view of the city. It had an unobstructed view of the mosque, which was believed to be the location of the insurgent forces. Mack and Sergeant Durham began setting up positions and dialing in their scopes. Mack was on the fourth floor facing the apartment complex where the fighting was the most intense while Sergeant Durham was on the fifth floor facing the mosque.

The radio started crackling just about the time Mack had dialed in his sniper scope to a range of 100 meters. It was the exact distance to the front door of the apartment complex and battle zero. His .300 Win Mag would only move a few millimeters at that range, so he didn't even bother to check the wind. The first platoon commander from Lima Company had just tried to push into the building across the street but had been turned back. Somebody's mic was hung up, and all that Mack could hear was gunfire over the radio. He scanned the building but didn't see any targets.

A panicked voice came over the radio reporting that there were two missing Marines in the building. The voice on the radio belonged to Lieutenant DeFord, and he sounded panicked. "There's Hajis everywhere; they're using civilians as human shields."

Mack felt his anger swelling as he searched desperately for somebody to put a bullet in. Lieutenant DeFord was requesting supporting fire as his Marines withdrew from the building. Mack aimed his rifle at street level and saw the Marines pouring out of the building. Just then he heard louder gunfire, and he realized that the Hajis were firing down from the windows across the street at the Marines exiting the building. Mack saw a man firing an AK-47 out of the third-story window directly across from his building. Mack squeezed the trigger on his rifle and watched the .300 WinMag round tear a hole in the Iraqi's neck big enough to put his fist in.

Forty-two, Mack said to himself realizing that the man was dead. He wasn't even ashamed to know his number anymore, he just started looking for contestant number forty-three. He scanned the building from top to bottom and almost squeezed the trigger at what he saw on the fourth and final floor, but something in the back of his brain stopped his trigger pull. Two insurgents were standing over another man who was lying on the floor. The man on the floor looked like he had been hog-tied, and one insurgent was kicking him.

Mack focused in with his scope, and his blood ran cold when he realized what he was looking at. The man on the floor had Marine Corps' digital fatigue trousers on and was stripped naked to the waist. His face was a bloody mess, and his entire torso looked bruised and broken. Mack checked the rest of the room before placing the crosshairs on a bearded man carrying an AK-47. He knew the bullet would tear through the man without even slowing down, and he didn't want to injure any non-combatants. He pulled the slack out of the MK13 and let loose another round that turned the Iraqi into a cloud of blood, beard, and brains. The blood sprayed all over the second insurgent as well as the Marine on the floor. The MK13 barrel moved backward after Mack pulled the trigger, so he had to take a second to bring the crosshairs back online. Mack didn't even have to think; he adjusted his aim and repeated the process. The second insurgent turned into a vapor of red and white blood cells and slowly splashed down to the floor.

The Marine was wild-eyed as he looked around the room. He instinctively braced for the same treatment but was relieved when it didn't come.

Now what? Mack thought. *Who's going to go get that guy?* It was a rhetorical question, as Mack was already on his feet.

"Where are you going?" Sergeant Riggin, his spotter, said sarcastically.

"There's a Marine over there, and I'm gonna go get him."

"What the ..." Sergeant Riggin started to say, but Mack cut him off.

"Just cover me. You got it?" Mack said, grabbing Riggin's M4 before making his way to the door.

Riggin rolled over and pulled the twelve-pound rifle toward his chest and started scanning. "I see him," he said. "You can't just go walking into that building," but Mack had already left the room.

Mack keyed his mic and told Spencer what he was about to do and then switched his mic off. He knew Spencer would never allow that kind of recklessness, but he didn't care. There was a Marine in that building, and he was gonna get him. Like a TV commercial, the typical flurry of thoughts and emotions invaded Mack's brain. It was like the war had paused to let Mack contemplate his life. He let the thoughts play on as he took the stairs four at a time. He couldn't save his wife and girls, but he could save a fellow Marine. He could not do anything about the men who had murdered his family, but he could unleash hell and fury on the Iraqis shooting at his friends. He couldn't change the past but allowed himself to feel like he could dictate the present. His head was very much in the fight, even as his brain whirled with regrets.

Thirty seconds later, Mack was crossing the street. Lieutenant DeFord watched him running across the street and yelled, but the sound of gunfire had drowned him out. Spencer saw him through the window and let out a steady stream of cuss words. He told the remaining four Marines from Force Reconnaissance to verify all targets before engaging. They had all heard Mack on the radio and didn't need to have it explained to them, but Spencer felt helpless and needed to do something. He changed frequencies to communicate with the platoon commander of Lima Company. He needed to tell him to cease fire as they had a friendly in the building.

"Say again, over," came the voice of Lieutenant DeFord, the platoon commander.

Spencer repeated his traffic, and Lieutenant DeFord's voice came back immediately.

"That was one of your guys?" DeFord yelled into the mic.

"Damnit," Spencer yelled. He keyed his mic and said, "He's one of ours. He said he had eyes on a Marine on the fourth floor." Spencer changed frequencies and tried Mack again. "Mack, get out of there. Get out *now*," but there was no response. Spencer wanted to scream, but he knew Mack too well. He knew that Mack would never purposely take his own life, but he wasn't sure he wouldn't welcome it if an Iraqi offered to take it for him.

The building had two wings with three staircases. Two on the outside of the building on either end and a central staircase. Mack had gone into the middle of the two buildings and was heading for the central staircase. The Marine was being held in the North Wing, but Mack had noticed gunfire from both wings while searching for targets. He hoped it would be possible to move up the staircase without getting caught in a crossfire. *Only one way to find out*, he thought. He burst through the front door and immediately came into contact with three Iraqi soldiers. They didn't see him at first, so he dispatched two before they even knew he was in the room. The third insurgent squeezed the trigger on his AK-47, and the automatic rifle coughed out five rounds as Mack pulled his own trigger.

Mack saw the insurgent's head snap back just as one of the five rounds found his own trauma plate center mass. The 7.62 mm round knocked Mack backward about three feet, forcing the air out of his lungs. He was fighting for breath before he hit the floor. It seemed like a year and half before the oxygen slowly trickled back into his lungs. He was vaguely aware of some shouting behind him, so he willed his body to pivot. Just as he had turned around, he saw a young woman come running into the room carrying an AK-47. A million feelings went through Mack's head in the time it took to squeeze the trigger.

He had never killed a woman. Would it feel the same as killing a man? Would somebody feel as though his world had been shattered when they learned of her death? Would somebody feel like he had when he had lost Renée? Would somebody dream of how good it would feel to torture and eventually kill Mack in revenge? The last feeling he had was recoil as his bullet found the frontal bone of the Iraqi woman in the doorway. The 5.56 round shattered the bone and pulled brain matter and blood with it out of the back of her head before continuing into the plaster wall behind her.

The air poured back into his lungs, and he was on his feet. Two floors later, he encountered another group of Iraqi's. They saw him at the same time and opened fire just as Mack was diving for cover. Bullets slammed into the wall sending shards of wood and plaster over his head. He grabbed a grenade off his vest, pulled the pin, and threw it backhand into the room. The second the grenade detonated, he was on his feet, moving through the cloudy room. Seven shots and four dead Iraqis later, he was back in the staircase. He made it to the fourth and final floor without any contact. He heard automatic gunfire, but it was coming from below. Not hearing any sounds from the other side, he recklessly plowed through the door and into the room where he had seen the Marine minutes before.

The first thing he saw was the Marine, still on the floor in the middle of the room, trying to wriggle himself loose from the zip ties holding his wrists together. The second thing he saw were three more Iraqis pointing AK-47s at him. He didn't hesitate as he dove to the ground to make himself a smaller target. He hit the floor and rolled to his side, firing his M4 in the process. One Iraqi went down as a hot burning sensation tore through Mack's left thigh. He rolled again as a line of bullets ripped past his head. Mack fired again, and his own bullets found their target as a second Iraqi fell to the ground. He felt the familiar feel of the bolt locking to the rear as his magazine emptied.

He dropped the M4 and began trying to pull his Beretta from the holster, but he realized he was too slow. He locked eyes with the Iraqi, who allowed a small smile to creep over his face as he pulled the slack out of his own trigger. Mack closed his eyes and waited for the pain. He heard a bullet slam into the wall next to his head as a splash of hot liquid painted his face. An instant later, he heard the unmistakable boom of the .300 Win Mag in the distance. Mack slowly opened his eyes and saw the body of the third Iraqi lying in the middle of the floor and what was left of his head rolling to a stop on the other side of the room.

Mack jumped to his feet and went to the window. In the distance, he could see Sgt. Riggin giving him a thumbs up from behind the barrel of the MK13. He gave him a thumbs up in return before spinning back to the center of the room. He scanned the room and then pulled his K-Bar from his waist. He cut the Marine loose and asked him if he could move.

"I'm good to go," the Marine Sergeant said wildly, getting to his feet. "Are you alone?" he said, realizing nobody else was in the room. "This place is crawling with Hajis."

"I've got a bunch of friends across the street. Let's get out of here," Mack said as he keyed his mic back on. *It was always easier to get forgiveness than permission,* he thought. He wanted to let Spencer know he would be coming out of the building soon and not to shoot.

"Wolfpack, this is Blackfoot. I'm on my way out of the building," Mack said, using the call sign that Spencer had given him five years ago in Afghanistan.

"Blackfoot, don't move. Lima company is about to breach the building now. Maintain your current position. You have friendlies in the building. How many tangos are left in there?"

"Not sure. I didn't go much past the staircase until I got to the fourth floor, but I still hear gunfire below me."

The Marine, who had been taken prisoner, grabbed Mack by the arm and swung him around. He grabbed the microphone and started yelling into it.

"Negative, Wolfpack, negative. Call everyone back. This place is wired to blow, and I'm pretty sure it is remote. They were using me to draw you in. I repeat, everyone pull back."

"Say again," Spencer said.

The sergeant pointed at the corner of the room, and Mack's eyes followed his finger. Det cord was strung along the floor and disappeared through the wall into the hallway. Mack ran to the staircase and looked down. The same det cord ran the whole length of the staircase along the ceiling with improvised explosions wired neatly every five feet. The whole building was one gigantic IED. He couldn't believe he hadn't noticed it on his way up the stairs. The reality slammed into Mack like a freight train. It was pretty ingenious, he had to admit. The Iraqis had to know by now that they couldn't win a fight against the Marines, but they could get them all in one place and blow the whole building to hell, taking every Marine and Iraqi with it.

"Wolfpack, this is Blackfoot. *Pull back. I say again, pull back now.*"

Spencer peeked into the ground floor of the building and looked up at the ceiling. He cursed loudly before ordering the Marines to pull back. It went against every ounce of his training to leave Marines behind, but better to leave two behind temporarily than to lose a dozen instantly.

Mack handed the Sergeant his M4 and a fresh magazine as he pulled his sidearm and said, "We gotta go."

"You're hit," the sergeant said, pointing to Mack's leg.

"Merely a flesh wound," Mack said in an exaggerated Monty Python British Accent.

They were taking the stairs three at a time on their way down. Gunfire was tearing up the walls all around them, sending shards of wood, plaster, and metal at them every step. Mack realized that the Iraqis above them were coming from the South Wing and firing down into the stairwell. The Marine sergeant was about ten stairs below him when Mack saw her. A little girl who couldn't have been much older than five was squatting in the doorway on the second floor. He told the sergeant to keep moving as he ran back up a few stairs to grab the little girl. He instinctively knew that he had probably just killed her mother, and he couldn't leave her there.

Ever since returning to Iraq, he had been taking too many risks. His superiors knew it; he knew it, and now it was about to cost him his life. What exactly was that worth, he had wondered a thousand times lately. No wife, no children, no parents, a few friends, and an estranged brother who hadn't even sent him a condolence card when his family was murdered. None of it mattered. He couldn't let an innocent child die in this bloody game. Not if he could stop it.

Gunfire ripped the staircase as he reached the second floor of the apartment building. He scooped up the girl, who didn't even put up a fight. He was firing his Beretta at anything that moved. He knew he had probably shot more than a few Iraqis. Whether they were combatants or not didn't matter to Mack; they were in his way. Mack yelled to the sergeant ahead of him, who skidded to a stop on the landing. The sergeant saw Mack hurl the girl over the railing at him, so he dropped his rifle to catch her. The rifle clattered to the ground an instant before the little girl landed in his outstretched arms. He hadn't anticipated the weight of the little girl, and she slid right out of his arms, landing hard on the floor. She screamed loudly, but the sergeant didn't know if it was from pain or from being thrown down a staircase.

"Get out of here. I'll cover you," Mack yelled over the gunfire and began firing up the stairs until his magazine was spent.

The Sergeant retrieved his rifle and headed down the remaining stairs and out the front door of the building as bullets rained down on him from the floors above.

Mack rounded the landing on his way to the last floor just as the call to prayer began blaring over the city's loudspeakers. Mack looked up and realized that the gunfire had stopped. He saw several Iraqis running from the North Wing to the South Wing, not even taking time to fire at him as he stood in the hallway. Mack spun toward the staircase as the entire building shook with a fury that left no doubt that the explosives had been detonated. The force of the explosion shook the entire North Wing of the building with a force that sent Mack's body hurtling across the floor before slamming into the metal staircase. He lay on the floor in disbelief that he was still alive. He looked up and saw daylight on the western side of the building that hadn't been there seconds earlier.

The explosion had taken down the entire western side of the north wing of the building and threatened to collapse the entire structure. Mack looked up and saw the explosives above him and the detonation cord still intact. The staircase would be next, he realized. His first instinct was to admit defeat and welcome his own death with open arms. But his first instinct was overruled by the man who was Mack Murphy.

He bolted to his feet and crashed through the doorway onto what he thought was the first floor. The concussion left him disoriented, and nothing looked familiar. He didn't take time to figure it out. He just kept moving forward. He saw a broken window with daylight beyond, and his mind was made up. He took two giant steps and hurled himself through the open window into the courtyard below. Just as he cleared the windowpane, a second explosion rocked the staircase, and a ball of fire engulfed his entire body. With a few quick calculations in his head,

Mack realized he was looking at a full twenty-foot free fall. About the time he was finished doing the math in his head, his feet found the hot sand of the middle courtyard, followed by his knees. Stinging pain shot through his legs as he rolled to his side to break his fall and to extinguish the flames that had engulfed his body. He had done it a hundred times before in Airborne training at Fort Rucker but never remembered it hurting as much. As his body rolled over and over, he saw the building collapsing in, and it was coming for him. The explosion had ripped the staircase and supporting beams into shreds, and the rest of the north wing of the building came crashing down.

He thought about the tiny fingers and toes that he would never hold again. He thought about the perfectly aligned set of teeth behind the softest lips that he would never kiss again. He thought of Spencer, how much he loved him, and how sad he would be. He thought of his brother strangely enough and how he regretted not staying in touch. The last thought he had, though, was of Renée. He missed her more than ever. All his thoughts gave way to a sense of excitement. He realized that he just might get to see them all again soon.

He let a small grin creep over his face as the steel and concrete came for him. The thought of seeing his girls again filled him with such peace that he didn't dare move. Mack soon found himself annoyed at another thought invading his moment of solitude. It wasn't a welcome thought, and he tried to force it from his mind, but it wouldn't budge. The thought grew in intensity until it was the only thing that Mack could think of. It took a moment to give the thought a name, but when he did, it stung. *Failure.*

Time had slowed to a crawl; Mack watched the building crash to the ground as thick clouds of smoke and fire began to engulf the air around him. *Failure.* He had made Renée a promise sitting at her grave that day, and he felt guilty for accepting the easy way out. He had made himself a promise sitting in that cold prison cell, and he was embarrassed at how easily he had broken his word to himself. He ordered his feet to work, but they were slow to respond. He only had to make it another twenty feet, and he would have relative safety. Somehow, his legs began moving, but his eyes quit working as the dust engulfed him. His legs pumped, but he had no idea where he was going.

A violent force slammed into Mack's back and hurled him once again forward into the unknown. He felt his body come to a stop against a concrete wall, but all he saw was blackness. The pain in his thigh seemed to be gone, and the gigantic bruise that had already started forming on his chest was barely noticeable. He felt a hot, sticky liquid flowing down his eyes and the back of his neck. His breathing was labored, but strangely enough, he was calm. The explosions had stopped, and the sound of gunfire was soft in the distance. Mack stopped trying to make his eyes work, and he allowed the darkness to wash over him. He whispered a silent prayer for his fellow Marines and went in search of the most beautiful woman he had ever met.

CHAPTER 24

Spencer watched in horror as the concrete and steel collapsed to the earth below with no sign of Mack. The dust was settling over the building, and the sun was slipping below the skyline in Ramadi. The Iraqi forces were crawling all over the place just as the call to prayer finished blazing over the city's remaining loudspeakers. Spencer knew all too well that the call to prayer sometimes doubled as a call to arms among the jihadist Muslims. Small arms fire was erupting everywhere, and Force Reconnaissance had been pulled back. The little ground that had been gained that day had been lost. The death toll was sitting at thirty-seven US and coalition troops since the battle for Ramadi had begun. He shuddered as he realized that Staff Sergeant Mack Murphy may soon be added to the list.

Sergeant Glenn, the Marine Mack had rescued, said there was no way he could have survived that explosion. The last thing Glenn saw was Mack firing his pistol up the stairs after throwing the little Iraqi girl over the railing. The sergeant had made it out of the building, but the explosion had thrown him clear across the street before landing next to the Humvee that Force Recon had arrived in earlier. He had received a head wound that needed immediate attention, so he was evacuated to the rear before Spencer could get any more intel from him.

Lima Company had pulled back and linked up with the Force Recon team to hold the line, but when no further insurgents exited the building, the brass had called them back. Two Marines were still unaccounted for, but they would search for bodies as soon as they were able to regain that property from the Iraqis.

Spencer felt a murderous rage welling up inside him when the Major had ordered the Marines to return to base. He had argued vehemently over the radio but stopped short of outright insubordination. A large civilian structure had just been destroyed, and who knew how many innocent lives had been taken? The Iraqis would undoubtedly say that coalition forces had attacked a civilian apartment complex, and the brass were running damage control. A mosque had been accidentally attacked in Fallujah two years before, and a number of civilians had been killed. Commanding officers had been relieved for that mess, so nobody wanted to be in the crosshairs of public opinion.

As the Marines rode back to base, Spencer held the hand of the little Iraqi girl who had curled up in his lap and fallen asleep. He kept stroking her cheek and playing with her dark black curls in the fading sunlight. She would never know how lucky she had been to have a guardian angel named Mack Murphy watching over her. Spencer hoped she was too young to remember anything, but if he ever saw her again, he would remind her that his best friend died so she could live. He shook his head at the incongruity of it all. Here he was, holding a little Iraqi girl who had just lost her parents, and the only thing he could think of was to remind her that his best friend died saving her life. What Spencer didn't know was that it was probably Mack who had taken their lives in the first place.

Spencer fought the sorrow as he realized he would never see Mack again. Staring at the faces of the men surrounding him, he knew they were all thinking the same thing. Losing brothers was not what they had signed up for, but they knew it was bound to happen. It wasn't something they talked about openly, but it was something they all carried with them like a talisman. Spencer knew that every man in that Hummer was wrestling with emotions. They were all thankful that it hadn't been them, but they were wishing it had been all at the same time. None of it made sense, so he stopped trying. He just closed his eyes and thought of his friend.

Twelve hours later, the Marines from Force Recon and Lima Company were back in the same Ramadi neighborhood searching for the two lost Marines. The neighborhood was eerily quiet as the civilians looked on with indifference at the Marines sifting through the rubble. Recon was running overwatch for the search party, and every window for miles was empty. Spencer knew that a quiet Iraqi village was a powder keg. When the people went silent, the enemy was gearing up.

"Heads on swivels, boys," Spencer said into his throat mic.

"Wolfpack, this is Hoosier, I need you to come see this," Sergeant Riggin said. He had been named Mr. Basketball in Indiana and was on his way to Indiana State University when the twin towers crashed to the ground. Every Marine had a nickname and every nickname had a story.

Spencer stood to his feet and made his way to the rooftop where Riggin and Durham were both lying prone. He stayed low across the roof to avoid making himself a target and then low crawled the last few meters before pushing himself up onto his elbows to look through Riggin's spotting scope. Spencer stared through the spotting scope for several minutes before he realized what he was looking at. When the young Iraqi boy came into focus, Spencer's blood ran cold. He was wearing a University of Montana baseball hat.

"Go get that kid now," Spencer said through gritted teeth.

Twenty minutes later, Riggin pushed the little Iraqi boy through the front door of the abandoned apartment building that Lima Company had just taken the day before. He was probably only twelve years old, but that didn't mean anything in Iraq.

"Where did you get this?" Spencer yelled.

The boy stared at him in confusion. Spencer shook the hat in front of his face and yelled it again. The interpreter stepped in and translated for the little boy, but he had understood Spencer's second attempt at communicating.

The little boy started speaking a 1,000 miles an hour, and the men all turned to look at the interpreter.

"He said he found it just inside the concrete barrier this morning on his way to his friend's house."

Spencer pointed to the front door, and the group walked outside and toward the collapsed building. "Tell him to show me where he found it," Spencer said to the interpreter.

"He will show you, but he is asking for food in exchange for the hat."

Spencer gave an exasperated look but finally dug in his pocket, handed the boy an MRE bag of peaches, and shoved him forward. "Win the hearts and minds of the Iraqi people," he said sarcastically to nobody in particular.

They arrived at the back of the building a few moments later. After Spencer had deployed his men to a new overwatch position, he followed the boy into the compound. The boy stepped over a few concrete blocks and pointed at the ground. Spencer began tearing away concrete debris and told the interpreter to redirect the search party to the rear of the building. They had been operating on the suspicion that Mack had tried to make it out of the front of the building, but if what the boy was saying was true, his body would be in the back courtyard. Twenty minutes later, one of the Marines yelled that he had found some blood. The other Marines dropped what they were doing and joined him. The search party went on well into the afternoon before the Major ended it. They hadn't found any bodies, but they had found a lot of blood. If the blood was all from the same person, the lifeless body would not be far away. Several blood samples had been collected and sent to the rear for analysis, but the search was being called off. They would need much heavier equipment to search the rest of the wreckage, and the war wasn't over. Spencer realized it might be months before they had the ability to search the entire area. Sitting on a small chunk of concrete, Spencer tried to make up his mind. He wasn't sure how to feel. If they had found Mack's body, he would have been able to grieve and move on. The whole day he had been hoping to find his body but silently praying that they wouldn't. He couldn't make sense of it all.

War was nothing but a giant cesspool of conflicting emotions. You don't want to see the enemy, but you want to kill him. You want to fight, but when it starts, you just want it to end. You know people are going to die, but when they do, it seems so unfair. You know you are being changed every moment, but you just want to go back to the way things were. It was one giant dichotomy. Spencer let a little optimism trickle in when he realized that Mack could very well be alive, but if he were alive, then where was he? The fact that Mack was still unaccounted for sent a chill down his spine. That could only mean one of two things: Mack Murphy was either still under the giant pile of rubble or he had been taken POW.

Night was falling over the debris as Spencer ordered his Marines back into the building for the night. They would be covering Lima Company again as they tried to push farther into the city. It was going to be a long night, and they needed to get some rest. Spencer took one more look at the rubble before turning to leave, and his heart sank. He realized that this may be as close to Mack as he would ever be again. Yesterday's despair at losing his best friend had been replaced by that old familiar hatred he had been trying to make peace with ever since that crisp September day so many years ago.

*****

The phone next to Maxwell Kaine's bed was buzzing and blinking as he reached for it in the dark. "This is Kaine," he said, still half asleep.

"Sorry to wake you, Director. This is Mike Planicka. Our assets on the ground in Ramadi have informed me that Staff Sergeant Murphy has been killed. He had apparently charged into a building just before it detonated. The entire building was destroyed, and eyewitnesses are saying that nobody could have survived that explosion." The line was quiet for close to twenty seconds. "Did you copy that, sir?"

"Yes, I'm thinking," Maxwell said, fully awake now.

After another twenty seconds of silence, Mike asked if there were any new orders, but the silence stretched on.

"Have we recovered the body yet?" Maxwell finally replied.

"No, sir. The area is still too volatile. The Marines are pushing farther into the city, but it has been tough."

"Until we have the body, everything stays the same. Is that clear?"

"Yes, sir."

Maxwell hung up the phone and thought about going back to sleep, but he didn't. He was up now, so he might as well get going. He had some important phone calls to make, and he couldn't use his cell phone. He slowly stood, slid his feet into the slippers next to his bed, and switched the light on. He walked to the portrait of his family hanging on the wall in the hallway and stared at it for a long moment. His wife had died over ten years ago, and his children were all married and spread out across the country. The only thing keeping him going anymore was the work.

He finally swung the painting outward to reveal the wall safe recessed into the plastered wall. It was a relatively small safe, but it was large enough to hold the things it needed to. He slowly placed his left eye over the soft, glowing red light and allowed it to scan his retina. A moment later, a small keypad slid out under the safe, and he put in the long chain of numbers and letters. After a few more seconds, the safe popped open, and he retrieved a small satellite phone. He pulled the cord that released the drop-down stairs from the ceiling in the hallway and slowly climbed up into the attic. He sat on an old chair directly under the large skylight window in the roof as he meticulously began inserting the battery into the satellite phone. The window gave him an 87 degree view of the northern sky, and it was almost 5:00 a.m. The Mossad satellites would be directly overhead in an hour, and he used the time to think.

As the satellites screamed across the northern sky, Maxwell powered the phone on and then pushed the numbers. The phone was answered on the first ring.

"I trust there is a very good reason for this call, or you would not have made it," the Israeli voice boomed.

"Yonah, it is good to hear your voice," Maxwell said. "I need to pass on some information that I just learned minutes ago."

"Does it involve the death of a certain Marine Staff Sergeant?" Yonah replied.

Maxwell was caught off guard. He knew Mossad (the Israeli equivalent to the CIA) had spies in every government in the world, but this was a bit fast. "How did you know that?"

"We have men on the ground in Iraq too my friend. We intercepted the radio transmission from your Force Reconnaissance commander yesterday evening."

"Does Esther know?" Maxwell replied, still confused. He knew Mossad was a powerful force; he had helped build it, but its capabilities were becoming a little frightening lately. If Mossad had the technology to intercept intelligence briefings at the highest levels of the military, that meant the technology was available to their enemies as well. Maxwell made a mental note to be even more cautious moving forward.

"Yes, Esther knows. I just spoke with her, and we are coming up with contingencies as we speak, but thank you for the call."

Maxwell hung up the phone and sat there in the dark for a few more minutes before making his way back downstairs. He had a growing sense of apprehension as he stepped into the shower for his morning ritual. Ten minutes of blistering hot water followed by ten minutes of ice-cold water, and he was ready for another day. His driver was right on time, so he grabbed his briefcase and headed toward the garage. As he slid into the back seat, he had a smile on his face. The apprehension from earlier was gone, and had given way to a new emotion. The meticulous planning had begun paying off, and his fifty-year career with the CIA was about to become worth every second. The long years of sacrifices, the time away from home, his troubled relationships with his children, and the loss of his wife were about to pay off.

*****

Seven months later, Spencer Williams and Basmina Shaw stood in the Rose Garden as the president read the citation for the Medal of Honor. It was the fastest Medal of Honor ever awarded to a United States serviceman. The Medal of Honor Ceremony was held the day before the burial, and the president laid the medal across Mack's flag-draped coffin. The only thing inside the coffin was a small blood sample taken from the wreckage. The sample matched Mack's DNA so he had been declared killed in action. Mina had insisted that Spencer accept the medal in Mack's place. The president spoke in a soft but sincere tone as he read the citation.

"For conspicuous gallantry and intrepidity at the risk of his own life, above and beyond the call of duty, while serving as Assistant Team Leader of Charlie Team, First Force Reconnaissance Battalion during the battle of Ramadi. Charlie Team was tasked with overwatch for the 3rd Battalion 8th Marines who were engaging the enemy on the outskirts of Ramadi. Staff Sergeant Makoyii Kanati Murphy, with no regard for his own wellbeing, charged into an enemy-held building that had been fortified with explosives in search of a fellow Marine who had been taken POW. Drawing intense fire immediately upon entering the building, Staff Sergeant Murphy killed four enemy combatants before proceeding farther into the building. Making his way up four flights of stairs while drawing constant fire from the enemy, Staff Sergeant Murphy entered the room where the Marine Sergeant was being held and killed two more insurgents before being wounded in the leg by enemy fire. Sniper fire from Force Reconnaissance eliminated the third insurgent in the room allowing Staff Sergeant Murphy and his fellow Marine to make their exit from the enemy-controlled building. Before reaching safety, Staff Sergeant Murphy spotted a five-year-old Iraqi civilian caught in the crossfire and, with no thought for his own life, ran back into the stairwell amid enemy fire to rescue her. While the Marine Sergeant and the little Iraqi girl made their way to safety, Staff Sergeant Mack Murphy held off the Iraqi forces long enough to allow their escape. While Staff Sergeant Murphy was holding back Iraqi forces, the entire building exploded from multiple IEDs placed at critical structural locations. The building collapsed, and Staff Sergeant Murphy paid the ultimate sacrifice. In a selfless act of bravery in which he was mortally wounded, Staff Sergeant Makoyi Kanati Murphy saved the lives of at least twelve fellow Marines. Through his unwavering courage, heroic fighting spirit, and selfless devotion to duty, Staff Sergeant Murphy gallantly gave his life for his country, thereby reflecting great credit upon himself and upholding the highest traditions of the Marine Corps and the United States Naval Service."

The President lifted the medal off the coffin and handed it to Spencer. The President and first lady spoke quietly to Mina and Spencer in private for many moments. The President had been the one who had taken the US into war with Iraq, and Spencer could tell that the decision weighed heavily on him.

The following day, as the entire Marine Drum and Bugle Corps played "Taps," six Marines from the Marine Corps Barracks in DC, commonly referred to as 8th and I, carried the casket of Mack Murphy across the immaculate grass toward his final resting place. Spencer Williams silently willed himself not to cry. He had lost friends in the war on terror, but none had been as close as Mack. He was closer than his own brothers had been, and he had been the closest thing to family Spencer would ever know again. He watched as his fellow Marines walked in perfect cadence toward the grave. Spencer looked around at his fellow Marines and noticed that they were all fighting back tears. Mack had been more than a friend to them; he had been their brother. It brought home the sacrifice that good men have had to pay throughout America's history to ensure that lesser men could live in peace. It wasn't until that moment that Spencer understood the meaning of patriotism. An overwhelming sense of pride consumed him as he looked over Arlington Cemetery at the thousands of grave markers that seemed to flow outward in perfect alignment forever.

How many lives had been given in the name of freedom? How many more lives would it take to ensure that men could live in peace? Spencer knew he would never answer the steady stream of questions that lined up in his mind. He just watched as they lowered his friend into the earth while the Marines all saluted and the bugles played.

*****

On the shore of Lake Erie, Marco Bertoli and Sal Rigo pulled their van to the dock and killed the headlights. They waited there in the dark, smoking cigarettes and talking about the things they would buy with the money they were about to make. Another seventeen units were on their way across Lake Erie, and the two men felt invincible. Marco's phone rang, and when he answered it, all he heard was, "It's a nice night for a boat ride."

Four hours later, the produce was secured at Marco's newest warehouse on the city's lower West Side. The methamphetamine business was booming, and Marco was having trouble of late keeping up with the demand. It wasn't that raw resources were a problem; it was finding enough employees to churn out the final product. Selling the girls was the plan, but when it came time to re-home them, he always lost an employee. The local harvest was getting more and more difficult due to the public awareness surrounding human trafficking. An increasing number of girls were finding ways to escape, and the public was getting savvy about what to look for. More than once, Marco had lost employees who gave out subtle distress signals in public.

The business was almost totally dependent on foreign produce now, and the risks were starting to outweigh the benefits. Despite the risks, Marco and Sal were making more money than even the two of them could spend, and they showed no signs of stopping. Marco's father had indeed handed the reigns to Matteo before retiring to the Italian countryside to pursue 'other goals' as he would call it. Marco knew it was coming at some point, but the five murders his father had gotten him off for had accelerated his departure. Days after the trial, Vinny and Matteo had taken Marco to an abandoned warehouse to break the news to him. They gave him the option of remaining on the family payroll, or striking out on his own. To remain on the payroll, he would have to submit to Matteo's leadership, but Vinny knew in his heart he never would. Matteo had argued for the outright elimination of Marco, but Vinny's soft spot for his oldest son finally prevailed.

When Marco realized that his father's money was tied to his obedience to Matteo, he went on a bender filled with every illicit substance he could get his hands on. Three days later, he passed out in a motel room, clutching his nickel-plated Tokarev to his chest. He had tried to pull the trigger several times, but he couldn't do it. When he awoke almost a full day later, he determined that he didn't need Matteo or his father anymore. He was his own man and would show them both that he could make more money than either of them. He called Sal, but Marco could tell he was holding something from him. Sal had brushed Marco off on the phone, so Marco went looking for him. He found his car two nights later parked at the Foxxy, but the new bouncer refused to let him in. Obedience to Matteo was the price of admission, and everyone on the payroll knew it. Sal finally agreed to step out and talk to Marco when he saw that things were quickly escalating. Marco was disappointed when Sal informed him that he was not to have anything to do with him anymore. Matteo offered to keep him on the payroll too, but he had the same stipulations. In the end, Sal had stayed on the payroll and pledged his allegiance to the youngest Bertoli brother.

Marco stood there in disbelief. He scanned the parking lot before pulling his Tokarev and pointing it at Sal's head. Sal didn't flinch.

"Your dad can't save you if you pull the trigger this time."

That was the exact wrong thing to say to Marco, and his mind flashed back to the last time he pulled a gun from his waistband. "So you sold me out too?" Marco's eyes went wild as he pushed the gun closer to Sal's forehead.

Sal just stood there staring at him and shaking his head. "You could be twice the boss that your father is if you could ever get that anger in check," Sal said, and he meant it.

Marco turned away and tucked the gun back in his waistband. "What are you saying, Sal?"

"I'm saying that I am not allowed to have anything to do with you if I want to stay on the payroll. That is what your father and Matteo told me." Sal shifted a bit in the gravel parking lot before speaking again. "If you could harness all of that anger into something productive, then we would be unstoppable."

"Did you say *we*?"

"Yes, Marco, I like my father about as much as you like yours, but they don't know what we are capable of. If you would just stop to think a little, we could be richer than both of our families put together."

"I like the sound of that." Marco stood there for a long time, considering what Sal had just said. Finally, Marco turned to Sal and put out his hand. Are you with me, Sal?"

"Always."

Two weeks later, Marco was laying the groundwork for an entirely new enterprise. It would be easy at first, but once turf lines started to get crossed, it was bound to get bloody. Marco pushed the thought from his mind and focused on celebrating the arrival of seventeen new products who needed to be re-homed.

They were back at Marco's new strip club on the city's East Side drinking more Stoli Elit vodka while Mack Murphy's lifeless body lay under a pile of concrete and steel.

THE END

EPILOGUE

Mack's body lay motionless under the concrete and steel that had crashed down all around him. He was dreaming of Renée and his baby girls as he floated high above the wreckage. His body didn't feel pain anymore, and he was acutely aware that he was looking down at the ruins of the building he had just been in. He tried to make his body go higher into the air, but something kept him there. He heard a voice, and he strained his eyes to see where it was coming from, but all he saw was wreckage.

"Renée?" Mack said, but there was no response. He heard the soft giggling of little girls, and his arms ached to hold them. The voices kept growing louder with every second, and Mack couldn't take it any longer. None of the voices was Renée's, he realized, but he somehow recognized them. The voices were soft and sweet, and Mack instinctively knew they were children. The voices seemed to float through the air, and Mack realized he wasn't hearing them with his ears; they were speaking directly to his soul.

"Who are you?" Mack said without moving his lips.

"You know who I am. You have just never heard me speak," the voice said.

"You know who I am, too," came a second voice. The second voice was just as sweet but somehow reminded Mack of himself.

Mack was growing more anxious every second, and he was now desperately trying to find the bodies that belonged to those sweet voices.

No matter what Mack tried to do, he felt his body inching back toward the earth and the ruins of the building. He tried to scream out for Renée but couldn't find his voice. Mack started panicking as he wondered where he was and why he couldn't see Renée or his babies. Finally, he heard the soft voice of a child, and it sounded like it was right next to him.

"Not yet, Daddy. There is much more to do."

"But I want to be with you," Mack implored.

He heard her voice again saying, "Not yet," over and over.

"We will be right here when all of your work is done," the second voice said.

It dawned on Mack that the girl had called him *Daddy*. The implication pounded on Mack like a hammer. He struggled even more to stop his body from dropping back toward the earth.

"Where is your mommy?" Mack begged. "I want to see your mother. Is she with you?"

"You will find her, Daddy. You will find her. You will find her. You will find her."

A roaring noise started low and steady in the back of Mack's brain. It sounded like a deep horn being blown from a long distance away. It kept getting louder, but Mack tried to push it from his mind. He fought to find the girls again but knew the battle was futile. He cried out one last time for Renée, and then he heard a voice.

> *"I tell you, hopeless grief is passionless;*
> *That only men incredulous of despair,*
> *Half-taught in anguish, through the midnight air*
> *Beat upward to God's throne in loud access*
> *Of shrieking and reproach. Full desertness,*
> *In souls as countries, lieth silent-bare*

Under the blanching, vertical eye-glare
Of the absolute heavens. Deep-hearted man, express
Grief for thy dead in silence like to death—
Most like a monumental statue set
In everlasting watch and moveless woe
Till itself crumble to the dust beneath.
Touch it; the marble eyelids are not wet:
If it could weep, it could arise and go."

Mack awoke to total blackness. The roaring he had been hearing was growing steadily louder. The sound was like a siren blowing directly into his ears so loudly that it drowned out every other sound. The first thing he felt was the pain in his chest where he had been shot moments before, or was it hours? Was the darkness due to the time or because he had been buried alive? Mack felt something hot and sticky in his left ear and wondered what had landed on him. A few very cloudy seconds later, he realized it was his blood.

The ringing in his ears continued, and it was getting impossibly louder. After a few moments, he realized that it was indeed a siren. It was so loud, he thought he was standing next to it. A few more seconds, and he realized that the siren was the adhan's call to prayer. He blinked several times to clear his head and force his eyes to focus, but all they saw was darkness. He quickly took inventory of all his assets. Hands worked; brain was obviously working; feet were still a little slow to respond, but he could move them. Chest felt exactly like it was supposed to after taking a 7.62 mm round to the chest. He still had his camouflage University of Montana trucker's hat, so things couldn't be that bad. He closed his eyes and remembered the day Renée had given it to him just before deploying to Afghanistan the second time. He wasn't dead, or was he? He was pretty sure he had been moments earlier, but two small children had urged him back to the land of the living, and he had reluctantly obeyed.

He had never been dead before. How was he supposed to know what it felt like? He remembered his last thoughts of Renée and his girls, and he fought to find the girls again and let himself be washed away. He wanted to die so badly that he couldn't stand it. He wanted to see Renée so desperately; he could think of nothing else for several moments. Slowly, however, the pain started trickling back into his legs and chest, and he decided he was not dead. He started moving body parts and was surprised that more of them didn't hurt. He tried rolling onto his side, but there was something wedged against his shoulder. He tried to shimmy his lower body to free his shoulder, and it worked. A few moments later, he was able to roll onto his stomach and feel the ground beneath his hands. He decided to keep pushing his luck and tried to stand. His head hit something hard before he had even gotten to his knees, and he winced in pain. It was sharp too. He put his hand above his head and felt some rebar sticking out of a slab of concrete.

Mack's body lay under a couple hundred tons of brick and mortar, but a large metal beam protected him from more serious injury. Renée always used to say he was the luckiest Marine she had ever met. He knew he was lucky, but this was a bit over the top. He could hear the call to prayer, and he thought for the millionth time how much he hated that sound. He wondered if his friends were out looking for him, but he dismissed the thought when he remembered exactly what had just happened. He had run into a building that was wired with enough Soviet-made explosives to blow the whole city back to Baghdad. He knew for certain that his friends assumed he was dead.

Mack slowly crawled in every direction, trying to find a hole small enough to squeeze into, but he couldn't. *Just my luck,* Mack thought. Survive a building exploding right onto my head and then die of asphyxiation under the rubble. *Wait a second*, he thought. I have been crawling around down here for a while now. Why haven't I suffocated yet? He shoved his hands deep into his cargo pocket and dug around for his Zippo lighter. Mack rolled his finger quickly across the metal roller on the Zippo, and he was rewarded with some precious light. He was just blown up by a couple thousand pounds of explosives, but his Zippo still worked. He would have to write a letter to the company when he made it home.

Home, Mack had thought, and then it hit him. *What home? What if I do get out of here? Then what? Go back to the States and try to rebuild my life?* No matter how often people told him, time would heal his pain, Mack knew that there were some things that even time couldn't fix.

They all think I'm dead. Nobody is coming to save me. Hell, if I saw somebody run into a building that just got obliterated with an IED, I wouldn't hold out any hopes for them either. The wheels in Mack's brain started turning. The playbook that he had been living out for the past six months had just changed. Mack low crawled some more, but in the back of his brain, he was calling an audible. It was too good to be true. He had been virtually handed the missing piece of the puzzle that had been plaguing him for months. How was he going to kill that many people without being caught? *Because I'm already dead,* Mack said aloud to himself and smiled.

They have to assume I'm dead. There won't be a search party. If I make it out of here alive, Marco Bertoli and his whole sorry family will pay. The thought that began racing through his mind gave Mack a moral dilemma. Surely, nobody would think he survived that. His death would be an unusually good turn of fate. He knew his Marine Corps career was over; there was nothing left for him in the States. He had three murders to avenge, and he had just been handed a get-out-of-jail-free card. Could he just turn his back on his friends in Charlie Company? Could he allow his friends to think he was dead, mourn him, have a funeral, all while he was very much alive?

The lighter flickered, showing Mack a pile of concrete and metal completely surrounding him. It flickered again, but it didn't go out. He watched intently to see which way the flame was blowing to give him an indication of where the air was coming from. He called the audible, and started crawling in a completely different direction. As he crawled, heaved, and kicked at the concrete, the air began to blow across his hands.

Four hours later, Mack's hand had pushed through the debris. He felt a cool breeze blow across the back of his hand, which gave him a new burst of energy. Twenty minutes later, Mack was sitting with his back against the wall of the courtyard he had landed in after he had jumped. He realized he had indeed been on the second floor, but the courtyard was a full story below the street level. There was almost a full moon when Mack finally pulled himself from the rubble. It lit up the night sky enough for Mack to find the street on the opposite side of the building. He saw a few dead Iraqi bodies lying in the street.

Mack's mind was made up in an instant. He grabbed the knife that had miraculously made it out of the building with him and started pulling off his chest rig. He plunged the knife under the seam in the back of the chest rig and started ripping. He had sewn the passports that Renée had made for him into the lining of the chest rig along with three thousand US dollars and a few hundred thousand dinars. The three passports were right behind the trauma plate and looked brand new with the exception of a slight dent in the kangaroo on the Australian passport. *Proper prior planning prevented piss poor performance*, he could hear Renée saying to him. She would be so proud of me. He quickly pulled off his desert fatigues and pulled on the white, dishdasha (the traditional Arabic robe), from the dead man he had pulled off the street. He dropped his Montana hat on the ground and tied the keffiyeh (traditional Arab head scarf) around his head and picked up the AK-47. The boots would have to stay on for now. He spoke the language; knew the surroundings, had a motive. Now he just needed a plan.

He saw a Toyota pickup truck down the street that didn't look like it had been damaged in the explosion. The thought occurred to him that he looked like an insurgent, so he slipped the AK-47 under his robe and pulled his Beretta out instead. No sense making it through all that and then getting shot by his own guys on the way out of town. He slowly picked his way down the street, staying in the shadows until he was behind the wheel. He realized the truck had clearly been stolen when he saw the ignition wires stripped and hanging loose from under the steering wheel. *Luck of the Irish*, Mack said to himself and touched the wires together. It roared to life, and twenty minutes later, Mack was driving North on Highway 12 out of Ramadi. There was heavy US presence between Ramadi and Syria, so Mack had to pull over a dozen times and kill his headlights when he saw approaching vehicles. Five hours and two more vehicles later, Mack was approaching the Syrian border.

Mack knew Syria was just as chaotic as Iraq, but the absence of any US or coalition forces gave him hope. He hoped that his language skills and disguise would allow him to make it to Damascus. He knew he was pushing his luck. He knew better than to drive after dark on an Iraqi highway, but he had made it all the way to the border with no great difficulty other than running out of gas shortly after making it out of Ramadi. He had to ditch the pickup since he couldn't just pull into a gas station and fill it up. He hotwired a Toyota min-van in Khauza before resuming his trek toward the border. Mack pulled the van to a stop along the highway about five miles south of the Al Qaim border crossing between Iraq and Syria. A copse of trees just off the highway gave him perfect cover for a while to sleep before setting off on foot to cross the northwestern border of Iraq into Syria. He decided it would be easier to just steal a car once he made it across the border and drive to Damascus rather than driving a stolen car across the border.

Two days later, an Australian news reporter by the name of Jonathan Franklin Turner boarded the British Airways flight from Damascus to Heathrow. A few hours layover, and he boarded another flight to Sao Paolo, Brazil. The hardest thing for Mack was switching from an Arabic to an Australian accent when he made it to customs. Another two days later, Mack had checked into a motel on the outskirts of Sao Paolo. *What better place to get lost than the world's fourth largest city?*

he thought. The irony wasn't lost on Mack. The name Sao Paolo was Portuguese for Saint Paul. Just as Paul had been forever changed on his road to Damascus, so had Mack. He would need a new name, a new occupation, and a new language. He would have to learn Portuguese quickly if he were going to blend in. Mack knew what he had to do. He needed to become the most lethal man on the face of the earth, and training started today.

Printed in the USA
CPSIA information can be obtained
at www.ICGtesting.com
LVHW010717030724
784517LV00002B/2/J

9 781963 102147